THE PRODIGAL SISTER

"Tiffany!" she hollered.

The girl pivoted at her car door. Those black-rimmed eyes dared Rachel to challenge her.

So who was she to argue? "Do us all a favor and go back where ya came from!" she snapped. "Don't go upsettin' Mamma's applecart ever again, hear me? With Dat gone, we don't need any more nasty surprises like you!"

Rachel hugged herself tightly as the scarlet car sent gravel flying behind it and then surged onto Route C. "Didn't even look!" she muttered when the vehicle sped around a horse and buggy clip-clopping up the road.

But someone else was looking: first thing Rachel noticed when she turned to go inside was Micah's face at the café window. And he wasn't watching *her*.

Don't miss any of
Charlotte Hubbard's Amish romances:

A Mother's Gift
A Mother's Love

Seasons of the Heart series

Summer of Secrets
Autumn Winds
Winter of Wishes
An Amish Country Christmas
Breath of Spring
Harvest of Blessings
The Christmas Cradle
An Amish Christmas Quilt

Promise Lodge series

Promise Lodge
Christmas at Promise Lodge
Weddings at Promise Lodge

Simple Gifts series

A Simple Vow
A Simple Wish
A Simple Christmas

SUMMER
of
SECRETS

Seasons *of the* Heart

Charlotte Hubbard

ZEBRA BOOKS
KENSINGTON PUBLISHING CORP.
http://www.kensingtonbooks.com

ZEBRA BOOKS are published by

Kensington Publishing Corp.
119 West 40th Street
New York, NY 10018

All Kensington titles, imprints, and distributed lines are
available at special quantity discounts for bulk purchases
for sales promotion, premiums, fund-raising, educational,
or institutional use.

Special book excerpts or customized printings can also be
created to fit specific needs. For details, write or phone the
office of the Kensington Sales Manager: Attn.: Sales Department. Kensington Publishing Corp., 119 West 40th Street,
New York, NY 10018. Phone: 1-800-221-2647.

Zebra and the Z logo Reg. U.S. Pat. & TM Off.

First printing: February 2012
ISBN-13: 978-1-4201-5117-6
ISBN-10: 1-4201-5117-7

ISBN-13: 978-1-4201-2782-9 (eBook)
ISBN-10: 1-4201-2782-9 (eBook)

10 9 8 7

Printed in the United States of America

ACKNOWLEDGMENTS

All thanks and praise to You, Lord, for showing me what I can do—who I can be—when I trust You completely.

Thanks, as well, to my editor, Alicia Condon, and my agent, Evan Marshall, for once again entering into a new series with me! Your encouragement and belief in my work mean so much.

Many thanks to Jim Smith of Step Back in Time Tours for his incredible assistance as I researched this book in Jamesport, Missouri—the largest Old Order Amish settlement west of the Mississippi River. It's a pleasure and a privilege to work with you, sir.

Much love to Neal, my husband of thirty-five years: truly the wind beneath my wings. Where would I be without *you*?

For Johnny Lynn, for—yes!—fifty years of friendship that's found us ambling along some of life's most fascinating roads . . . and for the laughter we've shared every step of the way!

So when they had dined, Jesus saith to Simon Peter,
Simon, son of Jonas, lovest thou me
more than these? He saith to him,
Yea, Lord; thou knowest that I love thee.
He saith unto him, Feed my lambs.

He saith to him again the second time, Simon,
son of Jonas, lovest thou me? He saith unto him,
Yea, Lord; thou knowest that I love thee.
He saith unto him, Feed my sheep.

He saith unto him the third time, Simon,
son of Jonas, lovest thou me? Peter was grieved
because he said unto him the third time,
Lovest thou me? And he said unto him, Lord, thou
knowest all things; thou knowest that I love thee.
Jesus saith unto him, Feed my sheep.

—John 21:15–17

Chapter 1

"And what shall I bring for your dinner, Micah?" Rachel Lantz grinned at the broad-shouldered blond seated at the back table of the Sweet Seasons Bakery Café. "We've got an order or two of Naomi's meat loaf left, and Mamma's chicken and noodles—and *jah*, those stuffed peppers ya like so well."

Although he knew their daily menu by heart, he pretended to study the specials she'd written on the dry-erase board this morning. His hair showed a slight ridge from his straw hat, now hung on the nearby wall peg, and she felt the heat of his sturdy body after his morning of building cabinets with the other Brenneman boys, in their shop. It was his steadfast strength that appealed to her, even if he took his sweet time deliberating over decisions. "I'm thinkin' I had the hash browns Tuesday at lunch and Thursday for breakfast . . . hmmmm . . . kinda warm for those heavy slabs of meat loaf . . ."

Rachel stood as close to him as she dared, watching her twin sister, Rhoda, set two plates of the meat loaf in front of Bram and Nate Kanagy at a table across the way. "The stuffed peppers, then? Leah picked us a basket of red ones, fresh this morning. They look mighty *gut*, smothered in all that cheese."

Micah glanced at his brothers, Seth and Aaron, who were piling their plates high at the salad bar. "*Jah*, but I'd rather have a double order of hugs with a side of your kisses, Rachel. When can you dish me up some of *those?*" he murmured.

When his deep green eyes sparkled up at her, Rachel's cheeks tingled. He'd finally proposed to her last week! Would they hint at their plans to marry at next weekend's ice-cream social, or maintain Old Order Amish tradition and keep it a secret? No doubt the rest of the summer would pass by mighty fast if she had dresses and household linens to make— quicker than this carpenter decided on his lunch, it would seem! Yet how could she fault Micah for pondering his menu choices each day, when it gave him a few extra minutes to gaze up at her with such fondness lighting his handsome face?

His older brother, Seth, sat down across the table and forked up a mouthful of cucumber and onion salad. "We've gotta get back to the shop sometime *today*, ya know," he teased.

"Ah, but time means nothin' to a fella stuck on the likes of Rachel," Aaron, the youngest Brenneman, chimed in. "Sweeter than this wonderful-*gut* frog-eye fruit salad, she is. Like havin' your dessert first."

Rachel wound a string of her kapp around her finger, grinning despite the heat in her cheeks. That cold, creamy salad, made with tiny pasta BBs, was her favorite on a warm summer day, too—not that sharing this opinion would make Aaron stop teasing her. These brothers kept her on her toes, but they were as solid as the lustrous tables and chairs they'd built for the café, which served as a showcase for their custom craftsmanship here in Willow Ridge, Missouri. She nodded at the lady at table two, who tapped her empty iced tea glass. "Back in a minute, Micah. By then you oughtta know—"

"Bring me whatever ya think looks best, Rache," he said as she started toward the counter of filled pitchers. "With a side of green beans and a big slice of your lemon icebox pie."

"Bring me some of that pie, too."

"Me three," his other brother called after her.

Jah, jah," Rachel murmured as she refilled all the glasses at table two. She smiled politely at this trio of older English ladies, who had sacks from the adjoining quilt shop beside their feet. "Will ya be havin' anything else today?"

"Is that a rhubarb pie in your bakery case?"

"Yes, ma'am. Mamma baked it fresh this mornin'." Rachel flipped through her ticket tablet to figure their bill, noting the van full of customers pulling up outside. This summer's tourist business would be brisk, if today's lunch crowd was any indication.

"Wrap that pie, then. I'll take it home to my husband—as his reward for not coming along with us today."

Her friends giggled and continued chattering as Rachel strode toward the front counter. While she put the pie in a carryout box, she called her order through the serving window. "A plate of the peppers for Micah, side of green beans. Three pieces of the lemon icebox pie—and ya got any more rhubarb pies, Mamma? I'm boxin' your last one here."

Her mother glanced up from the work island in

the middle of the kitchen, where she was slicing an assortment of fruit pies for a customer's family reunion this evening. She'd rolled her black sleeves above her elbows and her face was flushed from working in the heat of the ovens since three this morning. "I'll have to look, honey-bug. Rhoda just took down an order for ten dozen zucchini corn muffins, plus sandwich buns, goin' to a barbecue. And Naomi's been scurryin' to make more meat loaf and the fillin' for another pan of peppers."

Naomi Brenneman, her mother's partner in the café—and Micah's *mamm*—flashed her a brown-eyed smile. "What a day it's been! Busier than Leah's bees, we are."

"*Des gut*, ain't so?" Rachel fetched a lemon pie from the refrigerator and quickly plated the three biggest wedges. "Better than wonderin' if we'd make a go of it, like when we opened this time last year, Mamma."

"Can ya catch table three, Rachel?" her twin called from the crowded doorway. "I'll be pullin' four tables together for all these folks comin' in from the senior center's van."

The Kanagy brothers jumped up from their lunch to assist her sister as Rachel delivered Micah's meal and the slices of lemon pie. "Back in a few, boys," she murmured. "Help yourselves to tea and lemonade refills, will ya?"

Inhaling deeply to catch her breath, Rachel wondered if they should hire another girl for the summer . . . Naomi's daughter, Hannah, perhaps. She stopped beside table three and quickly reminded herself not to judge a book by its cover: the young woman who focused on the laminated menu sported short, spiky hair dyed witch-black. She wore tight black jeans with a matching tank top that revealed two tattoos on her back. And was that a little barbell piercing her eyebrow?

"Oh, gimme the meat loaf, I guess," she muttered.

"I'd recommend the stuffed peppers or the smothered hash browns. If ya can wait, though, we'll have more meat loaf in maybe fifteen minutes. Sorry," Rachel replied. Thank goodness not many of their English guests looked like something the cat dragged in. Or something left over from a Halloween party gone to the Devil, judging from those black fingernails and the heavy silver rings linked by chains to a leather band around her wrist.

"*Fifteen minutes?* You gotta be—"

The girl's curse word made Rachel grip her tablet to keep from dropping it. But when this guest raised her face to stare rudely, with blue eyes lined in coalblack eyeliner and heavy mascara, Rachel's mouth dropped open: Was it her imagination, or was that Rhoda beneath all that makeup? Why, scrubbed clean and framed in a fresh kapp, that could well be the face she saw in her own mirror each morning! Her breath left her in a rush, as though her mare had kicked her in the chest. Rachel backed away, stammering. "Excuse me, but I—I'll be back to take your order in—"

The bottom dropped from her stomach as she rushed toward the kitchen. Didn't matter that Micah and her friends might be wondering about the girl's outburst, or about the way Rachel ignored two guests who called for their checks. She hurried through the Dutch door, seeking sanctuary—from what, she wasn't sure. She fanned herself with her tablet, too upset to help Naomi take a big pan of sizzling meat loaves from the oven.

"Rachel? Ya look like you've seen a ghost!" Her mother's knife paused halfway across the cherry pie she was cutting.

What could she say? Rachel felt silly for that little flash of imagination, thinking the girl in black looked like . . . yet her stomach had tied itself in a knot and her pulse pounded as though warning her of something ominous. "I—I don't know what to—" She shook her head to clear it. "The girl at table three, by the window, well—she looks exactly like Rhoda. Or *me*, if ya don't count her ghouly clothes and hair."

Naomi's eyebrows rose as she glanced at Rachel's mother. Mamma stepped sideways to gaze into the café's crowded dining room, and then she walked slowly toward the serving window for a better view. The color left her face. Her knife hit the floor. "How on God's good earth—? Can it *be*?" Her expression vacillated between confusion and disbelief and . . . fear. But what would her mother have to be afraid of? Mamma wrung her apron in her hands, and with a whimper like a startled pup's she headed into the main room of the café.

Rachel looked at Naomi, feeling stupid and inconsiderate. "I shoulda stayed out there. Didn't mean to come in here upsettin' Mamma, what with her finally recoverin' from Dat's passin'."

"Let's go with her, then," her mother's best friend said. "Even if Miriam doesn't need our help, I'm thinkin' your sister could use a hand with that group that just came in."

Dear God, give me the strength to handle this. My toes feel ready to curl right through my shoes.

Miriam Lantz approached the girl in black slowly, feeling trapped inside a bubble that kept out the café's loud chatter and the aromas of cooked beef and onions. Were her mind and eyes playing tricks on her? Rachel had described the face beneath that spiky black hair to a tee, and while Miriam knew she was staring, she couldn't help herself. She had no words for the whirlwind of emotions that raged in her heart and soul, just as the river had raged in a flash flood eighteen years ago . . .

Once again her leg muscles clenched with the effort of clambering up that slick, muddy riverbank during a sudden downpour, as adrenalin and terror raced through her—but not as swiftly as that swollen river had risen up its banks. Her arms ached with the memory of clutching her frightened toddlers, Rachel and Rhoda, as she cried out to Rebecca, who had wiggled out of her grasp. Nothing could match the horror—the abject helplessness—she'd felt when the wild water snatched her baby girl and carried her downstream. Her little body, in a pink dress, was never found. Friends going door-to-door in the towns downriver returned without her precious child. Most in Willow Ridge had filed this incident far back in their memories, and her two remaining girls had been too young at the time to recall that fateful day.

But a mother never forgets. And she never forgives herself . . . forever wonders if God took her baby as a sign that she was too inept or unworthy to be raising His children.

Wouldn't a *good* mother have had better control of her girls? Wouldn't a competent wife have paid closer attention to the rapid rise of those flood waters? Her marriage to Jesse Lantz had never been quite the same afterward, for even as he, too, grieved the disappearance of their daughter, a cloud had hovered over their home as the years went by and she'd been unable to conceive again.

Miriam swallowed hard. Her heart hammered in her chest as somehow one foot found its way in front of the other, past guests who asked for more coffee or their checks. Though she found the young woman's spiky dyed hair and heavy makeup distasteful—and why would anyone have a skull tattooed on her shoulder—? Miriam couldn't look away from those pale blue eyes and the facial structure the girls had gotten from their *dat*.

How she wished Jesse were alive to help her now! This Englisher was a brazen one: she stared outright at Miriam's sweaty black dress, her kapp, and the dark apron smeared with flour and filling from a day of baking pies. Her attitude announced itself as blatantly as that tight, skimpy shirt accentuated breasts the same size as her sisters'. This sort of confrontation wasn't something her other girls had ever gloried in; wasn't something most Plain folk tolerated or brought on.

But she had to find words. She was the adult here . . . and there was a chance she was mistaken.

Vaguely aware that Naomi and the girls were seating a large group behind her, Miriam cleared her throat. She clasped her hands to keep from crumpling her apron. "I—I don't mean to be nosy, but—"

The girl smirked. "Okay, look, I said I wanted meat loaf, but forget it. I can't wait that long—"

"—when my daughter Rachel remarked on how *close* ya resemble Rhoda—"

"—so lemme outta here, will ya?" the young woman

demanded as she grabbed a Walmart sack from the chair beside her. "This was a huge mistake. My bad."

Miriam sidestepped quickly when the girl stood up so fast her chair struck the one behind her. Why was she so angry? And why had she come here in the first place? Willow Ridge was a quiet little community where Plain folk farmed and sold their handmade items to supplement their income. Tourists with piercings, wearing black leather wristbands, rarely ate here.

When a wad of pink fabric fell from the sack, the young woman swore and grabbed for it, but Miriam snatched it from the floor just that fast. Every fiber of her body vibrated with recognition of that little dress before this ungracious stranger could shove it back in the bag. Miriam cried out, clutching this memento of the worst day of her life.

"Dear God, can it be? It's nothin' short of a—it's a miracle!" Before Miriam realized it, she was laughing and crying hysterically while she embraced the young woman.

The girl jerked away in disgust. "Hey, I didn't come here to star in a big scene!"

"Mamma, are you all right? Whatever's makin' ya act so crazy-like?" Rhoda glared at the girl in black as she flung an arm around Miriam's shoulders, while Naomi stepped up beside her, as well. The entire café had gone quiet: the Kanagy boys and Naomi's sons had stepped closer, and all the customers lingering over lunch had stopped eating. Rachel, too, watched her mother warily from that big table of customers who'd just sat down.

Swiping at her eyes and still shaking, Miriam studied

the young woman more closely. If she were going to demand answers she had to ask the right questions, even if her mind was in such an excited muddle she couldn't believe what she was seeing. "Where'd ya get this little dress?" was all she could whisper.

Those black-lined eyes flashed, yet their crystal-blue color softened for a moment. Then she glared around the dining room. "Okay, look—show's over! Got it?" she announced loudly. Her gaze lingered on Naomi and Rhoda, but she didn't tell them to leave. Once the Brenneman boys and their friends returned to their tables, the girl in black took her seat again. She pointed to the chair across the table.

Don't forget about that help I asked for, God.

Miriam sat down, dazed. She smiled gratefully when Naomi poured her a glass of lemonade and then eased away, to wait on the folks who'd just come in. Nothing could possibly have prepared her for this moment: nearly eighteen years she'd dreamed of it, not daring to hope it would ever come to pass. But there was no denying the little dress she'd sewn with her own hands, and she couldn't help herself: she buried her face in the faded, yellowed fabric. It smelled faintly of cedar, but what did that matter? The only other person on this earth with a connection to this dress was now seated across from her. Looking as flummoxed as she felt.

"I didn't believe what my old man told me." The young woman leaned on the tabletop to nail Miriam with a doubtful gaze. "I was going through Mom's stuff after . . . after her service last week. Found this at the very bottom of her cedar chest. That's when Dad said I wasn't their natural-born daughter—that he rescued me from a tree being washed down the Missouri River in the flood of '93."

The young woman's eyes misted over and she looked away. "I don't know *what* to believe, now that I'm here. But it's, like, obvious they've kept some *really* huge secrets from me."

Chapter 2

Miriam choked on a sob. Silently she reached across the table to grip the girl's hand. "But you're alive," she rasped. "And to me, that means everythin'."

There was an awkward pause. In her peripheral vision, she saw Rachel, Rhoda, and Naomi watching this exchange even as they busied themselves with that big bunch of people at the pushed-together tables. What on earth would she say to the daughters she'd raised all along?

One thing at a time. Word by word—somehow. Miriam sipped her lemonade, hoping to clear her throat.

"Yeah, well, this wasn't quite what I expected, ya know? I mean, I've stopped at a lot of places this week, trying to get a handle on this thing." Some of the edge had returned to the young woman's voice, but she still looked as stunned as Miriam felt. "Never in a million years did I figure I was adopted, much less related to *your* kind. Jeez."

With an inward sigh, Miriam reminded herself that even the best-intentioned Englishers had no real understanding of Plain ways and beliefs. Thank goodness she also had two girls who'd been baptized into the church and who'd never given her a speck of trouble. "*Jah*, that must've been a shock—and findin' out after ya lost your . . . mother, too. I'm sorry about her passin'. Hardest loss there is."

How odd it felt to say that. She wanted to jump and sing for joy and tell everyone here *who* she was talking to! How could she not grab this young woman's bare shoulders and shout *I am your mother*?

But as she searched her long-lost daughter's face, Miriam sensed it was best not to alienate the girl further with a misplaced word or . . . another display of affection. Even though at such a time, *love* was the only response that made sense to her.

Across the table, her daughter swiped at her eyes with a napkin, which made raccoon rings appear beneath them. Had she no idea how beautiful she was without all that paint?

"So you're saying that flood story is true? When Dad told me about it, I laughed in his face," she replied defiantly. She plucked at the dress, which was on the table between them. "I mean, get *real!* How could a kid this little survive the ride from here to Morning Star on a tree trunk? In all that fast-moving water?"

"I honestly don't know." Again Miriam sipped her lemonade, gripping her damp glass carefully. Her whole body was shaking. "But I do know this, Rebecca: as I watched that river wash ya away from me— as I clutched your two sisters and lost my hold on ya—the water knocked a hole in my heart I knew would never be filled."

Had she gotten too melodramatic? Miriam stood, looking for Rhoda and Rachel in the crowded dining room. She beckoned to them, her heart hammering, because their faces said it all: What was going on here? Who was this stranger who had made her laugh and cry and go a little crazy, as none of them had ever seen her do? She'd shown little emotion since Jesse's passing. It took all her energy just to get from one day to the next, keeping herself too busy to think. Or to feel.

"These are your sisters, Rhoda and Rachel," she said in a thick voice. "They, like you, have no idea about that dreadful day because your *dat* and I rarely spoke of that storm, it upset us so. I have a lot of—of explainin' to do to them."

"What're ya tellin' us, Mamma?" Rhoda's eyes looked as round as china saucers in her flawless face as she studied the young woman who remained seated. In her deep green dress, made from the same pattern as Rachel's maroon one, Rhoda looked so . . . untouched by the world. Curious, yet confused.

"It's a long story, best left for when we're not dealin' with the lunch rush." Miriam sighed, noting doubt and maybe denial in Rachel's face. "Girls, ya were born as triplets, and—and this is the sister we lost the summer ya turned three. Her name is Rebecca—"

"Uh, that would be Tiffany." Those ice-blue eyes, so dear yet so defiant, assessed two kapps and two modest dresses and two faces identical to her own—at least before she put on her makeup each morning. "Look, I'm not even sure why I stopped here. Just took out driving around, trying to sort this out in my head. But it's a sure bet I won't be hanging around. I mean—talk about two different worlds!"

When Tiffany stood to go, Miriam's heart lurched. "Please, stay and eat! Rhoda, that meat loaf's ready now, and we have fresh green beans—"

"No way. Don't know what I expected," she muttered, removing Miriam's hand from her arm, "but this'll never work. Sorry."

Miriam bit back a cry as the too-slender Tiffany brushed past her and strode to the door. She almost ran after her—surely God hadn't brought her daughter back home only to drive her away in a matter of minutes!

But Miriam stood rooted to her spot. Her heart welled up and she wanted to cry as she hadn't since they'd buried Jesse, but what would that accomplish? And in front of all these friends and lunch customers?

Leave it be, her soul whispered. *The Lord works in mysterious ways.*

Rachel clenched her fists beneath her apron to keep from grabbing the rudest, crudest girl she'd ever met. Tiffany, was it? She'd seen beautiful lamps in catalogs with that name on them, but this creature—this grotesque specter in black and tattoos—had nothing in common with a creation that gave light. Why had Mamma carried on so, over a total stranger with a little pink dress in a Walmart bag?

And why was Micah standing at the back table with his mouth hanging open? Like his brothers, he'd put on his straw hat to leave, but instead of coming up

toward the cash register he went to the window closest
to the parking lot. Kept gawking after that spectacle
their mother had dared to call Rebecca—her sister!

Didn't Rhoda and Naomi feel it, the way the earth
had just tilted on its axis? The way this total stranger
had shown up just long enough to intrude on them
before declaring they had nothing in common? And
that she wanted nothing to do with them? Any fool
could see that! How dare she disrupt their lives and
then brush them off as though their feelings about
her surprise appearance didn't matter? Something
snapped inside her, and Rachel rushed out the door.

Tiffany was hurrying toward a flashy red convertible, pushing some sort of button in her hand that
made its lights flash. The skull drawn on her shoulder,
which clenched a long-stemmed rose in its teeth,
seemed the lewdest sign of all that this Englisher intended to provoke or offend people everywhere she
went. And what was the point of allowing that?

"Tiffany!" she hollered.

The girl pivoted at her car door. Those black-
rimmed eyes dared Rachel to challenge her.

So who was she to argue? "Do us all a favor and go
back where ya came from!" she snapped. "Don't go
upsettin' Mamma's applecart ever again, hear me?
With Dat gone, we don't need any more nasty surprises like you!"

Rachel hugged herself tightly as the scarlet car sent
gravel flying behind it and then surged onto Route C.
"Didn't even look!" she muttered when the vehicle
sped around a horse and buggy clip-clopping up
the road.

But someone else was looking: first thing Rachel

noticed when she turned to go inside was Micah's face at the café window. And he wasn't watching *her*.

And what's that all about? Seems Mamma's not the only one with some explainin' to do!

"Let's get this talked about, girls. Your sister Rebecca came and left in the blink of an eye, but the situation's landed in our laps like a load of horse apples, ain't so?"

Miriam sighed tiredly as they entered the kitchen of the big white house Jesse and his friends had built while he was courting her. Her days of baking began around three each morning, and she usually stayed until after the Sweet Seasons closed at two. Never had she imagined herself a partner in such an all-consuming business, but goodness knows it kept her from fretting over the death of her husband—not to mention the loss of his income as the only blacksmith in Willow Ridge.

And never had she imagined coming face-to-face with her lost daughter. *Lost in more ways than one, by the looks of her.*

"I got worried about you, clutchin' this little dress, Mamma," Rhoda murmured as she took the garment from Tiffany's Walmart bag. "It's not your way to shout or throw your arms around complete strangers."

"And this one is stranger than most!" Rachel muttered. "Who does she think she is, bargin' in durin' the lunch rush to gawk at us like *we're* the odd ones? And did ya see how Micah was eyeballin' her?"

Rhoda snickered. "Everyone was starin' at her, Sis.

Amongst all the folks on God's lunch menu, Tiffany's not exactly the blue plate special."

"So if she just now found this pink dress, why'd she come *here*? Today?" The daughter in maroon shook her head scornfully. "I'm not sure I believe it. I'm thinkin' she's after somethin'. Thinkin' she can trick us Amish into fallin' for her fancy scheme. After all, Morning Star is *up*river from Willow Ridge!"

"Why did her—the woman who raised her—tuck that dress into her trunk? Why did I think your *dat* was at the river fishin' that day the floodwaters rose so fast?" Miriam replied as they climbed the stairs to the second floor. "Life's full of questions, girls. And we find out, sooner or later, that some things're best left as mysteries for God to solve in His own *gut* time. The bishop we had before Hiram insisted we handle the accident that way all those years ago and . . . I believed he was right. Mostly."

And when was a good time to face up to these mysteries? To deal with the disappointment that burned so deep when things hadn't worked out the way she'd hoped? The six bedrooms along this hallway had often mocked her, a reminder of plans to fill them with the rest of the children she and Jesse had both hankered for . . .

Perhaps Rebecca's surprise return would bring a piece of her grief into the open air so she could release it, like picking a sliver of glass from a festering wound. High time. But, of course, nothing ever went easy, when it came to explaining past tragedies tucked away like little dresses in a trunk. Miriam gestured for Rhoda to open the square doorway built waist-high in the wall of the room where they did their sewing.

The attic's dry heat enveloped them as they stooped into the cubbyhole and then went up the short flight of stairs, lit by afternoon light from the windows on opposite walls. How her girls had loved to play here on rainy days, among old grocery crates full of odds and ends and cast-off furnishings that had belonged to Jesse's parents and her own. Rachel and Rhoda had no idea that a battered steamer trunk behind their grandmother's sewing cabinet kept such a sad secret.

"I looked for a way to tell you girls ya had another sister," Miriam whispered as she snapped open the latch of the trunk. "But as years go by, some things just don't seem as important. And explainin' them sure doesn't get any easier. Not many of the People recall that day, on account of how your *dat*'s parents and mine have all passed now, and Naomi's bunch moved here to Willow Ridge a couple years after the accident. The other elders insisted we not involve the police or outsiders in the search effort and as the deacon, your *dat* went along with them."

"Oh, Mamma." Rhoda picked up a handful of little green dresses and the white aprons folded in with them. "You saved our clothes—"

"*Jah*, thinkin' they'd be worn by other babes comin' along. I wasn't but twenty when . . . when Rebecca wiggled away from me and headed into the river." Miriam studied the expressions on their dear, identical faces and sensed her girls had enough to digest. No good would be served by revealing the other heartache she'd endured as a result of that ill-fated walk through the storm to find Jesse.

Rachel nipped her lip then. "There are . . . three of these green dresses." She lifted other sets of clothing, as well, as though counting and searching for evidence to back up her earlier accusations.

"*Jah*. Three of most everything in here, except—" Closing her eyes against fresh tears, Miriam lifted the layers of clothing in shades of plum and grass green and sky blue until she came to dresses of pink. "Here's the ones ya wore durin' that awful storm. Which is why I have to doubt Tiffany—our Rebecca—is tryin' to put one over on us. How else would she have a dress identical to these?"

Rhoda blinked, stroking the fabric that had gone soft with much wear. "And think, Sis, how hard it must've hit that poor girl when she found a dress made from this Plain pattern in her mamma's cedar chest. With only her *dat*—who's not really her father— tryin' to tell her the truth about it, after the fact."

"She had no reason to come here buzzin' like a wasp! Nor to make such a show of shockin' Mamma!" Rachel retorted.

Miriam smiled despite the way her heart had been torn in so many directions today. No one could fault her girls for the way they'd stood beside her, in the presence of a stranger whose ways had upset them all. "I can't imagine the man who raised her as his own is feelin' much better, or gettin' any more consideration from Tiffany than we did. She's sad after her mother's passin', and angry and . . . troubled in a lot of ways, I suspect."

"*Jah*, well, she'll know trouble for sure and for certain if she bats those black lashes at Micah—or comes back to haunt us again!" Rachel hastily re-placed the sets of baby clothing and slammed the trunk shut. "Let's go down and start somethin' *gut* for supper. Then I'll be ready for a big piece of Katie Zook's birthday cake and a ride in somebody's new courtin' buggy."

Rhoda followed her sister toward the dim stairs, but then turned to smile at Miriam. "Don't wait up for us tonight, Mamma. I'm thinkin' ya could use some quiet time and a *gut* night's rest, ain't so? Tomorrow's a new day."

Chapter 3

"Thought ya could use a little somethin' sweet after such a day," Naomi Brenneman said as she approached the porch. "Somethin' ya didn't bake yourself."

"Is that chocolate I smell? Oh, *denki*, Naomi. You're the best friend a woman ever had!" Miriam set aside the pillowcase she was embroidering to pat the swing's cushion. She smiled at the blonde whose eyes shone like dark, sweet tea. After her full day of cooking at the café, Naomi had changed into a fresh brown dress, and she held up a pan of the most heavenly smelling dessert, still warm from the oven. "Your chocolate zucchini cake calls for forks and plates—"

"And maybe a little time for talkin', what with all the kids bein' at the Zooks'? Sit still, Miriam. I know where everythin' is."

Miriam closed her eyes, exhaled wearily, and let the breeze blowing in from the river soothe her like the sweet perfume of the blooming mimosa trees. How could everything around her seem so normal, after the way her world had tipped like an overloaded wheelbarrow today?

"Didn't want to be nosy this noon. I could see you were havin' a time of it, though, talkin' to that . . . girl in the black getup." The porch swing creaked and shifted as Naomi settled into its cushion next to her and then handed over a generous square of cake. "I'm guessin' she's yours, and ya thought she was—"

"Long gone, *jah.* Didn't see how any toddler—not yet three years old—could've survived bein' carried off in that flood," Miriam murmured. "And I lost count of the nights I fretted and prayed when we never found her little body. Couldn't even say a proper good-bye . . . couldn't close the lid and move on. Not for the longest time."

The moist cake was a balm to her battered soul. Miriam savored its dense sweetness as she considered how to share such a story with her dearest friend. The bishop and the preachers at that time had advised them to grieve in private, and after a while Jesse had plain-out told her to devote her time and thoughts to caring for Rhoda and Rachel—and him, of course—instead of dwelling on the little one she'd lost.

No doubt in her mind this long-ago ordeal would've been easier to handle had Naomi Brenneman lived in Willow Ridge back then. Some things only a woman— a mother—could understand. "Sorta fits that Rebecca acts so much the rebel now, when ya consider she was always the feisty one," Miriam recalled softly. "When the river rose so fast that day, it was all I could do to grab those three girls and struggle back up the muddy bank with them—"

"And you've spent all these years thinkin' she drowned. And that it was all your fault."

"*Jah.* And believin' Jesse blamed me, too, though he never came out and said so." The cake on her plate blurred as she set down her fork. "Thing is, I got it in my head that God was showin' me what a poor excuse for a mother I was—"

"Oh no, Miriam! My own kids shoulda been so lucky as to have *you* for a *mamm!*"

"—and both of us figured it for the reason we couldn't conceive again," Miriam finished with a hitch in her voice. "What I couldn't tell the girls today, when they were lookin' at the two little pink dresses I'd put away, was that . . . well, I was carryin' that day I heisted them up the slippery riverbank. About five months along, I was."

"Oh, Miriam. That's just the saddest thing I ever heard."

When Naomi's arm flew around her neck, the tears finally came. All afternoon she'd faced up to folks watching her every move, her every reaction, and finally she let loose of the fear and pain stored up in her soul. With her head on her friend's shoulder, Miriam released a world of hurt and guilt no one else had ever seen. "Ain't no use in cryin' over somethin' so long past—"

"If ya can't cry about lost babes, what's left? I'm thinkin' God cried right along with ya that day, Miriam." Her friend sniffled loudly and swiped at her eyes. "Ya couldn't have been, what? Twenty at the time?"

"Twenty, *jah.* Same as Rachel and Rhoda are now."

"Well, then. Seems the Good Lord saw fit to bless ya with three girls at once and another babe only half-baked, yet He only gave ya two arms. . . ." Naomi cleared her throat, mischief sparkling in her dark eyes. "Even on a good day, that won't add up. Only a man would leave ya that shorthanded, Miriam. But don't go tellin' Bishop Knepp—or the Good Lord— I said that!"

Miriam gaped. Naomi's remark bordered on irreverence, and yet . . . all these years and she'd never considered that angle of her tragedy. Most women she knew had more children than hands—but most of them had never dealt with the survival of two children along with the loss of one wee, wiggly girl, either.

Only a man would leave ya that shorthanded, Miriam. She hiccupped and then a giggle welled up from deep inside her. "Oh, *denki*, Naomi. I can't thank ya enough for—all these years I've been blamin' myself for not bein' quick enough, or smart enough, to corral Rebecca—"

"And don't go thinkin' that'll happen anytime soon, sorry to say. She's a hard nut to crack, that one." The blonde fingered a string of her fresh white kapp, lost in thought. "Who can say how English ways might've fostered her rebellious attitude . . . and what that unsuspectin' couple went through after they rescued her. She musta been a real handful."

"There's that, *jah*." Miriam dabbed her eyes, feeling greatly relieved.

"I think you're a blessed woman, Miriam," her friend continued in a thoughtful tone. "You've had two fine daughters to raise, and now you've learned that your third girl is a survivor, after all. Stronger than any of us knew—even if her witchy face paint and clothes scared the Devil out of us for a bit. Had everybody watchin' her, that's for sure and for certain."

Miriam closed her eyes again, letting these positive thoughts cleanse the secret wounds of the past eighteen years. At least a little. "*Jah*, the term 'Devil's spawn' came to mind, at first glance," she said ruefully. "But that's my flesh and blood, Naomi. My little lamb lost. I can't help wantin' to see more of her—to *know* the girl beneath the ghoulish getup. To help her, if I can."

"Give it time, dear. By the looks of it, she was as shocked to learn the truth as you and the girls were."

"Came at a hard time for her, too." Miriam caught the last of her cake crumbs with the tines of her fork. How was it that the rows of sweet corn in her garden seemed greener now, in the rays of the setting sun? The soft perfume of the mimosa trees wafted over her again, and three hummingbirds buzzed in to light on the feeder in front of her. "*Denki* ten times over, Naomi," she murmured, feeling blessed indeed. "What would I do without ya?"

"You'd do the same for me." Naomi patted her hand. "Get some *gut* rest tonight. By the looks of your front garden, Leah'll be pickin' us a load of zucchini tomorrow."

As the mantel clock chimed half past eleven that night, Miriam's thoughts still simmered. The shock of her long-lost daughter's visit had worn off, but as she lay with her arm across Jesse's empty half of the bed, she felt anything but sleepy. What kind of childhood had her Rebecca known? What interests and talents had God given her? While Rhoda and Rachel looked identical, they were cut from different bolts of cloth, as far as their personalities went, so it only made sense that Rebecca—always more active and vocal than her sisters—had different strengths and interests, too.

And what of her *dat*? Was he put off by the girl's black clothing . . . her dyed hair and tattoos? He surely couldn't have envisioned her looking this way when he'd rescued the toddler in the pink Plain-style dress. Had he and Tiffany been close before his wife died? Or had the woman's death driven more of a wedge between them? A parent's passing always put a family out of kilter, even when everybody got along.

Was there a chance she could reach out and re-cover the lamb she'd lost?

Better watch me, Lord, or I'll go and do somethin' stupid. Might hurt people without meanin' to.

The quiet footsteps on the stairway told her Rhoda was home from the birthday party. And why that girl hadn't long ago settled on a beau was beyond her. Certainly wasn't for lack of interest amongst their young men, the way she'd heard it. Rachel was no doubt out enjoying Micah's new courting buggy on this fine summer night, although Naomi's boy was most likely getting an earful.

And what sort of boys did Rebecca like? Her im-modest way of dressing didn't bode well for the repu-tation a mother wanted for her daughter—but then, what could Miriam do about that?

Might as well get up, rather than lettin' my mind spin like the café's electric meter. Miriam listened to Rhoda's quiet preparations for bed . . . gave her another twenty minutes to fall asleep. Then she rose quietly to wind her hair into a fresh bun and dress for another day. It was hours too early to start baking pies and rolls, but two years without Jesse had taught her the value of hard work—not just for the income, but for releasing her worries, as well. The solitude of the Sweet Seasons kitchen . . . the soothing rhythms and scents of making her pastries while the rest of the world slept around her, were a balm to her soul. Almost like chocolate.

And if her sister Leah was bringing them a load of zucchini this morning, they'd be processing it to freeze for winter, as well as cooking some for lunch. And there were those two gallons of extra milk Lydia Zook had brought from the store . . .

It felt like a chocolate pie kind of a day.

Chapter 4

"Micah Brenneman, ya haven't heard a thing I'm sayin'! I don't *know* the answers to your questions about Tiffany—or Rebecca—or whoever she is. And I don't really care!"

Micah let the reins hang slack in his hand so Rosie, his mare, moseyed along in front of the buggy. He smiled in the darkness. Rachel cared plenty about their surprise visitor, or she wouldn't be railing at him this way. It was almost worth the tongue-lashing she gave him, to ask her the questions that made her eyes widen so and got her dander up. Nobody in this world stirred him the way Rachel Lantz did, and a fellow always knew where he stood with such an outspoken young woman. "I still don't understand about her comin' from Morning Star if she got carried downstream—"

"Exactly what I said to Mamma!" The girl beside him scooted closer, to take his chin in her hand so there was no missing what she was about to say. "Never underestimate an Englisher's tricks, Micah! Just ask

Tom Hostetler, now that his Lettie's run off with that fancy man! And him a preacher, too!"

"*Jah*, he's takin' the heat for that one." As he adjusted his hat, Micah thought it might be a welcome diversion from Tom's troubles to let the grapevine vibrate with talk of Miriam's long-lost daughter. "But your *mamm*'s not gonna let go of this one, Rache. That wild child named Tiffany mighta breezed in and blown right on out, but Rebecca's the lost sheep the shepherd Jesus rejoices over, even when He's got the ninety and nine safe in the fold."

"And why're you so all-fired fascinated by her, then? Ya haven't stopped talkin' about her since we got to Zooks'."

Well, she had him there. Micah clucked to his mare, keeping his arm on the edge of the buggy seat behind Rachel. If he weren't careful, she'd be giving him what his Mennonite electrician partner called the *kiss-off* instead of the kisses he'd been hoping for. She'd smiled through tears of joy last week when he'd said he loved her, even though their intentions wouldn't be published until later this fall—and that wasn't something a smart man messed with. Especially since he'd soon be twenty-five and had spent his time building his carpentry business with his brothers while most of his friends had wooed the community's courting-age girls.

"What's your answer to that, Micah?" she insisted in a low, tight voice. "If you're tellin' me you'd rather chase after that heathen in the indecent black clothes—"

Well, there was that thought. But he knew better than to take it seriously.

"—then don't let me stand in your way, mister!"

"Rachel!" He dropped the reins to take her pretty face between his two hands. "When I said I wanted *you* to be my woman—my wife—I meant it."

"And surely you can see my family needs a man, Micah. So don't go breakin' my heart, lookin' at that ghouly-girl with the hair lickin' her head like black flames."

He kissed her softly, all the way around her lips, the way she liked it. Rachel was young and sweet, yet impetuous. Not a girl to cower in the face of a challenge. She'd worked hard alongside her mother and Rhoda to make the café a thriving business, ever since Jesse had passed when a spooked stallion trampled him. And one of these days she'd understand why Tiffany's reappearance was a blessing rather than a bad omen, but right now Rachel was too rattled to hear his reassurances.

Micah held her close, inhaling her clean scent. "I've got a busy day, what with raisin' a barn over at Jim Kanagy's in New Haven tomorrow—and you'll be on your feet all day at the Sweet Seasons," he reminded her. "How about I take ya home now and see ya over breakfast . . . like I dream of doin' when you'll serve it up in our home every mornin', just for me?"

Rachel sighed softly and lowered her eyes then. "Are ya sayin' we'll have a place for just us two? What with Mamma bein' alone, I feel responsible for—"

"She'd never expect ya to put your happiness on hold until she finds her own, honey-girl."

"—and Rhoda! Like a butterfly flittin' from beau to beau, with no place to land. Can ya see those two makin' it from one day to the next without me to keep them on the steady path?" Rachel laughed softly as she shook her head. "With all those rooms upstairs, might be easier for *you* to just move in with—"

"With all you biddy hens?" Micah teased. He could do worse than take up residence with Rhoda and Miriam Lantz, but it wasn't his sweetest dream. "I've got better ideas for us, Rache. Can ya trust me on this and be patient awhile longer?"

Like a deflating balloon she let out her breath. Weariness replaced the excitement he'd seen just moments ago: Was she tired of his talk? He'd been courting her for a long time, compared to most couples they knew. "It's been a . . . tirin' day, *jah*," she murmured. "Best take me back, I s'pose. She won't admit to it, but Mamma doesn't sleep until Rhoda and I are both home."

"Wants all her sheep in the pen. Just like you and I will someday."

They rode in silence along the main county road that led to the Lantz land. Just past the café and quilt shop they turned off, to head down the long unpaved lane that led to the tall house, glowing white in the moonlight. Odd that a light burned in the Sweet Seasons kitchen at this hour.

Past Jesse's vacant smithy and forge they rode in silence . . . alongside the large, flat garden where sweet corn stood in rows like sentinels with tassled hats. On the other side of the lane, melon vines wound around the dark, shiny fruits that burst with red sweetness at the touch of a sharp knife. All was orderly and tidy, like Miriam Lantz herself. Micah steered Rosie in a circle when they came near the porch.

He hopped down, helped Rachel to the ground, and dared to kiss her full on the mouth even though her mother or sister might be peering out from behind the curtains. She tasted faintly of cake and root beer and all those homey pleasures he planned to share with her for years to come, and with her moonlit kapp framing her face, she enticed him with her expectant innocence. Would he live up to the sweet dreams shining in her eyes?

"G'night now, Rachel," he whispered. "See ya later, for breakfast."

She nodded and slipped out of her shoes, to pad silently up the front porch steps.

Miriam kneaded the batch of warm, soft dough into a ball and turned the big crockery bowl over the top of it so it would rise for this morning's cinnamon rolls. While she still rode this burst of energy, she stirred the butter she'd melted into a big bowl of graham cracker crumbs and began to form shells for those chocolate pies. Rhoda would be happy to stir up the pudding when she arrived, as the cool, thick filling resembled soft fudge when it set up: this was her favorite cream pie, while Rachel preferred butterscotch.

And what did Rebecca like? Had her mother even made pies or rolls? Hard to believe most fancy folk chose store-bought pastries and breads . . . handling dough was therapy to ease troubled souls and tense muscles—not to mention a surefire way to bring the family to the table together. Little of that went on these days in the outside world, she'd heard, and once more she felt ever so thankful for the Old Ways that kept families in Willow Ridge together.

Well, except for the Hostetlers. Now there was a sad sight: Tom slinking into the café these past few mornings to eat in the back corner, as though his friends wondered what he'd done to make his wife run off. Miriam could well imagine the talk *that* had caused in the quilt shop next door, where Mary Schrock and her husband's biddy aunts kept abreast of such situations. Recently widowed Priscilla, and Eva, a *maidel* as starchy as the doilies she crocheted for dresser scarves, had nothing better to do than speculate about how Lettie Hostetler had carried her suitcases out to the road under cover of a moonless night, to be whisked away by a man in a fast, flashy car. As Mennonites, the Schrocks were a little freer with their activities—and their imaginations. But she'd be forever grateful for the way Mary had partnered with her, providing the electricity and equipment the health department required, so she and the girls could run the café.

Miriam blinked. Listened for the noise out front to repeat itself as she stood here alone in the kitchen. Who would be coming into the café in the wee hours?

"That you, Miriam?"

She let out the breath she'd been holding. "Micah? Come on back, dear," she called. "But what brings ya here at this late hour?"

"*Early* hour, ya mean." He peered around the side of the tall stainless steel fridge, taking the straw hat from a full head of dark blond hair that made him resemble the picture on a Dutch Boy paint can. "Close as this place sits to the road, ya might wanna lock up when you're here by yourself. Saw your light. Everythin' all right?"

Miriam smiled at her best friend's middle son. No need to ask why her Rachel had been crazy for this one since they'd first sat in the schoolroom together. "When

I need to sort through my thoughts, I bake. Lots better than rollin' around in that lonely old bed—"

She flushed and quickly resumed pressing the buttered graham cracker crumbs into pie pans. "More than ya wanted to know. Sorry."

Micah shrugged. He opened the fridge and pulled out a pan with the two last pieces of lemon icebox pie in it. "Anybody's name on these?"

"Yours, now. How was Katie's birthday party?"

He smiled over the wedge of pie he'd crammed into his mouth. "Heavy on the girl side, but Jonah and I survived it." Micah swallowed, as though considering how best to continue. "Your girls had a lot to talk about tonight, what with their sister showin' up outta the blue. Must've been a shock to *your* system, too, but—but I'm real happy ya got to see her, Miriam."

Miriam rested her sticky fingers on the edge of a pie pan to take in what he'd just said. "*Denki*," she murmured. "It's troublesome to the girls, I think, but—"

"It'll work out." He lifted the pie to his lips again, closing his eyes over the huge, sweet mouthful as though he'd gone days without eating. Then he focused on her intently. "Got a secret, and I think you're the one to keep it for me. Got a big favor to ask, too—but if it ain't to your likin', I want ya to tell me straight-out!"

What could he be asking of her? Micah's quiet voice and the way he talked so freely to her felt encouraging, yet her insides fluttered with nerves.

"A while back I overheard ya sayin', after a Sunday meetin' when ya sat amongst your women friends, that ya might live in the loft above the smithy once your girls got hitched, and—" The young man's suspenders stretched over his broad shoulders as he shoved his hands into his pants pockets. "Well, maybe I shouldn't've been listenin', but it struck me as a mighty promisin' situation. If I were to remodel your upstairs there, in the evenin's after my shop work, would ya consider lettin' Rachel and me—"

"So you're gonna get hitched?" Miriam laughed softly and placed a large pan of pie shells in the oven. It was tradition for young folk to court in secret until they declared their intentions to marry, yet she admired Micah for making his plans . . . and for including her in them.

"Ya didn't hear that from *me*, ya know!" he replied with a conspiratorial grin. "But I'd make ya a real cozy nest upstairs—"

"Make a room for Rhoda, too. Ya surely don't want her around when—"

"Nah! We can all of us live in that big white house, if ya want!" he insisted. "Plenty of rooms to go around. I could just as easy remodel that place, so you could—"

"It's wonderful-*gut* of ya to offer that, Micah. *Denki* for your thoughtfulness, but when I had this building constructed, I figured on makin' my own little *dawdi haus* above Jesse's shop." She smiled at the sturdy young man before her, imagining the fine wee ones he and Rachel would make. "Newlyweds need some time for just the two of them. I wouldn't wanna interfere with your makin' me some grandbabies, now would I?"

Micah grinned, his cheeks the color of strawberries.

"Truth be told, unless I get old and feeble sooner than I think—"

"Oh, you're not nearly there, Miriam!"

"—I'd like some privacy, too, ya know. It's different for us, what with all the older ones in our families gone," she added pensively. "While I wish you and Rachel all the solid, steadfast kind of lovin' Jesse and I shared. . . ."

Miriam paused, wondering how to express the thoughts swirling in her mind. Would a young man like Micah understand? Or would he send her unconventional sentiments along the grapevine, where they'd likely come back like bees to sting her? "Well, now that I'm up before the roosters crow, bakin' for this business, I kinda like settin' the day's schedule around my work instead of around somebody else's. Does that sound horrible selfish? Like I don't need or want a man anymore? Or like I didn't live a fine, happy life with my Jesse?"

Micah's deep green eyes were fixed on her in the most quizzical way, as though he'd never considered the possibility of a woman declaring a bit of independence. That wasn't done amongst the People, where women submitted to their men's decisions . . . except in the quietest, subtlest ways. Because once women were left alone, they often discovered they were perfectly capable of tending their affairs. Perhaps were better at it than their husbands had been! *Deliver me, Lord, from uncharitable or self-centered thoughts. Thy will be done* . . .

"Sounds to me like both of us'll get the kind of happiness we're lookin' for, if we honor each other's intentions," he replied quietly. "Lots of women—my *mamm* included—appreciate the chance to make extra money here. Dat's not so fond of her cookin' at the café insteada at home in the mornin's, but a man in a wheelchair has to adjust his attitude about a lotta things, ain't so?"

"We all know Ezra'd rather be buildin' with you boys than pushin' papers at the hospital's admittin' desk," she said with a nod. Nobody plans on falling through a rotten roof they are repairing, after all. Truth be told, the accident had taken as much toll on Naomi as it had on her burly husband. Miriam understood that her best friend worked here as much to keep her spirits up as to bring in more income.

She brightened, noting the wall clock. "You'd best be gettin' some shut-eye, young man! But when you're ready to work on my new apartment, I am, too! And *denki* ever so much for thinkin' of me—and for sharin' your little secret!"

He fished a tape measure from the deep pockets of his trousers. "Think I'll have me a look-around and get a few dimensions. Get my head workin' on the plans so's I can really steam along once I start the remodelin'."

Who could argue with such a sensible way of approaching a project? And who could've guessed that beneath Micah Brenneman's quiet ways dwelt a man who thought things through, and considered others' needs? Rachel got mighty impatient with him, but she was luckier than she knew to have a prospective husband who had put his ducks in a row before he courted her seriously.

Miriam lit a lamp for Micah to take next door to Jesse's empty shop, and then quickly pulled her pie crusts from the oven. Again her gaze flitted to the clock.

Nearly five. Did she have time to call Sheila now? The Englishwoman often drove her around to deliver her pies, and a call this early—before the girls and Naomi arrived to cook—was her best chance to make the arrangements that had popped into her mind as soon as she'd started baking. Sheila Dougherty was another widow who got her best work done before dawn, and she'd be washing jars or stirring up a batch of strawberry jam before her day of driving the Amish began.

Hearing Micah's footfalls fading away, Miriam hurried to the telephone before she lost her nerve. Bishop Knepp allowed the café and the quilt shop to share a business phone in a little booth outside their back doors, but every now and again some personal business needed tending, too. Her finger stumbled over keys as she punched the familiar numbers and she had to start again . . . held her breath as it rang, hoping Sheila had her cell phone handy if she was fetching jars up from the basement.

"*Jah*, Sheila? It's Miriam, and I'm wonderin' could ya drive me someplace Sunday afternoon, early?" she said in a low voice. She waited while the efficient woman grabbed a pen and paper. "I also got a big favor, on account of I'm not sure where we'll be goin'. I'll explain all that later—but I need to find where a girl named Tiffany lives. Don't know her last name— sorry! But her *dat* lives in Morning Star, I'm thinkin', and her mother passed just a week or so ago . . . *jah!* If ya could check the obituaries in the paper, that'd be *gut*, Sheila! Thanks ever so much, and I'll see ya Sunday around one, then."

Miriam hung up, her heart pounding. Had she really arranged to see Tiffany again—and on Sunday, when the *Ordnung* forbade them to ride in cars? To find out where her daughter lived and possibly meet the man who'd rescued and raised her? It was a bold move, perhaps presumptuous, to show up unannounced at their door—if she had the gumption to knock! But what better opportunity? This Lord's day wasn't a preaching Sunday, and the girls were joining their cousins and friends at the Schrocks' to finish quilts for Mary's daughter's first baby . . . a bee where the younger women could enjoy each other's company, along with homemade ice cream, before the singles gathered for a singing that evening.

Plenty of time to see for myself how Rebecca grew up, and a chance to thank that poor bereaved man for raisin' her. I'll take a hamper of easy-to-heat food and fresh bread . . . catch another good look at the girl who left here too soon, before we could recover from her appearance enough to really see her.

Miriam suddenly felt so much joy she shivered. It wasn't like Rhoda or Rachel would want to go, anyway. And if they found out where she'd gone, well—Sundays were for visiting family, weren't they? With Sheila along, no one could question her calling on an Englishman, either. And her driver, who'd become an even better friend after Jesse's passing, would help her through any awkward spots of spending time in a non-Amish household, with folks who might feel uncomfortable about her Plain way of dressing and speaking.

After all, who could fault a mother, so long denied the presence of her child, for making this effort? Miriam wished Rebecca would return to Willow Ridge to visit, but in her heart she knew it was unlikely. To a girl Tiffany's age, the differences between Old Ways and her modern-day life would seem irreconcilable. She hoped Tiffany's *dat* would understand her reasons for coming . . .

And if he didn't? Well, nothing ventured, nothing gained. Miriam felt such a longing to fill the hole that had hollowed her heart for eighteen years now—felt such gratitude to God for this miracle, and to the earthly man who'd carried it out, she could no more remain at a distance than she could remodel the smithy's loft by herself. She glanced outside before returning to her work. Micah was vaulting onto the seat of his buggy, barely visible beyond the square of light from the kitchen's window.

Grinning, Miriam punched down the sweet, yeasty dough for this morning's orange knots. She'd mixed the crust for her usual weekend order of pies for three nearby restaurants, too, and would soon stir up muffins and cookies to sell in the front display case. It was going to be a wonderful-*gut* Friday, what with those chocolate pies for lunch, and Naomi and the girls working with her . . . even as her mind flitted like a happy butterfly toward Sunday afternoon's secret mission.

Chapter 5

"I'm writin' the specials on the board, Mamma," Rhoda called in from the dining room. "What're we havin', exactly? *Gut* mornin', Naomi!"

"*Jah*, it is, missy! Those sausages and the mornin's rolls smell so wonderful-*gut*, I might have to sample some." Their other cook came in smoothing her fresh apron, ready for another busy day. "And like I told your *mamm* last night, here comes Nate Kanagy with a wagonload of zucchini and sweet corn. A bushel of cukes and onions, too."

"No chance of the Devil findin' idle hands here today!" Miriam replied with a laugh. "We'll be servin' up Italian stew with that zucchini for noon, then. Fresh corn alongside the pork steaks. Those are the specials, Rhoda—along with your secret-ingredient chocolate pie. Tell your cousin Nate he can have a couple extra orange knots if he fetches me five pounds of hamburger and three dozen eggs from Zook's straightaway."

"*Jah*, I'll tell him, Mamma. Maybe if I also promise him a big slab of warm zucchini bread, he'll help me shuck all that corn," she added. "Rachel wasn't steppin' any too lively when I left home this mornin'."

"The consequences of courtin', ain't so?" Miriam greeted her partner with a smile and then turned on the exhaust fan to create a breeze in the kitchen. "Your boy's wagon's likely to be draggin', too, I'd think. Ah, to be their age again, knowin' what we know now."

Naomi's brown eyes sparkled with mischief. "And what would ya do different, Miriam?"

Miriam peered into the largest gas oven, slipped on her long mitts, and removed the first batch of orange knots. Their citrus sweetness filled the kitchen, and as she placed the pan alongside the cinnamon rolls she'd baked earlier, she stopped to think. What *would* she change? At twenty-one, would she have asked a driver to locate a total stranger's home, planning to go there unannounced?

Jah, if it meant findin' my baby girl, I'd've swum that ragin' river or done anythin' else in my power. Then again, when Rebecca had disappeared, she'd had two other toddlers and a husband who needed her at home, alive. Time changed how a woman looked at things.

"Tough question, that one," she murmured when she saw Naomi was waiting for her answer. "Maybe I wouldn't let fear get in my way of doin' what needed to be done. I'd like to think I'd've trusted God more, insteada worryin' so many mole hills into mountains."

Naomi's smile looked pensive. "*Jah*, there's that. I can tell ya I'd've been frantic—all done in and *ferhoodled* about the future—had my Ezra taken his fall when we were that young. Still haven't figured out what purpose God had in mind for it, but I'm waitin' Him out."

"And meanwhile, ya had three sons to step in and take over the shop."

"*Jah*. Guess it's all workin' out for the *gut*, like the Bible promises." Naomi measured powdered sugar into a bowl and then drizzled orange juice into it. As she stirred the frosting for the orange knots, a fine white haze drifted around her smoky-blue dress and apron. "There's times Ezra needs convincin' of that, when the phantom pain in his missin' legs gets him down. What with him havin' to take a desk job and me workin' away from home, life's not like we planned it when we first married."

Miriam sighed along with her best friend. "Who'd've thought I'd find myself alone, and not yet forty? Ah, but here comes a chuckle, yonder!" She pointed outside. "Your boys musta stopped to give Rachel a ride, and she's lookin' none too happy about comin' to work!"

Naomi stepped to the window beside her. While Seth drove, Rachel sat between Micah and Aaron on the bench seat behind him. Her arms were tightly crossed and her voice carried shrilly across the melon patch.

"Say all ya want about that Tiffany in her black paint! She may be one of God's children, *jah*, but she won't pay *you* boys any mind!" the slender brunette declared. "You'd best get that moony-eyed look off your face, Micah Brenneman! Stick with the one who'll make your favorite cookies for the ice-cream social, week from Saturday, and who's sewin' a new dress for the occasion, too!"

Naomi laughed softly. "She makes a *gut* point. I

doubt a girl like your Rebecca will have much time for the likes of us, sorry to say."

Nodding, Miriam opened the other oven. "Now there's somethin' I coulda done different," she murmured. "We shoulda found a way to tell the girls about losin' their sister. Woulda saved us a lot of trouble yesterday."

"Ya did the best ya could at the time, dearie. No sense in dredgin' up the past." Her blonde friend dipped a pastry brush in her bowl of glaze and expertly swirled it over the warm rolls. "Meanwhile, I'm thinkin' Rache and Micah are soundin' like an old married couple. Ya think they'll get hitched this fall? We've been waitin' long enough for *that!*"

Miriam busied herself shifting the large pans of rolls into the metal baker's rack to clear some counter space. Never let it be said she couldn't keep her mouth shut, even with her best friend!

"Micah never gives me a clue about whether this'll be the year," her partner chattered on, "even though he's mighty proud of that new buggy. And even though folks're sayin' the economy's still not the best, the boys've had a real *gut* year with their carpentry shop."

Recalling the talk she'd had with Naomi's son earlier, Miriam merely smiled. "Can't tell ya a thing about that."

"Rachel doesn't let on, either? She surely must be fixin' linens and whatnot for her dower chest!"

"My lips're sealed, Naomi." Miriam flashed her friend a mischievous grin as she took the large cast-iron skillets from their pegs on the wall. "We'd best get to cookin' breakfast so's we can open on time."

* * *

Would this day never end? Rachel took the orders at table four, forcing a smile to cover her exhaustion, and then refilled Preacher Hostetler's iced tea.

"*Denki*, Rachel," he murmured. Poor man kept his eyes down, as if he was ashamed to eat his dinner here with folks knowing how his wife had run out on him a few weeks ago. "Quite a crowd today. Give your *mamm* and Naomi my compliments on the pork steaks and corn—and can ya bring me more of the same to take with me?"

"Sure thing. Lemme get ya a carryout box—"

"And a slice of that chocolate pie, too." He nodded, lifting his eyes to smile ruefully. "So what's that secret ingredient ya list on your board?"

"If I told ya that, it wouldn't be a secret, ain't so?"

When Tom Hostetler laughed aloud, the locals looked up to see what was so funny. And wasn't it interesting that Priscilla Schrock turned clear around in her chair to gawk at the preacher, who was seated alone? That's when Micah smoothed back his dark blond hair to give her one of his meaningful green-eyed gazes, too—probably because his brothers and the Kanagy boys were filling second plates at the salad bar.

"*Jah?* What'll it be?" she demanded, of Micah, as she went to the boys' table.

"Was it somethin' I said?"

Rachel stopped stacking their dirty plates to scowl at him. "How do ya mean?"

"You're snappish today. Not your usual cheery self," he remarked with a shrug. "Just hopin' I didn't disappoint ya last night, stayin' too long—"

"Matter of fact, Mr. Brenneman, I didn't get a minute's sleep on account of I was havin' a dream about you and that—that Tiffany!" Silverware clattered noisily onto the dirty plates she snatched from the other boys' places, and it was all she could do to keep from giving Micah the blow-by-blow of what her imagination had served up last night.

"Now let me get this straight," he said in a low voice. "If ya didn't get a wink of sleep, how were ya dreamin' about—?"

"Just never you mind, all right?" she snapped. "If you're gettin' pie today, I'd like ya to say so, instead of piddlin' around about it."

"Soooo . . . lemme see." Micah gazed at the specials board for the longest time, unaware he was scratching the ridge his hat made in his hair. "Chocolate pie . . . or that strawberry cream cake, or . . . got rhubarb custard pie today? With a scoop of ice cream?"

She rolled her eyes, exasperated. "I'll have to check in the kitchen—"

"Meet me out back with it," he murmured as he scooted his chair from the table. "I've got somethin' you need."

"I've got no time for—can't ya see how busy we are, Micah?"

"That's why it's time for Mamm to spell ya, honey-girl. Can't have ya bitin' the customers' heads off, now, can we?"

With a gasp, Rachel hurried into the kitchen, clutching dishes she'd stacked too high. Had Micah not been following her, reaching around her at the right moment, the plates would've toppled into the dish tub, too—and his efficiency frustrated her all the more. Without waiting for him to speak to his mother, Rachel grabbed a slice of pie, bustled past her sister and slammed the back screen behind her. She stood in the shade between the kitchen entrance and the delivery door to the quilt shop, so upset she wanted to scream and cry and stalk back to the house as fast as her legs would carry her.

"And what was this dream about, sweetie pie?" Micah stepped outside, Rachel giving him the slice of pie as he did so. "It's got ya all *ferhoodled* and we need to—"

"Will ya stop it with the lovey-dovey names? I've had enough for one day!" she exclaimed.

Micah's smile sagged and his fork stopped halfway to his mouth. "Sorry, Rache. Tryin' to wipe that frown from your perty face, is all."

She sighed loudly and looked away. Why couldn't this man understand that sometimes she just wanted to be left alone? "In my dream, Tiffany showed up again."

"*Jah?*" Micah took a large bite of the rhubarb custard pie and then offered her a forkful.

Rachel turned her head. "The Kanagy boys egged ya on, and ya took their dare," she continued in a strained voice. "Not only did ya put your hand on her back, ya kissed her, too! Full on the mouth! And she grabbed on to ya like she wasn't lettin' go. Like she was hookin' her claws into ya!"

His face sank a notch lower. "But by the light of this day, ya surely see that I'm doin' no such thing, Rachel. Nor do I want to."

"Are we still goin' to the ice-cream social, then?"

"Where else would I be goin'?"

She sighed impatiently. Micah was being extraordinarily nice, yet his kindness scraped at her like the steel wool they scrubbed pans with. "I don't know! I just—ya wanted to hear about that dream, so there it is! I shouldn't have told ya, probably, as it just gave ya ideas about that ghouly-girl in black."

"She's your sister, Rachel. And she can't help that any more than you can."

"So? Why'd she come buttin' in on us that way? Did she think we'd act all overjoyed and throw a party, like the father did for his prodigal son?"

Micah offered her the last bite of his pie: creamy pink rhubarb sandwiched between golden layers of pastry, with ice cream melted over it. As though she could think of dessert at a time like this! "I'm sorry she's got ya so upset, Rachel. But ya know, Tiffany's not really doin' this to ya. You're doin' it to yourself."

Her face fell. This kind, handsome man spoke the truth, but there was just no believing what she didn't want to now, no matter how right he was! "I'm sorry, Micah. Truly I am!" she rasped. "But I'm fresh outta patience with—can't think any good will come of— oh, forget it! Things ain't been right since that surprise *sister* of ours showed up!"

Rachel slammed the back screen so hard, Micah nearly dropped his pie plate. But she'd hit the nail on the head, hadn't she? Tiffany's appearance had over-turned her applecart and now, in her soul, Rachel felt too scattered to get her act together. Not *gut*, considering she didn't have any idea how to turn her attitude aright again.

But he *knew* things, didn't he? Miriam's voice had drifted outside this morning during her phone call . . . and if he could use what he'd overheard to help Rachel, shouldn't he do that? She'd be furious if she

knew of the plan forming in his mind right now. But
then, if Rachel's own mother had arranged a meeting
with Tiffany and her *dat*, why couldn't he use the information from such a visit to make his girl feel better—
about herself, mostly?

He'd never seen her so upset. That was *fear* talking,
because Rachel seemed to believe he found Tiffany
more appealing, more exciting, than she was. How
silly and wrong was that? Yet Rachel's dream had
seemed real, and she believed what she'd seen in her
overactive imagination last night.

Micah went back inside, smiling at Miriam as he
passed through the steam from a pot of fresh corn
boiling on the stove. His mother was running fresh
green zucchinis through a grinder to make bread.
Rachel and Rhoda were going to a hen party Sunday
afternoon, so now he had a plan of his own . . . and
since most ablebodied men in Willow Ridge would be
spending tomorrow raising a new milking barn in
New Haven, it would be a Saturday night when Rachel
didn't expect his company. More importantly, those
hours of physical labor would allow his mind to lie
fallow so his best thoughts about this Tiffany situation
could develop.

Micah grinned as he fetched his hat from the peg
on the wall. His brothers and the Kanagy boys had already gone back to work, figuring him for a lovesick
fool who deserved to be late. But they had no idea: he
was about to solve the mystery of what made women
tick. And after he proved to Rachel how much he
loved her, she'd never again pester him about being
slow or clueless.

Chapter 6

"*Jah, des gut.* On goes the lid!" Rhoda positioned the skillet of chicken pieces on the gas burner of their stove at home, while her sister put the seasonings back into the spice rack beside the cookstove. "That makes us enough spaghetti squash, chicken, and green beans for supper—and for tomorrow, too. I'm ready to be out of the kitchen for a day. What a week it's been!"

"Glad for the party at Schrocks' tomorrow, too. *Gut* to get out amongst friends." Rachel took three plates from the cabinet. "And nice to go somewhere and be guests instead of servers, ain't so?"

Rhoda laughed. As she placed the silverware and cloth napkins at their places, she glanced at the head of the table, where Dat used to sit, and at the length that went unused unless they had company. Everything about this house had been designed for a large family, yet now there weren't but the three of them. And if Rachel moved out when she and Micah married . . .

Gut thing Mamma and I enjoy each other's company. Our two voices won't nearly fill the spaces left empty. But there was plenty of time to think about that: nearly half the summer left, and autumn yet. And who could tell what might happen by the time Rachel and Micah published? Why, she might've found a steady beau herself by then!

"What would it have been like, to have three girls while we were growin' up, instead of just us two?" Rhoda mused aloud. "It's for sure and for certain Mamma and Dat figured on havin' a raft of kids—"

"She said Rebecca was the feisty one. I'm thinkin' we'd've had a lot more cat fights, with her stirrin' things up amongst us." Rachel rolled the wringer washer out of the pantry closet and fitted the hose end to the faucet. She started the air motor to make it agitate. "And it would've been two against one, most likely, when it came to choosin' fabric for new dresses or what kind of pie to make."

Rachel reached under the sink for the laundry detergent, still considering this question. "Wouldn't take as long for three to redd up the house. But when we were little, if one weren't holdin' up her end of the chorin', we'd've all caught Mamma's switch across the backs of our legs!"

Rhoda chuckled as she separated their dark dresses from the underthings. "*Jah*, all things considered, you and I have never fussed much. Thick as thieves when it comes to keepin' our secrets and keepin' track of each other. Probably would've been some hurt feelin's if one of us would've become the snitch. . . ."

"Well, it wouldn't've been me or you!" Rachel added borax powder to the water, her mouth set in a tight line. "Maybe Dat would've taken Rebecca out to the shop, since he had no boys to help him. Seems she *likes* metal and leather—"

"Rachel! You need a saucer of milk for makin' such a catty—sourpuss—remark!"

"*Jah*, well, *somebody* needs to see things the way they are! That girl showed up and wrapped Mamma around her little finger—even while she insulted her!" Rachel stuffed one dress and then another into the washing machine, as agitated as the sudsy water. "And Micah took one look at her—"

"Micah and everyone else. Even the other Englishers."

"—and off his mind raced, like a spooked horse!" her sister ranted. "Only took two minutes for the pot to boil over, and now, two days later, we're still cleanin' up the mess she made of us!"

Rhoda sighed, sorry she'd speculated about growing up as triplets. "Listen to yourself, Rachel!" She jerked away her hand as her sister clapped the lid on the whirring washer. "You're the one who's so—I think you're *jealous* of Tiffany!"

Her sister's eyes flashed icy-hot. "Why would I want to be like her? Why would *anybody?*"

"Because Micah took his eyes off you for two seconds to gawk at her, that's why!" Rhoda struggled to restore their harmony—that seamless state in which no one knew where one of them ended and the other began. "This isn't at all your way, Sister! I'm as *ferhoodled* about your reaction to Tiffany as I am about her showin' up in those nasty black clothes."

"You think *you're* upset? This is my future we're talkin' about, so—"

"Stop it! Just *stop.*" Rhoda placed her hands on either side of her sister's hot, flushed face, startled by the emotions she saw there—yet again. Rachel was wound up so tight her kapp quivered like a pale leaf. "Look at us, Sis! We just said how we've never fought, and ya nearly cut off my hand with that washer lid just now! What's goin' on here, really?"

The kitchen rang with stunned silence.

Rachel's gaze locked into hers. Then, with a little sob, she squeezed Rhoda's wrists and shook her head miserably. "Don't rightly know," she murmured. "Last two nights I've been havin' the most wicked nightmares about that girl—"

"*Jah*, she looks like somethin' that stepped out of a bad dream," Rhoda commiserated.

"—and I can't seem to stop thinkin' on her—on the whole fact of her existence," she confessed. "So I'm not sleepin'. I—I'm truly sorry, Rhoda. Last thing I want is to upset you or Mamma."

"Mamma's got a lot on her mind." Rhoda plucked a towel from the sink and gently blotted her twin's tears. "But remember when we were wee little, cuddlin' in the dark so's the monsters under the bed wouldn't eat us?"

Rachel's quivering grin shone through her tears. "*Jah*, we reached our limit callin' out in the night for Mamma. Dat had no idea how lonesome—and scary!—it got when he moved us into separate rooms and told us to stay put."

"And then it got *really* scary when he passed, ain't so?" She let out a shaky breath, wondering how long it would be before she could discuss their father without wanting to cry. But that sadness wouldn't serve her purpose now. "Who'd've thought we'd be runnin' a restaurant with Mamma? Payin' all the bills and gettin' by better than anybody predicted. All our friends thought we'd just go to pieces, but we showed them what we were made of! And what we could do with God's help."

"*Jah*, there's that. Mamma's a strong woman."

"Well, so are *you*, Rachel. And no matter what happens—Tiffany or bad dreams or whatnot—you'll always have me." Rhoda smiled, drawing the corners of her sister's lips up with her fingertips, like they'd done when they were kids. "Even after ya get hitched, and ya need to steam like a teakettle, I'll understand ya like nobody else can."

"*Jah . . . jah. Fer gut* and forever, Sister."

"*Fer gut* and forever."

For a moment the two of them hugged each other hard, surrounded by the rhythmic thrum of the washer and the rich scent of chicken and vegetables. Together they sighed. And together they eased apart. "Better splash your face," Rhoda murmured. "Mamma always knows when we've been cryin'. She'll be here any minute."

Nodding, Rachel went to the sink and ran cold water into her hands. As she patted her face, Rhoda looked toward the lane to see if their mother had finished for the day. "*Jah*, here she comes. I'll keep her talkin' a minute—see if we've got a nice ripe tomato in the garden. Ya gonna be all right?"

Rachel resembled a little girl who'd just been pulled from a raging river—even if those waters only raced through her mind as emotions. But she nodded and motioned for Rhoda to go on outside.

"Feels *gut* to set a spell," Mamma murmured after they'd cleaned their plates. "The chicken and veggies tasted mighty fine, girls. But then, like I've told ya, even a peanut butter sandwich seems a feast when somebody else makes it!"

Rhoda widened her eyes playfully. "*Ach*, Mamma! Had I known ya wanted peanut butter instead of—"

Their mother smiled and reached across the table for their hands. "Ya can't know how I appreciate comin' home to find the house redded up and the laundry goin'. *Denki*, daughters."

For a moment they held the connection—affection like they hadn't shown when Dat sat at the head of the table and decided how their days would proceed, and what they'd do when the day's work was done. Truth be told, the work never seemed to *be* done, yet a satisfaction passed along the triangle of their joined hands with the gentle rhythm of their pulse.

"Dishes or laundry?" Rachel murmured.

"I'll hang the clothes." Rhoda stood, then pointed imperiously toward the porch before steering her mother out there. "Mamma, after such a busy week as we've had, you're due for some time in the swing with your feet up, ain't so?"

Mamma waved her off. "Comes a time I can't help with—"

"*Nee!* Ya better be out there supervisin' me! Can't have the neighbors cluckin' over how I hung your underthings toward the road!"

"Or on the side where Preacher Hostetler'll see them when he milks in the mornin'," Rachel joined in as she stacked their plates. "We cause enough talk, bein' three hens without a rooster in charge."

Mamma laughed as she removed her shoes and stockings. "Guess you girls'll just have to get hitched then. Don't go tellin' anybody, but I kinda like my life right now."

Rhoda smiled. It *was* nice, this chatter the three of

them shared after a busy week at the Sweet Seasons . . . yet Mamma was a far cry from being old or unattractive. Truth be told, some of the unattached fellows here in Willow Ridge came to the café as much to enjoy Miriam Lantz's company as her cooking, she suspected. And once she and Rachel started families, who would their mother spend her evenings with? Or did she figure to become the *mammi* of the family— the grandma—with all of them living *here*?

"Those are deep thoughts goin' through your mind, Rhoda," Mamma mused from the swing. "You and Rachel were jawin' about somethin' when I came home, ain't so?"

Rhoda cranked the pulley, moving their dresses away from the porch so she could fill another section of clothesline. "When are we *not?*" she hedged. Last thing she wanted was to bring up the subject of Tiffany again, what with Rachel just on the other side of the open window. "We were sayin' how it's *gut* tomorrow's not a preachin' Sunday, so's we can go to the party—and eat goodies we didn't bake ourselves! Sure ya don't wanna come?"

Mamma let out an exaggerated sigh as she stretched out on the swing, propping her bare feet on the armrest. "Peace and quiet . . . maybe somethin' as sinful as a nap. That's what these tired feet need, more than all the gossip you girls'll be hashin' over. But *denki* for offerin'."

A *nap*? When had her industrious mother ever slept during the day?

Rhoda almost challenged her, yet when Rachel came out with the big Bible for their evening reading, she let it go. Mamma rose several hours before the sun

every morning except for nonpreaching Sundays—
made her daughters look like laggards, getting up by
five to join her at the bakery. Truth be told, a little
extra rest would probably do them all a favor.

"Your turn to read tonight, Rhoda," Rachel reminded her. "Looks like Mamma's already in listenin'
position."

"*Jah.* Pick me out somethin', and I'll be right there."

When her sister lit the lamp on the sturdy little table,
its glow gave the summer night a peaceful feeling.
Used to be Dat who chose the selections, when it came
time for the actual reading, he always handed the
Good Book to Mamma. In every other family she knew,
the men read, and yet . . . the Scriptures took on a
warm, personal tone when a woman gave them voice.

"Here—I did like Dat and just let it fall open to the
place." Rachel handed her the Bible, mischief twin-
kling in her smile. "Like God decidin' what we need
to hear, he used to say."

Rhoda sat down so the lamp's light fell across the
page, then closed her eyes and put her finger down
on the spot where she would start. Silly, perhaps, yet
these simple traditions felt comforting now that Dat
was no longer alive—and after a week that had delivered a startling surprise to their doorstep. "I'll be
readin' from First John, the fourth chapter, startin' at
verse eighteen," she said reverently. "'There is no fear
in love; but perfect love casteth out fear . . . because
fear hath torment. He that feareth is not made perfect in love. We love Him, because He first loved us.'"

She paused to ponder this, to let the meaning
soak in.

"*Jah,*" Mamma said quietly. "It's like that sermon a
few weeks ago, where Preacher Tom said that if you're

feelin' afraid all the time, ya got no real faith that God's takin' care of things."

"Ya s'pose he sees Lettie's takin' off as . . . God workin' things out?" Rachel asked quietly. "That sort of thing's not s'posed to happen if a woman really loves her man—and if he really loves her. Ain't so?"

"Now *there's* a question best left to God." Mamma's tone suggested they might've veered from the Gospel into gossip. "Keep goin', Rhoda. You're a fine reader, child. Ya don't just rush over it, mouthin' the words, like some folks."

Rhoda nodded and focused on the dark, dense print again. "'If a man say, I love God, and hateth his brother, he is a liar: for he that loveth not his brother whom he hath seen, how can he love God whom he hath not seen? And this commandment have we from Him, that he who loveth God love his brother also.'"

She sighed, looking out into the night where the insects sang their summer song. "The Word only mentions menfolk and brothers, but it would work the same for a sister, I'm thinkin'. So . . . she who loveth God loves her sister, also?"

"Ya just said a mouthful, honey-girl."

In the porch chair on the other side of the lamp's glow, Rachel shifted until her face was lit by the lamp. "Like God decidin' what we need to hear," she repeated in a faraway voice.

For just the slightest moment, Rhoda had a vision of Tiffany—their Rebecca—in a kapp. Clean faced and smiling ever so gently.

Chapter 7

Out by the county highway on Sunday afternoon, Miriam waved at the familiar van pulling onto the shoulder. She opened the back door to put her picnic hamper on the floor, and then hoisted herself into the front passenger seat. "*Gut* afternoon, Sheila! And how are ya this fine day?"

"Doing well, thanks." The stocky woman behind the wheel smiled and adjusted her sunglasses. She wore brown slacks and a beige short-sleeved sweater, simple yet becoming for a woman her age. "I found that obituary we talked about, and I confess to being *very* curious about where we're headed today. That is, if you care to share!"

Miriam fastened her seat belt, wondering how much to reveal. Over the years this kind, careful woman had traveled many miles with her—over the roads, as well as into the uncharted territory known as widowhood—and she trusted Sheila Dougherty nearly as much as she did Naomi. "Well, I might be askin' ya to go inside with me, to keep me from losin' my nerve. So . . . you found out where Tiffany lives?"

Sheila nodded as she looked right and left before making a U-turn onto the road. "The funeral notice was for a Janet Oliveri, and her husband Bob—and Tiffany—are listed as survivors. Had to check the phone directory for an address, but it's just up the road in Morning Star, as you told me on the phone."

"*Jah*, that matches what she told us, even if we don't understand it." Miriam took a deep breath and released it to quiet her jangling nerves. Was she really on her way to meet the man who'd raised her Rebecca? And maybe to see her daughter again? She felt all twitchy and had to make herself sit still.

"The family suggested donations and memorials be made to the hospice in New Haven, or to the American Cancer Society," her driver went on in a somber voice. "So I'm guessing this Janet might've had a nasty time of it, like my Rick did."

"Sorry to hear that, but it helps us understand the situation. Poor Tiffany. Awful hard to watch that happenin' to someone ya love." Miriam shifted in her seat belt, feeling the waves of curiosity Sheila was too polite to express. They rode in silence for a couple of minutes, past the familiar places of folks she knew . . . Henry Zook's market, closed on this Lord's day . . . Holsteins grazing at the Hostetler dairy farm . . . the turnoff that led to the Brenneman shop. "Seems we all take our turns at dealin' with tragedy, ain't so? But—well, I had my very own miracle served up at the Sweet Seasons, this Thursday past. Would ya believe it, Sheila? That Tiffany ya read about is the little daughter I thought we'd lost in the flood, back in 1993. Except she's not so little any more."

The floodgates opened once again. While Miriam shared her excitement at finding Rebecca, along with the shock of seeing this Tiffany Oliveri decked out in so much black dye and clothing, she smiled and cried a little and answered Sheila's surprised questions. "*Jah*, it's a blessin', all right," she agreed as she dabbed at her eyes. "And I hope Rhoda and Rachel will come to see it that way real soon. I . . . over the years, I couldn't seem to find the right words to tell them about their lost sister, and Jesse urged me to just leave it be. So I've got some fences to mend."

"But what a story! What a joy, to have your long-lost daughter restored to you!" Sheila blotted her eyes on her sleeve and sniffled loudly. "That's the nicest thing I've heard in a long while. So you're taking a hamper of food to them today? To get better acquainted and to meet Mr. Oliveri?"

"That's the plan, *jah*. Hope it won't blow up in my face, for stickin' my nose into their business."

"But it's your business, too, Miriam. And the fact that Mrs. Oliveri saved the dress Rebecca was wearing, the same as you saved Rachel's and Rhoda's, tells me you two women have been on the same wavelength all along, without even knowing each other. That's just—well, it *is* a miracle, Miriam. And I'm really honored that you're sharing it with *me*."

"*Denki*, Sheila. Can't thank ya enough for sayin' it that way." She nipped her lip as they came to the turnoff for Morning Star. "I just hope Bob Oliveri is half as understandin' as you've been."

Sheila steered off the county road and then entered Morning Star, a well-kept little community where a mix of Amish and Mennonites lived amongst the Englishers who ran most of the local businesses on Main Street. As the van ventured farther into town, past the car dealership, a Laundromat, and the post office, Miriam reminded herself to breathe . . . to keep Mr. Oliveri's concerns foremost in her mind so she didn't run off at the mouth with her own questions and concerns—if he was even home, that is.

She gazed nervously ahead as Sheila turned down a street of modest older homes. "Probably woulda been the polite thing to call ahead, to be sure he didn't mind me comin'. But I . . . wasn't sure I could stand it if he said no. Even so, Tiffany might not want to see me again."

Her driver reached over to squeeze her arm, smiling kindly. "Who could refuse *you*, Miriam Lantz? Not only are you bringing a hamper of your wonderful food, but you're the kindest woman I know. I'm guessing this fellow will be relieved you broke the ice. Quite happy to talk to you."

"About earlier days, anyway. I'm guessin' the Tiffany who showed up at the café with her black hair standin' on end and eye makeup that could pass for road tar isn't the same sweet child he snatched from the river." Miriam's smile faltered as they pulled into a driveway at the end of the street. "I've been so blessed, havin' Rhoda and Rachel helpin' me all their lives. Especially after Jesse's passin'."

"And they'll stand by you no matter what comes of this surprise reunion, too." Sheila turned off the ignition, encouraging her with a smile. "Shall I wait here? Or come to the door with you?"

"I—I'll knock. But would ya mind terribly comin' inside if they're home?" she asked in a wavering voice. "Just seems more proper, and maybe more comfortable for them. Tiffany—my Rebecca—gawked at our Plain dresses and kapps as much as we tried not to stare at her black clothes and metal jewelry."

"It'll all work out fine, Miriam."

Be in my mind and in my heart, dear God. You know how I want this to go well for all of us. Miriam carried the basket of food to the front door, noting how the petunias in the hanging baskets could use a good drink . . . probably one of many things Bob Oliveri was at a loss about, now that his wife was gone. She held her breath and pressed the doorbell. It occurred to her that in her black mourning clothes, second nature to her now, she wasn't exactly a ray of sunshine—

The door opened and a pudgy, balding man of fifty-something blinked in the sudden daylight. "Yes? I—if you're handing out religious tracts, I don't want any!" He was ready to close the door before Miriam found her voice.

"Please, I know this must seem strange to ya," she blurted out, "but when Tiffany came to our café in Willow Ridge this week, I—I just had to meet ya! And I hope this food will—" As she held out her basket, Miriam's heart fluttered so frantically she could barely breathe. "How can I possibly thank ya for pullin' my little girl from the river eighteen years ago? I—I thought I'd never see my Rebecca again, and her comin' back is nothin' short of a miracle!"

The man's mouth dropped open. He blinked rapidly, and then glanced at the van in the driveway before focusing on Miriam again. "You'll have to excuse me if I seem—I lost my wife last week—"

"And I'm so sorry about her passin'. Lost my husband a couple years ago, and I'm still not all the way over it." Miriam caught herself running at the mouth and paused for a moment. "And if I'm intrudin' by comin' here, I'll just leave ya this food—"

"—and when Tiffany stormed out of the house with that little dress she found, I was afraid she might do something—" He swallowed hard and made a futile swipe at his thin hair. "I'm Bob Oliveri, by the way. Won't you come in—?"

"Miriam Lantz. Thank you ever so much, sir!" Eagerly she beckoned Sheila, and then stepped into the house as he held the door for her. "I can't tell ya how overjoyed I was to see her—to know she survived— even if she wasn't, well, *pleased* to find out she has Amish roots. And she has two sisters who look exactly like her—if ya don't count the clothes!"

He shook his head as he quickly cleared the sofa. "I've never understood why Tiff ruins her pretty looks with all that black getup. Goth, they call it. I hope she didn't say or do anything offensive. Tiffany—Rebecca, you called her?—always had a mind of her own, but when Janet was diagnosed with a malignant brain tumor a couple years ago, it was like our . . . the delightful daughter we'd always known turned into an alien creature who seemed determined to self-destruct."

"*Jah*, kids go through that." Miriam tried not to stare at the dirty dishes on the coffee table, until an arrangement of photographs on the wall drew her eye immediately. "Oh my," she breathed, her hand fluttering to her mouth. "She . . . except for the hairstyle and the clothes, she's the image of Rachel and Rhoda, ain't so, Sheila?"

The presence of her driver settled her. Miriam gazed eagerly at photos taken during her Rebecca's school days . . . several alone, and some with Mr. Oliveri and his wife. They made such a . . . nice-looking family. Happy. Like they belonged together.

"I'd know her anywhere," Sheila agreed, shaking her head in amazement. "This whole story is giving me goose bumps, it's so wonderful."

"And I've forgotten my manners! Mr. Oliveri, this is Sheila Dougherty, who was kind enough to drive me here today. You see, we Amish have no cars—no photographs, either, as we believe such graven images go against the way God wants us to focus on Him alone. But I can tell ya . . . I'm thankful for these wonderful-*gut* pictures. I can see you were a—a close-knit family, and I'm so glad for that."

She dabbed at her eyes with a tissue Sheila pressed into her hand. For a moment the three of them stood gazing at the wall of smiling faces, allowing the images to settle their nerves. Bob Oliveri let out a long sigh and began to point at them. "This was when Tiffany played T-ball in grade school. Quite a little athlete she was, too!" he said proudly. "And this was her dog, Ozzie. Just a mutt, but we were devastated when we had to put him down a few years ago."

"*Jah*, I can understand that." Miriam couldn't stop gazing at her daughter's face: the hairstyles changed and she wore a little striped uniform, or a checkered dress with a large white collar, or later a red cap and gown at her graduation, but those eyes . . . those dimples and that smile spoke volumes that only a mother's heart could hear. "I gotta tell ya, though, it threw me for a loop when she told us ya lived in Morning Star. Last I saw of her, she was caught up in the current, racing downriver—"

"We lived south of New Haven then." Bob's face

tightened and for a moment he seemed unable to speak. "Couldn't believe my eyes when I went chasing after Ozzie that day. He was just a puppy and scared of such a storm—"

"*Jah*, it was an awful day! Blew up so sudden-like, I grabbed the girls and hurried up the muddy river-bank—"

"—and there on a big tree trunk was a little girl in a pink dress!" he said in a rush. His pale face flushed with his excitement as he relived that fateful moment. "I grabbed a leafy branch and hauled her in, and—well, Janet said it was a sign from God! We . . . we'd lost a little girl about a month before and . . ."

When he hung his head, Miriam gently grasped his hand. "I know all about how hard that is," she whispered. "Thought it was my fault when Rebecca broke away from me that day. Blamed myself that I was near the river, lookin' for their *dat*. When our friends and family searched in all the towns downriver from Willow Ridge, and came back without her, well . . . we assumed the worst."

The man beside her pressed his lips into a tight line. "What we did probably sounds . . . unthinkable to you, ma'am. But we loved her so much—so immediately— we didn't try to find where she might've come from. The timing was too perfect to be coincidence. Janet had just gotten a new job a little ways north of here, so we moved away from New Haven. A fresh start as a new family, you see."

Why didn't they contact the local authorities? Say they'd found a child washed away by the river? she thought harshly. But then she blinked back more tears. *My side of the story no doubt sounds just as unbelievable to him. We*

Amish keep our problems to ourselves. The bishop insisted we not notify the police, either . . .

Miriam held her breath. Bob Oliveri was not only a man who'd lost his mate and, long ago, a baby daughter; he was a man who'd apparently kept a secret even more complicated than her own. She nodded mutely to encourage him. If she interrupted with questions, he might never finish what felt like a confession welling up from a troubled soul. "We all gotta move on," she murmured. "Hard as that is sometimes."

With a grateful nod, he blew his nose in his damp handkerchief. "Please understand, we didn't act as we did to hurt *you*, Mrs. Lantz," he continued in a strained voice. "But because this little girl was so like our own lost lamb, we called her by the same name . . ."

His eyes took on a faraway look. "She said right off she *liked* the name Tiffany, when we told her about our other little girl. We—we would never have forced her to go by something different, had she insisted on her real name."

Miriam laughed softly. "She couldn't say her *R*'s. Rachel and Rhoda were ahead of her learnin' to talk, too, and she didn't like that one little bit."

"So by moving to a new town, you met new friends who believed Tiffany was—had always been—yours?" Sheila inquired gently.

"You'll never know how that little girl restored our spirits—our will to get on with new lives, because God had blessed us with her in such . . . miraculous circumstances." Bob hesitated and then gently grasped Miriam's hand. "Please accept my apologies for not trying to find you and your family. What we did was wrong, but it felt so . . . providential. I don't suppose you could possibly understand or forgive—"

"We thought she was dead, ya know. Thought her little body musta rushed miles and miles downriver, and got hung up underwater, where no one'd find it." Miriam sniffled loudly and patted the hand wrapped around her wrist. "I couldn't share this with anybody at the time—not even my sister Leah—but I believed it was God's way of tellin' me I wasn't fit to raise that little girl—"

"No, that's not true! I don't even know you, Miriam, but I can see—"

"—so I accepted the consequences as His will." She let out a long sigh, heavy with the burden she'd borne for eighteen years. Sheila put an arm around her shoulders, crying quietly. And in Bob Oliveri's eyes, Miriam saw the same relief and release she felt, now that he had admitted his own deep secret. "And how could I see things any different, standin' here with you? God delivered my Rebecca to a family who needed her, and who took *gut* care of her. And now she's come back to find me—"

"And how did that happen?" he asked with an incredulous shake of his head. "Even if she'd given me a chance to explain, I had no way to tell Tiffany about her birth parents. The only clue we had was the style of that little pink dress."

Miriam blinked. The whole story defied explanation. But who was she to demand more answers or make accusations when things had turned out so much better than she'd hoped, so long ago? "Gotta be God workin' out His purpose again, ain't so?" she murmured. "Even if we can't know what that purpose might be now, any more than we knew back then."

Bob exhaled loudly. He looked like a man exhausted by grief, yet his eyes had a sparkle in them now. "Please accept my apologies for anything Tiff might've said or done that offended you—"

"She *surprised* us. That much is for sure and for certain!"

"—and I can't promise you she'll come back to hear your side of the story," he continued with a resigned shrug. "She hasn't been home since she stormed out of here with that little dress. Thank goodness her best friend's mom called to say she's staying there for a while. Tiffany's very upset about her mother's death, and she's always had a mind of her own."

"*Jah*, since the day the girls were born, she was the one testin' my patience and runnin' off when I called her," Miriam confirmed with a rueful laugh. For a few moments a comforting silence settled in around them. She gazed again at the photographs on the living room wall, sensing she'd gotten enough answers for now and that, if she needed to, she could talk to Bob Oliveri another day. "You've been ever so gracious. I'll pray ya get some rest and find peace about your wife, after an illness that's left *you* tired and sad, too."

His final attempt at composure gave way to a brief bout of tears, and as Sheila walked with Miriam to the door, Bob followed them. "I'll do my best to convince Tiff—Rebecca—to visit you when she's let go of her negative feelings. And thanks so much for the food. It smells wonderful, Miriam. Lots of stuff in the house, but I'm not in the mood to cook."

"Least I could do for ya. God bless ya, Bob," she whispered. "Take care of yourself, now."

After they stepped outside with a final wave, he closed the door. Sheila went around to open the passenger door of the van, and Miriam blinked back fresh tears as she stepped up into it. "Well, now. Don't that beat all? I've got lots to think about."

Sheila smiled and swiped at her eyes. "But it's all good. An amazing story, Miriam, and I'm so honored that you included me in it." She twisted the key in the ignition, still shaking her head. "Never heard anything like it. And to think your other girl has lived just up the road a few miles all these years."

Chapter 8

Micah watched from behind a massive old oak tree as Sheila Dougherty's familiar van pulled away from the house in Morning Star. Tiffany's Mustang wasn't parked in the garage, so while the two ladies had been inside, he'd driven around Morning Star looking for it. He'd parked his buggy among the others at the Mennonite church, so now he walked toward the pool hall where he'd seen a convertible like hers. During his *rumspringa*—his "running around" time—he'd ridden in his English friends' cars out on the highway . . . he recalled the way his pulse had raced as they roared down the road. Such reckless excitement, all through his body—the sense of *freedom* he'd felt—had warned him that if he learned to drive a car, he might never go back to the Old Ways or to Willow Ridge.

Rachel would never understand that. And she would never understand or approve of him snooping around in Morning Star, looking for the sister who so closely resembled her yet was different in some very basic ways.

What *was* he doing here, really?

Walkin' across the Devil's backyard, the elders would say.

Micah strode past some other storefronts, telling himself he needed to find Rebecca—to quiz Tiffany— as much for Rachel's sake as to satisfy his own . . . curiosity. This was the sort of prying their preachers, Tom Hostetler and Gabe Glick, and Bishop Knepp warned them about in Sunday sermons; poking around that would get him in trouble for sure if anyone back home found out about it. But if his investigation would resolve the doubts Rachel had about this whole alarming situation, wasn't it worth the risk of punishment?

Playin' with fire, his thoughts warned as he walked alongside the shiny red car. The top was folded down and the black leather interior gleamed richly in the afternoon sun. The silver emblem on the trunk didn't resemble any horse he'd ever ridden or worked with: far too fancy and fast for Plain folks. Quickly Micah entered the pool hall, before his nerve left him.

His eyes took a moment to adjust to the dimness. As he studied the men of various ages leaning intently over the green pool tables, bathed in light from swag lamps advertising liquor, the smoke stung his eyes. In the shadowy corners of the room, other fellows slouched over small tables, glass mugs and cigarettes in their hands. The dank musk of beer made him sneeze loudly—and then *he* was the one everyone eyed.

"Hey, farmer boy! You lost or somethin'?"

"Where'd ya get that *fine* hat, Mr. Hayseed?"

"Yeah, I've been wantin' me a sun hat like—"

Micah gasped, swiping at the air above his head: somebody behind him had poked his straw hat off, and now it dangled on the end of a pool cue, just beyond his reach. The man who tormented him appeared to be around thirty—old enough to have better manners. But then, the grimy bandanna around his long hair, and faded jeans with split-out knees, suggested he didn't much care how he looked. "Whaddaya think your hat's worth, blondie?" he jeered.

"Oh, it's these suspenders *I* want!" A fellow behind him grabbed the back crosspiece of his suspenders as though he intended to lift Micah from the floor. "Get the feelin' your kind don't belong here?" he asked with a harsh laugh. "Or did ya come in to find out how real men pass a Sunday afternoon?"

"Came lookin' for Tiffany!" Micah blurted out. He knew better than to grab for his hat or struggle against his captor, because then they'd only torment him more.

"Tiff Oliveri? Now what would a rube like you want with a hard-core babe like her?" The guy dangling his hat glanced toward a smoky corner of the room and then smirked at him again. "Like she'd waste her time on such a wuss-boy!"

A movement at one of the tables caught his eye, and through the haze Micah saw a girl with spiked hair wearing a black T-shirt. She gawked at him before downing the rest of her beer and sticking her cigarette in her mouth. Then she slumped against the wall, choosing to ignore him.

His heart thudded hard. He'd come this far, after finding her mother's obituary at the county library. He wouldn't likely get another chance to speak with Tiffany about her sisters—or anything else. A more aggressive man would have marched between the tables and start a conversation, even though the long-lost Lantz sister appeared peeved that he'd spoken her name. But what would he accomplish by embarrassing her in front of her friends?

Micah jerked free from the guy who still gripped his suspenders. "If you'll gimme my hat, I won't bother ya further. Just wanted to express my sympathy about Tiffany's mom and answer any questions she might have about her sisters, that's all."

"Looks like you're runnin' somewhere between *fat* chance and *no* chance, plowboy." The guy in the bandanna laughed at his own turn of phrase. He dropped the straw hat onto a table, where a couple other guys yanked it from their plate of nachos and tossed it toward the door.

Micah didn't have to be told twice. He stepped quickly between the tables, grabbed his hat from the dirty floor, and headed out into the muggy afternoon. With his handkerchief, he wiped the smeared cheese from the woven straw, striding up the road toward the parking lot of the Mennonite church. Why had he believed he'd accomplish anything in a pool hall?

And why was Tiffany there? Are those the people she called friends?

He could certainly never relate any of this to Miriam or the girls: they'd seen and heard enough in their café from that—what was the term?—hard-core babe? While it was true enough that something about Tiffany's brash attitude attracted him, Micah had no further desire to find out what she was like beneath her dyed hair and that tattoo of a skull on her shoulder.

Sometimes the cover *did* show what the book inside was like.

"Hey. How'd you know about me? And where to find me?"

Micah's breath caught. He stopped next to the red Mustang that had purred up alongside him while he'd been lost in his troubled thoughts. Tiffany sat stiffly behind the wheel. Her eyes were hidden behind large, dark sunglasses, but he felt the gaze she fixed on him. Challenging him. How should he answer, considering the way she'd spurned him just moments ago?

"Saw ya last week at the café in Willow Ridge. Miriam Lantz and her girls are . . . family friends." Why couldn't he bring himself to say he intended to marry Rachel? Was it because he couldn't back up his feelings with words? Or was his curiosity about this defiant, demanding young woman overruling his common sense? She was nothing but trouble, judging from her tattoo and her black attitude, but hadn't God said His people weren't to judge each other? Jesus and His Father would do the saving or condemning, and meanwhile humans were created to love and forgive . . . unconditionally.

This has nothin' to do with the Good Book and you know it! But don't write her off just yet.

"So why didn't you tell Becker where to get off?" she demanded. "Should've punched him out for grabbing your . . . suspenders, for starters."

Micah put on his hat, despite the greasy spots on its rim. He badly wanted to retuck his shirttail, but that seemed inappropriate with Tiffany studying him so intently. "It's not our way. And what would I have accomplished with violence?" he pointed out. "One punch, and I'd've been knocked to the floor, outnumbered about twenty to one. Totally at their mercy. Not my kind of odds, thanks."

Tiffany removed her sunglasses to gawk more intently at him. Her shimmering blue eyes looked so much like Rachel's yet so . . . icy hard. "So you *are* a wuss, like they said?"

"Is that why you came after me?" Micah crossed his arms, scrutinizing her in return. Why had he even entered into this sparring match? Tiffany's expression told him all he needed to know: she found him odd and out of place in her world. Somebody to make fun of, now that he was standing close enough that she could see all the reasons not to take him seriously.

Isn't that why you came today, without tellin' anyone? To get a closer look at this girl who appears so alien? An outsider in more ways than one?

One corner of her mouth lifted. "Get in. Unless that's not your way, either."

His pulse pounded. Tiffany was inviting him for a ride in this car that glowed like hellfire, which would put him at *her* mercy . . . odds he liked better than those he'd had in the pool hall. Yet he hesitated with his hand on the door. The *Ordnung* expressly forbade riding in cars on Sunday—let alone with a brash Englisher like this one. He'd known that law all his life and had sworn to abide by it when he'd been baptized into the church.

Micah's throat went dry. Still those blue eyes taunted him. Tempted him.

"Suit yourself," she said with a shrug. "I thought we could compare notes about what my old man told me and what you know about that lady at the café. She was gawking at my clothes, but ya know . . . *she* was wearing all black, too."

"Lost her husband—your *dat*—a couple years back. She still misses him." Before she could change her mind and roar off, Micah climbed into the seat beside her. "Are ya sayin' you don't remember anythin' about bein' washed downriver? Let alone recall your own mother and sisters?"

"Hey! I was only a little kid!"

"And I intend to see that ya don't hurt those folks any more than ya already have," Micah went on. He turned in the seat to look at her, unflinching. "Our people no doubt appear odd and out of step to ya, but your *mamm* suffered horrible-much when she lost ya that day—and again when Jesse died and left her and his other two girls to make their way without him. I won't allow ya to tromp all over their feelin's, *Rebecca*."

She winced at the name. "When I asked the shrink last week, she said I probably repressed the whole episode. Was too freaking scared to let my mind recall what happened—or remember anything about that day," she muttered. "Don't expect me to come crawling back, acting all grateful or apologetic, or—"

"If ya can't be grateful for a mother who loves ya, don't come back at all."

Where was this stern, Old Testament side of him coming from? Micah settled into the low-slung seat, reminding himself that this *hard-core babe* might just order him out and never speak to him again . . . which wouldn't accomplish a thing, would it? Micah glanced at her delicate hand as she shifted into DRIVE again. Except for the black fingernails and the chains running between the metal ring on her finger and the leather band around her wrist, it could be Rachel's hand. Could he convince this black sheep of the Lantz family to open her heart to the mother who'd missed her for so many years? Could she at least come to see Rachel and Rhoda as young women who were *like* her in so many ways?

"Answer me this, then, Micah: When I went to the library to check out the newspapers from back then, there were no accounts of a little girl getting washed downstream." Tiffany focused on the road then, as though she could turn her attention on and off with a switch.

Micah suspected that beneath her big, dark sunglasses some tears were gathering. And why wouldn't she cry? It had to be frustrating, figuring out whom to believe when she'd learned the Oliveris weren't her natural parents—and this after the woman she'd called her mother had passed on. "I don't have an answer for that," he replied beneath the rush of the wind. "My family moved to Willow Ridge from Lancaster County a couple years after the flood. My *mamm* is Miriam's best friend, and she was completely *ferhoodled* when you showed up last week. Had no idea the Lantz girls had been born as triplets."

"And you don't find *that* hard to believe?" Tiffany shot back. "Why is it, when I ask these questions or go looking for evidence, it's like my ride down the river never happened? Like I—I never existed, until I got rescued by Bob Oliveri? Or so he says!"

Micah resisted the urge to hold the hand that rested on the shift lever between them. Her voice had risen into a register that threatened to crack, and he couldn't imagine what she must be feeling. "Maybe you need to ask him more about—"

"How can I trust what he tells me? These are the people who faked my identity—called me the same name as a little girl they'd lost, and used the same birth certificate, even! What's wrong with this picture?"

He let out the breath he'd been holding. As she got more upset, Tiffany's ringed fingers gripped the wheel tighter and they flew down the road even faster. What had he done, putting himself in her hands? Was he risking his reputation—his standing in Willow Ridge as Rachel's beau—by allowing himself this secret taste of forbidden fruit? Was he risking his life, riding with Tiffany? He saw now why Amish men believed it was a bad idea to allow a woman to take the lead, or in this case, take the wheel.

Yet she was asking important questions. He prayed things wouldn't go terribly wrong while Tiffany was this upset. He said nothing more, so as not to distract her.

"Okay, something else I don't get." She said above the rush of the wind. Tiffany obviously loved the open road: after a few moments of calming silence as she sped down the highway, she lifted her face to the sun with a mystifying smile. "How come your women wear such dull dresses, all made in the same dumpy style? And what's with those little hats with the dangly strings?" she demanded. "You can't tell me Amish guys wear suspenders and straw hats as a *religious* ritual! I mean, *really!* Do you believe you'll go to hell if you wear plaid pants—or go to a barber for a real haircut? Or that your women will be condemned if they sewed a dress from a neon leopard-skin print?"

Micah's breath left him. While she sounded genuinely curious, she could obviously fillet him with her sharp tongue even faster than Rachel did when she got upset. When a gust of wind popped his hat from his head, he grabbed it and held it on his lap . . . not proper behavior, especially in the presence of an Englishwoman, but what else was he to do? "When we are baptized into the church—as adults, so we *choose* to live the Old Ways—we agree to follow the *Ordnung* our congregation has agreed upon."

"*Ordnung*? You mean like rules and regs?"

"*Jah*. And it reminds us to not be distracted or misled by worldly things like electrical appliances and—"

"That is so freaking weird." From behind her sunglasses, Tiffany stared at him as though he had two heads. "So then, how do they cook at the café? And how on earth do those women conduct business without a phone?"

"Bishop Knepp allowed Miriam to partner with Mennonites—her husband's cousins—who wired the buildin' for electricity after she had it built. So she can run the Sweet Seasons with a kitchen that's up to code," he added in a voice that sounded none too confident. "The two shops share a phone in a little booth out back—"

"You let one guy decide who gets electricity? That's nuts!"

The bishop had insisted they use pneumatic tools and a generator in their carpentry shop, rather than more convenient electrical power, but he and his brothers hadn't protested or challenged Hiram's judgment. "He was chosen by God to lead our district—"

"So you're saying *God* lets you Amish have phones, but only outside? Get real!"

"Only because the café brings in tourists that

supplement all our incomes. We don't have telephones in our homes because—"

"This is unbelievable! Freaking uncivilized!" Tiffany looked at the road again and then swerved to get back into the proper lane. They were going way too fast, yet she seemed able to control the car . . . as though she enjoyed driving with the wind whipping her short, spiky hair.

And he enjoyed watching her.

Micah shifted. Recalling this same rush of excitement when he'd ridden hell-bent down the highway with his English and Mennonite friends a few years ago. The wind was blowing his chin-length hair into a tangle, but he didn't care: it was enough to feel these moments of glorious speed with no one from Willow Ridge to witness how he'd spent his afternoon. He'd pray about it tonight. Talk to God about staying on the straight and narrow way he'd sworn to uphold, because Rachel deserved a man who kept his word—to her and to God.

As Tiffany slowed to make a U-turn in the middle of the road, he tried desperately to speak of his faith, of the strong family ties fostered by Old Order ways . . . family ties and a birthright she could reclaim, if she chose to. But he was bungling it badly when she took a tiny phone from a holster on her belt and began talking into it, oblivious to his presence for several moments. How could she negotiate this turn with one hand, and talk at the same time?

Tiffany made a face at the cell phone before she slipped it back into its holster. Then she focused on him instead of watching the road. "So where's your car?" she demanded.

"Don't have one."

"You *what?*" She jammed her foot on the brake, to stare at him as the Mustang idled right in the middle of the county highway. "So you don't even know how to drive? And you're *how* old?"

As Micah watched the incredulous emotions play across her face, he felt like a little schoolkid. Tiffany's sudden mood switches intimidated him—and they might not be too safe at the speeds she'd been traveling, either. But, of course, if safety was a concern, what was he doing here with this English-raised daredevil? "*Jah*, I drive," he insisted, "but without a license, I'm limited to farm machinery and horse-drawn carriages."

"Let me guess: your bishop decided that, too."

Micah cleared his throat, grateful that she was driving again rather than sitting in the middle of the curving road. "Ownership of cars fosters envy and competition. Takes us too far from home—"

"So how'd you get to the pool hall? Didn't see a horse outside—not that there was a hitching post, either!" An unladylike snort escaped her, and once again Tiffany became his interrogator, his challenger.

"I parked amongst the rigs at the Mennonite church."

"And why weren't *you* at church today?" she shot back.

"It's not a preachin' Sunday, so—"

"Look, forget it." Tiffany turned left so suddenly the tires squealed on the hot pavement as she headed back toward town. Micah grabbed the door handle and the console to keep from being knocked around. His arm brushed against hers, and he was suddenly too aware of her—and also aware that her laughter was at his expense. The car shot across the other lane of traffic and into the church parking lot, where she gleefully stomped the brake to skid to a halt.

The ruckus made Rosie, his mare, dance nervously and toss her head. All the other carriages had gone home, so it was very obvious the new courting buggy was his—not that Tiffany would be impressed.

Micah's heart felt heavy in his chest. At least folks weren't coming out of church to witness the end of this fruitless little adventure where the joke had been on him: he knew some of the young Mennonite men who attended service here, and they'd never let him live it down that a girl like Tiffany had spurned him. Through her dark glasses she was gawking at him as though his next move should be obvious, so he stepped out to the pavement. As he closed the shiny red car door, he resigned himself to reality. "Look, I'm sorry we couldn't reach any solutions, but I hope ya realize Mr. Oliveri—your *dat*—wasn't makin' up that story about the flood and findin' ya in the river. And I wasn't lyin' about how your mother wants to—"

"Yeah, well."

That's all she had to say? *Yeah, well?* With a sad nod, Micah turned toward his horse to soothe it. He wasn't having much effect on the other female he'd been dealing with, so—

"Whaddaya say you come see me next Saturday night, Micah?"

He turned, staring. Was she sincerely interested in spending time with him? Or was this just another chance to entertain herself at his expense? Seemed like there was something else he was supposed to do . . . yet when Tiffany flashed him a bright smile and batted those black eyelashes, he forgot all those reasons he shouldn't be wasting his time with this exotic, irreverent young woman. "*Jah*, I could do that, if—"

"I'll wait for you here, then. Say, sixish? We can get something to eat and talk some more."

Micah nodded, fighting a silly grin. As Tiffany revved the engine of her car and then sped back onto the highway, he felt like a kid who'd just won a prize at the mud sale. What was he, five years older than this unconventional young woman? Yet his mind raced ahead to ways of engaging her in more meaningful conversation—ways to convince her it wasn't such a horrendous thing, having Plain roots and a family who was truly interested in knowing her again. "Ya know, Rosie, we might just soften that hard-core shell she hides behind—"

"Can I help ya, young fella? As you can see, you're a little late for the service."

Micah pivoted then forced a quick smile. The gray-bearded man coming out the front door of the church was a preacher, whose sharp little eyes were looking right through to his soul. No sense in making up some cockeyed story about what he'd been doing just now. "What might ya know about that gal who just drove off? Tiffany Oliveri, her name is."

The older fellow's thin shoulders rose expressively and his demeanor spoke volumes. "Don't know her, son. Not the type who'd come to services."

Because you wouldn't let her in? Tiffany could use the comfort and strength that comes from spendin' time with God, among His people. And that's what he needed to do right now, as well, so Micah didn't challenge the preacher's remark. "I'll be headin' on home, then. The Lord's been workin' in some mighty mysterious ways—"

"Don't be misled, son. The Devil tempted Jesus, too, with ideas that seemed reasonable, under the circumstances."

Micah held back a remark. He hopped up into his buggy and clapped the reins lightly across Rosie's back. "Thanks. I'll keep that in mind."

Chapter 9

"Miriam? *Gut* mornin', Sister! Ya look all flushed and overdone, like rhubarb cobbler just come from the oven!"

Miriam glanced up from the double batch of oatmeal-flax dough she was mixing for her favorite bread. It *was* hot in the café's kitchen: she'd been running the ovens for hours, and July mornings in Missouri were always sultry. "Takes some doin' to work in the last of this whole wheat flour. Ya been pickin' us more veggies this mornin'?"

Her sister wore an old choring dress with a bandanna tied over her hair, and she was barefoot. *Mighty sweaty herself*, Miriam noted smugly. As Leah set baskets of lettuce and spinach on the far counter by the sink, her expression seemed . . . purposeful. "*Jah*, best to get the greenery in before the sun wilts it. Been wonderin' about that girl who stopped in last week—"

"My Rebecca! *Jah*, she's alive! And I've learned all sorts of—"

"—and I'm just now findin' a minute to see how

you're doin' with that. Musta been quite a shock."
Leah leaned a hip against the counter where Miriam
worked. "I stopped by the house yesterday, when ya
didn't come to the quiltin' frolic with the girls."

Miriam paused, her hands clamped around the
bowl and her spatula. With all those boys to raise, bees
to tend, and the huge garden plots she watched for the
café and several farmers' markets in the area, Leah
Kanagy had little time to chat—and less inclination
toward needlework, truth be told. "*You* spent the day at
a quiltin' frame, Sis? Amongst all those chirpin' girls?"

She shrugged. "Stopped with a wee gift for Daniel's
niece, due any minute now, and then stopped by to
see *you*. Tell your big sister, now, Miriam: Were ya out
courtin' and keepin' it quiet-like? High time, I say!"

"Nothin' like that." Miriam paused, partly for effect
and partly to decide how much of her secret to reveal.
If word of her Sunday excursion reached the wrong
ears, there'd be trouble . . . but if she couldn't share
this family matter—this unexpected joy—with her
own sister, whom *could* she trust?

Miriam smiled. Took two to play cat-and-mouse,
and she'd always enjoyed putting one over on Leah,
making her gawk and beg for details this way. "I was
gettin' acquainted with Bob Oliveri, over in Morning
Star! Can ya believe it?" she asked happily. "He pulled
my Rebecca out of the river eighteen years ago!
Raised her as their own, he and his wife did—I saw
pictures of her on their walls, and—oh, Leah!" she
added with a wistful sigh. "Never in my life had I
thought to see my lost girl again."

"They say she looks hard. One tough-talkin' customer, too."

"*Jah*, that she is. No patience for Plain ways." Miriam pinched the brown dough into four equal sections, to shape them into loaves. Her sister had never been one to gush or show emotion, so she proceeded carefully. "But it was like my sins were forgiven . . . all those years of blamin' myself for lettin' her get loose, put to rest! Even Sheila proclaimed it a miracle. We were all of us in tears."

"Don't go gettin' your hopes up. Hate to see ya hurt again, dredgin' up so much from the past, Miriam."

Miriam chuckled wryly. She could count on Leah to see the glass as half empty rather than believing it would run over with goodness. "*You* recall how devastatin' it was when I lost little—"

"She's not so little now, and she's not the wee girl ya were raisin' to follow our ways!" Her sister's damp brow furrowed sternly. "No tellin' what she might try, now that she sees how well the bakery and café're doin'."

Miriam blinked. Even for Leah, this conversation seemed cold and hard. Such suspicious talk reminded her of another blessing: she was all too glad that her sister had such a talent for raising food while she was the one in the kitchen, cooking it! It was nearly five. She glanced out to see if her girls or Naomi were on their way down the lane. "I doubt Rebecca will come back to see us again, but it's good to know she's alive, Leah! Surely ya can let me have *that* to smile about!"

"*Jah*, of course, I'm happy about that." Leah washed her hands and then ran water into a stainless steel sink to clean the greens. "But Mary Schrock was sayin' this version of Rebecca had everybody gawkin' on account of her black-rimmed eyes and witch-dyed hair. And a sketch of a skull on her back, for land sakes!"

"Well—we all know the gossip from the quilt shop's always true, ain't so?" Miriam fought a sly grin. "I can recall when Mary and the aunts had you steppin' out with the UPS man, on account of him stoppin' every single day for a week to deliver your onion sets and beekeepin' gear."

"Oh, go on with ya!"

"I'm tellin' ya, the café was buzzin' like a hive of your bees, Sis!"

Leah lifted a double handful of deep green spinach from the water to let it drain. "Word of this situation with Rebecca is bound to reach the bishop, ya know. He'll not want the story gettin' out of Willow Ridge, bringin' in reporters or television cameras—"

"You'd be singin' a different song if *your* wee one had washed away all those years ago! Now hush with ya!" Miriam gestured toward the window. "The girls are nearly here and this ain't been easy for them."

Her sister's grin turned catlike. "*Jah*, your girls were more in the spotlight than the expectant mothers and their babies yesterday, and they were none too happy about it."

"My girls? Or the new mothers?"

Leah's lips quirked. "*Jah*, them."

Miriam fought the urge to shoo Leah Kanagy back to her garden plots. Had her own sister—Rebecca's aunt—nothing positive or encouraging to say? Only sunrise, and already Leah had put a damper on the day—not that things had changed since they were girls growing up amongst five other sisters. She patted the fat, brown loaves into their pans and set them by the ovens to rise. Then she opened the large refrigerator door to assess the makings of today's breakfast offerings.

"Well, I can see my big-sister advice is gonna blow right by ya." Leah gently squeezed the last of the wet spinach and dropped it into the colander. "Take care, Miriam."

"*Jah*, you too, Leah. Careful out there in the heat of the day—and *denki* for the fine-lookin' greens. I'll add them to my tab, end of the month."

Her sister wiped her wet hands and then left by the kitchen exit, her greetings to the girls drifting into the kitchen with them. Rhoda, in blue, hugged her mother warmly while Rachel, in faded brown, appeared as pinched as a robin on a parched summer lawn. Miriam gazed at their dear faces. How would her daughters react if they heard she'd been to see Mr. Oliveri yesterday? Especially if they learned it secondhand? She hadn't gone to Morning Star to spite them or hurt their feelings . . . didn't want yet another secret to make them doubt her boundless, unconditional love for the both of them.

"So Aunt Leah brought us more work, did she?" Rachel remarked shrilly. "Seems to be the only time she comes around."

Miriam blinked. Where had *that* come from? Such an uncharacteristic question warned her that everyone's morning would go downhill from here if she mentioned her trip to Morning Star right now. "*Jah*, the work—and the fresh veggies—keep comin' at us, thank goodness! So we'd best make our way through it with a smile, instead of whinin'," she replied as lightly as she could. "We'll be needin' silverware bundled first thing.

And I'm thinkin' we've got more ham than sausage this mornin'—at least until the Zooks send us any surplus from the weekend. "What sounds *gut* for the breakfast specials?"

Rachel beelined into the dining room, to the big tub of clean silverware beside the coffeemakers. Rhoda sighed and tipped her head toward her sister. "Got a bone to pick with Micah, I'm guessin'," she murmured as she stood beside her mother, gazing into the refrigerator. "He didn't come to the singin' after our quiltin' frolic, and she's mighty put out about it."

"Was he s'posed to? Did he say he'd pick her up?"

"Well, in Rachel's mind, the poor fella's to be spendin' every spare moment with her now." Rhoda glanced out the serving window to where her sister was tightly winding white napkins around silverware. "I try to remind her he's got outside jobs, and he puts in extra hours this time of year, but she'll hear none of that. All wound up about the ice-cream social next Saturday, too."

Miriam smiled to herself. Micah Brenneman had bought paint, lumber, and other building supplies and stashed them in the smithy Saturday morning so he could begin the transformation of the loft this week. "I hope she don't get so pouty and pushy he changes his mind about her. Micah's a man with a *gut* solid plan for his future—and hers, if she'll give him a little breathin' room."

"*Jah*, and he's got eyes for only Rachel, ain't so? Always has." Rhoda took out cartons of eggs and a jug of milk, her expression thoughtful. "I'm in the mood for bacon and flapjacks this mornin'. Could mash those spotty-ripe bananas and add some walnuts to the batter . . ."

Miriam smiled. This daughter had a true talent for creating wonderful-*gut* meals out of whatever food she found—a gift she'd certainly use, if ever she'd settle down and start a family. "So who's got eyes for *you* these days, honey-bug?"

"*Ach*, Mamma! Do ya think I'd tell ya if I knew?" Rhoda flashed a teasing grin over her armload of groceries.

"Ain't like you're sixteen anymore. And the fellas seem to flock around the new crop of courtin'-age girls—"

"The frolic yesterday was proof of that, for sure and for certain. Not a one of those expectant mammas was yet eighteen." She began mashing the overripe bananas with a vengeance and then looked out the window, toward the lane. "Naomi not comin' today, I wonder?"

"Takin' Mammi Adah to the eye doctor, clear to Columbia."

"Guess I'll be your chef then. *Des gut*, too," she added with another glance toward her sister in the dining room. "Best we stay outta the way, in case forks start flyin' when Micah comes for his breakfast."

Two hours later, it was Hiram Knepp who came in first, with Tom Hostetler, and old Gabe Glick—not that it was unusual for any of them to take meals at the Sweet Seasons. The bishop's wife had passed last spring, and Preacher Tom's wife had vamoosed with a fancy man, and Gabe often came when his ailing wife didn't feel up to cooking. Seeing them all enter together and take a table in the back, however, made Miriam's insides tighten. "Now why do I feel like those three are doin' more than just eatin' together?" she asked Rhoda, who stood at the griddle flipping pancakes. "All we need's Deacon Reihl and we'd have us a meetin' of the elders. Do ya . . . s'pose they've heard about our Rebecca comin' here last week?"

"And what if they have?" Rhoda replied with a shrug. "Not like we *invited* her to cause such a ruckus. And not like we're stirrin' the pot amongst her English friends or tryin' to get our story in the papers, either."

Miriam nodded as she poured the glaze over the lemon pound cakes she'd made for today's lunch. Had somebody seen her going to Morning Star with Sheila yesterday? Or had last week's gossip at the quilt shop—and yesterday's talk at the quilting frolic— made its way to Esther Reihl and her husband by way of their greenhouse? How would she answer if those men started asking pointed questions about her long-lost daughter and what plans she might have for their reunion?

Lord God, You know my heart! Let my words and thoughts reflect the truth as only a mother can know it. And let my girls understand that my actions are based on love. That's how it would have to be. She'd been asking after her lost child's welfare and comforting Bob after he'd lost his wife. No one could fault her intentions there. And since Sheila had refused her money, it wasn't like she'd hired a driver on Sunday. Not exactly, anyway . . .

A few minutes later they got another surprise altogether: Micah entered the café, grinning at Rachel as he headed toward an empty seat with the Kanagy boys. Rhoda looked up from the eggs she was scrambling. "Best hold on to your kapp, Mamma. There goes Rachel to—"

But before Rachel could express her irritation or take Micah's breakfast order, Hiram Knepp rose from his table to approach Micah, as well. Tom and Gabe slipped out through the hall connecting to the quilt shop, their expressions grim. Thank goodness Rachel knew better than to voice her complaints when she overheard what the bishop said to Micah: indeed, the fellows at his table looked as *ferhoodled* as the blond carpenter himself when Micah followed Hiram outside. He looked like a boy being called behind the woodshed for a spanking.

"And what's *that* about?" Rhoda murmured to Rachel as she carried Nate Kanagy's loaded plate to the dining room. The girls exchanged concerned looks, and then Rachel hurried through the kitchen. After she glanced out the window, she turned off the big exhaust fan.

Miriam nearly protested about the heat—until she saw the three bearded men huddling around Micah, near the back of the building where the horses and buggies were hitched. Silently, she and Rachel positioned themselves out of sight as her daughter opened the back door just a crack.

Hiram Knepp wasn't a man to waste time on social niceties. "You know what this is about, don't you, son?" he asked sharply. "You're fully aware it's wrong to ride the roads in a car with a young Englishwoman, now that you've made your vow to the church. And on a Sunday, no less."

Rachel's face paled. When she looked ready to cry out—or just cry—Miriam pressed a finger against her daughter's lips because the men would hear anything they said. Her insides tightened. What had possessed Micah to go and find Tiffany? Could it be coincidence that he'd gone to Morning Star yesterday, too?

"Care to explain to us why ya went?" Preacher Tom asked a bit more gently. "I can tell ya firsthand, it's not a *gut* thing when our paths get too crossed-up with outsiders."

Micah cleared his throat. His cheeks resembled bright pink geraniums. "You've no doubt heard that Miriam's daughter Rebecca, the triplet washed away durin' the floods of '93, came by here last week," he said in a low voice. "After the way she showed such disrespect to her *mamm* and upset her sisters—especially Rachel—I felt it my duty to set the girl straight. I'm thinkin' Jesse woulda done the same, if he were alive."

"The way I hear it, you went into the Morning Star pool hall, and then spent a good half hour joyriding in a red sports car with a disreputable-looking young woman," Hiram countered. "Is that true, Micah?"

Miriam scowled. While it was the bishop's place to keep his flock on the straight and narrow, she was touched that Micah had talked with Tiffany on their behalf: an attempt to prevent further conflict. The café had been crowded the day of the surprise visit, yet who else among the People had gone to the trouble of telling Tiffany how she'd offended them with her sass and outrageous appearance?

Of course, Rachel would never see it that way: Micah had betrayed her trust and risked his standing with the People. The girl stood glued to the wall by the window, hugging herself as though her slender arms were all that kept her from shattering at this revelation. And, truth be told, such behavior could put Micah under the ban, if the bishop chose to make an example of him—especially now that Lettie Hostetler had run off with an Englisher.

And what would Bishop Knepp do if he learned Miriam had been to Morning Star, as well? And how would Rachel and Rhoda react if *they* found out their mother had fibbed to cover her secret visit, to learn more about her daughter . . . a child she'd lost in a raging storm and who'd now kicked up another kind of storm altogether, merely by showing up again?

We did what we did for our own reasons, God. Help us all to do Your will now, rather than makin' a bigger mess of things.

Even in prayer, Miriam's pulse and thoughts raced so frantically, she wanted nothing more to do with the conversation outside. She pointed toward the dining room, a signal for Rachel to return to her tables. Then she dished up the double servings of smothered hash browns two English fellows from down the road always ordered when they came to the café.

"They're still talkin' out there?" Rhoda asked quietly as she took the two loaded plates from her mother. Rachel must have told her sister what she'd overheard.

"*Jah*, and considerin' your other sister is the main gist of the conversation, could well be Hiram questions me next," Miriam replied in a breathy voice. Once again she wondered if she should tell the girls of her visit with Bob . . . but right now it would only irritate Rachel more. And they'd all pay for that! "Bishop Knepp came to Willow Ridge some years after the flood, so I'm sure he's got questions about the whole thing. Questions Micah has no way of answerin'."

"Let's hope Hiram won't talk with us until after we close. Can't he see we're shorthanded, with Naomi gone?" Rhoda's sigh and expression reflected Miriam's own exasperation, but it wasn't a matter of anyone's *convenience* when such blatant behavior as Micah's came to the attention of their religious leaders. And if Hiram had somehow heard of *her* excursion . . .

On the assumption her work would be interrupted later, Miriam cut up two of the large watermelons and the cantaloupes Nate Kanagy had brought in before his breakfast. Best to get ahead of the lunch preparations so the girls could handle things if she had to speak to the brethren this morning. Her heart went out to poor Rachel, who looked for all the world like a baby bird who'd lost its mamma. "You all right, honey-bug?" she murmured. "No cause for jumpin' to conclusions or—"

"But Micah didn't deny what the bishop was sayin'," Rachel replied in a faraway voice. "Which means that instead of takin' me to the singin' last night, he was ridin' in that bright red car with—with Tiffany! He knows better than to— If he keeps this up, he'll get himself shunned for sure and for certain!"

The pain in her daughter's voice pierced Miriam's heart. Rachel had waited a long time—had set her young heart on Micah Brenneman years ago—and from all appearances, he'd been cavorting with the Devil's own girlfriend. But appearances could be deceiving.

"Best you talk with Micah himself, when it's just you and him. He's not the type to go back on any promises he's made—to you, or to the church,"

Miriam assured her stricken girl. "You should be aware of his true intentions, instead of believin' your own conclusions, Rachel. We all see things from our own—"

"I didn't just fall off the wagon yesterday!" Rachel whispered vehemently. "I know the difference between seein' and believin'!"

As her daughter stalked back to the dining room, where the preachers and Micah were seating themselves again, Miriam smiled ruefully. For Micah's sake—and her own—she hoped Rachel could also *love* without having to see, just like her sister had read to them from the Good Book the other night. And she certainly hoped her peevish daughter kept control of her temper while those elders were here eating their breakfast. Men had ways of showing their irritation when their meals got interrupted—especially by women who challenged or defied them.

So much trouble brewing, like a summer storm, and it wasn't yet eight in the morning.

Chapter 10

Rachel started the dishwasher for the last load of the day's plates and then quickly removed her white café apron. "Guess ya know who I'm gonna go talk to," she murmured to Rhoda. "And he better give me the right answers, too!"

Off she strode, down the lane behind the Sweet Seasons and then across Kanagy's pasture. If it was Micah's duty to set Tiffany straight, well—shouldn't *her* mission be to watch after *him*? Sheep and a few floppy-eared goats watched her, munching their grass, but today she had much more pressing business than pondering four-legged creatures too dense to understand the way her heart pounded.

Not that Micah will understand, either. The way he was starin' at Tiffany the other day . . . whatever possessed him to seek her out? In a pool hall, of all places! And there'll be no lettin' go of this, now that the bishop will be watchin' him like a hawk.

She took the next gravel road and approached the carpentry shop more slowly. It wouldn't do to corner Micah while his brothers looked on, for Seth and

Aaron would side with *him* and then poke fun at both of them. And Micah's wild ride with that misfit Tiffany was anything but funny!

Rachel eased the shop door open, grimacing when the bell jangled gleefully overhead. From various areas of the shop, the Brenneman brothers turned to look at her. The shrill whine of Seth's large saw ceased, and Aaron stopped his spray painting to flip the switch on his compressor. The silence hung around her like the summer heat.

"Afternoon to ya, Miss Rachel!" the youngest blond called across the large room. "I don't s'pose ya brung us any of that fine lemon cake from lunch?"

"Don't s'pose I did," she replied, fixing her eyes on Micah. Was it her imagination, or did he hide a wagonload—a carload—of secrets behind the smile he flashed at her? He approached her as though nothing had happened, but when he grabbed his hat from its peg by the door, he seemed hesitant about stepping outside with her.

"Can't spare ya much time. We gotta deliver these new shelves for the Schrocks' quiltin' shop before four, or there'll be some ladies complainin'—"

"The Schrock women got nothin' on me when it comes to lettin' folks know I'm peeved!" Rachel spat out. She crossed her arms, driven by a desperate need to know exactly where she stood with—what she meant to—the handsome man standing beside her. "So what's this about you settin' Tiffany straight yesterday? Ridin' in her car and goin' to the pool hall, no less?"

Micah's grin withered. "How'd you know about—"

"The kitchen's got ears, Micah."

He let out a bemused laugh. "*Jah*, and it seems the Mennonite preacher in Morning Star felt compelled to report to Hiram, too. What he saw and what I did are two different things altogether."

Rachel turned her head slightly, waiting him out.

"I wanted to see where your sister lived . . . what sorta life she had all those years she was away from her Plain family, Rachel."

Was he holding out on her? He seemed to know things he didn't want to share. "And what did ya learn while ya coulda been at the singin' with me?"

He blinked. "I was home long before then, honey-girl, because if you'll remember, I hadn't figured on *goin'* to the singin'. You'd already said the hen party might take all day on Sunday."

Rachel pressed her lips into a line. "A girl likes to hope her beau will surprise her sometimes."

A smile softened his handsome face. "Oh, I got a surprise I'm gonna show ya real soon, Rache. But last night I was thinkin' about what to do next . . . hopin' I hadn't stepped outta line, tellin' Tiffany not to come back here unless she could mind her smart mouth around her mother—and you girls." He lifted her chin with his finger until she focused on his eyes. "A lotta lives and beliefs got upset like applecarts when she showed up outta nowhere. And it's not like Tiffany's the only one hearin' stories that seem . . . far-fetched. Ain't so?"

He appeared to be telling God's own truth: Micah's deep green eyes shone as steady as tall pines in the forest as he rested his large hands on her shoulders. Rachel sighed. "I—I was just disappointed, not seein' ya at the singin', after a day with so many girls younger'n me, havin' second and third babies . . ."

"All in *gut* time, love," he murmured. "And *jah*, I rode in Tiffany's red car, on account of it was the only way she'd talk to me. Found her in the pool hall amongst a buncha bad apples, and I walked out, figurin' it for a lost cause. But when she drove up alongside me . . . I thought it might be my only chance to get through to her."

"And?"

He exhaled, considering his words. "She's not so impressed with our Plain ways. I answered her questions about the People as best I could, but she wasn't really hearin' what I said, Rache. Could be she's good and mad at her English mamma for dyin' too soon." He paused, looking pensive. "Could be she's as confused as you and Rhoda, about bein' your sister. Must be tough, learnin' that everybody she trusted most didn't tell her this one huge, important detail about who she really is."

Rachel felt a little embarrassed about nailing him this way, but a girl saw what she saw and she had her feelings about it, too. Better to find out *before* she hitched up with Micah Brenneman, if he was the sort to chase after women. Especially brazen, black-haired girls of a world far beyond the Plain folks of Willow Ridge. "Don't go forgettin' about the social next Saturday night," she reminded him with a sweeter smile. "You know I've got my heart set on goin', and I've cut out a new dress—gonna make a couple platters of the *best* cookies, Micah. You say I'm your girl, and I want to believe it."

"*Jah*, I meant that with all my heart, Rache."

"*Gut.* So don't go givin' the bishop any more reason to talk like you'll be under the ban for spendin' time with Tiffany. She might be my sister—as close as Rhoda, by blood—but she'll never be one of us," she added with a sad shake of her head. "I know Mamma

wants Rebecca back in the fold, or at least on speakin'
terms. But I don't see that happenin'. And I don't
wanna lose *you* over it, neither. 'Nuff said."

"*Jah.* 'Nuff said."

Rachel smiled up at him, suddenly aching for his
kiss—but the wood shop, like the kitchen at the Sweet
Seasons, probably had ears. "Better get crackin' on
that shelvin' for Mary Schrock, then. Can't have her
and Priss and Eva squawkin' at ya, now, can we?"

She started for home, turning to wave at the handsome, broad-shouldered carpenter as he watched her
go. Mamma was right: she felt better after hearing the
story from Micah's side . . . believing what she saw in
his face and heard when he spoke of his feelings for
her. Tiffany was no real temptation to him, after all.
And wasn't it wonderful-*gut* that he saw beneath the
surface of this confusing situation, which had changed
things for everyone involved? Most men had little tol-
erance for women's emotions—much less for women
who spoke their minds, as she just had.

And meanwhile, she felt ever so much happier
knowing she had a new plum-colored dress to wear to
the ice-cream social . . . and it was no secret that
Micah couldn't resist her butterscotch brownies or
dark chocolate cookies studded with chocolate chips.

Maybe Mamma was right: she'd catch a lot more
flies—or kisses—with honey than with vinegar. And
chocolate made pretty good bait, too.

Early that evening, as Miriam baked pies to supply
Zook's grocery store and Leah's stand at the farmers'
market the next day, she was pleased to find Rachel

peering in at her. Smiling again. "Well, now! There's a face I love to see!"

"If ya got room in the ovens, I thought I might bake up cookies for Leah's market stand—and to freeze for the social," her daughter began. "But if the other ladies're comin' to—"

"It'll be just us two. Seems Lizzie Glick's baby came—"

"*Jah*, she was mighty antsy at the party yesterday."

"—so her *mamm* and aunts won't be makin' bread today. Glad for your company, Rachel!" Relief swelled within her, seeing her daughter more at peace after she'd talked with Micah. Miriam quickly shaped five more crusts in disposable pie pans, glancing across the kitchen now and again to enjoy the easy way this daughter worked with food when she put her mind to it. "Micah answered your questions, I take it?"

"*Jah.* Sounded to me like the bishop overstated his case—or else the Mennonite preacher in Morning Star stretched the story out of shape." Rachel dropped spoonfuls of dark chocolate dough onto her cookie sheets and then slid them into the oven. She looked up at Miriam, her blue eyes wide. "Guess I've done some stretchin' of that story myself—about Tiffany and how terrible she surely must be. I—I'm sorry about that, Mamma. Didn't mean to cause ya more grief—"

"Oh, honey-bug, anybody'd be upset to learn she had a surprise sister—and that her own *mamm* had kept it from her, too." Miriam crossed the kitchen to wrap her arms around her daughter, suddenly aware of how long it had been since they'd hugged this way. "I don't tell ya this near enough, Rachel, but I owe the success of this whole business to you. 'Twas your idea for me to start a café after your *dat* passed."

"Well, who better to do that?" Rachel replied as she tightened her embrace. "*Nobody* bakes like you, Mamma!"

Miriam blinked back a tear, savoring the sturdy feel of her daughter's body. "*Jah*, there's that," she said with a chuckle. "But if I didn't have you and Rhoda, I don't know how I'd get from one day to the next. It was ever so *gut* of you girls to give up your chance for teachin' at the school or workin' for pay someplace else."

Rachel eased away to swipe at a tear. She shrugged, unable to speak.

Miriam smoothed her girl's kapp, straightening its strings. Her heart felt filled to the brim with gratitude. She should mention her trip to Morning Star now, while Rachel was busy and happy. "Better check your cookies, don't ya think? They're smellin' mighty *gut*."

"*Jah*, that Dutch cocoa and the dark chips'll have Micah eatin' out of my hand for sure and for certain!" When she glanced out the window, her grin was a sight to behold. "And would ya look at who's comin' down the lane, even as we speak? Now, why's he stoppin' *here*?"

Seeing Micah's familiar build and stride silhouetted against the sunset, Miriam had a pretty good idea—but it wasn't her place to reveal the young man's secret. When the broad-shouldered carpenter knocked before entering through the back door, she kept her chuckle to herself. "Come on in, Micah! Could it be the smell of Rachel's cookies that lured ya here?"

For a moment he looked like a fellow caught between going and staying: he held his tool bucket in one hand and a can of paint in the other. The sight of

Rachel bending over to check her cookies apparently made him reconsider. "Seems timin' is everythin', ain't so?" he teased. "Could be, Miss Rachel, that when ya finish your bakin', ya might want to join me next door. I could use your . . . expert opinions."

Rachel raised her eyebrows. Flushed with the heat from the oven, carrying two trays of hot cookies, she was the picture of anticipation and the homely arts; a fitting helpmate indeed for the man whose eyes shone with mischief as he plucked a cooled cookie from the rack on the counter. "And what might ya be doin' over there in Dat's smithy?" she asked coyly.

Micah shrugged, and as he lifted the key ring from the peg near the door, he winked at Miriam.

Miriam poured cherry filling into her pies, smiling as though she had no idea what they might do in Jesse's vacant blacksmith shop. Not surprised that her daughter finished baking the cookies lickety-split and then carried a double handful of them out the door. The sound of their laughter drifting on the breeze, as Micah revealed his secret project, was a balm to her soul. Maybe Tiffany would never resume her Plain place as Rebecca, but having Rachel and Rhoda happy, healthy, and here with her felt like such a blessing.

Miriam deftly arranged strips of dough into lattice-work top crusts, then placed the pies in the oven with a satisfied sigh. Running the Sweet Seasons while also baking for other places kept her mighty busy . . . but it felt providential that she was supporting herself at last, in the absence of a husband. Interesting, too, that so many fellows—Tom Hostetler and Matthias Wagler, the harness maker, and the bishop himself—had lost their women this past year, yet she had no desire for any of them to become more than the friends they'd always been.

"My word, Miriam. I can't recall the last time my house smelled this wonderful. Do you never leave this kitchen?"

She turned with a start, to find Hiram Knepp leaning against the doorframe. She nearly asked him who fixed his dinner these days—and who was minding his many children right now: his eldest, Annie Mae, escaped those chores every chance she got. But something made Miriam hold her tongue.

"Cookin' is what I do," she said with a shrug. "Seems my purpose on this earth is to feed people, so *denki* yet again for agreein' we should have these wonderful-*gut* gas appliances. Not to mention lettin' us partner with Jesse's cousins, to run the exhaust fans and dishwasher with their electricity."

As the bishop's gaze lingered on the large freezers and ovens, Miriam waited him out. The dark hair beneath his black hat contrasted sharply with a pale face somewhat older than hers, yet his beard had gone more salt than pepper. Hiram's sonorous voice and his elevated way with words were surely *his* gifts, underscoring his position as their moral and religious leader—chosen by God's holy will to carry out the Old Ways and the *Ordnung*. No doubt in her mind he was here to do that rather than to compliment her cooking.

Miriam scraped the fragments of piecrust together. A huge bowl of sweet yeast dough awaited her, and even though she felt the weight of Hiram's penetrating gaze, she scooped half of the soft, fragrant mass onto the floured countertop. Beneath her rolling pin, the dough became a large rectangle.

"Seems your surprise visitor last week has stirred up a lot of trouble. I hadn't arrived in Willow Ridge when she was swept away by the river," he said in a low, even voice, "so perhaps you should explain to me what happened that day. And why you felt compelled to seek out the man who raised her."

Two spots burned in her cheeks. She hadn't shared this secret with anyone except Sheila and—

Leah! Did my own sister tell the bishop about this after she was here this mornin'?

Miriam concentrated on spreading butter over every square inch of the dough, giving her answers time to bubble up like yeast. "You're a father, Hiram," she began carefully. "Surely you can imagine my shock and—and *fear* as I watched my runaway toddler bein' carried away by the risin' river."

"Why were you so close to the water? Didn't you see the storm coming?"

Miriam had asked herself these questions a hundred times, pointing the finger of blame at herself. But Naomi's assurances—and speaking with Bob Oliveri and Sheila—had freed her heart of its guilt. And she refused to invite it in again. "Jesse was fishin' that day, and I went to fetch him when I saw the weather blowin' in," she replied quietly. "Had to take my triplets, of course. They weren't quite three that July. At a wiggly age and gettin' worked up by the weather, especially when the rain started pourin' down on us."

She sprinkled sugar and cinnamon liberally over the dough and then dotted the surface with raisins. "I was heavy with child at the time, too. And when I grabbed the girls to hurry up the bank to safety, Rebecca broke away . . . and fell in. I—I knew I couldn't stay ahead of the risin' water, so all's I could do was holler after her . . . and watch her disappear around the bend as I clutched my other two cryin' babies."

Hiram ambled toward the counter and picked up one of Rachel's chocolate cookies. "And you searched for her, no doubt."

No sign of empathy in that voice. No allowance for her pregnant condition, or the fact that Jesse hadn't been there to help with the girls. Was Hiram giving her enough rope so she could hang herself with her own words?

Miriam sprinkled the raisin-studded surface with more sugar and cinnamon. "*Jah*, Jesse and the neighbors looked all along the riverbanks, clean into New Haven and beyond," she replied around the lump in her throat. "My husband was torn up, but as ya know, he was also the deacon. So when Bishop Byler decided against callin' in the police and firemen to help us search, we went along with his decision—even though it broke this poor mother's heart."

Broke our spirits for a gut *long while, too. But this is no time to get all weak and watery-eyed.*

He closed his eyes in pleasure as he bit into the cookie. "That's the way Preacher Hostetler and Gabe Glick recall it, too. And—just as we Amish wanted no interference from the authorities or outsiders before, we must insist this incident remain buried in the past. For the People's safekeeping, as it were."

What exactly did he mean by that? Miriam's throat tightened around a retort as she carefully rolled the dough lengthwise away from her, tucking as she went. "*Jah*, I see no purpose in callin' in reporters or such, to cause a hoopla in the papers," she replied in a controlled voice. "Is that what you're sayin', Bishop?"

Hiram cleared his throat and came to stand beside her. "We've already seen how a single visit from this Tiffany—your Rebecca—has led young Micah to seek out her company. And she's compelled *you*, a pillar of the church, to sneak away for a meeting with the man who raised her," he said, placing a hand firmly on her shoulder. "These are prime examples of how English-ers entice us away from the *Ordnung* and from God's holy purpose for our lives, Miriam."

She shrugged from under his hand to fetch her sharpest knife. Oh, how this man made her insides simmer and stew! Had Rachel and Micah seen the bishop come in? Would they wonder why he was here, and come over? Miriam reminded herself of the warning she'd given her daughter about letting her temper get the best of her.

"Beggin' your pardon, but it's not like we invited Tiffany to come here. I didn't know she was alive!" She sliced the dough log into separate rolls with quick, practiced strokes. "And no matter what the brethren consider as holy purpose, ya can't deny that Tiffany is my long-lost daughter. Nor can ya keep me from lovin' her as my own, no matter *what* she looks like or what comes of it!"

Even as her words rang in the kitchen, Miriam knew she'd crossed the line. Said too much, too insistently—and with a knife in her hand, no less.

"Be still and *listen* when I'm talking to you!" Hiram stepped behind her to clap his hands on her elbows, pinning them to her sides. He wasn't hurting her, but as the bishop stood behind Miriam, his low, sonorous voice left no room for doubt—just as his grip kept her from wiggling out from between him and the kitchen counter. "Living without a husband for two years—running this business—has given you a dangerous sense of independence and lack of humility, Miriam Lantz. And it's clouded your judgment, as well. I advise you to leave your black dresses behind and cleave to a new husband. *Soon.*"

You, for instance? She knew better than to defy Hiram Knepp, but neither would she agree with him. Miriam let the knife drop to the counter as a sign of submission, but she made *him* continue the conversation. She hoped Micah and Rachel had become aware of her visitor and would come over soon . . . even if it meant Rachel would learn her most recent secret.

"You're a woman in your prime yet, Miriam. Created by God to keep a man's household and bless him with children." The bishop stood so close she felt the tickle of his breath upon her neck. "You believe that, do you not?"

Now *there* was a noose with her name on it! Miriam turned to meet his gaze. "Not a soul in Willow Ridge can deny that I fulfilled those promises while I was Jesse Lantz's wife," she replied. She couldn't just stop there, so she prayed God would give her words to get Hiram Knepp off her case and on his way.

"The day we lost Rebecca, I also lost the babe I was carryin'. And we could conceive no more," she added sadly. "So I have three daughters and I love them all—even if that love's not the same for the English-raised girl who's returned to learn the truth of her Amish roots. By this I'm not defyin' your advice, Bishop. I'm statin' things the way they are. Didn't Jesus preach that when we feed and help 'the least of these' we help Him, too?"

Hiram's dark eyes flashed like coals rekindled. "Could be I need to remove you from this kitchen for a while," he said coolly. "It brings you into contact with tourists and other outsiders. It fills your days with labor—with the earning of income—rather than with the wifely duties that would fulfill you as a woman of God."

Oh, there was no missing his message. Many times the grapevine had vibrated with the news of yet another Knepp baby on the way . . . never mind that Hiram's second wife had been only half his age. While Miriam had never considered it a hardship to bear Jesse's children, it seemed God had declared her unfit to create any more. She had accepted her lot faithfully: she'd had more time and energy to fully love Rachel and Rhoda, not to mention her husband.

But that was not what the bishop wanted to hear, nor did she care to share something so close to her soul. Not with him, anyway.

"If you take away the baker, you have no bakery." It irked her that Hiram kept his hands on her, kept her from putting these sticky buns into pans before they swelled out of shape. "And if you close the bakery, you affect the welfare of the Brenneman family, and the Kanagy bunch, and all the other wives who bake here to sell in so many places. The Sweet Seasons attracts folks to Zook's Market, too—and other stores and roadside stands where English folk buy our handmade crafts and garden produce."

Hiram's smile flickered above his beard. "Is this *pride* I'm hearing in your voice, Miriam?"

Ah, yet another sin he was pinning on her. This time she kept her mouth shut and she wished fervently that Micah and Rachel would peek in the kitchen door— *that* would surely make the bishop back away. Yet he seemed as unlikely to change his physical position as to change the opinions he was forming during this uncomfortable chat.

Next door, a pneumatic tool whined shrilly, once . . . twice . . . three times against a wall.

"What's that? Is someone working in Jesse's shop?" Hiram kept his hands on her arms, but as he gazed through the glass in the door he eased away from her.

To Miriam, the driving of those screws sounded like an answer to her prayer—even if her reply might further nail her to a cross, of sorts. "Truth be told, Micah Brenneman's buildin' a little place for me—and for Rhoda—in the loft, on account of how he's thinkin' to marry Rachel this winter. But ya didn't hear that from *me*, of course."

"He and Rachel should live with you. Plenty of rooms in that house, now that your parents are gone."

"*Jah*, or I could live there with *them*, dependin' on how ya want to look at it. But I'm thinkin' every man deserves to be king of his own castle—at least for a while." She smiled sweetly and inched him back enough to resume her work with the cinnamon rolls. "And when *you* find another wife, Bishop, will ya want your oldest, Annie Mae, movin' into your house with her husband? My girls are sayin' she and Yonnie Stoltzfus are gettin' mighty thick. Could be they'll soon publish their intent to get hitched, if things keep on the way they're goin'."

"Yonnie Stoltzfus isn't fit to wipe manure from my Annie Mae's shoes—if she were stupid enough to step in it." Hiram scowled, and then looked up again when the drilling next door sounded louder and more insistent. "I can see I need to be asking her some questions—but you and I aren't finished with our conversation, Miriam. You'd best consider your response to your disruptive daughter, as well as to my advice concerning your courting and re-marrying in a timely manner. Your soul's welfare—how you obey our God—is my highest concern, of course."

Of course! she retorted silently as the bishop made his way toward the smithy. Miriam quickly arranged the spirals of dough in her pans, inhaling their cinna-mon sweetness to soothe her troubled heart. No doubt in her mind, Hiram Knepp could close the café if he took a mind to it: he could work the "evidence" of her ruination into a case to convince the other brethren it was best for the community, too.

But could he force her to marry again? And was he positioning himself to be the man who courted her? *If he tells Rachel and Micah where I went yesterday, I'll have no end of explainin' to do . . .*

Exasperated, Miriam covered the pans with clean towels and shoved the rolls into an oven, where the warmth of the pilot light would help them rise. Indeed, she and Hiram weren't finished with this con-versation. She'd talk nonstop until God's Judgment Day to keep from getting caught with any of the lines Hiram had been casting.

Chapter 11

"Is Mamma all right, do ya think? Twice today, she forgot to set the oven timer—burned two batches of pecan rolls," Rhoda remarked in a concerned voice. "I've never known her to act so distracted."

"Stunk to high heaven, too," Rachel agreed. "Didn't help that she forgot to put baking sheets under a couple pies, either. Bubbled over in the oven and not even the exhaust fan could suck out that awful smell."

"*Jah*, Nate Kanagy asked if we were doin' burnt offerin's, like in the Old Testament. Said he had a few sins he wanted to throw on the fire."

They laughed together as they stood at the kitchen table that afternoon, spooning peanut butter no-bake cookies onto long sheets of wax paper. Like clockwork, from working together all their lives, they formed the fragrant mounds from opposite sides, filling the sheets toward the middle before moving down a couple steps to start a new section. As Rachel's hands went through the repetitive motions, she considered how best to answer her sister's question.

"I'm thinkin' Mamma's still got her mind on the bishop's visit last night," she began. "Like I told ya, we couldn't hear every word they were sayin', but once I slipped over to stand outside the kitchen, the gist of his lecturin' came through loud and clear."

"And ya think he wants to close the Sweet Seasons? What would that accomplish, considerin'—"

"Exactly what Mamma told him. If he decides she's spendin' too much time workin' there, insteada findin' a new husband, all of Willow Ridge'll suffer for it." Rachel scowled as she recalled listening with her ear against the door, then scurrying back to the smithy just in time to avoid being caught. "And when he saw how Micah was fixin' the loft of Dat's shop for—" She bit back the rest of a sentence that would give away her man's secret about their futures. "Well, let's just say I wasn't any too keen on bein' held responsible for Mamma and Micah *both*, as far as how things're goin' with Tiffany. Nothin' like it when Hiram puts ya in charge of somebody else's salvation."

Rhoda scraped the sides of the bowl with a rubber spatula so they could dip out the last of the cookies. "And he's thinkin' we could've kept her from showin' up? Not like we asked her to come—and besides, he's goin' on hearsay, ain't so? He's never laid eyes on Tiffany, yet he's forbiddin' Mamma from seein' her own daughter—"

"*Jah*, that's the message I got. But some pieces of the puzzle're missin'." Rachel fetched the second bowl of dough while her sister ran water into the one they'd emptied. "Once Micah started drivin' screws into two-by-fours, their talk got drowned out."

Across the table, her sister's face lit up with a cat-like grin. "Ya might as well tell me what Micah's doin' up there, Sis. I'll worm it outta one of ya sooner or later. Or I'll just go see for myself when you're not watchin'."

Rachel laughed out loud and then looked down the lane. "Here comes Mamma—"

"If it's her you're keepin' the secret from, ya *know* I won't let on!"

Rachel hedged . . . but why *was* she keeping Micah's project a secret from Rhoda? Might not hurt to get her sister accustomed to the idea of living above the vacant blacksmith shop: they could use her coolheaded way of handling the situation, if Bishop Knepp came calling again to say they were veering too far from the People's path. "Oh, Mamma already knows. 'Twas her that gave Micah the thumbs-up about us livin' here, in the house, after we get hitched—not that he's told anybody else that part. So he's fixin' an apartment in the smithy's loft for her and you, Sis."

The kitchen went still. Rhoda's lips pursed into a pale pink rosebud as she considered this information. "Well . . . *that*'ll be different, not havin' my room next to yours. But I s'pose—"

"We're *not* doin' it to keep ya outta my life, Rhoda! Never that! 'Specially not after the way Tiffany's got us all on pins and needles!" Rachel reached across to stop the hand that was so stiffly, automatically dropping dough: she'd inflicted a wound she hadn't intended. "'Twas Mamma's idea, makin' a little *dawdi haus,* to give Micah and me a chance at bein' newlyweds, I'm thinkin'."

Rhoda smiled wryly. "The bishop had a few words to say about *that*, then."

"*Jah*. Said there was plenty of room here for us all—but there was no missin' the way he was suggestin' Mamma needed to find a new husband—"

"Meanin' she should be considerin' *him*?"

"Uh-huh." Rachel peered through the glass in the door again. "She's on the steps. Let's not trouble her with this anymore."

Again they busied themselves with the dough, staging an unspoken race to see who could form the most cookies the fastest. As the door opened, they focused intently on their hands, spooning up dough and then pushing it to the wax-papered table with a finger to form mounds of peanut butter sweetness made chewy with oatmeal and coconut.

Mamma sighed as she crossed the kitchen, but she was smiling. "Got us a cookie frolic goin', do we?" she asked as she peeled one from the far end of the paper.

"*Jah*, Aunt Leah says these go real well at her farmers' market stand," Rhoda offered cheerfully.

"We haven't had any of these in the front case lately, either," Rachel chimed in. "And they don't heat up the house with the oven."

"*Jah*, there's that. Had my fill of ovens today—*cleanin'* them, that is. Broke my heart to throw out two big pans of pecan buns, but they were too far gone to use for bread puddin', even." Their mother's eyes closed over the fudge-textured cookie as she let out a tired sigh. "Mmmm! Like chewy, salty-sweet candy.

Maybe we could sell them all in the café . . . Leah's got lots of veggies these days, and we wouldn't want our goodies gettin' runny in the hot sun. Or squished, from her pilin' other stuff on them."

Rachel glanced sideways, matching her mother's expression as she talked about Leah. It was yet another sign Mamma had something weighing on her mind, when she sounded less than generous—and critical of her sister.

"Leah been givin' you a piece of her mind lately, Mamma?" Rhoda ventured.

What was that flickering across their mother's face? Irritation? Resentment? As Mamma pulled out a chair, she landed with a sigh that said she was heavy of heart . . . maybe about something she'd tried not to bother them with. As the youngest of seven sisters, she'd tolerated a lot over the years—and what did it say about her family's growing-up years, that Mamma and Leah were the only two whose families stayed in Willow Ridge after their parents had passed on?

"You girls're too sharp for your own *gut* sometimes," she murmured as she pried off her shoes. "Which is why I'd better be tellin' ya what's what, before ya hear it elsewhere."

Rachel glanced across the table, her eyebrows arched. Rhoda, too, looked up from the dozens of cookies they'd been forming.

"Understand when I tell ya this—that I wasn't aimin' to upset anybody or to show favoritism or whatnot. But there's things a mother's just gotta know."

Two spoons stilled on the wax paper. Rachel knew without asking how Rhoda's heart was fluttering like a hummingbird's wings, hovering above the doubt and fear their mother's words brought on.

Mamma sighed and took another cookie. "While you girls were at the quiltin' frolic on Sunday. I . . . went to see where Rebecca lived—to see how she grew up, and what sort of family she had and—well, I'm sorry I kept it from ya. Can ya forgive me?"

"Oh, Mamma." Rhoda's fingers fluttered to a string of her kapp.

Rachel felt a retort spinning like a storm cloud and bit it back. There was more to Mamma's bad mood than she and her sister had imagined. "So . . . after the way Tiffany practically *spat* on ya the other day, ya went to her house?"

"There's reasons for the way she is—the way we *all* are," their mother said in a rush. "And sure enough, her *dat*—the man who raised her—is upset about her wearin' those chains and black fingernails and whatnot, too. His wife lost her fight with cancer . . . a sad story, and I was glad, afterward, that I went to meet him."

Mamma paused to beg their forgiveness with her wide chocolate eyes. She looked older, as if she'd been bearing the world's weight on her shoulders. "Rebecca wasn't home, and that was all right, too," she remarked. "I think she moved out to spite him. Or on account of bein' upset with the world after her *mamm* passed."

"Micah says she's livin' with a friend—and that girl's boyfriend." Rachel's spoon clattered on the table. She crossed her arms, tempering her words so they'd get the whole story. "Seems he went to the trouble of seein' her—figurin' her out, like you—but all he got for his efforts was a lecture from Bishop Knepp yesterday. And again last night."

"*Jah.* And best I can figure, it was your Aunt Leah who told him I went. She and Sheila were the only ones who knew." Mamma stood up to rub Rachel's shoulder. "I'm guessin' it was his foot in the door, far as tellin' me I'm gettin' too tied up in workin' at the bakery when I should be devotin' myself to a husband again. But that's another thing altogether."

Rachel's thoughts were still spinning as their mother slipped an arm around her shoulders. "I'm sorry this is all blowin' up while you and Micah are makin' your plans, honey-bug. S'posed to be a happy time, your courtin'—even if most of us know about it already," she added with a laugh. "And ya probably think I'm spoilin' things by chasin' after a Rebecca who exists only in my mind. But I won't be goin' back to Morning Star. Saw what I needed to see, and came home to be with the girls who've been my pride and joy all their lives. I hope ya believe that?"

"Oh, Mamma." Rhoda hurried around the table to slip beneath their mother's other arm, to be the final side of their triangle. "How could we think anything different? Ya poured yourself into the Sweet Seasons mostly for us—to keep from dependin' on charity after Dat died, ain't so? If that's not love, I don't know what is!"

"*Jah*, there's that," Rachel murmured. She pulled Rhoda and her mother closer, grateful for her sister's gentler way with words. This situation with Tiffany was by no means behind them—never would be. But at least Mamma had spoken her truth and told them about her visit, and they stood once again in each other's arms . . . a comfort they'd not shown so freely until it was the three of them without Dat. "And we'll always be your girls, too, Mamma. *Fer gut* and forever."

"*Jah. Fer gut* and forever," Rhoda echoed solemnly. For a moment the three of them stood linked, savoring the quiet of this kitchen . . . the solidity of their bond. Rachel realized just how different things would be once she married—or if the bishop insisted Mamma find another husband, or if he closed the café. And considering how they loved working there—even though their days were long and tiring— it would be a shame for all of them and for Willow Ridge, too, if the Sweet Seasons closed.

But the bishop had the final say. It was their way, the church's *Ordnung*, and they followed it.

"We're seein' now how hard it's been for ya, knowin' ya lost our sister when we were wee little," Rhoda said with misty eyes. "And it hardly seems right that Hiram expects ya to just push her aside, outta your life—"

"Well, he didn't say that exactly," Mamma clarified. "And I for sure and for certain didn't agree to do that! Told him he couldn't control what that troubled, grievin' young girl did—"

"*Jah*, no tellin' how she'll act now, knowin' who her real family is."

"—and he couldn't tell me who I was gonna love, either!" Their mother looked purposefully at each of them, pulling them closer in her embrace. "It was sass, most likely—as he saw it. But I wanted him to know he couldn't go tellin' me what man I was gonna settle down with, either. Because at my age, I refuse to settle. For anybody."

Rachel nodded emphatically, as did her sister. "It's one thing to tell ya the mournin' clothes've gotta go. Another thing altogether to make like you're to marry *him*, just because he's the bishop and he says so!"

"*Jah*, Mamma, truth be told, I can't see that workin' out so *gut*," Rhoda said with a shake of her head. "You followed the Old Ways, far as submittin' to Dat and the church, but you get plenty riled up and *ferhoodled* when Hiram Knepp tells ya how things have to be!"

"And that won't change." Mamma glanced down at her flour-smudged baking apron. "Told him I'd found my life's purpose—feedin' people—and that my café is helpin' a lotta our families here in town, too. He wasn't so agreeable to all that."

"Not used to a woman who thinks for herself, ain't so?" Rhoda replied. "But with Dat gone, who else is gonna do the thinkin' and decidin' around here?"

"Gotta be all of us, workin' together," Rachel agreed.

"And that's why I've held back from marryin' and mixin' you girls in with somebody else's kids—in another man's house." Mamma smiled then, as though she felt herself rising above the questions Hiram Knepp's visit had forced her to deal with. "It's a lot to ask of children, not only to get along with another family—actin' like everything's all well and *gut*—but it's another thing altogether to give up your home place, as well."

"*Denki* for thinkin' that way, Mamma," Rhoda whispered, sniffling.

"*Jah*," Rachel chimed in solemnly. Then she thought for a moment. "And what would happen to this place, were you to hitch up with another man, Mamma?"

Their mother's eyebrows rose expressively. "S'pose that depends on the man. With land bein' so precious, and this place borderin' the river, I'm thinkin' plenty of fellas would farm it or bring in livestock again." Mamma smiled. "*Gut* thing your *dat* insisted on payin' his way, so he owned this place free and clear. That's one reason we were able to get a loan to build the café and grow our business, without worryin' about where our daily bread would come from till we turned a profit. Didn't have to go beggin'."

"So . . . what would happen to Dat's smithy if ya got hitched again?"

"I locked it up and left it just as it was when he passed, on account of how this town could use another good blacksmith. Didn't want another fella tearin' it down or clearin' it out to use for somethin' else. It was just a . . . feelin' I had, like God has another plan for that forge, just like he does for me." Mamma smiled at them. "And Rachel, honey, I mean for you and Micah to live here in this house, same as I said before. No matter what I do about gettin' hitched."

"You can live here, too, Mamma. You and Rhoda always have a place—"

"I'll keep that in mind, on the chance the bishop says I'll no longer be bakin' at the café. And if he does that, it's for sure and for certain I won't be marryin' *him!*"

They all nodded, considering these things, until Rachel glanced at the bowls on the table. "Ya know, we're gonna have us one big useless blob of sugar and peanut butter and oatmeal if we let that dough set up."

"Just one more thing, while we're talkin' this way." Mamma smiled at them again, pride shining in her mellow brown eyes. She looked relieved . . . restored. "When I was your age, courtin' and decidin' which man to marry, I didn't know a lotta things. But now I see it all from a different angle, and marryin' a man's a lot like puttin' your money down on a big grab bag of fabric in Schrocks' quiltin' shop. Ya see on the outside how full it is, and how solid, and ya got a pretty *gut* idea that even if all the colors don't suit, ya can make them work for somethin'.

"But with a husband, ya don't know what's inside that grab bag until you're hitched," she went on wistfully. "Sometimes ya find pieces that rub ya the wrong way, or that just don't go too *gut* with anythin' else . . . like when ya learn he's got a short fuse, or he doesn't so much want a wife as he wants a mother to clean up all his messes . . . or worse, he mostly wants a draft horse that'll work without complainin' till it just drops over."

She kissed Rachel's cheek then. "You've got a *gut* young fellow, honey-bug. I know how ya fussed about him goin' to see Rebecca, but ya patched it up and went on. *Des gut*, and that's what it takes to make a marriage work—long as he can do the patchin' when you do somethin' that doesn't suit *him*."

She looked pensive then. "Your *dat* was a solid sort and we had a *gut* life, mostly. Only thing he never really got over was the way I let Rebecca wiggle loose that day at the river. Didn't want her to be dead on account of my carelessness—"

"Mamma, that wasn't so!"

"Ya did your very best, Mamma!"

She sighed and released them with a hug. "*Jah*, I know that now. Made the best I could of it all those years you were growin' up, too, and . . . and seein' how Rebecca wasn't dead at all has kinda restored my faith in myself—and in God. There's a plan at work here, girls. And someday we'll figure out what it is."

As she glanced at her sister, Rachel saw the same determination in Rhoda's eyes as she felt welling up within herself: determination and a rightness that went beyond anything she could do by herself, whether with her long-lost sister or with Micah. "We'll make it all work out, Mamma. We want ya to be happy."

"*Jah*, ya deserve the life ya want, no matter what plans the bishop has."

Mamma nodded and wiped a tear from one eye, but her smile was bright. "*Denki*, girls, for helpin' me through the rough spots. Couldn't do it without ya." She reached for one more of those peanut butter patties and closed her eyes over its deep sweetness. "I'll fry us up some bacon for BLT's while ya finish your cookies. I feel lots better about all of this now."

"Me too, Mamma," Rhoda said, at the same time—in the same way—Rachel did.

Hard to imagine how things would be different, had Rebecca not run off that day so long ago—and if she'd not come looking for her original family this past week, too.

Whatever she's doin' right at this moment, God, I hope she knows we're thinkin' about her . . . wantin' life to work out for her, too, Rachel prayed. It seemed like a good idea—and it made her feel like smiling again, too.

"So, Sister," Rhoda said from across the table. The cookie dough was set enough that they were rolling it into balls between their palms now, letting the warmth from their hands soften it. "What-all's inside that grab bag named Micah? What're ya thinkin' you'll find when you open it, after you're hitched?"

Rachel's lips curved. "That's for me to know and you to wonder about! Ya just wish ya had a grab bag half so fine as mine, ain't so?"

Chapter 12

Micah glanced at the gray clouds rolling in and wondered if God was telling him something. He lightly clapped the reins over Rosie's back to hurry her along, past the Lantz house where Rachel would be getting dressed for the ice-cream social about now.

Why are you breakin' her heart again? Is this really such a gut idea?

The first raindrops splattered on his shoulders, cold and wet through his clean shirt. Maybe he was defying the bishop, keeping his date with Tiffany to prove he knew better than Hiram Knepp—to give the lost Lantz sister a chance to reveal her positive qualities or to ask him more questions and settle herself about who she really was. The bishop had chided him for visiting Tiffany right in front of Rachel the other night in the smithy. Knepp had warned Rachel that her mother might need assistance, as well: such a troubled Englisher could only wreak havoc upon their family and infect Willow Ridge with her dubious influence, he'd said.

And Rachel stood by you in spite of how you'd sneaked out on her . . . insisted this fascination and curiosity would pass because Tiffany was obviously as repelled by our ways as we were by hers. And you went along . . . not lettin' on for a minute that you were meetin' Tiffany on the same night as the social. Liar! LIAR!

Damnation in disguise, the bishop had pronounced her. And maybe Tiffany was more of a bad apple than Micah could see in the surface of that shiny red car.

Yet something told him Rachel's sister was hiding behind her black clothes, dyed hair, and tattoo, waiting for someone to shine some light on answers she could believe in. Wasn't he supposed to be an example of God's power and protection in this earthly life? Being older and more responsible, wasn't he supposed to do right by both of these Lantz girls? And if he didn't keep this date, he might never get another chance.

Rachel, however, had no idea how his curiosity had intensified since he'd ridden in that Mustang. And truth be told, keeping his date with Tiffany while he left Rachel waiting announced his confusion about the issue, didn't it? As he imagined Rachel's blue eyes gazing at him with such trust and love the other night, he nearly turned Rosie around in the middle of the road. Why did Tiffany attract him so? She'd probably forgotten all about that dinner invitation she'd made in such an offhand way . . . even if her eyes glimmered like a pretty summer sky, same as Rachel's did.

But he kept going up the highway, toward Morning Star. Toward answers he had to find even if he got shunned for spending time with her again . . .

* * *

Rachel glanced out her upstairs window for the dozenth time. Fresh from her Saturday bath and wearing the new plum cape dress she'd sewn, she felt happier than she could ever recall. Over and over in her mind, she imagined how wonderful-*gut* it would be to sit with Micah at one of the long tables, where his deep green eyes would shine with a love as bright as her own while they enjoyed homemade ice cream with their friends from around the district. While they wouldn't openly announce their plans to marry, she intended to make it clear that she was spoken for. No more waiting around as the crowd dispersed, wondering if any of the boys would offer her a ride home. Micah Brenneman would be holding her hand, along with the key to her heart.

"I'll be goin' now, Sis. You're sure ya don't want to ride over with—*ach*, but ya look real perty in that color!" Rhoda stepped into Rachel's room then, her eyes a-sparkle. Rhoda's dress was a deep shade of rust, as they had long ago decided not to dress alike, especially at social events.

"Thanks, but Micah's comin' for me. I'll fetch my cookies and walk with ya to the road, though."

As they passed through the kitchen, she picked up her tray from the table. Those dark chocolate chip cookies would surely be different from what the other girls brought, and the butterscotch bars were Micah's favorite. "Seems kinda dim in here—"

"Rainin' out!" Rhoda announced. "Sure hope Jonah hitched up the covered carriage, or we're gonna get soaked!"

From the big front porch, they looked beyond the yard and the large garden, down the lane. A single window glowed in the back of the Sweet Seasons. "Just as well Mamma's bakin' this evenin'. She gets kinda blue when it's dreary like this. Reminds her of the day we buried Dat."

"*Jah*, and the bishop didn't help that any, tellin' her to forget about Rebecca!" Rhoda peered between the side porch pillars, farther down the road. "Here come the Zooks now. Sure ya don't wanna join us? Katie always loves tastin' your cookies and talkin' about recipes."

Rachel chuckled slyly. "Got better things to talk about, thanks."

As Rhoda grabbed an umbrella and hurried down the lane to meet her ride, Rachel remained beneath the porch roof. Micah would be along any time now, as he was never late . . . would her sister ever find someone who made her as happy? Rhoda seemed content to accept an occasional ride with one fellow or another, but before much longer she'd be the oldest unattached girl at the singings . . . destined to be a *maidel* if she didn't hitch up with somebody soon. Maybe tonight, mingling with youth groups from New Haven, Morning Star, and districts beyond, some young man would be bowled over by how special Rhoda was. It would be wonderful-*gut* to marry on the same day this winter, twins that they were!

But you're really triplets. And Tiffany won't care about sharin' a wedding day. Will she wear black pants and black fingernails when she gets hitched?

Rachel glanced at the kitchen clock. A little past six, it was. No sense in wearing a path in the porch floor, so she sat on the swing to watch for Micah. He'd probably gone back home for an enclosed carriage when the rain started . . .

By six thirty, Rachel was swinging so fast the cookie

tray nearly slipped off the cushion. She grabbed it, scowling. What could possibly be making him this late? The turbulent sky was reason enough for him to stay off the road with Rosie, of course—and times like this were when she resented the *Ordnung*: if they had phones in their homes, Micah would have let her know he was waiting out the storm. Little chance he'd be phoning the Sweet Seasons from his carpentry shop, either, knowing she wouldn't be at the café to answer it.

A whoosh of wind and rain sent her inside, peeved as a wet cat. No sense in soaking her new dress, so she waited by the big window in the front room. Didn't turn on the lamps, as Micah would surely be here any moment. He wasn't one to miss homemade ice cream, and they were to serve dessert at six thirty. As the minutes ticked by, marked by the old mantel clock, Rachel became so upset she dropped down into a chair with her back to the lane, her arms crossed tightly.

Micah could just come in and get her. He'd know why she wasn't eagerly awaiting him outside. Rachel closed her eyes against the sting of tears, determined to hold herself together on this night she'd waited for so long.

Uncountable minutes later, the kitchen door opened and closed. With her face turned away from him, Rachel sat stiffly, anticipating his stammered excuse. Micah was polite and accommodating to a fault . . . had probably seen Mamma's light in the café and stopped to check on—

"Rachel! What're ya doin' here in the dark, honey-bug?" her mother exclaimed, bustling to light a lamp.

"Thought ya left for the social long ago, with Rhoda and the Zooks!"

Rachel clenched her jaw to keep from crying. "Why would I do that when Micah was to come for me?"

Mamma studied her as the light rose in the glass globe. "Well, then, he's run into somethin' unexpected. Couldn't ask for a more dependable fella. He worked all mornin' on the new apartment without me even askin' him."

"*Jah.*"

"Nice enough to carry all those boxes of glass jars in from the wagon, too. Saved *us* a lot of totin' before the cannin' frolic, for sure."

"*Jah.*"

Her mother raised an eyebrow and then sighed tiredly. "Goin' to take my bath now and sit a spell. They say hard work's the antidote for dwellin' too much on our disappointments, but this gloom's got me stewin' over what the bishop said about our Rebecca—even if I did bake the ten pies and twelve dozen wheat rolls for the Zook's Market order tonight." Her brow furrowed as she held a hand in the small of her back. "Not Tiffany's fault she didn't get raised amongst the People, like you and Rhoda. Tried to tell him that, but he wasn't hearin' any of it."

As if Tiffany would submit to the Ordnung—*or any other rules,* Rachel thought with a frown. *As if I give two hoots about someone who dresses like the walkin' dead.*

"So what do you want for toppings? Probably an extra large, huh? I bet you farm boys really scarf it down." Tiffany widened her eyes at him . . . blue, blue eyes that looked far too familiar despite a face that seemed so foreign. So . . . exotic.

Micah blinked. Rachel would be pretty peeved with him by now, waiting at home in her new dress, so he focused on the present moment—and on the Lantz sister who sat close enough that their arms brushed every now and again. Was it possible Tiffany had worn even more black stuff on her eyes tonight than before? And why would any girl wear earrings with little skulls dangling from them, when she was meeting a fellow for dinner? "Uh—what're my choices? For toppings, that is."

She rolled her eyes. "You want pepperoni? Sausage? Black olives, or green—"

"Don't rightly know. What do *you* like?" Seemed the polite thing, to defer to the lady's taste, since he could count on one hand the times he'd eaten pizza.

"I—what*ever!*" she said with an exasperated shrug. "What I *like* is a guy who can make up his mind and say what he wants! It's *pizza*, for crying out loud!"

"Ah. Well, maybe that comes from my bein' a carpenter rather than a farmer. Not as smart about food choices, ya see." Micah smiled patiently. He hadn't expected their conversation to go smoothly, so—all things considered—he felt he was holding up his end pretty well.

"So is this how you are with Rachel? Waffling all the time?" she demanded tersely. "And she's still hot for you?"

He swallowed hard: Rachel would be hot, all right—under the collar. Tiffany nailed him with those blue eyes, a mere foot away, and his heart lurched. Her tone and voice sounded exactly like her sister's . . . and so had her complaint. Woodworker that he was, he should be building an ark, by the looks of those storm clouds on her face.

"Never mind then! I'll just get what I want." She went back to stroking her fingertip across a small black screen she held, making the images flicker sideways before he caught on to what she was doing. But she'd write him off mighty fast unless he sharpened his strategy.

As Micah sneaked gazes at her, sitting just inches from him on the couch in her best friend's apartment, he still had more questions than answers about this girl . . . so much like Rachel and Rhoda, yet from another galaxy altogether.

And so distracted by worldly gadgets. But maybe that was for the best: he'd arrived looking like a drowned cat, so rather than go to a restaurant Tiffany had taken him to where she was staying. Loaned him jeans and a T-shirt that belonged to her roommate's boyfriend, while she ran his for-good shirt and trousers through her dryer. He couldn't count the ways he'd gone against the *Ordnung* in the past hour—grounds for a shunning, no doubt. His best hope was that because Tiffany seemed to think nothing of this odd, dangerous arrangement, no one back home would ever know how he'd compromised his church vows.

"Yeah, gimme a large meat-pleaser special, extra cheese . . . you got it, Hayden. You know where I'm staying, baby."

Micah gawked. By all appearances she was talking to herself, yet he had the idea she'd somehow ordered their pizza. "So . . . how'd ya do that?"

Tiffany blinked, closing the curtains of her black eyelashes for a moment to keep from laughing. "Bluetooth technology," she explained, tapping a pointy little gadget hooked to her opposite ear. "Don't guess you Amish are into wireless, hands-free communications, eh?"

Oh, but he wanted to communicate with his hands! Mostly wanted to ruffle the top of her spiked hair to see if it felt as bristly and stiff as it looked. Instead, he humored her with a patient smile. "Don't laugh, but I've never had a pizza delivered to my house, either."

"*That*'s against your rules, too?" She shifted to sit cross-legged then looked up from the screen resting against her ankles. Her expression suggested he might have sprouted a second head—or horns.

And maybe he had, at that, flirting with the Devil the way he was. "Don't s'pose food delivery is so wrong . . . your *mamm* gets food delivered from Zook's Market several times a week, for her bakery. But she— and all the other women—cook at home. Fresh stuff from the garden in summer, and what they've pressure canned or frozen durin' the winter. Get our meat at Zook's locker, or from another fellow who butchers the local cows and hogs and sheep."

"So, like, you don't even shop for groceries?"

Micah shrugged. "Not much need, except to buy flour and other such stuff to make our bread and desserts. Your *mamm* and sisters, now *those* gals make pies like nobody's business!"

"No microwavable meals, I bet. Man, I couldn't live without a microwave or my computer."

"No electricity at home, remember? It's only on account of the health department and their Mennonite partners that they've got electricity at the Sweet Seasons."

Tiffany nodded absently. She'd already gone back to staring at the pictures that flickered across her handheld screen, which gave him yet another chance to feel guilty about standing Rachel up. He could be eating her butterscotch bars with a big bowl of home-made ice cream now, basking in the adoration of her sky-blue eyes, as they chatted with their friends . . . planning a long ride home along the quiet country roads, now that the rain had stopped.

"So what's that you're lookin' at? Mighty tiny to be a computer, ain't so?"

Tiffany's grin crinkled her nose, as though she thought his accented speech was too quaint for words. Probably thought he was really stupid, too. "It's an iPad. Sorta like a computer, 'cause you can check e-mail and go online to . . . not that you have any clue about those things, probably."

"*Jah,* not so much. You're right about that." Micah paused for but a moment before saying what had been on his mind all along. What could it hurt to have another girl mad at him when he'd surely broken the only heart that really mattered to him? "But I've got a clue or two about *you,* Tiffany. I think you're hurtin' worse than you can say—maybe worse than you even know. And I bet ya feel like those folks who raised ya really dropped a pile of it, and ya stepped in it before ya knew how . . . stinky it would get."

For just a moment her mask slipped. Tiffany looked as *ferhoodled* as her sisters when they'd learned about her—except this poor girl had lost her mother and felt like her father had betrayed her, and then found out that's not who the Oliveris were at all. Who could she believe? What did she have to hold on to as she slipped in that pile of emotional horse hooey?

"You can't tell me you came here to play shrink, Micah. Why *did* you meet me tonight?"

Now *there* was a question! Just like her sisters, Tiffany had a sharp mind and a quick tongue. Micah shifted, feeling the unfamiliar tug of the tight jeans around his thighs and the way this girl watched the T-shirt hug his shoulders. "I'm curious about ya, for sure and for certain. But I . . . I just have this feelin' there's more to ya than makeup and skulls and such. And when I dig deep enough—find our girl Rebecca underneath all that—I bet I'd like to be her friend."

Her hand slipped into his. For a moment she looked vulnerable . . . almost fragile. "So then . . . why aren't you kissing me? Touching me like you're interested?" she pleaded. "I *know* you've been checking me out! Don't tell me you big, stud-puppy Amish boys don't *do* it! I mean, my God—*look* at you!"

Was that how she was used to being treated? Pawed at and played with like one of the girls' faceless dolls, and then dropped when the game grew tiresome? Micah wished his clothes weren't in her dryer, for he was being sucked into this quicksand of his own making . . . drawn deeper by those wounded blue eyes that watched him so closely. Eyes that widened and apparently liked what they saw.

"That's not how a decent man treats a woman. Especially one he barely knows," Micah replied in a tight voice. "*Jah*, I've thought about it some—doin' it, as ya say. And I decided, long time ago, that Rachel was the girl for me."

"So you're saving it for her? Yet you came *here*?"

Tiffany crossed her arms, challenging him with her incredulous gaze. "No way am I falling for that one."

Micah shrugged. "Got a lotta fences to mend, for leavin' Rachel on the sly tonight. I hope she'll forgive me, on account of how I'd be a sad, sorry man without her." He paused to gather his courage: it wasn't the easiest thing, to talk about deeply personal matters with someone dressed like Tiffany, showing so much skin and shape. But if he didn't try to reach her, he'd made the trip through the rain and upset his Rachel yet again for no good reason.

"I wanted ya to know, Rebecca, that your Amish mamma and sisters love ya and nothin' can change that," he murmured. It felt like praying out loud, and he sure hoped God was listening even though he'd gotten himself into a sticky situation. "That love's yours, if ya care to accept it. But once again, I'm tellin' ya: if ya go meddlin' and messin' with their lives for the fun of it, because ya think we Amish are simple-minded instead of just simple . . . you'll be real sorry. And so'll we."

Tiffany's eyes widened until he once again couldn't miss the resemblance to Rachel. And one more time he kicked himself for betraying her trust. This look-alike seemed ready to say something—

"Pizza man!" somebody cried as the door flew open. In walked a guy carrying a flat black bag, grinning at Tiffany—until he saw Micah. "Hey, dude. Love the shirt and jeans."

"Uh, Micah, this is Hayden, my best friend's guy . . . our other roommate," she explained as they stood up. "He sorta loaned you those clothes."

"And I thank ya for that," Micah said as he extended

his hand. Easy enough to see this fellow wanted to laugh at his longish, hat-flattened hair, just as he knew Hayden was jumping to the wrong conclusions about why he wasn't wearing his own clothes. But that didn't really matter, did it?

He excused himself to wash up, leaving Tiffany and her housemate to talk in low voices. When Micah caught his reflection in the bathroom mirror, he laughed sadly. Who did he think he was, trying to convince this young woman she had another family . . . more love in her life than she knew? And why did he think she'd listen to a fellow like him? He was a fish out of water here, flopping around awkwardly when it came to saying and doing what he should.

When he returned to the main room, Tiffany was sitting on the couch with the pizza box open on the coffee table. She held a cheese-draped wedge in one hand while she kept looking at that iPad gadget . . . sure was more interested in that than she was in him, or his message.

Time to get your clothes on and leave, he thought, realizing how suggestive this whole situation had become, even though he'd not so much as held Tiffany's hand. Was she worth the risk of shattering Rachel's trust in him? It didn't appear that he'd made any progress at all.

Micah cleared his throat. "I'd best be gettin' my shirt and pants—"

"But you've gotta help me eat this huge— Here! I . . . guess I've been kinda rude, haven't I?" Tiffany looked up, holding out a huge slice of pizza on a napkin. Was she offering him an olive branch, as well?

He sat on the edge of the sofa, farther away from

her, taking the pizza without touching her hand. "Well, it does smell wonderful-*gut*—"

"And you're a carpenter, Micah? There's this cool YouTube piece—" Once again she was flicking her fingertips across her iPad screen and then tapping it. "It's true what they say about so much junk being on the Internet, but this guy in Hong Kong—here, look what he's designed!"

Micah closed his eyes over a mouthful of chewy crust, seasoned meat, and warm, gooey cheese. He *must* ask Miriam or Rachel to make pizza sometime. Music burst from the iPad and then a voice, telling about a young Asian fellow who'd converted a tiny old apartment into a sleek modern home for himself.

He sat glued to the quick-moving images of walls that rolled on wheels and ceiling tracks, converting one main room into a sitting area, a bedroom, a kitchen, a small office. All by shifting these walls— with built-in shelves and nooks for appliances—to the other side of the small apartment. His bed folded up into the wall. His huge TV screen came down from the ceiling. He had created this compact space for himself by taking what he already had and organizing it so only the things he was using at the time were out. Then he tucked them away—everything into its place—and moved another wall when he needed the function of a different room.

Form and function. Wasn't his life work centered on those interwoven concepts?

The little movie ended too soon. Micah chewed, thinking. "Can I see that again?" he asked breathlessly. "Maybe a couple more times?"

His mind was spinning with ideas. Amish farmhouses

were huge and sometimes unshapely from numerous additions: three generations of a family often lived under one roof. The downstairs rooms of the larger ones were often fitted with removable wall partitions to accommodate benches for a couple hundred people on preaching Sundays, so the compact form and function he'd just witnessed were impractical. Yet if a builder approached an Amish home from a nontraditional angle . . .

As Tiffany touched the screen to show the piece again, Micah sensed the *rightness* of this moment— sights and ideas that could change his work forever, brought to him from a most unlikely source while he was where he wasn't supposed to be. And wasn't that how the biggest things had happened in the Bible, to God's movers and shakers throughout humanity? They might've been liars and cheaters—or even murderers, like King David—yet the lessons they learned prepared them to accept greater responsibilities and a higher purpose from their Creator, when next He sought them out.

Let it be this way for me, God. Show me what You'd have me do with this fascinatin' idea. It was too providential to ignore, this five-minute peek at such innovative thinking.

Spellbound, Micah paid closer attention to the nuts and bolts of how this Asian architect had designed his system of wooden walls that rolled silently, effortlessly . . . oh, this was gonna be so good when he measured that loft again and convinced Aaron to custom-weld him some hardware . . .

"Micah? You want your clothes now?"

Micah blinked. He could've kissed Tiffany, he was so excited, but he would go back to Willow Ridge instead. The ride would be a good time to let his thoughts jell while he also figured out how to win Rachel back. He had no doubt she was fuming right now, and she had every right to give him a talking-to. Micah hoped the inspiration he'd gotten these past few minutes would give him ways to impress his girl, too—not to mention how it would prove he loved Rachel even more than before.

He dressed quickly, unconcerned about the wrinkles in his white shirt and dark trousers. After he put on his hat, he offered Tiffany both hands. She rose to grip them, her expression wary yet hopeful. "*Denki*— thank you—ever so much for puttin' up with me and showin' me that movie," he said in a husky voice.

"Well, I'm glad *one* of us had a good time."

Micah's lips curved. Better to leave that line alone and not fall for the *wanting* he saw all over her so-familiar face. "I wish ya my best as ya come to grips with your *mamm*'s passin' and figure out what comes next."

And before those beautiful blue eyes could lead him any closer to perdition, any farther from where he needed to be, Micah headed home to whatever Rachel would dish up.

Chapter 13

Tired of stewing at home, Rachel watched Mamma drift off on the couch and then slipped quietly out into the night. The rain had stopped, but her personal storm still rumbled within her. The later it got, the more she believed Micah might not stop by: If he'd gone to see that witchy sister with the black hair and mascara, why would he bother with *her* tonight? He'd no doubt sneak in his own back door and avoid her altogether.

She wouldn't give him that chance! As she strode down their lane, Rachel didn't care that her shoes got wet and muddy . . . far worse if Micah Brenneman's soul got soiled from his association with that free-wheeling girl her *mamm* had claimed as one of their own. What was the attraction there? She'd known Micah most of their lives, yet now she wondered if she hadn't paid close enough attention to the man behind those serene green eyes.

What would she do if he renounced his Amish ways? Forgot his promises to her? While she hadn't yet whispered to her friends that she was working on wedding plans, folks in these parts *knew* she and Micah had been sweet on each other for years. How would she stand it if he backed out on her now? How would she endure the humiliation of facing her friends . . . going to singings and hoping, like a sixteen-year-old, that a nice fellow from around these parts would drive her home?

I'm too old for that now. What if I end up a maidel *like Eva Schrock . . . grim and unsmilin', peckin' away at everyone like a biddy hen?*

The stark image made her walk so fast her leg muscles ached, yet she needed this release. Along the dark highway she strode, ducking behind the bushes at the intersection of the Brennemans' lane when she heard laughter and young voices coming from an approaching buggy. Never mind who it was! They mustn't see her walking alone. Once the courting couple had passed, Rachel headed for the large farmhouse up ahead, beyond the small orchard where pears and apples glowed in the moonlight. Suited her fine that the lights were all out: she'd simply park herself on the front porch, so's not to miss Micah's homecoming.

But when she was within earshot of the two-story house, a familiar voice called to her in the darkness. "That you, Rachel? What're ya doin' out and about at this hour?"

Naomi. And now that her eyes were adjusting to the shadows beneath the overhang of the porch roof, Rachel saw the shape of Ezra's wheelchair, too. No way to act as though she hadn't heard the question, so she countered it with one of her own. "Micah home?"

"Why, no, dear. Thought he'd gone with you and the others to the social in—"

"Well, he never showed up." It wasn't the time to spew her suspicions about where Micah had spent the evening, but there was no turning around and heading home, either. "Not like he didn't know I made his favorite cookies and a new dress—"

"He's been mighty quiet this week. Tuckered out, I'm thinkin'," Naomi remarked. "The boys've been workin' on a big job east of New Haven. Tables and chairs for a lodge conference center and—"

"Glad for the business, too," Ezra cut in. He leaned forward in his wheelchair to peer at her from the shadows. "So ya didn't bring any of them cookies?"

"I should think not! Micah's got some explainin' to do before I feed him treats!"

Ezra grunted but then raised his head to look toward the road. "Looks like you're about to get your wish, missy. Try not to whittle him down with that tongue of yours. Took us this long to see him baptized into the church—"

"Ezra! We're goin' inside so—"

"—so I don't wanna hear about him jumpin' the fence to live amongst outsiders if ya scare him off!"

Rachel clapped her mouth shut. It was always hard to tell when Micah's *dat* was teasing, even as Naomi grabbed the handles of his chair to wheel him inside. Did the Brennemans know their boy had gone to visit Tiffany, or was Ezra pulling her leg? She'd hoped not to bring this sensitive subject to light in front of anyone else, so she turned to watch the approach of the courting buggy.

Her heart pounded. She hated nagging him . . . would rather not pick a fight at this late hour. But didn't she have a right to Micah's reasons for leaving her behind tonight? After all, if he'd been visiting her sister on the up-and-up, why hadn't he asked *her* to go? Rachel stood a few feet in front of the deserted porch, watching him: Micah handled the reins and Rosie with such expertise, he appeared not to be driving at all but merely along for the ride.

He stopped about ten feet in front of her, with his mare between them. "Rachel," he said with a nod.

"So ya still recognize me. *Des gut.*"

He grimaced. "I owe ya an apology, *jah*. And I'm hopin' what I learned tonight will prove why I love ya even more than—"

"How'd your clothes get so rumpled, Micah?"

"—before! And it's lookin' *gut* for your *mamm*'s relationship with Rebecca, I'll have ya know!"

There it was, like that imaginary elephant in the front room folks avoided instead of talking about. She fought back a sob, wrung out from this endless evening of having her highest hopes dashed. "Seems to me *you're* the one workin' on that relationship. Am I right, Micah?" she blurted. "That's where you've been, ain't so?"

He gazed down at her from the buggy seat, daring to smile kindly at her. "Wait'll ya hear about what I saw on her little computer gadget! Somethin' so perfect for the little nook Rhoda and your *mamm*'ll have above the smithy—"

"Well, hoop-de-do! I'm hearin' everyone's name but mine, Micah!" Rachel scowled, detesting that selfish whine in her voice. She sounded like she was six years old, having a hissy fit over not getting her way. And she certainly hadn't been raised to *expect* her way from the man she would marry! Yet the fellow in that buggy had the nerve to babble on about—

"—so when we get hitched, we can—"

"Ya sure about that, Micah Brenneman?" Like steam building up in a teakettle, she felt herself ready to blow, and there was no holding it back now. "I'll be twenty-one in a couple months!" she spouted. "Most of my life, I've been *waitin'* for ya to get established in your family's business! That's happened now, *jah?* But I've been waitin' for ya to latch on to property, too, so's you could build us a home—except the way I understand it, Mamma's givin' ya full run of *our* place!"

She stepped backward, blinking rapidly. Powerless against the rant that bubbled over like pie filling in a hot oven. "How long do I have to *wait* before ya see this Tiffany's nothin' but trouble, Micah?" she continued in a terse whisper. "The bishop's warned ya—twice now! The property and the house don't mean a thing if the People bring the ban down on ya for spendin' more time alone with that Englisher who wears all the makeup and that skull tattoo!"

Still Micah sat there, watching her. Waiting for her to run out of steam . . . to unwind and fall silent, like a top whirling at full speed eventually slows and topples over. "I understand why you'd feel this way, Rache, and I—"

"You understand nothin' of the sort!" she cried. "Sometimes I think ya just enjoy windin' me up and watchin' me spin this way. Ya *knew* how I was lookin' forward to the ice-cream social—with *you*—and yet . . . and yet ya left me alone all night without so much as a fare-thee-well."

He glanced at the house behind her and then patted the buggy seat. "Got an audience," he murmured. "Let's take this somewhere else, Rachel, on account of how

I want to share so much more than what I learned at Rebecca's—"

"And what might a man like you learn from a girl wearin' chains and witch-black hair?" she challenged.

Micah leaned down, beckoning her forward with a bent finger. "All I saw in her fridge was beer, Rache. Not that she could cook if she had any food—and she admitted as much." He tried to rest a hand on her shoulder, and smiled again when she jerked away. "And I learned how precious you are to me, with your Plain ways and your sweet, clean face. We're travelin' through this world at the same pace, you and I, and I want it to be *you* I travel with from here on out, honey-girl." Again he patted the buggy seat. "Please? It's you I love, Rachel Lantz. Even if your sister looked just like ya, I could never care for her serious-like."

Was he wearing her down? Or was she finally ready to listen to what this handsome, if rumpled, man had to say to her? With a sigh, Rachel clambered up into the buggy and sat beside him, leaving a conspicuous space between them.

Micah cocked his hat farther back on his head, smiling now. He clapped the reins lightly against Rosie's back and waited until they were halfway down the lane before he spoke again. "Have I ever mis-treated ya, Rache? Or forsaken ya? Or lied to ya—except for this visit to Tiffany's tonight?"

Rachel stared warily at him in the darkness. The buggy swayed over rough spots in the road, making her bump into him now and again. "We . . . we've been sayin' for weeks we'd be goin' to the social—"

"And it was wrong of me to keep my intentions to myself, after your sister invited me last week to see her again tonight. I knew you'd feel betrayed—anybody would," he added with a heavy sigh. "And I'm sorry I wasn't straight with ya, Rachel. Knew it was the wrong thing to do, even if I told myself I was seein' her for the right reasons."

He steered the mare into a right turn at the county road, away from her house. "But all week, while I was thinkin' about why Tiffany dresses and acts that way, that Bible verse from Micah reminded me about how the Lord requires us to love mercy, do justice, and walk humbly with our God. I maybe wear that out, on account of how I was named for that prophet," he admitted, "but those words spell it right out—how we're supposed to treat other people even if they're not our People. And even if they don't treat us the way we'd like to be treated."

His voice wafted over her like the night breeze. It wasn't her favorite thing, to hear Micah talk about how well such a brazen intruder should be treated . . . and Bishop Knepp disagreed with this way of applying that Bible verse to outsiders. If the brethren heard Micah had gone to see Rebecca again, she fully expected them to discuss a shunning—as much because he'd disobeyed the bishop's dictates as for chasing after the likes of Tiffany Oliveri. Rachel tried to formulate an answer as he pulled the buggy off the road into a little grove where they'd often sat talking in the moonlight.

"I won't be goin' back, Rachel," he said firmly. "Truth be told, she paid more attention to her iPad and a phone contraption clipped to her ear than she did to me."

"Ah! None of that second-fiddle stuff for *you, jah?*" she blurted. "So how'd it feel to be ignored, Mr. Brenneman? And ya still haven't told me how your clothes got so rumpled. A girl could get ideas about that, ya know!"

"Got caught in the downpour on the way to Morning Star. Sat around in the apartment she's sharin' with her best friend and that gal's boyfriend . . . wearin' the boyfriend's jeans and T-shirt while my clothes were in the dryer." He looked her straight in the eye. "I know that sounds mighty suspicious. But I hope you'll believe me when I say your sister's got a lotta important pieces missin', far as what I want and need in a wife, Rachel. Coulda had whatever I wanted—more than pizza— on account of that's what she was offerin'. She laughed at me when I said I was savin' all that for marriage. For *you*."

Rachel's eyes widened. She sniffled, wiping her nose on her sleeve. Was there such a thing as too much honesty? As Micah described his evening, the pictures in her mind were anything but flattering, yet . . . his voice and his tone sounded sincere. Weary of the outside world after just two visits with Tiffany.

"I love ya, Rachel," he murmured. "Will ya still give me the rest of our lives to prove that to ya, every single day?"

She closed her eyes, wanting to believe such sweet words from the man who sat beside her. So many fellows went wild with women during their *rumspringa*, yet Micah had not. So many of her friends, married for a few years and balancing babies on their hips now, acted as though the romance they'd known during their courting days had evaporated like morning dew . . .

After tonight's episode, she had a lot to consider about things she'd naively taken for granted, lost in the haze of new love. Never before had she doubted

Micah's intentions. It didn't feel good, assuming the worst about where he'd been and what he'd done this evening while she fumed at home in her new dress with her tray of cookies.

Micah gently lifted her chin with his finger. He scooted closer and draped an arm loosely behind her, on the seat. "You're not much on hearin' about this, I know, but Tiffany—Rebecca—has a lot in common with you and Rhoda right now. She's not only lost a parent, she's learned that some mighty disturbin' secrets were kept by the people she trusted most. Gotta be tough, findin' out you're not who ya always thought ya were."

Rachel gazed into the eyes that were focused on hers. "Not easy findin' out that Mamm and Dat kept that secret, either, ya know."

"I suspect the brethren had a say in that. Since your *dat* was a deacon and all." He cleared his throat, thinking. "I'm guessin' it's takin' a toll on your *mamm*, too, havin' to bear the brunt of this alone. She's looked a little worn around the edges this week, even though she's wantin' to catch up to her lost daughter."

"The bishop's got ideas about that, too." Rachel made a face in the darkness as she recalled Hiram Knepp's stern reprimands when he'd cornered the two of them in the smithy the other night . . . not to mention how upset Mamma had been after he'd left.

Micah smiled gently. He ran a tender fingertip alongside her face. "*I've* got ideas, Rache," he whispered, "and they've got nothin' to do with anybody but you and me. Know what I mean?"

A little shimmer went through her and she dropped her gaze.

"If you're wantin' me to kiss and make up with ya, honey-love, ya better give me the go-ahead," he murmured. "I don't wanna take somethin' ya don't wanna give me, just because *I* want it so bad. Your forgiveness, that is. And then your kisses."

Rachel gazed into his handsome face. Where would her dreams be if the brethren banned Micah from speaking and eating with his family and friends in the church—and her? What would happen to their anticipated wedding day? And what would happen if she didn't forgive him right now? Would he look for someone else on the outside?

Is that somethin' you really want to find out?

Rachel nipped her lip. Micah had explained and was apologizing, after all. He'd been very calm and compassionate—about her feelings and Tiffany's, as well. Where most men would expect her to go along with their own wishes—or wouldn't have admitted going to see Tiffany at all—Micah had confessed even the questionable details of his situation. He'd tended to business he felt was far more important than an ice-cream social . . . and wasn't it, after all? Hadn't her sister's appearance changed all their lives, whether they liked it or not?

He's takin' the high road here. Are you gonna walk it with him, or get left behind?

Rachel smiled and cupped his jaw. "How do ya put up with my whinin', Micah?" she whispered with a sigh. "Sometimes I get so wound up, I—well, your *dat* irritated me right off by sayin' not to whittle ya down too far—"

She stopped there. No need to go into Ezra Brenneman's rant, because this moment *was* just between her and Micah. Softly she kissed him, and felt the sweet relief of his affection easing away the tension of this entire evening. Why had she doubted him? As he wrapped his strong arms around her, settling in for the kind of kissing they both so enjoyed, Rachel smiled inside. Mamma was right: Micah was steadfast and gentle, a man with a plan for taking care of her for all their lives. A man who could rise above her petty remarks and excuses for not being the best woman she could be. He deserved a wife who would support his ideas and believe in him . . . believe he had the best of intentions, no matter how things might look on the surface.

Rachel sighed as he held her close. Being *in* love felt so much better than fearing she'd been left out of it.

Chapter 14

Miriam smiled as she drove the wagonload of Mason jars and canning supplies to the back entrance of the café. The Sweet Seasons had done a brisk lunch business for a summer Monday, and after they'd gone home for dinner with their families, she and Naomi were returning to hold a canning frolic. What with the larger cookstoves here, the commercial dishwasher, and the tables and chairs in the dining room, the café was the perfect place for the women of Willow Ridge to put up large quantities of vegetables from their gardens, which were now in their peak season.

It pleased her to offer her friends a place where this work would be easier, a way to repay their many favors since Jesse had passed. The evening wasn't as humid as usual, and with the long, late rays of the sun illuminating the trees after a gentle rain, Miriam felt as shiny as the green leaves all around her. Maybe it was this recent reuniting with her Rebecca, or maybe time had finally eased her grieving heart: she felt *good* again. Happy. At peace with her situation, and confident God would show her what came next when the time was right.

"And here we are again, dearie." Naomi smiled as she came through the doorway holding a tub of fresh watermelon slices for their break. Mammi Brenneman entered with her, carrying deep baskets of canning lids and rings. "I hear tell we've got bushels and bushels of tomatoes comin' tonight. My Hannah corralled the younger Zook kids, and they picked and snapped string beans all day long. Hope we've got lots of pressure cookers comin'."

Miriam looked up from the first load of hot, shiny jars she'd run through the dishwasher. "Mighty *gut* to see ya, Adah!" she said, greeting her best friend's mother-in-law. "Probably best to do tomatoes on one stove and beans on the other. Maybe keep the tomato mess here by the sinks whilst we pack beans into their jars over by the serving window."

"*Jah.* Did that last year, as I recall. Worked out wonderful-*gut*." Naomi's brown eyes sparkled as she set her watermelon in the refrigerator. "Micah said he and Aaron had some weldin' to do tonight for a special project. You wouldn't know anythin' about that, would ya?"

"Can't say as I do. Just glad Rachel was in a good mood this mornin'," Miriam replied with a chuckle. "She was fit to be tied when Micah didn't show Saturday night."

"*Jah*, he heard about that from his *dat* and me, too. It's one thing to reach out and be kind to your Rebecca," her friend said with a nod, "but he's invitin' another kinda trouble altogether, gettin' mixed up with sisters. Especially considerin' . . . well—"

"You can say it out loud, Naomi. She's not the same Rebecca that Jesse and I woulda raised, but it's mighty fine to see her alive, ain't so?" Miriam grinned and then nodded toward the window. "Grab the door, will ya? Leah's got an armload of tomatoes!"

And behind Miriam's sister came Mammi Kanagy and the three Schrocks, along with Lydia Zook and her two older girls. Rachel and Rhoda arrived with Hannah Brenneman and the huge washtubs of green beans they'd cleaned today. Most of these women had worked together through so many garden seasons that they fell into small groups, chattering as they boiled and peeled the tomatoes on the north side of the kitchen or processed beans at the serving window counter. The little girls prepared lids and rings while their big sisters and mothers formed assembly lines that filled the hot jars and then loaded them into the cookers like clockwork.

Wiping her damp brow on her rolled sleeve, Miriam smiled with satisfaction. While any one of them could've hosted this frolic in her kitchen, they had so much more space to work with here at the café— and to put out the hot, finished jars on towel-covered tabletops in the dining room. In the café's back corner, the smaller children played or wrote on the whiteboard while the two grandmas, Adah Brenneman and Essie Kanagy wrote out date labels for tonight's jars. It was a wonderful thing, the way every woman could join in and feel welcome and useful.

Come time to go home, everyone would have several quarts of beans and tomatoes, the work made easier because it was a form of fellowship . . . a time to ask about Rebecca, too, and then speculate about how Preacher Hostetler was faring without his wife, and to share ideas about how to use up the overabundance of zucchini in all their gardens.

"I'm thinkin' a freezin' frolic's in order," Lydia suggested. "Henry cleared me some space in the butcherin' locker to store rhubarb or corn or grated zucchini. Whatever you've a mind to bring, if your own freezers are full."

"Don't know about your house," Leah chimed in, "but we've about reached our limit of stuffed zucchini and sautéed zucchini and zucchini fritters and—"

"*Jah*, mine are turnin' up their noses at limas and yella squash now, too."

"There it is! Got all our canners filled and cookin'!" Naomi announced above the chatter. "I'm thinkin' a slice of cold watermelon sounds mighty *gut*."

"*Jah*, let's all sit a spell and—"

The exhaust fan overhead stopped. "Miriam, I'd like a word with you."

All eyes turned toward the doorway, where Hiram Knepp stood as though he were silently taking attendance at a Sunday church service. Miriam sighed inwardly, but there was no putting off the bishop: after the way he'd suggested the Sweet Seasons might be leading her away from her true purpose, she knew better than to challenge him in front of all these women.

"When would be a *gut* time?" she asked with more patience than she felt. "We're smack in the middle of our cannin'. Got lots more to go yet."

His dark eyes singled her out in the middle of the crowded kitchen. "Deacon Reihl, Preacher Hostetler, and I have discussed how the café might be keeping you from finding a husband . . . fulfilling yourself as a woman in God's holy order of things," he intoned.

"We'll be here when you close tomorrow afternoon. Two o'clock sharp."

Miriam's friends looked at her, silent questions in their eyes, and then focused on the bishop again. They knew better than to object or to stand up for her—if indeed they felt Bishop Knepp was overstating his case. She and Naomi and the three Schrocks were the only women here who ran shops full-time, so the rest of them had no such worldly concerns taking them away from their families. Lydia and Henry Zook simply brought their children to the market: the older ones had worked there since they'd been able to make change and reach the cash register.

"I'll be here," she replied. Why did she feel like a sinner being ordered to her knees? She detested the way her heart flailed in her chest while her pulse galloped like a runaway mare.

"And you, Annie Mae, are coming home with me!" Hiram continued sternly. "Your dear mother taught you better than to race out of the house with the kitchen in a mess."

"But, Dat, I asked—" The dark-haired girl who was rinsing tomato seeds from the sink let out an exasperated sigh. "Nellie said she'd redd up because she didn't want to come cannin' with us—"

"And as the eldest, are you not ultimately responsible for the household?"

Miriam sighed, feeling the painful burden the bishop's daughter bore. Not only had Annie Mae lost her own mother when she was a young girl, she'd also begun her *rumspringa*—her running-around years—after her father remarried: Hiram's second wife had been but a few years older than Annie Mae when the bishop started a second family. At nineteen, this

sensitive young woman appeared worn beyond her
years and . . . bitter. A troublesome combination of
traits now that she had to nurture her two full sisters
as well as four motherless half siblings, who'd always
seemed exempt from the rules and responsibilities
her father imposed upon her.

"Coming, Dat," Annie Mae murmured.

An uncomfortable silence rang in the kitchen, un-
derscored by the bubbling of the pressure cookers.
When Bishop Knepp had walked most of the way to
his buggy, someone flipped on the exhaust fan again
and the women resumed their conversations in a qui-
eter tone.

"I'll bring your beans and tomatoes by on my way
home," Rhoda assured her friend.

"Jah. Denki." Annie Mae left the kitchen, her lips
pressed into a tight line as she wiped her hands on
her apron.

"That one's gonna be trouble if Hiram don't watch
how he handles her," Eva Schrock predicted dourly.

"And what's he sayin' about *you*, Miriam?" Lydia
Zook asked with a scowl. "If he's thinkin' women have
no place runnin' a business—insistin' they stay home
to clean and cook and make babies until they die—
well, I could tell him a thing or two about how our
store *really* gets managed!"

"*Jah,* and you can be sure Reuben, my cousin on
the Reihl side, is gonna understand just how much
business the Sweet Seasons brings the rest of us with
shops in Willow Ridge," Mary Schrock piped up. "Out
here in the sticks, if we don't have a place for tourists
to eat, or just wet their whistles, they most likely won't
bother stoppin' at all. Just as easy to go to the convenience store at the gas station up the way."

Miriam nodded her thanks to these friends, ever so grateful for their understanding and support. Surely if Mary told her cousin, the deacon, about the financial implications of removing her from this roadside eatery, where the Brenneman boys attracted so many buyers for their cabinet shop, and folks who'd finished their meals then wandered into the quilt shop next door . . .

But she knew better than to second-guess Hiram Knepp. The bishop and her husband, Deacon Jesse, had spent enough time out in the smithy with the preachers, discussing the business of the People, that she'd seen firsthand how this man of God conducted his earthly affairs.

Miriam sat down at a table, amongst her friends, and closed her eyes gratefully over her first bite of cold, crisp watermelon. *This business with the bishop is in Your hands, God . . . but I for sure and for certain would appreciate help with the right words.*

As she smiled at the children in back, who scribbled on the dry-erase board below the day's menu, it came to her: the way to a man's heart was still through his stomach . . . and a fellow who oversaw the welfare of hundreds of church members couldn't argue against a ledger filled with solid, black figures.

Could he?

Chapter 15

Come two o'clock the next afternoon, Preacher Tom and Deacon Reuben sat down in the café at the table in the far corner, followed soon after by the bishop—who made purposeful eye contact with Miriam in the kitchen before he took his seat. She waved and nodded—as though the Sweet Seasons ever closed when the sign on the door said it did! Rhoda poured the elders some iced tea and lemonade and then checked on the long table of ladies who'd arrived in a van from a senior center at one forty-five.

"Well, bite my tongue!" Naomi murmured under her breath. "Sometimes I wonder how those fellows can take off from their day's work whenever they please. But you didn't catch *me* complainin', Miriam, because you let me do that, too."

Brushing flour from her apron, Miriam chuckled. "Didn't hear a thing ya just implied, on account of those older ladies havin' such a fine, fun time laughin' over their lunch. Couldn't ask for a better cook than you, friend."

"So what'll ya say if he closes us down?"

There was worry peeking around Naomi's bright brown eyes, and Miriam was well aware of what her best friend's income meant to the Brenneman family. "Not sure he's aimin' to shut the doors, dear. Just wants me to behave myself, is all."

"And he thinks keepin' you home will do *that*? Puh!"

Miriam shrugged and cut a generous wedge of rhubarb cream pie, another of crustless fudge pie, and one of cherry. "It's all a matter of how you consider the act of *submission*, Naomi. There's the side where you roll over belly-up like a dog and always say *jah*, and there's the kind where you submit the work of your hands as an offering—especially to God."

Naomi watched as she plated the desserts. "Hmmm . . . no need to ask what ya plan to try, then."

"Might surprise ya." She added a scoop of vanilla-bean ice cream to the fruit pies and topped the chocolate slice with a dollop of whipped cream and a bright red cherry. "I learned things about Hiram Knepp while Jesse was deacon, and I'm askin' God to remind me of them at all the right times."

"You go along now. The girls and I'll redd up."

"*Jah. Denki*, Naomi. Couldn't run this place without *you*."

With her plates of pie on a tray, Miriam walked through the dining room. She chatted briefly with two of the white-haired ladies from the senior center, who asked what she'd used to season the fresh green beans. Then she set her desserts in the center of the brethren's table. After she took a plain black book from the drawer in the serving station, she sat in the empty chair. Couldn't miss the way Hiram had arranged it so she sat by him.

"Afternoon, gentlemen." She smoothed her kapp and folded her hands on her lap, waiting.

"Well, now, Bishop—we couldn't've picked a better place for this meetin', ain't so?" Reuben Reihl grabbed the fudge pie before anyone else could. Tom reached for the cherry, but then sat back to allow the bishop *his* choice.

Was Hiram holding out to prove he could resist her offering? Or did he consider it a bribe? "As I said the other evening, Miriam, I'm concerned about the long hours this business requires of you. I fear you focus your time and attention on the café rather than upon any man who might make you a suitable husband."

Bless him, Tom Hostetler glanced at the stern, black-haired bishop and then smiled cautiously at her as Hiram reached for the cherry pie. Miriam flashed him a grateful grin . . . she had an ally here, anyway—even if they'd have to go along with whatever the bishop decided.

"And what're you sayin', Bishop? As *I* mentioned before, the Sweet Seasons wouldn't be much of a bakery without its baker." She opened the ledger and slid the book in front of him, careful not to bump his pie plate. "Not a prideful thing to say, when ya consider the wages I pay Naomi for her long days cookin', and the way the café supports Leah's truck farmin', too," she explained carefully. "In exchange for those two women not always bein' in their own kitchens, their boys and Dan Kanagy get their breakfast here, on the house, nearly every mornin'. Not to mention the way I've kept myself and the girls goin', without havin' to request assistance after Jesse passed."

Hiram's eyebrow arched. "We are to trust in God's providential care—"

"*Jah*. And I'm pleased to be an earthly hand for the gracious arm of God's providence, too." Miriam ran her finger under a line item she was particularly pleased about. "I made this extra donation to the church's emergency fund last spring, on account of how Ezra Brenneman wouldn't accept my money when he had that bad reaction to his new medication. Ended up in the hospital for more'n a week, he did. And when Reuben took a check to the hospital, my donation covered a *gut* part of what Ezra owed."

The bishop perused the handwritten entries for a few moments, absently chewing a large bite of pie. "These are impressive figures, Miriam. Almost too good to be true, considering what I've seen from some of our other local businesses of late." He looked across the table. "You're the money manager, Reuben. What do *you* think of these entries?"

Reuben sent her an apologetic glance as he accepted the ledger. "I can tell ya that Miriam's figure for that donation is accurate, on account of how she handed me the money personally."

"And how was the church ledger when you took it over after Jesse passed?" she asked quietly. "Were all the funds accurately accounted for?"

"To the penny. Had no trouble a-tall knowin' which amounts had been withdrawn, and from which accounts," the middle-aged deacon replied. "God knew what he was doin' when he had your husband draw that lot."

Miriam's insides fluttered. She had to proceed very carefully . . . walk a line as fine as the ones drawn beneath the columns of neatly written figures in her ledger. With trembling fingers she slipped an envelope out of the pocket on the first page. "You would recall,

then, the way Jesse wrote and formed his numbers? As
he did on this ticket he made out for shoein' your
horses and repairin' some garden implements?"

Beside her the bishop shifted, frowning. But Reuben's expression confirmed her hunch about present-
ing her facts and figures this way, thank God above.

"This don't look a thing like the records in the
church ledger." Reuben blinked and then glanced at
her café ledger again. "*That*'s the very handwritin' in
the church books, right there!"

"And how did *that* happen, Miriam?" Hiram Knepp
shifted closer to her, to establish his superior height
and position. "Women are not chosen as officers in
the church, so are therefore forbidden access to the
records!"

"*Jah,* Jesse knew that when the deacon's lot fell to
him," she murmured, praying she didn't further en-
danger her restaurant's fate by being honest. "And
God knew, too, that while my husband was a fine, up-
standin' businessman and committed to his responsibilities for the People, he . . . well, Jesse could tote
up a column of figures in his head faster than you ate
that pie, Reuben. But he was dyslexic. Somewhere between his eyes and his mind, his letters and numbers
got switched around, and the teachers in our Amish
school couldn't give him the help he needed, ya see.
So I did his readin' and writin' for him, from the time
we were courtin'."

Across from her, Tom gaped. "I—I had no idea
Jesse was—"

"Huh! Just like ole Jess not to beg off, on account
of somethin' bein' hard for him," Reuben replied
with a decisive nod.

"That's the most underhanded, dishonest—" Hiram's

raised voice carried all over the room. He stood, as though he were leaving in a huff. "It is not *our way* to allow women access to our accounts or the overseeing of church monies—and Jesse knew that all along, yet he never confessed to this wrongdoing!"

Miriam felt glances from the kitchen and the ladies from the senior center, who were getting their checks rung up at the door. The dining room was so quiet they heard Rhoda drop her pen at the cash register.

"The lot fell to Jesse, Bishop. Would've been a disgrace to refuse God's call, ain't so?" she asked in a still, small voice. "He and I prayed on it. Decided that since God knew of Jesse's disability—*made* him that way, for whatever reason—I was in the picture so my husband could carry out the work he'd been ordained to do. Womenfolk are to be their husbands' helpmates, *jah*? The Good Book says it's so."

Was that anger in Hiram's eyes? Or did he resent how she'd proven that her house—and her business— were in order? "I've seen and heard enough," he remarked as he plucked his hat from a peg on the wall. "Good afternoon, Mrs. Lantz."

Reuben and Tom scooted their chairs back, signaling the meeting's end. "*Gut* pie, too," the deacon murmured as he passed her.

"Mighty *gut*, Miriam," Preacher Hostetler echoed.

As silence filled the dining room, Miriam closed her eyes and hugged the ledger to her chest. Jesse had been a master at covering his disability: he'd been the butt of so many *dummkopf* jokes in school, he refused to let such indignities stand in the way of his being a successful blacksmith and church officer. He'd taken his church responsibilities very seriously, and not one penny had gone astray while he served as their deacon.

And ya stood beside me just now, when I needed ya most. Denki, dearest Jesse—and God, You, too! Even if the bishop's not finished with me yet.

"I got big plans—and a big idea workin' here—but ya gotta promise me ya won't peek into the smithy nor let the girls go up into the loft anymore. Can ya do that for me, Miriam?"

Miriam gazed up into Micah's unlined face, tanned from his outdoor construction work. What a fine, handsome man Naomi's middle son was as he stood in the kitchen doorway. "Well, it sounds easier to go along with than havin' the brethren here, takin' a fine-tooth comb to my accounts," she replied pertly. "Don't reckon anythin' you can surprise me with'll top that for today."

"It's like nothin' you've ever seen. And best of all, it'll prove that some good came outta my visit with Tiffany." He motioned to Aaron and Seth, who jumped down from a large wagon loaded with lumber and building supplies. "Seems you and I gotta help each other when it comes to dealin' with Hiram's attitude—and Rachel's. If ya have a little faith in my work—"

"Oh, I know whatever you're doin' to that loft'll be top-notch, Micah."

"—maybe you and I can prove that the Old Ways'll work even better for everybody if we give new ideas a chance now and again."

Nodding, Miriam stepped over to the smithy to hold the door open. The other Brenneman boys began toting two-by-sixes through the smithy and up the stairs, with Micah pointing the way. As their boots clomped up the wooden steps, her heart fluttered: What on earth was this surprise written all over their faces?

"And mostly I hope to prove to Rachel—and to you, Miriam—that only *gut* can come of this reunion with your other daughter. It was meant to be, ain't so?"

"*Jah. Jah*, it was," she murmured, suddenly moved by his fervent voice and the way he squeezed her shoulder.

"So you'll be keepin' my work a secret then?" he repeated with a grin. "My brothers know just enough that they're givin' me the next few days to work on this project, on account of how this might be somethin' new and really *gut* for our business, if it works like I've told them it will."

Miriam sighed happily and tweaked the brim of his straw hat. "Ya don't know how this pleases me, Micah, to see ya stretchin' yourself . . . riskin' your time and talent and all the while believin' things'll work out for the *gut*," she remarked quietly. "Reminds me of my Jesse when he was startin' his smithy business—breakin' away from the farmin' his family always did, because he saw we needed a new way of makin' a livin'."

"*Jah*. And he did us all a favor that way—and we still miss him and the *gut* work he did with our horses." Micah stepped out of the way to let his burly brothers pass, his green eyes shining. "So when ya hear me hammerin' and shiftin' stuff around, ya gotta resist the urge to come checkin' on me—and ya gotta keep my *mamm* outta there, too! When it's all done, *you* get to see it first. And if ya don't like it, well, I'll make it the way ya want it. Least I can do, for the way you're givin' up your home to Rachel and me."

After the ups and downs of this day, Miriam felt ready to cry—until she saw Seth and Aaron wheeling a refrigerator toward the smithy door. "*Ach*, I never thought to—you'll be needin' some up-front money to pay for your—"

"Least I can do," Micah repeated more emphatically, "for the way you're givin' the house to Rachel and me. And if you're gonna stand here and fuss over what we carry upstairs, then you can just go on home! Time you was takin' a load off, anyway, seein's how early you get here to bake each mornin'. Ain't so?"

His pointed expression left her no room to protest. A grin twitched on her lips and it felt good. Miriam reached into the drawer nearest the door and handed him a key. "No sense in leavin' yourself open to vandals, close as we are to the road. Like you're sayin', the Old Ways're fine—until other people get new ideas about takin' advantage of us. You're a good boy, Micah. I'm goin' home now, leavin' it all in your hands."

Chapter 16

"What *is* all that racket and poundin' over there?" Rachel, along with Rhoda, Naomi, and her mother, gazed out the door toward the smithy Wednesday morning as though they hoped to see through its sturdy walls to the carpentry work going on there before the café opened. "Thought Micah was only workin' after hours—"

"He's got a new project cookin'. Somethin' he got the idea for while he was at Tiffany's," Miriam remarked. "And I promised him we'd *not* be goin' over there to nose around. That goes for *all* of us!"

Naomi shook her head good-naturedly as she dumped a steaming pot of spiral pasta into the colander. "He was all hush-hush about it yesterday. Top-secret idea, he said—and even his brothers don't know enough about it to let on. Haven't seen Micah this excited over a job in a *gut* long while."

"Guessin' by the boxes they tore down and threw in back, he must've carted new sinks and a shower stall and who knows what-all up there after we left yesterday." Rhoda gently pressed labels on the fresh pies she'd wrapped for the front counter, her face alight with the guessing game they played. "Even saw a couple *big* cartons, flat, like for mattresses. Mighty excitin', to think of a whole new home up there. Like Christmas in July."

A rapid-fire series of high-pitched whines progressed across the entire smithy wall . . . screws being driven by a battery-powered screwdriver. Rachel raised her eyebrows at the noise; at the same time she was stirring her skillet of sizzling sausage. As she cut the larger clumps with the edge of her spatula, she wondered exactly how his visit with Tiffany had sparked such a burst of building. But hadn't Micah asked her to have patience and faith?

Patience and faith, she repeated to herself. *If I had more of those, life might be ever so much easier . . .*

Not that she felt any more confident, knowing where Micah had gotten his inspiration for the one-man work frolic going on next door. How could spending last Saturday night with her black-sheep sister give him such fine ideas that he was working in the smithy loft instead of with his brothers on their shop orders? Rachel bit her lip against her rising doubts. As she stirred the eggs, milk, and seasonings for the morning's breakfast pies, she planned her questions for when Micah came over to eat. Surely he'd tell *her* what he was building up there!

"Here's your glass pans, all sprayed and ready, missy! If you'll get your head outta the clouds, I'll put those pies in the oven when they're ready," Naomi teased.

Rachel realized then that everyone else in the kitchen was watching her. Had she done something absentminded? Or given away her jealous thoughts about Tiffany? "Won't be but a minute!" she blurted. "Have we got enough of the Cheddar Jack, Rhoda?

Tastes better on this spicy sausage than plain Cheddar, I'm thinkin'."

"Either one's *gut*, but we'll be needin' more, come time to make the Italian green bean casserole for lunch." Her sister joined her at the center island to top each of the pies with the cheese after Rachel had poured batter over the sausage. These pies made their own luscious topping and crust as they baked, and there was never enough to fill all the orders, no matter how many they made!

Is there a message here, about My patience and grace never runnin' out—no matter how many times you need it? Love is an ever-flowin' stream, you know.

Rachel stopped pouring batter to consider what this thought might mean. It wasn't a common, everyday thing to think such messages might come to her direct from God: Why would He be contacting *her*? Especially while she was making and serving breakfast, as she did every morning?

But if God *was* tapping her on the shoulder, maybe she should pay attention! Maybe the bishop was coming back to challenge Mamma—or propose to her. Or maybe Tiffany would make her next move. Or—

"You all right, Sis?" Rhoda waved her hand up and down, grinning. "For a minute there, ya looked a little *ferhoodled*."

Rachel blinked. Aromas of cooked sausage and Mamma's zucchini cornbread reminded her she was back in the café's kitchen . . . that she'd never left, even if her thoughts had taken her away. She shrugged and finished scraping the batter from the bowl. "We all get confused that way now and again, ain't so? Just hopin' there's a slice of this pie left come time for my break." *So maybe my faith and patience won't run out when I really need them.*

The breakfast shift was in full swing, most of the tables full, when Rachel realized no one had called to get more cheese for those Italian green bean casseroles on the lunch menu. As she headed for the phone shanty out back, she caught Naomi's eye. "Anythin' ya need from Zook's besides that shredded cheese?" she asked above the chatter in the dining room.

"*Jah*, have them send a couple bags of Italian seasoning and—"

The phone rang and Rachel rushed out to the little white building. Chuckling at herself, she answered on the third ring. "Sweet Seasons Café, this is—"

"Miriam, it's Lydia! Ya won't believe it, but I think your Rebecca's here in the store!" the grocer's wife said in a low, insistent voice. "She got black hair stickin' up like little pitchforks? And black fingernails, like she's a witch, ain't so?"

Rachel blinked. While Lydia Zook's description was accurate, it was anything but flattering. Nor would it make Mamma feel any better about the daughter who'd already raised the bishop's eyebrows. "*Jah*, that's our Rebecca. Goes by Tiffany now," she replied, somehow keeping her voice composed.

Why would Tiffany be in town? And shopping for groceries this early? Even as her heart pounded faster with suspicions and doubts, Rachel felt the urge to set Mamma's friend on the higher road as far as spreading stories about this surprise visit from her . . . her own sister. There might come a time when it was important for the Lantz women to stick together—and hadn't *she* always been the one to speak up?

"Tiffany comes from the same stock as Rhoda and me, so I'm thinkin' she's no real threat to ya," Rachel continued in a lighter tone. "The Lantz blood's thicker than that flood water that carried her off, too, so we're tryin' not to judge that book by her cover."

"Oh, Rachel, it's you! Well, *jah*, I wasn't meanin' to—"

Had she just defended the English girl who'd thrown her life into more than one tailspin lately? Did that explain the sense of calm she felt as she listened to Lydia's apologetic chatter?

Rachel turned to hide a smile from anybody who might be following this conversation, peering in from the kitchen or the quilt shop, mere steps away through both of the back doors. Not five minutes ago, Micah had come down from the loft for his breakfast. As he joked with Nate and Bram Kanagy, his smile had made something bubble up inside her. Why not surprise everyone by *daring* this situation to work out? Hadn't Micah already taken such a risk by spending time with Tiffany?

"Lydia, I was just gonna call ya for some shredded cheese—plain Cheddar, and some Cojack. Five pounds each. Need a couple bags of your Italian seasoning, too," Rachel said when Mrs. Zook had paused. "I'm thinkin' Rebecca's comin' here anyway, so why not ask her to bring our order? Mamma'll be real pleased to see her."

Lydia gasped. "Well, I reckon I could . . . ya don't s'pose she'll leave that cheese in her car too long on this hot mornin' and—"

"No need to be afraid of her, Lydia. Underneath

the dye and ghouly makeup, Tiffany's . . . well, she's a *lot* like Rhoda and me," Rachel reminded her. "But if she says no, send Jonah with it. Tell him Mamma made rhubarb pie today—and his favorite rhubarb crumb cake, too."

"*Ach,* I plumb forgot! We sold the last of your *mamm*'s pies yesterday! Got some fresh ones ya can spare?"

Rachel closed her eyes, recalling what they'd placed inside the glass case this morning, and what they'd already sold. "Couple of gooseberry and a couple of peach be all right? I don't want to run us any shorter than that till Mamma makes more."

"*Jah,* that'll be—oh . . . now where'd that girl get off to?"

Rachel heard voices in the background at Zook's store, and then the whine of Henry's saw as he cut some meat. She already sensed what Lydia was about to say, and her heartbeat sped up a notch.

"Gonna have to send the boy, I s'pose. Seems, uh, your Tiffany's up and left already." Mrs. Zook sounded downright relieved.

"That's fine, then. Your pies'll be waitin'."

"*Jah.* Tell your *mamm* hullo."

As Rachel hung up, she smiled at the scene that had just played out . . . at the way her sister had intimidated the storekeeper's wife so badly, Lydia had stalled to keep from talking to her. Tiffany hadn't done anything but show up, yet Lydia Zook was all in a dither—

Kinda like you, ain't so? Tiffany just showed up, and it's been you *gettin' all twisted around like a pretzel.*

Smiling at this revelation, Rachel returned to the café and circulated at her tables, picking up dirty plates and refilling coffee cups. Now that she realized how her sister affected Plain men and women—in different ways, but with the same effortless power—it might be fun to watch her come into the café this morning. Could get mighty interesting, too, considering how Hiram Knepp and Gabe Glick, their other preacher, were coming down the road in the bishop's buggy.

And sure enough, from the other direction, here came a bright red car. It slowed as it approached, but then passed on by . . . turned in at the next lane, and then headed back toward the Sweet Seasons again.

Rachel came away from the window and wrote out three tickets, resisting the urge to warn everyone in the kitchen about Tiffany's approach. It just seemed right to let things play out, without trying to direct or control this situation—and without getting upset about it.

Chapter 17

"Mornin' to ya, Rachel." Gabe Glick looked a hundred if he was a day, so stooped his pale beard came to the center of his chest. He squinted through his rimless glasses. "Me and the bishop'll be wantin' a table in back. Think Tom's gonna join us."

Rachel gently took his elbow. "Kinda tight between these tables," she said up close to his ear. "We've got a place in the back corner, right next to the buffet table."

"*Jah, des gut.* Noisy crowd today, ain't so?"

As she escorted the old preacher past the north window, she glanced outside: Tiffany was slamming her car door and looking toward the café. Not belligerent, exactly, but even in that bright pink shirt, her black hair, skintight jeans, and heavy mascara announced her as a challenge.

Rachel nipped her lip and pulled out a chair for Gabe. Why had she sensed this was coming? Would it be a showdown—a Willow Ridge version of Armageddon? The forces of good fending off evil? That seemed a little melodramatic, maybe, but it was for sure and for certain things could get mighty hot in a hurry. She felt surprisingly calm, almost eager to watch, as though she'd set this ball to rolling and been put in this time and place to witness an event that would set the course for her family—maybe even Mamma's café—by the time the breakfast rush was over.

"Good morning, Rachel." Hiram came in behind them, wiped his freshly washed hands on his napkin, and then focused on the whiteboard's menu for the day. "Bring us three plates of that sausage pie special and a pot of fresh coffee."

"Comin' right up. Got cantaloupe and watermelon on the buffet, *gut* and sweet, plus Mamma's special cornbread, so help yourselves." Rachel met his gaze and then made her way between the chattering ladies at the next tables to the coffeemaker. Nothing in Bishop Knepp's dark eyes suggested any more confrontation than usual . . . and it wasn't all that odd for these three elders to eat together.

Yet when the door opened again, Rachel stood straighter, listening rather than turning to watch people's reactions. "Need three orders of the sausage pie," she called into the kitchen as she filled a carafe for the brethren. "Gettin' low on cornbread, too."

"*Jah*, I got that comin'," Rhoda replied as she lifted a big basket of the muffins. She came quickly from the kitchen and then stopped, wide-eyed. "Oh. Looks like cornbread's not all we got comin', Sister."

Tiffany Oliveri stood by the cash register, gripping the big black purse slung over her shoulder, surveying the crowd. Preacher Tom stepped inside and stopped behind her. He spotted Hiram and Gabe in the back, yet was too polite—or too startled—to slip around the spike-haired young woman who stood out in this conservative morning crowd.

As one, Rachel and Rhoda went toward them.

"Tiffany, it's *gut* to see ya!" Rhoda said, extending her steaming basket. "How about one of Mamma's corn muffins while we find you a spot?"

"Your table's waitin', Preacher," Rachel said from behind her. "I was just takin' your coffee over there—but first I'd like ya to meet our sister, Tiffany. The one who found us last week! And Tiffany, this is Tom Hostetler. Runs a dairy farm when he's not conductin' services of a Sunday."

Neither of them looked certain of what to say, but good manners carried the moment. Tom nodded, smiling as he looked from one face . . . to another . . . to the third. "It's *gut* to meet you, young lady. Quite a story, about your washin' away all those years ago and now comin' back. And *jah*, it's a sure thing you three perty girls are sisters."

When Tiffany smiled, she looked altogether different—even with those dangly pewter earrings and three heavy chain necklaces. "Yeah, it was a big surprise to all of us. Nice to meet you, Tom."

He seemed relieved to follow Rachel into the crowd of familiar folks, several of them his Plain neighbors. Then he waved to his two companions. "I'll take this coffee on back. You've got other folks to see to."

"Thanks ever so much for understandin'. I'll be right there with your plates." Rachel exhaled: first encounter and all was well.

As she looked at Tiffany, still near the cash register with Rhoda, Rachel recognized *hesitation* . . . even fear,

beneath all that metal and makeup. Maybe, like the
Plains Indians long ago, her English sister wore so
much paint to appear fierce and invincible. Yet in this
roomful of strangers—where most folks knew who she
was—the girl in black didn't seem so bold or brazen.

What if it were me standin' there, not knowin' a soul?

Rachel wasn't sure where this idea came from, but
it seemed this day was made for surprises. She strode
through the crowd in Tom's wake, to pluck the fourth
chair from the men's table. "Be right back with your
food," she chirped, and then she carried the chair
over to where Micah sat with his friends.

"Best be on your *gut* behavior, fellas," she warned
as she motioned to Tiffany. "Not every day ya get to sit
with a guest like this one."

Nate, Bram, and the two other Brennemans seemed
utterly *ferhoodled* when the girl in black took the chair
on the end, next to Micah. Micah, however, grinned
broadly—first at Tiffany and then at Rachel. Was the
special glimmer in his green eyes for her . . . or for
her unconventional sister?

"Tiffany! This is Bram and Nate Kanagy," he said as
each of them nodded mutely, "and the two blond
jokers across the table are my brothers, Seth and
Aaron. What brings ya to Willow Ridge so bright
and early this mornin'?"

Before Tiffany could answer, Micah's arm shot out
to catch Rachel around the waist. "Time for your
break, so's you can join us, ain't so, Rache? I'm
thinkin' since Nate's finished eatin', he could spell ya
for a bit—"

"*Gut* way to get all your dishes broke!" their friend
protested.

"*Jah*, and the bishop might not like it so well if his

breakfast landed in his lap, either." Rachel grinned. Micah's arm was still around her, and he showed no sign of moving it. The big smile on her face surprised her, yet it felt like it belonged there as she focused on Tiffany. "If ya can stay till after this early rush, though, I'll be free for a bit. Gotta go now—but I'll tell Mamma you're here."

Second encounter and still no lightnin' strikes. Rachel strode quickly into the kitchen to place the three waiting plates of sausage pie on a tray. Rhoda was immediately beside her to garnish the steaming wedges with twisted slices of fresh orange.

"Did ya see the way Seth and Aaron looked ready to—well, I couldn't tell if they were ready to run on outta here, or to just gawk all mornin'," her look-alike teased. "That was the *last* place I figured you'd set her, Sis!"

Rachel shrugged. She didn't feel like getting into a deep discussion about her change of heart—not when the bishop was waiting for his breakfast. "Keeps her in Plain sight, ain't so?" she quipped. She looked over to where their mother was drizzling white icing over the cherry-pie bars for the noon menu. "Tiffany's here, Mamma. Preacher Tom's met her just now, and I'm thinkin' it won't be long till the bishop looks her over, too. I set her at Micah's table so she'd have somebody to talk to."

Was that amazement on her mother's face? Mamma set aside her pastry bag to wipe her sugary hands and smooth her kapp. "She say why she's here? This is—well, a nice surprise all around!"

"*Jah*, I told her you'd think so." Rachel hefted the tray to her shoulder. "Let's hope the brethren see it that way, too. This sausage pie oughtta keep them busy for a while, anyway—*if* you'd like to see her, that is."

"So how ya been, Tiffany?" Micah's smile broadened as he watched his four tablemates fetch their straw hats, like the day's work was suddenly calling their names. "Mighty *gut* to see ya. Didn't figure you'd be back."

"Yeah, well—things change."

He was no expert on women, but Tiffany's shrug told him more than what she didn't say: some mighty *important* things had changed. She fumbled with her muffin wrapper, focusing on it as though she'd find the right words written there. Micah brushed crumbs from the plate his toast had come on and put it in front of her. "Here—that cornbread's mighty tasty with honey on it. Rachel's aunt—*your* aunt—Leah supplies it from her own hives."

Tiffany's eyes widened . . . eyes so expressive, like her sisters'. For a moment an awkward silence stretched between them—or had the café gone quiet? Micah didn't look around. Whatever this girl had on her mind—whatever had brought her here—was more important than the opinions of the folks who might be gawking at them.

"I moved out of that apartment. Thought about stuff you'd said—"

Micah agonized while she lifted a chunk of honey-drenched muffin to her lips. When she closed her eyes over it, those long black lashes did something fluttery to his insides. Or was it that little moan, when she chewed and swallowed like she'd never eaten anything so heavenly? He cleared his throat. "So—if you're not livin' with your girlfriend—"

"*Former* girlfriend. You know the guy who brought the pizza? Hayden, her live-in?"

Micah nodded, his insides tightening as he thought of all the possible ways this revelation might go. She was easing another bite of that crumbly cornbread into her mouth with fingers that trembled.

"Well, when he got home that Saturday night, he freaked. Started throwing things at me because you were wearing his—"

"Rebecca—I mean, it's Tiffany now! It's so *gut* to see ya again!" Miriam Lantz bustled around the table and landed in the chair on Tiffany's other side, her kapp strings aflutter around a face flushed with pleasure. "And don't ya look perty in pink? I—I miss seein' you girls in that color, now that you're all grown up."

While Miriam made an excellent point—the deep rose of Tiffany's top gave her pale face a soft, healthy glow—Micah sighed inside. This mother had the right, and every reason, to take a rare chance for conversation, no matter how much he needed to hear the rest of this girl's story.

"Good to see you, too. Dad says hi."

Miriam's eyes shone like hot coffee. "So how's he doin' now? And what were ya sayin' about movin' out? Are ya home again, I hope?"

Micah blinked. Had mother's intuition kicked in just from the few words Miriam had overheard before she sat down?

Tiffany smiled, looking shy despite the dramatic black lines accentuating her eyes. "I was telling Micah that the guy—well, let's just say I realized I could do better than hanging with those two. They fight all the time, about really stupid stuff, and I'm tired of being in the middle of it."

"*Gut* for you! And ya know, child of mine, ya have a place to stay here if ya want." Miriam had lowered her voice and she leaned closer to the young woman beside her. "Ain't easy dealin' with a man who's lost his wife, and ya must have terrible-mixed feelin's about the whole situation, I'd think. Don't ya go livin' on the streets, gettin' yourself into places ya can't get out of. Promise me?"

It was almost more than Micah could listen to, this intense exchange. Yet he admired Miriam for cutting right to the bone.

Tiffany nodded as she searched Miriam's face . . . the flawless honesty in her sparkling eyes, framed by brown hair pulled tight beneath her kapp. Their smiles came out like the sun after a summer shower. "I came to tell Micah—and you—that I've gone back home, because it's Micah who made me see it as the better option. He was so . . . patient, so *decent*. Even when I was acting snotty and pretending not to listen."

Miriam flashed a smile at the burly blond beside her. "*Jah*, we kinda like Micah around here. When he says he'll do somethin', ya can believe it."

"I don't know any other guys like that." Tiffany paused, as though this statement summarized the thoughts she'd tried to pull together. "Those slackers in the pool hall, they—they made fun of his hat and suspenders, and—well, not a one of them cares what happens to me. They never said *boo* about Mom dying,

or—well, they're only after one thing." She winced
and looked away. "Sorry. That sounds really sleazy."

"You're here now, ain't so?" Miriam reached for
her daughter's hands, blinking rapidly. "I'm ever so
happy to see ya, and to hear you're givin' your *dat* another chance, too. Let me get ya some of that nice
sausage pie—"

"Could I have bacon and a couple eggs, over easy?
And toast with jelly? This cornbread's awesome, too,
and—" She looked down at her empty plate and
blinked. "Guess I'm hungrier than I thought."

"We got just the cure for that, honey-bug. Sit tight."
Miriam got up, grinning through her tears. "If
Micah's gotta leave, I know a couple girls who're due
for their break, now that the crowd's thinnin' out."

"I'm on my own clock today, remember?" Micah's
grin looked wide and confident. "I'll be here."

"Here ya be—bacon and two eggs, over easy. Mamma's homemade cinnamon-swirl bread for toast," Rachel
said as she set the plates before Tiffany. "And here's
that sausage pie I've been wantin' all mornin'. And
for you, Micah, one of the cherry-pie bars we're tryin'
out for lunch. Mamma wants your opinion on that, or
you'd be gettin' no such favors from her, ain't so?"

Rhoda joined them with a plate of melon wedges
from the buffet table. "Be back, soon as I refill the
bishop's coffeepot."

As Tiffany bit into the buttered toast, her gaze followed Rhoda to the back table. "So that's the guy who
says you get electricity? Or says you're not supposed to
hang with girls who wear makeup and drive fast cars?"

"*Jah*, that's Hiram Knepp. The dark-haired one." Micah took a huge bite and then licked thick, ruby-colored filling from his lips. "I'm guessin' he'll be over here to look you over when he's *gut* and ready. Nothin' shy about him."

"Oh." Tiffany's face fell and then she glanced around the dining room, which only had guests at a few tables now. "You got a restroom? Maybe I should go—"

"Nah, don't go hidin'. He'll wait ya out." Rachel closed her eyes over the first bite of her late breakfast, savoring the spice of the sausage and the way the warm cheese flooded her tongue. It was surprising how calm she felt, sitting here beside the girl who'd set her top to spinning so fast before. "And before the bishop says anythin'—about anythin'—I wanna apologize, Tiffany. I had no call to holler at ya last time ya came here. I was just, well—*ferhoodled* to find out we had another sister."

"*Ferhoodled?* What a funny word!" Tiffany looked her straight in the eye then, assessing her . . . yet not judging. She smiled as she spread jelly on her toast. "Like when your best friend lets her boyfriend pitch a fit at you, and you blow outta there before you can pack all your stuff? That's *ferhoodled . . . jah?*"

Rachel's insides tightened at this information, but she had to grin at Tiffany's attempt to understand their language. "*Jah*, it means you're all muddled and confused and chasin' your tail—like I've been lately. Well, ya know what I mean."

"Yeah, I do. Losing Mom stirred up a lot of stuff I didn't expect—besides finding out about you sisters and my birth mother, that is."

"We had a hard time doin' without Dat for a while,

too." Rhoda sat down to her breakfast, recalling their struggle as she gazed at them all, but her first sweet bite of cantaloupe brought back her smile. "Mamma's poured herself into this café ever since, and we're helpin' her make a go of it. And to think ya found us here!"

Rachel glanced toward the table in the back corner, sensing she didn't have much time to say things the way she wanted to. "We most likely seem real odd to ya, on account of our plain-colored cape dresses and our kapps. But understand, just because ya wear English clothes and those chains and whatnot? You're still family, Tiffany—part of us. Just like your one little pink dress matches up with the two Mamma had packed away. We understand that now."

"*Jah*," Rhoda chimed in. "And we won't be tryin' to make ya Plain—unless ya wanna be! It's tough for Englishers to change over to the Old Ways. Classes to take on our beliefs, before ya join the church, and a whole new language to learn—not to mention givin' up your jewelry and jeans and makeup!"

Tiffany laughed with them. "I've gotta say I like the guys in their suspenders, though," she remarked with a playful wink at Micah. "Do your brothers and the Kanagy boys all have nice Amish girlfriends?"

"Not that they admit to," Micah replied. "We keep our courtin' a secret, mostly, till we intend to marry. But ya can't miss who's drivin' which girls around in their buggies of an evenin'."

"And some couples aren't quite as *gut* at keepin' quiet about it," Mamma hinted as she and Naomi set their plates on the table. "Tiffany, this is Micah's *mamm*, Naomi Brenneman. My fine cook she is, too. Couldn't run this place without her!"

Tiffany smiled around a big mouthful of bacon and

eggs. And as the chatter continued among the six of them, Rachel realized how smoothly it was going . . . how nice it felt to sit and enjoy their food together rather than forking in whatever was left from breakfast while they prepared for the lunch crowd. A movement behind them made her turn: Tom Hostetler tossed his napkin onto the table and hurried through the center hallway into the quilt shop. *And it's a sure thing he's not shoppin' for fat quarters of calico.*

Mamma, too, took note of his exit and glanced over to where Hiram and Gabe remained seated. "I'd best see if they'd like fresh coffee, or—"

"I'll get it, Mamma. Ya just sat down." Rachel walked quickly between the sturdy oak tables, empty except for theirs and the brethren's, to fill a clean carafe. Something about the way the two men talked with their heads together warned her not to intrude . . . but she was doing her job, checking on their guests. Wasn't she?

". . . see what ya mean about that girl and her un-natural getup," Gabe was murmuring. "Lantz or not, her type could cause problems . . ."

Rachel ducked in quickly to set the coffee on their table. "Can I get ya anythin' else?" she asked brightly. "Got fresh cherry-pie bars Mamma made for lunch, to go with this coffee. Or if ya want your check—"

"We're fine. Thank you, Rachel." Bishop Knepp gave her a purposeful look.

She put on a smile. "If ya need somethin', holler. And when ya get a minute, we'd like ya to meet our sister."

Back to the table she walked, wishing she hadn't overheard that snippet of talk. If the elders wanted to talk about problems in their district, why didn't they do it private-like? Maybe she shouldn't have mentioned coming over to meet Tiffany—

"Everythin' all right, honey-bug?"

Rachel noted the glow on Mamma's face and decided this wasn't the time to spoil things with gloom and doom. "Wouldn't call it a tea party at the bishop's table, but *jah*, they got what they need for now."

Naomi and her mother exchanged a glance—but then Mamma smiled, suddenly excited. "And speakin' of parties, we need to be thinkin' about you girls turnin' twenty-one soon, ain't so? Especially now that our other chick's come back to the nest!"

"That's somethin' to celebrate, for sure and for certain!" Naomi agreed. "Must make ya feel mighty fine, Miriam, to have your three girls all at the same table again."

"*Jah*, it sure does." Mamma blinked rapidly and then grasped Tiffany's wrist. "Understand, we're not expectin' ya to give up your ways, or—we just love havin' ya here with us, Daughter. Not a birthday's gone by for Rachel and Rhoda that I didn't—just for a minute—think of you cuttin' into that cake, too."

Tiffany looked like a cornered cat, or maybe just flustered by this sudden upswelling of emotion. But then she relaxed again. "I've always loved birthday parties—"

"Us, too!" Rhoda blurted out.

"What a *gut* idea! Please say you'll come!" Rachel insisted as she sat down beside Tiffany again. "We'll make ice cream—"

"And strawberry cream cake—our favorite!" her sister added with a grin.

"—and you can see if ya recall anythin' about the house, and—well, because ya know how it is, after one sister gets hitched," Rachel continued earnestly. "Just won't be the same kind of party as when we're all still girls!"

"I'm thinkin' that might be a *gut* time to show off the apartment in the smithy, too," Micah joined in with a sly smile. "Was kinda hopin' for that to be part of the birthday surprise this year."

Tiffany's gaze flitted among them as she followed this happy chatter. She was sitting tall, looking pleased to be included in these out-of-the blue plans. Yet she was nipping her lower lip. "So . . . what day is our birthday, really? I'm guessing Mom and Dad celebrated on May fifth because, well—that's the date on the birth certificate, which we now know belonged to the first Tiffany."

A stunned silence fell. What did it feel like to be this old, yet to find out for the first time when your birthday was? And how . . . second-fiddle must it feel, to realize you'd been a fill-in for your parents' natural-born child? Rachel gripped Rhoda's hand, and then—hoping she wouldn't seem pushy—she took Tiffany's hand, too. "August fifteenth. Gonna be the nicest birthday we've had, too—for sure and for certain—if ya come meet our friends and—"

The loud scraping of chairs across the room made them all look up. Rachel reached for her ticket pad and then froze: Tom Hostetler had come back with Reuben Reihl in tow, and now all four of the brethren were looking their way. Even without their black hats and vested suits, their Sunday *fer-gut* clothing, they made a somber-looking bunch. Hiram Knepp approached with the others behind him, all of them with grim, bearded faces.

Like goats goin' to a funeral, Rachel thought. And

then she immediately added, *God, I hope you'll forgive my sass and stand beside us now. This looks like somethin' we won't wanna hear.*

"We've discussed this subject before," the bishop began, directing his gaze at Mamma and then at Micah. "But now that we've all *seen* this Englisher who's distracted you two from following your promises to the church, we must advise you that your sin won't go unnoticed. We're going into private session now, quite probably to initiate the required discipline at Sunday's service."

Chapter 18

Rachel's heart thudded. She gripped her sisters' hands—refused to let go when Tiffany tried to pull away. It was one thing to behave as a bishop, who took charge of keeping his flock on the path toward salvation; it was downright rude to talk about Tiffany as though she weren't sitting right in front of him.

"And just what are we talkin' about, exactly?" Naomi asked in a strained voice.

Hiram clasped his hands in front of him, as he often did when he was preaching. "This concerns matters I've discussed—twice now—with Miriam and Micah. Unfortunately, neither has heeded my strong suggestion to eschew the dubious company of—"

"How about ya say it in plain talk? I'm a Plain woman." Naomi's brown eyes flashed as she rose slowly from her chair. "And if you're meanin' to put the ban on my Micah—and maybe Miriam, as well—it's an obvious concern to me, too, ain't so?"

Rachel and Rhoda exchanged cautious glances. It wasn't like Naomi—or anyone else—to challenge Bishop Knepp. He did speak in an elevated tone and use a vocabulary they knew only from their dictionary work in school, because that was part and parcel of his esteemed behavior as their leader.

"Naomi, let it be," Mamma whispered. "We'll work this out—"

"This is the support of my family we're talkin' about!" Mamma's friend countered. She gripped the back of her chair—furniture from her sons' cabinetry shop— barely restraining her anger. "If ya shun Micah— don't allow him to go to jobs where Seth and Aaron gotta work with him—they can't make *gut* on their backlog of orders! And if ya force Miriam to stop her bakin' here, the Sweet Seasons'll close for sure and for certain!"

Naomi paused, but she wasn't ready to let the bishop have his say yet. Her face flushed with the knowledge that she was defying authority, with the preachers and Deacon Reihl as witnesses. "Say what ya want about Miriam and me workin' here insteada at home," she continued in a voice that shook with conviction, "but it's kept our families fed! My faith is everything to me, *jah*—and by workin' a job because Ezra can't be a carpenter anymore, I'm puttin' my faith into action! The Lord helps those who help themselves, and we Brennemans believe in payin' our own way!"

Micah, too, rose from his chair to put an arm around his petite mother's shoulders. "Ya think we boys like it that our *mamm* is workin' so hard here? The cabinet shop's doin' a boomin' business now, but if ya take me outta the picture, I don't know how we're gonna keep payin' on Dat's physical therapy and medications, Bishop."

"You knew the consequences of your waywardness

when you stepped off the path to visit this Englisher, did you not?" Hiram demanded in a low voice.

Micah glanced at Rachel and Tiffany, his expression grim. "Like I told ya before, I understood the risks when I went to visit Miriam's other daughter, and I'm not goin' back to see her again. If ya want my confession at service this Sunday, I'll give it. But I'm askin' ya not to burden my whole family on account of my behavior."

"You know our hearts, Bishop. Pardon me if I'm oversteppin', but I think you're misjudgin' our intentions here, about reunitin' with my Rebecca. And you surely must realize it's not our way to ask for help when we can help ourselves!" Mamma joined in. She rose to stand behind Tiffany, her hands on her daughter's shoulders. "And if comin' between me and my child—and then makin' me give up the mission that's sustained me since Jesse died—are your ways of convincin' me to come outta mournin' so's you can court me, well, that's a mighty strange way to win a woman's love! Ain't so, Hiram?"

Tom Hostetler's mouth dropped open, while Gabe and Reuben stared at the bishop as though his interest in Miriam Lantz came as a big surprise to them. Then Gabe, the eldest of the brethren, cleared his throat and looked sharply at them all.

"This defiance—this disrespect—for the man God chose as our earthly leader *appalls* me." Preacher Glick's voice reverberated in such a low tone they all had to lean forward to catch everything he said . . . but there was no missing his message. "I think every one of ya needs to be on your knees at a members' meetin' this Sunday. Such a raisin' of voices! Against a man who takes responsibility for your very souls! You should be ashamed, and ask the bishop's forgiveness. And then accept whatever discipline he and the People agree to after witnessin' your contrite confessions."

The dining room rang with silence and unspoken fear. Rachel's pulse nearly drove her to stand up and join in, defending her mother and the man she loved—except Rhoda grabbed her arm. The ominous way her sister shook her head, warning her to keep quiet, reminded her of the trouble her outspoken complaints had caused with Micah . . . how it wasn't always best to voice her opinions, even if she felt she had good reason.

And the tightness of Hiram Knepp's jaw, and Mamma's wide eyes, seemed reason enough to stay out of this. For now.

Naomi turned her head sharply, like a little girl about to pitch a fit. Then she let out her breath. "I apologize if I spoke outta turn, Hiram," she murmured. "Just my worry talkin' for me, is all. Wasn't my intent to offend ya, or to question your authority."

"Nor mine," Mamma echoed. "I'll go before the People Sunday mornin' to make my confession, *jah.*"

Bishop Knepp looked at them all, assessing. His gaze lingered longest on poor Mamma, as though to prompt a more elaborate apology.

"Didn't intend any disrespect, Bishop," Micah stated quietly, "but the Lord knows I'm not sorry for sayin' what had to be said. Like I told ya, I'll come before the People, to give my confession and accept whatever punishment ya decide—"

"Wait a minute! What am I missing here?" Tiffany brought the butt of her fork down hard on the table when she pounded her fist. She looked from Gabe to Tom to Hiram with an incredulous expression that would only provoke them more, but there was no stopping her. "You're going to excommunicate—or shun, or whatever!—Micah because he came to see me? Because I refused to listen to him anyplace except my car? Because I invited him to dinner and he told me how much my original family loved me?"

Mamma gripped Tiffany's shoulders firmly. "Daughter, now's not the time or the place to—"

"But I don't understand! Why was it a sin for Micah to tell me I needed a better class of friends? And that I needed to get my act together?" Tiffany demanded. "He was absolutely right! And who besides Micah and I *know* what went on and what was said? I don't know where you got your information, Bishop, but—"

Mamma clapped her hand gently over Tiffany's mouth, entreating Hiram with her wide brown eyes. "Englishers don't know our ways, remember."

"All the more reason not to spend time with them," Gabe replied tightly. "We're seein' firsthand the trouble it can cause, allowin' outsiders to have sway over our thinkin'."

Rachel's temples throbbed and her heart pounded so hard she could barely breathe. How had this conversation gotten so far out of hand so fast? With each passing moment, Hiram Knepp looked steelier . . . more inclined to require the strictest discipline. And why? Because Mamma had reclaimed her long-lost daughter?

Not Tiffany's fault she was raised outside the People's

influence. And Tiffany had only asked the question she herself had wanted to: How had the bishop *known* what Micah did when he went to Morning Star? This was yet another reason for her not to speak up or ask too many questions. The brethren had their way of finding things out.

"I've made my decision." Hiram Knepp clasped his hands again, focusing on each of them in turn. "Miriam, I now believe that the decision I made last year—to allow you to construct this building for your business—was a mistake. Once I went along with that, I made all manner of other exceptions for you, allowing conveniences and appliances—your partnership with Mennonites—so the facility would meet health department standards." Hiram let his stern gaze sink in along with his words. "Had I adhered to my original belief, that a woman shouldn't own property that will take her out of her home, away from her family, we'd have prevented many of today's problems before they arose."

Mamma's hand flew to her mouth. She closed her eyes against tears, composing her thoughts before she spoke again. "Are ya sayin' I can't bake? Can't support myself and my girls?"

Rachel glanced fearfully at Rhoda, Micah, and Naomi. They, too, looked totally stricken. What on earth was going on here? Had this really been discussed by all the elders? The way Tom Hostetler and Gabe Glick shifted, their mouths pressed into tight lines, suggested they'd had nothing to do with this decision . . . this *proclamation* that Mamma would no longer own the Sweet Seasons Bakery Café.

Bishop Knepp cleared his throat and waited for

Mamma to look at him. "As I mentioned the other night, I believe your independence—your pride in ownership—has blurred your vision. Misplaced your priorities. You must sell the building, Miriam."

Mamma's' whimper rang out in the empty café. "And what am I to do for an income? I've got no other family to fall back on, and I detest becomin' dependent—"

"Plenty of women bake and sell from their homes." He glanced at Naomi and then toward the door, where an elderly couple was coming inside. "With the business you've built up, you could surely cater from your own kitchen, as well."

"And what of the quilt shop?" Naomi demanded, pointing toward the other half of the building as she stared at Reuben. "Your cousin Mary and Zeb's aunts'll be hard pressed to find a better location—"

"I didn't say you had to give up your businesses," Hiram remarked more quietly. "If the building's new owner agrees to keep the café and quilt shop here, so be it. You may remain open until the building sells, which gives you time to formulate a new plan. A plan that honors God as well as your places in His earthly kingdom."

The sound of chairs scooting against the floor made them all look up. Rhoda excused herself to greet their customers, her face splotchy. Rachel felt she was coming out of a bad dream, back to the reality of cooking and serving their customers—a reality that might not be supporting them by the end of summer.

"I'll arrange a time at the bank in New Haven, and let you know when we'll be initiating the sale, Miriam."

With a nod, Hiram dismissed himself. Left them at the table, stunned silent, as he and the other three brethren exited the café.

"I'm outta here." Tiffany eased her chair back so as not to bump into Mamma, who stood with her fist pressed to her mouth, alongside a wide-eyed Naomi. "I don't understand this stuff, but if it's my fault for showing up—or the way I look—well, I don't know what else to say. I'm really, really sorry this happened, Mamma."

As the girl in pink and black hurried toward the door, Rachel jumped from her chair. With a grimace, she recalled the last time, hollering at Tiffany to leave and never come back. Now that *that* mistake had been reconciled, everything else in their world seemed to be crumbling around them. What a shame that her sister had called their mother *Mamma* now, when Tiffany was leaving again? Maybe for good this time.

"Wait—Tiffany! Rebecca!" she called out as she trotted across the gravel parking lot.

Her sister opened the car door and turned. Wet, black streaks flowed down her cheeks. "This is the most— Can't you *see* what that guy's doing?" she muttered. "*He's* going to buy the building, just you watch! Control freak that he is, he's pulling her strings like she's a puppet. Making her dependent upon him for—oh, forget it! This is just too freaking weird!"

Rachel bit back her reply. She'd had some of the same suspicions, but hadn't voiced them for fear she'd make the situation worse. "We meant it about the birthday party, though! Please come!" she pleaded, gripping the hot car door. "We *want* ya here! And please don't abandon Mamma, now that she needs us most."

Tiffany gazed at her for several seconds, maybe studying what she'd look like as a Plain girl. "I'll have to think about it. Seems I've been nothing but trouble for Micah and our mother, and I have enough hassles dealing with Dad," she said in a rush. "Can't make any promises. But thanks for asking."

Moments later Tiffany's car roared out of the parking lot, throwing gravel as she pulled onto the highway. She veered sharply to avoid hitting Bishop Knepp's buggy and then sped on down the road.

Rachel sighed sadly. Would they ever see her again?

Chapter 19

"Mamma, ya really should eat somethin'." Rhoda slipped an arm around Miriam's slumped shoulders. "Rachel's warmed some of those *gut* stuffed peppers, and I brought us home the last three cinnamon rolls from this mornin', so—"

"I'm hot and tired and so *ferhoodled* I could just—" Miriam rose from her chair at the end of the table, retreating to the front porch. Even here, though, the oppressive July heat made her clothing stick to her after the day's work in a hot kitchen: not a breath stirred the trees. She dropped wearily into the porch swing, regretting her words with Rhoda. Didn't her girls always look after her? Hadn't they all done the best they could these past two years since Jesse passed?

Wishin' won't bring him back . . . nor will fussin' at everybody solve the real problem here. His name is Hiram . . . and Lord, if we don't find a way to heal all these open wounds insteada pourin' salt on them . . .

Miriam peeled off her shoes and stockings and flexed her feet. She felt ninety years old, as limp and bedraggled as she had those first months of being a widow—and she was doing this to herself, she realized. As the girls came out to join her in the late rays of the sunset, she put on a smile for their sake. Rhoda carried the big family Bible and Rachel had quartered those cinnamon rolls and put them on a plate, which she set on the swing cushion. Little imp. Rachel knew she would eventually reach for just one piece of the sweet, cinnamon-rich pastry, and then another.

"Didn't mean to bite your heads off, girls," Miriam said sadly.

"*Jah*, well, it's been one of those roller coaster days," Rhoda observed as she handed over the Good Book. "Felt so fine to have Tiffany actin' like she wanted to be with us—"

"And then the bishop had to come and rain on our party." Rachel's sigh sounded far too old and sad for a girl about to turn twenty-one. "What're we gonna do, Mamma? Priscilla Schrock gave me quite an earful about *her* feelin's—"

"*Jah*, I saw the three of them listenin' in the hallway."

"—and said she was gonna give Reuben what for about the buildin' bein' sold," Rachel continued forlornly. "But when Hiram had his say . . . seemed to me he'd already made up his mind. No talkin' him out of it."

Miriam let out a short laugh as she turned the thin pages of the old Bible. "*My* talkin' didn't help matters. Only eggs him on when a woman states her case, like I did today and the last time I met with him."

"He's not keen on havin' his facts challenged by somebody else's." Rhoda reached for the first section of cinnamon roll.

"And I *know* that, ain't so? Yet I keep answerin' back like a smarty-pants who has no respect for God's holy ordinances."

"Mamma! Everybody knows you respect God!" Rachel objected. "It's Hiram and his string-pullin' we're objectin' to here. Even Tiffany could see that."

"Ya can't tell me you're gonna let him take away all you've worked for! *He* allowed ya to set up the Sweet Seasons, and now he's changin' all the rules!" Rhoda squeezed her piece of pastry into a tight ball before popping it into her mouth. "God strike me down if I'm speakin' outta turn here, but it's just plain nasty, the way he's backin' you into a corner so's you'll give in . . . maybe marry him. *Please* tell us you're not gonna do *that*, Mamma!"

Two sets of intense blue eyes were fixed on Miriam. The dusk deepened around them when the sun dipped behind the smithy, and then the quickstep of hoofbeats made them all look down the lane. "Micah and his *mamm.* Fast as they're comin', I hope nothin's wrong with Ezra," Miriam murmured. She waved and called out, "Hullo there, you two! Everythin' all right?"

"Puh! You're a fine one to be askin' *me* that!" Naomi replied. She clambered down from the buggy before Micah could assist her and then her bare feet slapped against the wooden porch steps. "Gave Ezra some extra meds for his phantom pain and left him snoozin'. Seems to get worse in this heat, and we're probably lookin' at another round of tests soon."

"Had to get her outta the house so's she wouldn't keep spinnin' like a tornado," Micah remarked gently. He sat on the step, leaning against the thick porch pillar. "Didn't feel much like workin' on the upstairs tonight, what with Hiram sayin' your buildin' is to be sold. So here we are. Misery loves company, ain't so?"

"Pass this young fella the plate." Miriam took a section of cinnamon roll before handing the sweets to Rhoda. "We were just gettin' ready for our readin', and I've picked out the Psalm Jesse used to rely on when things bothered him . . . mostly on nights when meetin's with the bishop tested his patience."

"We could use a dose of *that* medicine," Naomi agreed. "Keep tellin' myself all this frettin's not doin' us a lick of *gut*, but do ya think it stops me? I'm mighty wound up over this kettle of fish, I can tell ya."

Miriam smiled. Already she felt better, surrounded by those who loved her most and shared her deepest concerns. "Micah, it's been a long while since we heard our evenin' readin' in a man's voice. Would ya mind? It's number twenty-seven."

The sturdy blond removed his straw hat, looking honored that she'd asked him for this favor. He sampled a piece of the cinnamon roll, wiped his hands on his pants, and then took the large book from her. Rachel had fetched the lamp from the table and lit it, and they made a soothing sight as they sat together over the Word.

"'The Lord is my light and my salvation; whom shall I fear? The Lord is the strength of my life; of whom shall I be afraid?'" he began. He smiled at Miriam, sensing her reason for choosing this passage tonight. "'When the wicked, even mine enemies and my foes, came upon me to eat up my flesh, they stumbled and fell . . .'"

As Micah's confident young voice continued, Miriam

felt her whole body relaxing. She nodded at Naomi, both of them pleased at the sight and the sound of this devotional time they all shared . . .

"'Hear, O Lord, when I cry with my voice: have mercy also upon me and answer me. When thou saidst, Seek ye my face my heart said unto thee, Thy face, Lord, will I seek . . .'"

Thy face, Lord, will I seek, Miriam's heart repeated. Surely God wouldn't mind if it was Jesse's face she saw in these times when troubles confronted her.

"'Teach me thy way, O Lord, and lead me in a plain path because of mine enemies. Deliver me not over unto the will of mine enemies: for false witnesses are risen up against me and such as breathe out cruelty,'" Micah continued. His fervent voice added meaning to the phrases as they followed him with their hearts.

And while it pained her to place Hiram Knepp, the bishop God chose for them, in the same category as enemies and false witnesses, Miriam realized that others might well see *her* in that role at times: Didn't everyone take a turn bearing false witness and breathing out cruelty, after all? She bowed her head, allowing Micah to finish the familiar passage as a prayer she mouthed along with him.

"'Wait on the Lord; be of good courage and he shall strengthen thine heart: wait, I say, on the Lord.'"

Their collective sigh wafted like a breeze around them, welcome relief from the heat of a day that had troubled them and made them cry out, like the Psalmist, when it seemed the very basis of their lives—their daily bread—was about to be taken from them. But that hadn't happened yet, had it?

"Your Jesse knew how to pick them," Naomi remarked quietly.

"*Jah.* And I'm hopin' he'll stand by me when Hiram takes me to the bank. Can't think Tom or Reuben talked him outta that."

"Well, at least we can keep doin' what we do best . . . thinkin' of ways to work outta your kitchen if it comes to that." Naomi ventured. "We *do* have a good followin' built up, with lots of standin' orders and folks who ask us to do their receptions and whatnot."

"Could be, too, that since property's not sellin' so fast nowadays, the bad economy'll be in our favor," Micah remarked. "A lot of our carpentry jobs now are for folks who're fixin' up what they have or addin' on, rather than buildin' new homes and offices."

They sat in the deepening dusk, with only the creak of the swing punctuating the silence while they watched the flame flicker in Rachel's lamp . . . maybe deciding whether to voice more doubts or to keep their complaints about this situation to themselves while the Bible reading still held sway over them.

"Any idea how Hiram's horse business is doin'?" Miriam asked quietly. "Haven't been to an auction in years."

Micah seemed to follow her train of thought: his lips lifted at one corner. "Read in *The Budget* not long ago that he's now considered the top draft horse breeder in Missouri, Iowa, and Illinois. His stallions go for a hefty price, and Plain folk as well as English come from miles around to bid on them."

Naomi took Miriam's hand with a sigh. "Are ya thinkin' he'll hand over the cash when he takes ya to the bank, then? Just sign the new papers, and it's over and done with?"

"I don't know what to think. I guess we'll find out when God says it's time," she replied. "And meanwhile, like ya said this mornin', Naomi, the Lord still helps those who help themselves, ain't so?"

They nodded somberly.

"We're followin' the order of things, kneelin' before the People this Sunday to confess so's we can start with a clean slate," Miriam went on. "From there, we—"

"And just what have ya done, Miriam? Taken back a daughter ya thought was dead? Kept your other two fed—and employed?" Naomi demanded. "What do ya have to bring before *anybody* for doin' what any mother would've done?"

"Our way calls for obedience and submission . . . patience to wait on God's will for our lives, like the Psalm said," Miriam replied quietly. "We promise to put Christ and His church ahead of the world, includin' our own flesh and blood. So insteada turnin' this matter over to Hiram Knepp, I'm gonna entrust it all—my lost-lamb daughter and my bakin' business—to the Lord. The bishop answers to Him, too, ya know."

She smiled as an inner peace settled within her, recalling how often this simple, Plain plan had gotten her through the toughest times in her life. "Now— who's gonna join me while I help myself to those stuffed peppers Rachel warmed?"

"Been quite a day," Rachel murmured. "Just when we were havin' such a *gut* talk with Tiffany—hearin' her call our mother 'Mamma'—the walls came crashin' down."

Micah slipped his arm around her. It was a fine night for a moonlight ride, but even though they'd left the yard—and prying eyes—far behind to sit in the buggy, in their favorite spot, he seemed in no mood for kissing or cuddling. "*Jah*, I was surprised to see Tiffany. Knew somethin' had changed, when she came to visit again," he said with a sigh. "Poor timin', far as the bishop's decision about sellin' the buildin'. Mamm's fit to be tied and Dat's none too happy, either. While we all know your mamma's right about submittin' to God's will and obeyin' it, it's a lot easier said than done."

For several moments, the cicadas and crickets sang around them, but for Rachel, the summer serenade lacked its usual note of peace and contentment. Nothing seemed to match up right after Hiram Knepp had stepped in and decided their future: she wasn't so sure God had been given much of a say here. "So . . . what'll ya do if the bishop puts the ban on ya?"

Micah tensed beside her. "Oh, I'm havin' my thoughts about that, for sure," he muttered. "*Jah*, I went to Tiffany's, knowin' the consequences, but Hiram's seein' a lot more sin than was there. Not like I even kissed her, or touched her—or so much as thought about her that way. Told her I was givin' all of that to *you*, Rachel. You believe that, don't ya?"

She smiled sadly in the seclusion of their favorite little grove. "*Jah*, I do now. If it weren't for you goin' there, she wouldn't've come back, most likely. Still wearin' the dark eye-paint and dyed hair, but . . . well, she's not so stiff and standoffish now."

Micah sighed, fingering the long string of her kapp. "And what if I said I was leavin' this church? Goin' in with the Mennonites down the road, where our plumbers and electricians live?"

Rachel sat bolt upright, staring at him. He'd talked about branching off into his own shop, but never too seriously, on account of how it might split up his family. "Ya can't mean it, Micah!"

"I'd have to start up on my own—unless Seth and Aaron wanna come work for me there," he mused aloud. "Wouldn't wanna leave Mamm and Dat here in Willow Ridge, though—especially considerin' how sellin' your mamma's buildin' means such a cut in her income. Or, truth be told . . . the parents might go, too, if they see I'm leavin'."

Micah watched her reactions closely. "Hiram's never been high on Dat's list, but this *decree* today made him really itchy. He's not wild about Mamm confessin' on Sunday, either—confessin' to *nothin'*, to keep the peace with the bishop, he says. I'm thinkin' that's why his pain's so bad tonight."

Rachel swiveled her head, forcing herself to breathe. She could *not* face one more life-changing decision today! Especially one that might put the brakes on her upcoming wedding. If she married a man who'd left the Old Order, even to follow a different branch of Anabaptist Christianity, she, too, would be cast out of the fold. Shunned and avoided by her own family—in public, anyway. So she thought of something else to talk about. "Kinda calls a halt to your apartment in the smithy, too, ain't so?" she offered in a faltering voice.

"Not keen on buildin' it all sleek and perty—and then havin' the bishop forbid your *mamm* to live there." Micah sighed and forced a smile. "But we're puttin' the cart before the horse, assumin' the worst. That's not usually my way. Sorry I'm so glum, honey-girl."

As this situation sank in, Rachel's hands went

clammy. She shivered despite the July heat and the warmth of Micah's sturdy body against hers. He was speaking more slowly than usual, which meant he was building up to a point that might upset her even more than his talk of leaving the church.

"Would ya come with me, Rache? Would ya still be my bride if I jumped the fence?"

There was a question she'd never thought to face! From childhood they'd been taught that obedience to God and the church came before love of family . . . yet the man she'd always loved was asking her to choose. "Not wild about leavin' *my* mamma here, either, ya know," she whimpered.

What *would* she do? All her life she'd pictured herself living in Willow Ridge, and now she dreamed of raising Micah's family and relying on Mamma for advice and support while she and Rhoda worked with their mother at the Sweet Seasons. Maybe they'd even see Mamma remarry someday. "I . . . that's not an easy question, Micah."

"And not a fair one, expectin' a decision point-blank like that." He buried his face in his hands and sighed tiredly. "I'm sorry, Rache. Didn't mean to upset ya."

"Most of what we heard today wasn't fair," Rachel echoed. She rested her head on his shoulder, wondering bleakly how she'd decide whether to stay or to renounce her vows. If she left Willow Ridge with Micah, it meant being shut off from regular contact with her mother and Rhoda—unless they, too, did the inconceivable and decided to leave the Old Order.

"*Jah*, well, let's handle one thing at a time, shall we?" He kissed her temple and sat absolutely still beside her as he inhaled the night air and released it. "I thought it was so *gut* when you girls invited Tiffany to your party," Micah remarked quietly. "And I was proud to see ya treatin' her like a sister, too, Rache. Hope today's talk didn't scare her away from gettin' to know all of ya."

"Can ya imagine havin' birthday parties all your life . . . and findin' out they've been on the wrong day?" she mused in a faraway voice. Then she chuckled. "Hard to think of somebody who looks so steely and tough bein' afraid of Plain folks like us, ain't so?"

"Told ya she was hidin' behind that getup," Micah murmured. "She's not half so strong as you, Rache."

Pleased at his remark, Rachel recalled their morning conversation around the table at the café. What she wouldn't do to turn back the day's clock, to before their scene with the brethren. "Tiffany thinks the bishop's gonna buy the buildin'. As a way to pull Mamma's strings."

For the first time all evening, Micah chuckled. "Somethin' tells me your mamma's gonna get around that, honey. She didn't build up the bakin' business she has by bein' flaky."

"Like her pie crust?" Rachel giggled and snuggled closer to him. "I'm thinkin' Hiram doesn't really wanna close down a *gut* place to eat his breakfast—and Mamma's pies. I just don't like all this nasty back-and-forth between them. Especially knowin' he'll always have the upper hand."

"That's the sum total of it, right there. For all of us." Micah scooted lower in the buggy seat, resting his head against hers. "Your mamma's got the right idea, though, gettin' back to total trust in how God's gonna handle all this. Did ya see how much calmer she looked when she went inside to eat?"

"*Jah.* She's stronger than we know."

Micah kissed her softly on the cheek. "She passed some of that on to you, too, honey-girl. I . . . I feel a lot better about all this now, just talkin' things out, nice and quiet-like."

Closing her eyes, Rachel willed her whirling thoughts and earlier objections to settle with the peace of this summer evening. If this man loved her and believed in her, what else mattered, really? "So . . . if the bishop calls for a ban after your confession on Sunday, what'll ya do, Micah?" she asked quietly.

He exhaled and paused for a long moment. "We'll know the answer to that when God reveals it, ain't so?"

Chapter 20

Even though they scheduled the summer services in homes with basements to provide some relief from the heat, Rachel squirmed: the pews were tightly packed with the members of Willow Ridge's twenty-six families. She had the feeling Preacher Glick felt inspired to talk longer than usual on this day when three confessions would be heard during the members' meeting that followed the service.

"Let's not forget the Bible's warnin' against keepin' company with those who would stray from the path of the righteous," he droned. "Even as God placed Adam and Eve, the first man and woman, in a garden paradise, the Devil slithered in to whisper temptation! Eve fell prey to that silvery tongue, and by her original sin we're all condemned to repeat her mistake."

From across the crowd, Rachel met Micah's gaze: his green eyes lacked their usual shine. He always sat on the end of a pew, where he could maneuver his *dat*'s wheelchair—and Ezra Brenneman looked more peevish than usual as this service wore on. Micah's lips tightened in a straight-line smile that told of his resignation to accept whatever punishment the bishop delivered. Most Sundays they played a silent game of peekaboo or sent discreet air-kisses from their opposite sides of the room, but not today.

"And in the same way, the people of Israel railed against God while Moses led them out of bondage in Egypt, toward the Promised Land!" Preacher Gabe continued in a higher pitch. "Manna from heaven He sent them, providing for their every need! Yet they disobeyed like naughty children, clamoring for their own way and making idols!"

Beside her, Rhoda shifted. They shared a silent glance: *How much longer?*

Rachel shrugged wearily. If Preacher Gabe was only in Exodus now, it could take him another half hour to recount the Bible's examples of God's children falling short. Again she glanced at Mamma and Naomi, who sat among women older than she and her sister. From behind, their mother appeared as relaxed and still as she always did, while her best friend's shoulders slumped forlornly.

How would this day turn out, after Mamma, Micah, and Naomi made their confessions? What if Bishop Knepp insisted on even harsher punishment than making Mamma sell the Sweet Seasons building? Would Micah bring more discipline on himself by sounding resentful and angry as he spoke before the People? Or would he declare he was jumping the fence and taking her with him? If he didn't seem truly repentant, the members might vote that he deserved to be shunned.

But thinking such bothersome thoughts would only make her squirm more. Rachel studied the weave of her plum-colored dress fabric, telling herself not to close her eyes even for a moment, or the heat and Gabe's tedious sermon would make her doze . . .

When the sermon was over they fell to their knees for the final prayer. Then came the benediction and the final hymn chanted from the *Ausbund*. While the age-old order of their worship had taught Rachel a sense of patience, on this Sunday, when those she loved most would confess and then await the members' verdict, her heart beat in double-time to the un-accompanied hymn. A short silence reverberated in the airless room.

"Members, please be seated. We will tend to the business of the People and hear confessions from three among us who have professed a need for repentance." Bishop Knepp stood with his hands clasped while those who had not yet joined the church left the room with the small children in tow. Mamma and Naomi moved to sit on the pew at the front of the women's side while Micah shifted forward, as well.

As silence fell, the bishop's gaze swept the congregation. "Word has spread amongst us concerning the reappearance of Miriam Lantz's daughter, who, as a toddler, was washed away in the flood of '93. Three of our members wish to confess behavior contrary to the *Ordnung* and thus unpleasing in the sight of God," he began in a solemn voice. "As this situation developed, I saw the flaw in my own earlier decision: by allowing Miriam to build her café and partner with Jesse's Mennonite cousins, I enabled her to connect too closely to the outside world. Upon meeting her English-raised daughter, the other elders and I saw that immediate correction was necessary. I insisted that Miriam sell her building, and this provoked reactions from Micah and Naomi Brenneman, and Miriam herself, that we shall consider here today."

Those in the room exchanged glances. How would they cast their votes, when it came time to agree upon punishment? The story of Tiffany's outlandish behavior and looks had spread like wildfire in Willow Ridge, and while few had actually seen her sister that day, even fewer knew how difficult Rebecca's emotional situation was. Rachel forced herself to inhale deeply. She felt Rhoda do the same.

"Naomi Brenneman," Hiram went on in a stern voice, "when I spoke of selling Miriam's building last week, you became distraught about how this would affect your family's income. You then apologized for the tone you used with me, and I believe you are sincerely concerned for Miriam's welfare, and for the future of your sons' carpentry business, should the People bring the ban upon your Micah."

The bishop paused. The room got very quiet, as it always did when the subject of a shunning came up. "A sitting confession will suffice. Have you anything to say, Naomi?"

Mamma's closest friend covered her eyes with her hand. "I appreciate your understandin', Bishop," she said in a halting voice, "and I'm sorry I got so high-toned the other day. I—I confess that I have failed— should believe that God knows what's best for me and that He'll take care of my family. I want to make peace and continue in patience and faith with God and the church, so I can do better in the future."

A sitting confession . . . the most lenient type. As Rachel watched Naomi leave the basement, and then voted in turn with the others to accept her confession, she felt better. It was good to see Micah's *mamm* smiling again when she was invited back inside for the verdict, knowing she was right with God and with the other members.

When the bishop called Micah's name, however, Rachel slipped her hand into Rhoda's. The man she loved approached the center of the room, between the men's side and the women's, to kneel on the floor before Hiram and the other elders. When he bowed his head, his blond hair covered his eyes like a curtain.

Please, dear Jesus, lend him Your strength and wisdom, she prayed. *Help him keep his temper if the bishop says things that upset him.*

"Micah, because I learned of your transgressions with Miriam's English-raised daughter from someone other than yourself, you now kneel before us." Hiram's solemn voice carried to the corners of the basement. "You are confessing of your free will—the same free will God gives you, which can be as much a bane as a boon. Did you indeed ride in this Tiffany's automobile, on a Sunday afternoon? Knowing this goes against the *Ordnung?*"

"*Jah,* I did."

"Would you explain what led you to seek out the company of this brazen-looking young woman? To the extent that you also entered a pool hall on the Lord's day?"

When Rachel stiffened, Rhoda gripped her hand

in warning. It wouldn't do to blurt out that Tiffany didn't *know* how Micah's troubles would snowball if he responded to her invitations.

Micah cleared his throat. "She was born Rebecca Lantz," he replied matter-of-factly. "While it's true Rebecca's looks startled us all durin' that first visit—not to mention findin' out that she was Miriam's long-lost daughter—I felt I should know more about her, rather than sit in judgment."

He took in a breath to settle himself, his contrition echoing in the stillness. "And I also told Rebecca that her *mamm* loved her no matter how she looked—and that she'd better not go breakin' her mother's heart. Rebecca wouldn't talk to me in the pool hall, with the others lookin' on, so when she drove up alongside me I figured it for the only chance I had to say my piece."

"And you didn't take Rachel or Rhoda with you? Or Miriam?" Hiram quizzed him. "At least some sense of propriety would've been preserved, had this young woman's sisters or mother accompanied you."

Micah's head remained bowed. "No, sir, I didn't. The girls had other plans, and—well, Rachel thought I was payin' too much attention to this stranger, as it was. She was upset with both of us." He glanced at Miriam then, but said nothing about her visit to Morning Star that same day.

"So you went to see this young woman on the sly, Micah? In secret, so your sins would go undetected?"

Rachel's head began to swim. Confessions always made her feel like someone was offering up tattered, discolored underwear for all to see, and Micah might as well be waving some of *hers*.

"*Jah*, there was that. I knew I was breakin' the rules and breakin' Rachel's heart, too," Micah replied hoarsely. "And I confess to a curiosity about Rebecca that got the better of my good sense. Rachel's already forgiven me for this, and I thank God for that. I also admit to seein' Rebecca a second time, at the apartment where she was stayin'—"

The women looked up suddenly, while the men shifted on their benches. Rachel exhaled and held tightly to Rhoda's hand as Micah continued. He was speaking the truth, after all. Not really pulling her into the mire with him.

"—and I've also confessed this to Rachel. And bless her, she believes—as I do—that this whole situation has been guided by God's hand," he said in a reverent tone. "With all humility, Bishop, the Lantzes and I see Rebecca's survival in the flood all those years ago—and her reappearance now—as a miracle. I did wrong by breakin' our rules, *jah*. But I'm not a bit sorry I took that risk."

A few folks sucked in their breath. Rachel gazed carefully at Hiram Knepp's face to gauge his reaction. The black-haired bishop stood poised to point up more of Micah's sins, but Micah continued before their leader could lecture him further.

"I looked beyond the tattoos and the black, spiky hair to see one of our Lord's children, needin' compassion now that the woman who raised her has died," he explained earnestly. "She needed to hear that her Lantz family loved her, while she sorted out the confusin' parts of growin' up, under a different name, with the couple who rescued her from the river but didn't go lookin' for her real family. Any one of us would have a hard time dealin' with all that stuff."

Hiram's scowl had deepened. "You're walking a very thin line, presuming to know the mind of God while taking matters into your own very human hands, Mr. Brenneman. Such pride is the ultimate sin, and when I hear—"

"I couldn't sit by and watch a family be separated by religious differences! I saw the chance to reunite the Lantzes, and I took it!" Micah raised his head to look directly at Hiram, and then to entreat the People. "A lot of wounds are on the mend now, Bishop," he rushed on in a voice choked with emotion, "and I'm grateful that God has allowed me to be a part of that process. All that aside, though, I stand in need of the People's forgiveness for the way I started down this path."

The room vibrated with Hiram's power and presence as their bishop, and with Micah's heartfelt entreaty as a younger man who knew he'd done wrong. Rachel sat on the edge of her pew, ramrod straight. Surely Hiram wouldn't bring the ban down on Micah for doing what he felt was right . . . and if the bishop recommended such a punishment, surely the friends and family in this room wouldn't agree to it! *Would* they?

"I'm sorry I got irritated when we talked about this the other day, Bishop," Micah added quietly. "I—I hope now to behave in a way that makes me worthy of the Lord's love. I'm mighty grateful for the grace that gets me through each day."

The room seemed to breathe in deeply and then let out a collective sigh. Rachel let a tear dribble unchecked down each cheek: Micah had risen above the bishop's insinuations to walk the higher road. He had taken a potentially immoral situation and tossed it as a lifeline to Rebecca . . . and Rebecca had grabbed it. She seemed eager to know them now, to learn of Plain ways even if she didn't intend to join the Amish Church.

Rachel glanced around the crowded room as Micah rose from his knees. His shoulders looked straight and strong, his head high, as he started up the stairs toward the light of the open doorway.

"Is there further discussion?" Hiram asked tersely. "Preacher Gabe, has Micah rectified your earlier misgivings?"

The old fellow still appeared cranky and rumpled, as if he'd gotten up on the wrong side of his bed. "Young Micah has a ways to go to approach the *humility* we Amish aim for! Sayin' he followed God's lead, callin' this situation a *miracle*. And then ridin' on its coattails to claim he was takin' a *wrong* and makin' it right—"

"And I'm mighty proud of him for it, too," Mamma spoke up boldly. "He talked to Rebecca about our faith—even when she and her friends made fun of him. He went lookin' for answers instead of standin' on his *presumptions* and takin' her at face value. Because of Micah, my Rebecca came to visit us again last week—and she'll be celebratin' her birthday with her sisters for the first time in . . . in eighteen years."

Several sucked in their breath. Mamma's' remark sounded none too contrite, especially considering she was the next one to confess. But several of the women wiped at their eyes as they whispered of this unexpected turn of events—a celebration any mother would thank

God for. Hiram stood before them, assessing . . . taking his flock's emotional temperature as he considered what punishment to vote on.

"Preacher Gabe and I were concerned enough about the gravity of Micah's repeated offenses that I believed a shunning was the only effective way to—"

"How can ya say such a thing, Bishop?" one of the women pleaded. "What do ya hope to accomplish by separatin' Micah from his family, when he brought Miriam's family back together? He said he was sorry for the way he went about it, and I believe him!"

Hiram pivoted to face the women's side of the room. "Stand and be recognized! Our discussion must be open—transparent to all, before God!"

Rachel's jaw dropped. Never had anyone dared to challenge Hiram Knepp in such a tone! From the end of the pew in front of hers, a figure in dark brown slowly rose.

"Aunt Leah!" Rhoda whispered.

Rachel nodded, shifting on the hard bench. Their aunt stood, clasping her hands as though afraid to proceed yet compelled to by a higher presence. "My sister and I have had our differences over the years— and for that I need your forgiveness, Miriam," Leah said in a tremulous voice. "But, Bishop, I'm sorriest about bein' the one who told ya Miriam went to Morning Star to see Rebecca. It was my need to spread a juicy piece of news—my tattletale's heart—that started this whole unfortunate wagonload rollin' down the hill."

Heads swiveled. Whispers hissed in the dim room.

Leah's shoulders sagged. "And now Miriam's losin'

her buildin'. And Micah's family might forfeit both his income and Naomi's—"

"I heard about Micah's misbehavior from other sources, as well," Hiram pointed out.

"—so I'm sayin' if anybody's to be punished for this," she went on doggedly, "I oughtta be among them."

The room went silent again. Across the way, Leah's husband, Daniel, looked none too pleased about his wife's calling attention to herself. Her sons Nate and Bram sat taller, too, watching the emotions play over the bishop's slender face.

"You have confessed freely and spontaneously, Leah. I see no sin in bringing the questionable activities of other members to my attention, as you did." Hiram then squared his shoulders, looking stern as he stood before them in his black trousers and vest. His shirt was so white it glowed in the light from the basement windows. "What say you, the People? Shall we accept Micah Brenneman's confession, or does he require further discipline?"

Down the rows he went, listening to each man's vote in turn before turning to hear the women's replies. Rachel held her breath. No matter how long it took, the bishop would seek a unanimous verdict. As the young women along her pew chimed in with "*Jah,* I accept Micah's confession," her heart fluttered rapidly.

"*Jah,* I accept his confession. He's a *gut* man," she insisted when it was her turn, and Rhoda echoed her sentiment. Minutes later, when Micah was called inside, she wanted to stand up and shout about how wonderful he was, and how much she loved him. But, of course, that would be inappropriate in church. When he heard he was fully pardoned, his face lit up and he beamed at her. What a wonderful relief, that neither he nor his mother would be chastised for speaking and acting in a way that had raised the elders' doubts.

But that still didn't mean Mamma could keep her building. Hiram had already decided that, and as the voices around them quieted again, her mother stood. Mamma looked shorter . . . as vulnerable as anyone who'd ever gone before the congregation. She knelt before the bishop, in the center of the room.

See my brave mamma there, Lord? Rachel prayed as she gripped her sister's hand. *She needs our help and support now . . . needs Your guidance while Hiram leads her through his questions and answers. Give us all the strength to accept Your way.*

Chapter 21

"Miriam Lantz, what do you come before us to confess today?"

Rachel swallowed hard. Didn't the bishop usually announce why someone had come to kneel before them? By putting Mamma on the defensive from his first words, he had put the little woman in black at a disadvantage right from the start. She sensed Hiram Knepp had saved her mother's confession for last to make an example of her . . . or to show her, in front of everyone, that he was in total control of this situation.

Cleanse me from suspicious thoughts, God. You chose Hiram by holy lot to be our leader. It's my place to believe he carries out Your purpose for all of us.

Beside her, Rhoda tensed. Her sister's blue eyes were fixed on their mother, who lowered her head, facing the leader who held her future in his hands.

"I've come to confess my sins, Bishop, and to be made right with my God again."

"And what sins would those be?" he repeated. "It's important, when we petition for God's pardon, that we have a clear idea what we're asking for."

"Puh! Like the Lord doesn't know!" one of the women muttered under her breath.

Rachel suspected it was Naomi, voicing the exasperation Mamma surely must be feeling right now. A warning glance from the bishop stifled any further whispering.

"Even though it was on a nonpreachin' Sunday— our day for visitin' kin," Mamma pointed out in a wistful voice, "I disobeyed the *Ordnung* by hirin' Sheila to drive me to see my Rebecca and her *dat*—even though Sheila refused my money. Took along food for the fella who pulled my daughter from the river eighteen years ago, as he'd just lost his wife. And *jah*, I did this in secret. Had I known Micah was goin', I could've ridden along and saved us both some grief, ain't so?"

Rhoda grinned and closed her eyes. On Rachel's other side, Annie Mae Knepp stifled a snicker.

"Mrs. Lantz, this is a serious matter—"

"I'm as serious as can be, Bishop."

"—and I must ask you to come to your point with appropriate solemnity," Hiram warned.

Mamma lowered her head farther. "I'm givin' the full story, like you asked, Bishop. My point bein' that while I broke some of our rules, I felt I was doin' it for the right reasons," she said contritely. "Was it wrong to thank the man who saved my little girl's life? Or wrong to express my sympathy for his loss? Sundays are the only time I have for doin' that."

Rachel nipped her lip to keep from chuckling. The sparkle had returned to Rhoda's eyes, too, because their mother was trying Hiram's patience as only she knew how. It was good to hear Mamma stand her ground and state her priorities. Were the unwritten rules of their *Ordnung* more important than caring for

those who'd lost family members? More important than
expressing love—and thanksgiving—for a daughter
returned? It was an issue that seldom came before them
in such a dramatic way, and everyone in the room followed this discussion closely.

Hiram cleared his throat purposefully. "And you
have only Sundays for this purpose because you work
in your café the other six days. Which—as we have discussed several times, Miriam—has taken over so
much of your life that you've not opened your heart
to the love of another husband."

Mamma shifted on her knees. "My heart's open,
Bishop. But my head's sayin' the right man hasn't
shown himself yet."

"Miriam!" His voice rang like a thunderclap in the
low-ceilinged room. "This is precisely the sort of
hubris—the lack of humility—that has brought you
before us today! And the very reason I have insisted
you sell your building! Your dealings with the English
have eroded the basic faith, obedience, and submission we all witnessed when you were Jesse's wife."

Rachel held her breath. Once again the bishop was
exercising his power as their spiritual leader, and he
sounded like he might just slap a ban on Mamma the
moment she dared defy him again. *Lord, please help
those two come to Your understandin'*, she prayed with all
her heart. *It's not like either of them is wrong, but this isn't
soundin' right, either.*

"Things were different when I was Jesse's wife," her
mother stated quietly. "While I confess to enjoyin' my
business and *jah*, takin' pride in feedin' people, I
thank God that He has provided me a means of sup-
portin' my girls . . . while also showin' me just how
strong He created me to be. 'Tis a gift, to realize that

just when ya feel you've hit rock bottom, ya *have*—for sure and for certain—landed on the Rock, indeed. It's God's own hand you're sittin' in."

A hush went over the crowd. All present sat absolutely still. The bishop's knuckles went white. From in front of Rachel, Hannah Brenneman's stomach rumbled loudly, announcing the lateness of the hour in the absence of a clock. While their church services and members' meetings were lessons in patience and waiting, Rachel wondered how long Hiram Knepp might press his point for the sake of putting Mamma back in her place.

Apparently the other elders wondered this, too: Preacher Tom and Reuben Reihl, the deacon, took the bishop aside for a whispered conversation. Hiram didn't look happy about what they said, but when the two sat down he once again stood before Mamma. "Have you anything else to say before you go outside, Miriam? I sense nothing further will be accomplished if you continue to respond so glibly, rather than with heartfelt contrition."

Glibly? Did Hiram feel their mother wasn't stating her faith in acceptable, worthy terms? Or did he sense he'd lost the confidence of the congregation?

"'The Lord is my light and my salvation,'" Mamma replied quietly. "'Whom then shall I fear? Of whom shall I be afraid?'"

Rhoda squeezed her hand so hard Rachel nearly yelped—but she squeezed back. There was just no arguing with Dat's favorite Psalm. At a time like this, no one could deny the power of the Holy Scripture to answer every question and speak to any accuser.

"You may step outside, Miriam."

Mamma nodded, and when she struggled to rise

from the hard basement floor, Micah stepped forward to steady her. *"Denki,"* she murmured, and then she hurried up the stairs.

"Do you, the People, accept Miriam's confession as the true, contrite request for God's forgiveness?" the bishop asked. "If anyone doubts her sincerity, it's your Christian responsibility to speak up rather than to let her attitude pass because of your friendship with her or the lateness in the day."

Once again Rachel held her breath and her sister's hand as the vote followed the rows of men on the other side of the room . . . and then went quickly from one woman to the next. Did she dare celebrate this affirmation with the same joy she'd felt when Micah's confession was accepted? *"Jah,"* she said proudly, "I accept her confession."

"Jah, me too!" Rhoda echoed.

Happiness made her heart flutter like butterflies as Preacher Tom went to fetch Mamma. When their mother paused in the doorway to read the faces she knew so well, it was a joy indeed to see her smile return before Hiram Knepp announced their verdict.

At last the day began to move again. As everyone filed up the stairs and began setting out the long tables for their lunch beneath the trees, Rachel hugged her mother. With Rhoda on their other side, they formed the tight triangle they'd come to love, rocking each other with a love that would not let them go.

"Oh, Mamma, ya sounded so strong! So confident," Rhoda murmured. She thumbed a tear from their mother's cheek and then swiped at her own eyes.

"I was prayin' for ya," Rachel said in a voice that

wavered. "Askin' God to let the truth be told—held up for all to see, no matter how Hiram seemed to—"

"And that's all we'll be sayin' about the bishop and his way with words." Mamma gazed pointedly at Rachel and then at her sister. "Truth be told, my mouth's my worst enemy sometimes and I *do* sound like I'm makin' light of important matters. It's best we don't continue doin' that, ain't so?"

At least not here, Rachel mused as she saw friends coming across the yard to greet them. The same thought sparkled in her sister's eyes.

"I'm thinkin' the faster those tables get set, the sooner we'll eat," Rhoda remarked. As she looked over Mamma's shoulder, she smiled. "And I'm thinkin' Aunt Leah might want a word without us listenin' in, too. Mighty surprisin', when she stood up that way— and mighty *gut,* too."

"*Jah,*" Rachel agreed as they stepped toward the tables, "some days the surprises are better than others."

Chapter 22

Obedience . . . submission . . . patience, Miriam reminded herself as she rode in the bishop's carriage on Monday morning. *Obedience . . . submission . . . patience. Wait on the Lord and leave this all in His hands . . . the Lord is my light . . . whom then shall I fear?*

"You're awfully quiet this morning, Miriam. Considering the overwhelming support you received after your confession yesterday, I expected you to be more *pleased.* Happy to be in good standing with God and the church again." Hiram fixed his dark eyes on hers as they rolled down the highway toward New Haven. He was a master at waiting out people's answers—making them fill a silence that grew more uncomfortable as the seconds ticked by.

It was a skill she was learning, too: Obedience. Submission. Patience. And she refused to carry on about how *pleased* she was to be making this trip to the bank, or how he'd been right to take her down a peg or two by selling her building. Lying was a sin, after all.

"I didn't expect anyone to speak out against you, of course—nor did I believe anyone would fault you for reuniting with your daughter," he finally remarked. "What's her real name, again?"

"Rebecca," Miriam murmured.

"Ah, the three *R*'s—but much more personable than reading, writing, and 'rithmatic." He steered the horse left at the four-way stop, into New Haven. "You have a fine family, Mrs. Lantz. Truly a pity you can't have more children."

Was he toying with her? Trying to win her favor by tugging at her heartstrings? As he helped her down, in the lot reserved for horse-and-buggy customers behind the bank, Miriam focused on making a graceful landing rather than meeting his gaze. She wanted no part of the hands that lingered at her waist, nor would she give him the least bit of encouragement. This was her livelihood Hiram was messing with! It was one thing to beg forgiveness in church—obeying the bishop's command—and quite another to submit to this man's whims.

Obedience . . . submission . . . patience, she repeated as they entered the modern brick building. *To a point.*

Miriam let her eyes adjust to the cool dimness of the air-conditioned lobby. She was pleased to see Derek Shotwell, the same bank officer who'd made her the loan for the Sweet Seasons building. As he approached, she reminded herself that while she dared not challenge Hiram's decision, she didn't have to roll over and play dead, either. Derek was several years younger than she, very businesslike in his long-sleeved yellow shirt and striped tie. She clutched her ledger as he shook hands with her.

"A pleasure to see you again, Mrs. Lantz," he said as he gestured toward his office door. "Although I confess I was surprised when Mr. Knepp asked me to draw up the papers for the sale of your building. Anytime I've ever driven by, your parking lot's been full!"

Obedience . . . submission . . . patience, she repeated as she took a chair in front of his heavy desk. *Let the situation speak for itself—and let the Lord speak through it, too.*

Miriam smiled at him, liking him even more for the colorful photos of his three young children displayed on the credenza behind him. "*Jah*, we do a boomin' business with the bakery, and we're gettin' a steady clientele eatin' our meals, too."

Derek's high-backed leather chair bobbed when he landed in it, the obvious question in his eyes. She continued to smile at him, straight on but silent, as he took the paper clip from the documents he'd prepared.

"Just as the ownership of an automobile is considered worldly, the sale of this building is an exercise in humility: placing our faith ahead of the success that deters our progress on the path toward salvation," Hiram replied smoothly. "This is why, once the sale's arranged, we want no signs in front of the building. Word has spread through Willow Ridge already, and we prefer to give our members the opportunity to keep this property in Amish hands."

"I can understand that, yes, sir." Once again, the loan officer met her gaze as he turned the paperwork toward her so she could read it. "Our appraiser kept that in mind when he visited the property."

When had that appraiser been to the café? Didn't such dealings take time . . . require a certain amount of research into titles and records? Miriam sat forward, skimming the legal description of the Sweet Seasons, its size and location and then the asking price. "A hundred thirty thousand?" she gasped.

Hiram grunted and snatched up the paperwork. "How can this be? The original loan was only for—"

"A vacant building, sir. And with its custom finishing, its prime location on the highway, plus the installed appliances, it's worth much more than when Mrs. Lantz purchased it." Derek focused on her again. "Am I to assume you're moving your business, Mrs. Lantz? Does all that beautiful Amish-crafted furniture stay in the dining room? That would increase the asking price by quite a bit."

Oh, but she was liking the sound of this! "Depends on what the new owner wants to do with it," she replied, fighting a smile. "I'd love nothin' more than to keep workin' there—as would the quiltin' ladies in the other half of that buildin'. And *jah*, all that finishin' work and the furniture was done by our local Brenneman boys. Best quality ya can buy anywhere—ain't so, Bishop?"

Hiram looked up from the paperwork and then fixed his facial expression. "True enough. But the tables and chairs could be sold at auction—as could the kitchen equipment—if the new owner has something else in mind."

Miriam maintained her pleasant expression but her mind was racing over these details . . . the way the bishop had apparently arranged the appraisal—maybe let the fellow inside one evening while she was gone. Hiram's surprise at the asking price told her the appraiser had researched the contents and furnishings; had gone beyond what the bishop anticipated, either out of ignorance of the market price, or . . . personal interest?

Obedience . . . submission . . . patience. They seemed to be working in her favor, but she couldn't jump to any conclusions: too much was at stake here, and no one had signed on that line yet.

As the men discussed the contract terms, fees, and a possible time frame for when the building might sell in the current market, Miriam sat quietly. She wasn't pretending to be ignorant, exactly . . . just realizing her *place* in this conversation and staying there, for once. The men haggled over the asking price and the value of the building's contents—and wouldn't Micah be awestruck to know the retail value of his finishing work and his furniture? A sudden silence made her look up.

"Here's a pen, Mrs. Lantz. It's the line with the sticky note arrow beside it."

The price hadn't gone down. Her heart thundered as she dutifully looked to Hiram for his go-ahead. As he nodded, she signed her name to the biggest amount of money she'd ever dealt with.

"You realize, of course, that depending upon the market, we might lower the asking price to entice potential buyers," Derek informed her in a low voice. His gaze didn't waver. "But we'll contact you first. And we'll let you know the minute we have offers you might wish to consider, even if they don't meet the asking price."

"*Jah, des gut,*" she said, nodding.

Derek glanced at her signature and began stapling and folding the duplicates. He flashed an easy smile at the bishop as he finished up. "I hear your Belgians and Percherons took top dollar at a couple recent auctions, Mr. Knepp. Always good to learn about clients making good in this tough agricultural market."

Hiram brightened immediately. "Yes, my stallions

and draft horses are rated among the best in the country, not just around here."

"And while I know you Plain folks don't use computer technology, that ad I saw online—with the photo of your horses and the new barn—surely must generate some business," Mr. Shotwell went on.

Miriam's eyebrows rose at the mention of a computer ad and a photograph—both forbidden, although some of their local craftsmen had English or Mennonite friends handle advertising for their businesses. Hiram Knepp was as keen on his fine horses as she was on her cooking talents, yet he seemed unaware that his attitude could be construed as *pride*: the same sin as the one he'd instructed her to confess yesterday.

Instead of bringing this up, however, Miriam glanced at the two chatting men and slowly slipped her ledger onto a stack of manila folders on Derek's desk. If her figures could speak for her, perhaps they would compensate for her not talking much today, in deference to Hiram.

A few minutes later, she and the bishop were on their way home. While Miriam was even more convinced that this shrewd Amish man had made some arrangements behind her back, she felt a little better about the sale situation. She could leave it to the Lord and not believe she was forfeiting all she'd devoted to the Sweet Seasons. They arrived at the café minutes before noon, so she clambered down from the buggy as soon as he pulled his horse to a halt. "Appreciate the ride, Hiram," she remarked. "Gotta jump in on the lunch rush. Ya know how busy my girls and Naomi'll be about now."

His expression suggested he had other things to discuss. "Just be mindful of getting too involved—so busy with worldly pursuits that you have no time for the twins. Or to find a husband, like we've discussed."

Already halfway to the building, Miriam turned to look pointedly at him. "All *three* of my girls are at the top of my to-do list, Hiram. If you're not too busy sellin' the services of those prize stallions, you can join us for their twenty-first birthday party in a couple weeks."

As he adjusted his black hat, his nostrils flared like a horse's. "What're you implying, Miriam? Breeding draft horses is my livelihood."

"*Jah,* like bakin' is mine. And I'm guessin' those stallions of yours could find themselves a nice mare without you doin' the choosin' and takin' the credit, ain't so?" She'd crossed the line again, but she couldn't unsay the words. "Far be it from me to suggest you're actin' prideful and could use a dose of the same humility you're dishin' up to the Brennemans and me, Bishop."

Miriam fully expected him to follow her into the kitchen and deliver a sermon, but she had no time to fret over it: Naomi was forking hot, crispy chicken pieces from three cast-iron skillets while Rhoda scurried to remove pans of fresh biscuits from the oven. Rachel saw her first, over the tub of dirty dishes she'd hefted onto the counter beside the sink.

"Mamma! How'd it go?" She wiped her hands on her white apron, concern furrowing her flushed brow. "Did the banker think we'd be movin' out soon? Mary Schrock's been in a dither about where they'd display all their quilts and—well, we're gettin' a *lot* of questions! And I can't answer them!"

Miriam smiled at her daughters and Naomi, the three faces she loved most, here in the kitchen that had become her second home. Surrounded by the crackling of grease and the fragrant steam from the tastiest food to be found anywhere in these parts, she caught each of her girls in an arm and hugged them hard. "Not our job to answer all the questions, honey-bugs," she replied. "Wasn't my favorite trip, goin' to put this place up for sale, but I believe Mr. Shotwell will do his best for us."

Naomi finished filling the biscuit basket for the buffet. "I see them out there waitin' for more chicken. It's like they can't get enough of our food, now that the grapevine's shakin' with the news of the place goin' up for sale."

Glancing out into the crowded dining room, Miriam nodded. "I'll carry that for ya. Then I gotta get crackin' on those fifteen fruit pies for Zook's, and refill our front case, too. Hated bein' gone this mornin', but ya do what ya have to do."

As she approached the steam table, the Kanagy boys and the three blond Brennemans stood waiting to stab some chicken before she could put the pan in its place. "Can't have ya passin' out from hunger now, can we?" she teased as she stepped out of their way. Then she tapped Micah on the shoulder. "Can I have a word?"

"*Jah*, sure." He quickly grabbed two large chicken breasts and two more biscuits. "How'd it go at the bank? Was thinkin' about ya, Miriam, wonderin' if I should've come along."

"You've got your work, Micah. And I just wanted to

tell ya—" She waited for Nate and Bram to go back to their table, and then lowered her voice. "I feel real *gut* about this situation now, bein's how Mr. Shotwell's appraiser adjusted the sale price *way* up from what I paid—on account of your fine finishin' work and furniture, mostly. I want ya to go ahead and finish off the apartment in the smithy."

Micah nodded, listening closely as the crowd chattered around them. "*Jah*, probably not a *gut* idea to leave it half-done."

"When the buildin' sells—and . . . *jah*, I believe it will," she said with a hitch in her voice, "I'll pay ya for the materials and whatever ya want for your labor, outta the money I get for it. Investin' my profit in that upstairs apartment'll save me some income tax—and I still wanna live there when you and Rachel marry."

"And how was Hiram durin' all this? Ya think he's gonna buy it and turn ya out?"

Miriam's heart fluttered as she allowed herself to imagine a happier ending. "It snapped his suspenders but *gut* when he saw the askin' price!" she whispered. "I was flabbergasted myself, but it was the appraiser's say-so and we'll go along with that. This was Hiram's way of tonin' me down, remember. But he's gonna pay a perty penny if he sees this through."

Chapter 23

Rachel stopped halfway up the stairs to the smithy's loft, her heart pounding as steadily as Micah's hammer. She was glad he'd decided to finish these rooms: surely it would put an end to any thoughts about his moving out of Willow Ridge to live among the Mennonites. While all had been forgiven concerning his visits to Rebecca, as he'd said during his confession, there was still the matter of the café being for sale . . . the possibility that his *mamm* might lose her income. Kneeling before the People hadn't settled Micah's feelings about the bishop and his decisions, had it?

She breathed deeply to gather her courage, savoring the scents of sawdust and paint. Amish women didn't tell their men what to do or make their decisions for them—and she'd learned well enough that complaining got her nowhere except into trouble.

So it was time to act—and speak—like a woman mature enough to marry and raise a family. Because that's exactly what she intended to do. With Micah.

Rachel waited for a pause between bursts of nail

pounding to holler into the open doorway. "Micah? Ya gonna show me how it's all comin' together?" she asked in a teasing tone. "Or do I have to sneak up here after ya leave?"

"Only folks I'm lettin' up here'll get put to work!" came his reply.

"How soon ya forget!" she teased. "I was *born* to work, Mr. Brenneman. A hand that fits an oven handle and a broom can hold a paintbrush, too, ain't so?"

"Bring some of those brownies you were makin' this afternoon! Left home before dessert so's I could work here while there's still light."

Rachel snickered. Truth be told, Micah had even more of a yen for chocolate than she did. But who could fault a man for leaving Naomi's table to build her sister and Mamma's new home? Or at least she hoped it would be . . .

She galloped down the stairs barefoot, then crossed the café's back parking lot. Mamma looked up from making a batch of pastry for tomorrow's piecrusts as Rachel put half a dozen fresh brownies on a plate. "Don't follow me, now!" she teased her mother. Then she bounded back over to where her man was working, hoping to maintain this lighthearted attitude as she spoke her peace.

Micah was bent over to check a hardwood floorboard. When he grinned at her from between his sturdy legs, spread in an *A* shape, she giggled. "You're a fine sight, Micah."

"So're you and your brownies, Rache. Just what a man needs to get him through maybe two more evenin's of work."

"Me? Or the brownies?" She bit into one, to watch him react.

"*Jah.*" He righted himself, playing along . . . watching her chew with obvious interest, yet not moving toward her.

Will he look at me this way a year from now? Ten years? She swallowed the bite of chewy chocolate studded with walnuts. "Lookin' real *gut*," she murmured as she pulled her gaze away to check his progress.

"Me? Or the apartment?"

She snickered. "*Jah.*"

"Watch this." Micah stepped over to the shelves he'd built on the outside wall—except he pulled them effortlessly along tracks in the ceiling to reveal a wall about twelve feet long that rolled into the center of the big open room. It clicked into place. Then he went to what was *really* the outside wall and pulled down a panel that contained a bed. "Try the other one. If ya can reach it—and handle the weight okay—your *mamm* and Rhoda'll be fine with it. And we've got us two instant bedrooms, ain't so?"

Gaping, Rachel set aside the brownies and approached the opposite wall. She grabbed a decorative crosspiece carved at eye level in the paneling. When a second bed came down, her giggle echoed in the open, unfinished space. "Micah, this is—this is amazin'! Bedrooms that fold up and roll away when you're not sleepin'!"

"*Jah,* like the old Murphy beds they used to install in Craftsman houses. Great space savers, and both rooms have shelves, too. And here, for the bathroom—" Micah walked in front of the kitchen sink and rolled out a smaller wall segment that revealed a tub and shower unit. "Had to arrange these water pipes and drains to work with the ones in the smithy bathroom below us," he explained. "But this way, ya can use the toilet and hand sink here in the corner without takin' up the usual space for a full bath."

"And you've got the towel racks and whatnot on the movin' wall," she murmured. With a gentle push, that wall segment rolled silently along its ceiling tracks. It clicked into place near the stairway, to not only enclose the tub but provide privacy for using the stool, as well. Fascinated, Rachel tugged on it to see exactly how the wall system transformed this end of the apartment into a small kitchen with a full bath. "If you'd've tried to tell me about this, I couldn't've imagined it."

She rushed over to throw her arms around him. "Micah, this is the most wonderful-*gut* little place! I might wanna live here with ya instead of lettin' Mamma and Rhoda—"

"Careful what ya wish for, Rache," he said as he bussed her cheek. "Mighty tiny for a man my size. And where would we put the kids? Tape them to the ceilin'?"

His kissed her then, still laughing as he hugged her exuberantly. "Your mamma was right to have me finish this project. No matter what happens if somebody else buys the—"

"And this would be the perfect do-over for the attic—and maybe some of the other rooms at the house, too," she said in an excited whisper. "Oh, Micah, I've been thinkin'! If Hiram boots Mamma and Rhoda outta here, we can make them a *dawdi haus* in the attic and maybe—maybe rent some of the bedrooms, like a B and B. And if we expand the kitchen some, Mamma could do her bakin' there while Rhoda and I tend the guest rooms and—"

"Whoa, there! You're talkin' so fast my poor head's spinnin'." Still holding her, Micah smiled. The dimming evening light made his eyes deep pools . . . pools she wanted to see herself in for the rest of her days. "We'd still have to get the bishop's permission to run that sort of business, ya know. And then . . . there's still the matter of where to put all the babies I want to make with ya."

"Micah, there's *six* bedrooms there, and—" She exhaled, caught up in the words she so needed to say, hoping for the response she so needed to hear. "Micah, I know you're frustrated with Hiram makin' you and Mamma toe the line, but—but *please,* can we stay here in Willow Ridge?" she pleaded.

He gazed down at her, patient as always. But he looked none too convinced.

So she went on before he could protest, hoping he understood. "Mamma's other sisters, except Leah, all married fellas from other towns, and with Dat gone I just can't leave her, Micah. We're all she's got," Rachel pleaded. "And if she loses her café—well, I don't want to leave *your* mamma hangin', either, Micah!"

Rachel stopped for breath, hoping the right words came while she was on a roll. "We can't let our feelin's about Hiram chase us away from the home—the lives—we've always loved here!" she insisted. "We've gotta stand up and show him how God and our faith *do* come first—but that for us, *family* is part of that faith, too."

He cleared his throat, wrestling with what he wanted

to say. "I was plenty steamed up the other night when I talked about jumpin' the fence, Rache. But still, I don't like the way he's treatin' your mother. It's like he expects her to give up her business and hitch up with him so—"

"Micah!" Rachel pulled away to plant her fists on her hips. "Do ya really think Mamma's gonna fall for that? And if Hiram does decide she's leavin' the Sweet Seasons, do ya think she'll curl herself into a helpless little ball?"

"Never said your *mamm* was helpless—"

"For sure and for certain, she'll find a way to do what she loves—and to see as much of our sister as Rebecca will allow." She gripped his sturdy shoulders. "*Jah*, Mamma loves her café, Micah, but it's only a buildin'. She's got a home and a family and a heart bigger than all of this world. Do ya think lack of a *buildin'* can stop Mamma from doin' what she loves, with the people she loves?"

He gazed at her for a long moment before coaxing her into his embrace. "Truth be told, I wasn't feelin' any too *gut* about pullin' away from my family, either," he murmured. "But what ya just said? Well, now I know why I've gotta have ya in my life, Rachel Lantz. Ya listen to my bluster and see through it to what really matters. I love ya, honey. *Fer gut* and forever."

Her heart skipped in her chest. Wondrous enough that he'd said it so clear and sweet: *I love ya, honey*. But to echo the sentiment she and Rhoda and Mamma had shared since Dat passed was more than coincidence. It was a sign. Sure proof that with God—and this man in her arms—all things were possible.

"So . . . we're stayin' here? In Willow Ridge?" she breathed.

"Don't reckon I'm leavin'," he said with a soft chuckle. "It's for sure and for certain *you're* not, ain't so? And why would I go anywhere without you?"

Chapter 24

Early Tuesday morning, Miriam crimped the crusts on a dozen more cherry and peach pies. The familiar rhythm of baking had always soothed her: the tart fragrance of the cherries . . . the cool dampness of the unbaked crust . . . the peachy sweetness of filling licked from a spoon before she put it in the dishwasher . . . the silence and productivity of these predawn hours before anyone else arrived. What would she do if these simple pleasures were taken from her when the building sold?

Bake in my own kitchen again came the immediate answer, but *this* kitchen in the Sweet Seasons had become her second home. It went far beyond ownership of the physical building, this satisfaction in work well done. Although Miriam knew she and the girls would survive, it was such a disappointment to think this cozy haven might be taken from her. Had God allowed her to prosper here after Jesse's death, only to take her down a peg or two now?

Obedience . . . submission . . . patience, she reminded

herself as she positioned the pies in the ovens. The Lord would see her through this. He was teaching a lesson she needed to learn, and it was best to accept this as His way of enriching her faith.

She smiled as she recalled Rachel's bubbly enthusiasm over how Micah had transformed the rooms in the smithy's loft—and how her daughter had suggested transforming their home into a B and B. That pair would never lack for employment! Miriam itched to peek upstairs, to see Micah's project for herself, but she wanted to be truly surprised when he showed it to her. Such pleasures came seldom enough . . . and if she and Rhoda never got to live in those rooms . . .

Outside, a movement caught her eye. Here came Leah, driving her wagon through the pearl-gray haze of the morning.

Miriam closed her eyes against the buzz of other fretful thoughts. True enough, her sister had confessed to tattling about her Morning Star visit, and she'd forgiven Leah for that. But what would it take to really *end* the tension between them? How could she convince her older sister that her ideas about life and earning a livelihood were as valid as Leah's plan for *her* family? Years ago their mother had set the pattern, creating Miriam's place as the youngest—the supposedly most indulged and spoiled—daughter. But that was decades ago! Didn't she and Leah deserve to know each other for the women they'd become?

"*Gut* mornin', Leah!" she called outside as she opened the kitchen's back door. "Ya drivin' the honey wagon?"

Leah chortled. A "honey wagon" was a vehicle that carried away animal waste after the barns and chicken houses were hosed out. "*Jah*, brought some filled jars for the sale display, and comb honey for your tables, too."

Miriam dried her hands and hurried out to help her sister heft the twelve-gallon crock. "*Gut* timing. Just got the pies in, so I've got a while to do this before Naomi gets here."

"And how're the two of ya takin' to the news of the sale?"

Miriam sensed *this* was Leah's real reason for coming, because it put the Lantz family in yet another spotlight—a situation that kicked up speculation all around Willow Ridge. She shrugged, determined to put a positive spin on whatever her sister might say. "We're comin' up with some surprisin' ideas, actually," she hedged as they lowered the heavy crock of honey between them. "Necessity's the mother of invention, ya know."

"So it's a for-sure thing you'll have to move out, you and the Schrocks?" Leah's eyebrow rose. "The bishop's talkin' like this buildin' is already his and that you'll be cookin' at *his* place before the summer's out!"

How much of this was true? And how much was Leah saying to bait her? Miriam considered her answer as they gripped the wooden handles of the crock. As always, they hurried into the kitchen with it because it didn't seem so heavy that way. "Let me gather up the jars from the tables so's we can fill them—"

"You're stallin', little sister. Somethin' tells me there's more to this story about you and Hiram than you're lettin' on."

Something inside her snapped and Miriam closed

her eyes. *Obedience and submission aren't required here,
Lord, but I could use a big dollop of patience.*

She looked at her sister, taller and stockier than
she. Leah wore a wrinkled kerchief on her head and
a faded tan choring dress that rippled in the morning
breeze above her sturdy bare feet. "Ya know, it's that
kind of tongue-waggin' that landed me in the situation I've got with my Rebecca," she began in a low
voice. "But I forgive ya yet again for startin' all that
talk. Stirrin' up the pot."

Leah's brow furrowed as they carried a plastic dish
bin into the dining room to gather the honey jars. "I
don't follow ya. I had nothin' to do with that girl
comin' here—"

"That *girl* is your niece, Leah."

Her sister's frown flickered as she reached for a
half-empty jar of honey.

"But when ya told Hiram I'd gone to see Tiffany's
dat, over in Morning Star, that started the whole snowball rollin' down the hill, far as the elders sayin' this
café gets me too involved with the outside world," she
continued in a low, steady voice. "Not much of a
stretch to say it led to puttin' the place up for sale—
and you've admitted to puttin' the bee under Hiram's
bonnet. You're the only one I told, ya see."

Leah's features stiffened beneath her kerchief. She
tossed a couple of honey jars so hard they nearly
broke in the bin. "Here ya go again, Miriam, turnin'
things around to make it look like I'm pickin' on ya,
when—"

"But you're not listenin', are ya? I've already said I
forgive ya, Sister." Miriam's pulse fluttered in her
throat as she righted the overturned jars. "It's nobody's

fault Tiffany showed up lookin' like the Devil's own daughter that first time. I'm just happy she stopped in again last week, lookin' . . . not so hard. Wantin' to *know* us, as family."

Miriam grabbed Leah's tanned hand. "To me, that's rainbow enough to compensate for all this other stuff that's pourin' down on me right now. For once, I'd just like ya to be *happy*, and to see my silver linin'— even if ya can't feel it for yourself."

Leah grabbed both ends of the bin to carry it into the kitchen. Her bare feet slapped across the tile floor. "Are ya sayin' I'm a gossip? Disagreeable and hard to get along with?" she challenged.

Miriam cleared her throat, praying for diplomacy that wouldn't dilute her whole purpose here. "Remember how testy Mamm got with her headaches? And how you always had to be in charge of us littler kids while she was restin'—and then ya had to rush around, reddin' up the house and cookin' supper before Dat got home?" she asked in a faraway voice. Then she smiled. "Well, ya can leave that behind ya now! I'm not four anymore, and ya don't have to act like you're my mother! How's that for *gut* news?"

Her sister's expression shifted from denial to doubt to disbelief. She twisted the lids off the honey jars while Miriam fetched a wide-bottom funnel to fill them. "Puh! What's this got to do with Hiram buyin'—"

"Who says that's gonna happen? And who says my reunion with Rebecca's gonna be my ruination?" Miriam countered quietly. "Maybe you don't wanna change the way things are between us, but I thought I'd give it a shot. Okay, I'm done workin' on ya now!"

Miriam inhaled the musky scent of the amber honey, which Leah stored in covered crocks in her root cellar. She'd have to spin this chat faster, in a better direction, if they were to come out ahead . . . sisters and *friends*. "Thanks for bringin' this honey today, Leah. Calls for oatmeal pancakes and biscuits—and maybe a French toast special this mornin'. That'll make Rhoda mighty happy."

"*Jah*, my boys, too. They love eatin' their breakfast here, I'll have ya know." Her voice still had an edge to it, yet her features softened. She cut sections of honeycomb to drop into the jars while Miriam held the funnel. "And maybe I should be happy about *that*, instead of feelin' miffed that you've always been the better cook. Maybe I'll miss that extra time workin' my gardens, if Hiram turns ya out of here . . . because I'll have to make my men breakfast and noon dinner again."

"*Jah*, there's that."

They finished filling the jars in silence, but it felt like they were sisters working together instead of going head-to-head. Miriam wiped the sticky jars with a wet rag. She'd soothed the scabs on her soul that her sister so enjoyed picking at. *She* felt better anyway, which wasn't a bad way to start another morning at the Sweet Seasons.

"Been a long time since I thought back to Mamm's headaches. Didn't know them as migraines then, but that's what they were," Leah recalled aloud. "And if you're sayin' I act that same way—"

"Oh, not near so bad!" Miriam corrected. She slipped into her padded mitts and opened an oven door. "Just sayin' we can let go of that whole time. Lotta water under the bridge in thirty years, and we might as well go with the flow, ain't so?"

Leah looked around them, at the modern gas

cookstoves and the freezers that hummed against the wall. She stepped out of the way as Miriam quickly placed the bubbly hot pies on the center island. Then she stood gazing at the golden crusts, sparkly with sugar, and the leaf-shaped cutouts oozing with amber or ruby filling. "You always did turn out a pertier pie than anybody else, Sis."

"And you get the gardens to yield up the best veggies—and your honey's what *makes* my biscuits, truth be told. Seems like we're both doin' what we were made for, and that's a *gut* thing." Miriam inhaled the aromas of her morning's work, a sweet satisfaction indeed. She fetched a shallow box from the recycling stack by the door. Then she lined it with a dish towel and set the most perfect of the dozen pies in it, to hand across the counter.

"For me?" Leah blinked then grinned like a kid. "But I thought these were for—"

"Peach was always your favorite. Who better to enjoy it while it's fresh?"

As her older sister started back home in the wagon, waving, Miriam chuckled. For once, she'd had the last word—left Leah without a comeback. Even if nothing else of consequence came of this day, she'd gotten it off to a fine start.

Chapter 25

It was nearly ten fifteen when Miriam noticed him at the back table: Derek Shotwell closed his eyes over a mouthful of honey-drizzled biscuit, as though he'd passed through the pearly gates to sit at heaven's own breakfast table. He chatted with Rachel as she topped off his coffee, then protested amiably as Rhoda stabbed him a steaming oatmeal pancake from the batch she was adding to the buffet table.

Could he tell how her girls enjoyed their guests? They didn't know he was the banker who held their future in his hands . . . who pulled the purse strings, as far as how the sale of the building went. Though she could support herself for years on the money—even after she made a sizeable donation to the common fund, as Hiram would expect—Miriam prayed this young executive understood the difference between her love for this café and the income it generated.

Should she go out and talk with him? Miriam smoothed her apron, looking around for what needed to be done next. She decided to slice the pork loins so Naomi could stir up their gravy, and let Mr. Shotwell do whatever he'd intended when he came here. He'd surely found her ledger by now—and maybe she'd made a silly mistake leaving it behind, trying to influence this transaction. But it was too late for second-guessing.

"How's that pork lookin'?" Naomi inquired. She bustled to the stove with thickly sliced onions to add to a potful of boiling carrots and potatoes.

Miriam looked up from her woolgathering. "Real *gut*. Not a speck of waste and hardly any fat."

"Might be better if ya sliced against the grain, *jah*?"

She let out an exasperated gasp and changed directions with her sharp knife. "Glad ya caught me when ya did. Don't know what I was thinkin' . . . well, *jah*, I do," she admitted sheepishly. "That youngish-lookin' man in the necktie? He's the loan officer from the New Haven bank."

Naomi's brown eyes widened as she gazed through the serving window. "*Gut* thing he's likin' the food, ain't so? Why's he here, so soon after you and Hiram—"

"Don't know. But I'm suspectin' we'll soon find out."

Together they lifted the remaining loins from the pan so Naomi could make the gravy from the broth. Miriam fought the urge to stare at Derek as she sliced the pork . . . heard the *ding!* of the old cash register by the door . . . turned down the fire under that pot of vegetables. Anything to keep busy rather than fret about what might happen to her beloved bakery.

"Miriam, that meal was *almost* as delightful as your daughters."

She looked up. Derek stood at the serving window, grinning, with her black ledger on the counter in front of him. By some stroke of grace or luck he'd come well after the hour when the bishop ate: she had *not* looked forward to stammering out an explanation to Hiram for leaving her restaurant records at the bank yesterday. "Let me wash my hands. I'll be right out."

"No hurry. Looks like you're transitioning into lunch."

"*Jah*—and this is Naomi Brenneman. She's my cook—and her boy Micah was the carpenter I told ya about," Miriam went on, hoping she didn't sound desperate. "Can ya imagine it? Still best of friends, even after all the spills and ruined food and broken dishes between us."

"I doubt you've had many of those things go wrong. It's a pleasure to meet you, Naomi—a real treat to eat here and observe the way your business works, too." Derek nodded, turning to gaze around the nearly empty dining room.

Something inside her prodded Miriam to be bold. She'd left her ledger so this loan officer would come back with it, after all. "If ya want to see somethin' *really* special, have Rachel take ya next door to where Micah's been buildin' some rooms," she remarked. "But it's a secret he's keepin' from me and Rhoda until he's all finished, so ya gotta promise not to tell me what-all he's been doin' up there!"

Rachel brightened and set the bin of dirty dishes on the back counter. "*Jah*, come on up, Mr. Shotwell. I've never seen the likes of this anywhere, and I think you'll like it, too."

As they quickly crossed the lot to the smithy, Naomi smiled. "*Gut* to see our Rachel beamin' again. She and my boy seem to've patched up their squabbles over Tiffany."

"*Jah*, I believe they have."

"But I know you, Miriam Lantz. And that kitty-cat grin means ya been up to somethin'." Naomi set down the big bowl of cooked macaroni she was about to make cheese sauce for. "If that banker's here to tell us the place is already sold out from under us—"

"Not worryin' about that anymore. Said a lotta prayers and told God I was leavin' it all up to Him—" Miriam playfully raised an eyebrow. Hope bubbled within her like yeast in warm water, even though it seemed too early to hear an answer. "But ya know *gut* and well I didn't *forget* my ledger yesterday."

"Ah. And Hiram didn't notice." A sweet smile stole over Naomi's face. "Shoulda known to have faith in you, Miriam—and shoulda let God have his way with this situation, like you did. Goodness knows my frettin' hasn't improved it one little bit."

They worked alongside each other, Miriam peeling big, orange sweet potatoes as Naomi made the cheese sauce in her Dutch oven. Voices drifted from the smithy's open windows . . . Rachel showing the banker all around. The words weren't clear, but the tone seemed as light and happy as a summer's breeze. A good sign. And when Derek Shotwell stepped back into the kitchen, his expression defied description.

"That was the most creative—the *coolest*—conversion of space—" The banker stopped midsentence as though he couldn't think of enough wonderful things to say. When he grinned, he looked like the littlest boy in his office photographs. "Mrs. Lantz—Mrs. Brenneman—"

"Oh, but we're Miriam and Naomi to you, sir!"

"—you have an awesome surprise in store when

Micah unveils his project!" Derek confirmed. "And after I've talked with you, Miriam, I'm going to catch up with Micah, too. The bank's renovating a pair of fourplexes built in the seventies—senior housing— and what he's doing next door is, well, it's *perfect!* It's so—so innovative it'll knock the committee's socks off!"

Naomi shrugged, her face aglow. "*Jah*, my middle boy's always been the smarts behind the Brenneman cabinet business. The shop's just up the way, first right off the highway and down about a quarter mile."

Miriam glanced out into the dining room. "I'll put the fire under these sweet potatoes and we'll talk for a bit, Mr. Shotwell."

"That's Derek, please."

"Can I get ya anythin'? Just made fresh tea, and there's peach or cherry pie—"

"Can't hold another bite." He rubbed his stomach, smiling. "But I know those pies are like none my wife brings home from the store."

Now *there* was a gap to be filled. "I'll send one with ya, then. Cherry or peach?"

Derek's jaw dropped as though he'd never heard such an offer. "Any chance I could have . . . half of each kind?"

"For sure and for certain!" Miriam giggled as she grabbed her knife and a clean aluminum pie pan. "This way, you've got somethin' for everybody—"

"You think I'm going to *share* that?"

"—and those who take the pieces where the two fruits meet get a taste of both!" Quickly she arranged three wedges of each flavor in the pan and then put it in a carryout box with a clear lid. "Now—I've done my best, givin' you a fine surprise today, Derek. Your turn to do me the same favor whilst we talk about our business, ain't so?"

It was a cheeky sort of challenge, yet Miriam felt too good about this young man to restrain herself. If he liked Micah's work so much and was going to hire him for those fourplex renovations, hadn't a lot of good already come from this day? She firmly believed that one favor begat another—and it worked best if she gave first.

"I'll see what I can do about that," Derek replied in a more reserved voice. He accepted the heavy pie pan with a wistful look in his eyes. "You know, of course, that the sale of this property isn't as neatly sliced—or nearly as sweet—as the pies you make. Wish it was, though."

Into the dining room they walked, while Miriam's pulse thrummed faster. *Whatever he tells me, God, help me listen and follow Your way for me.*

Derek pulled out a chair for her and then sat across the cleared table. He ran an appreciative finger over its glossy surface. "The workmanship—the *love* in this place—makes me so glad I stopped by instead of relying on the appraiser's notes," he began earnestly. He folded his hands on top of her ledger, studying her with a kind smile. "We've received an offer on your building, Miriam."

The news slammed into her. She willed herself to breathe.

"And while this potential buyer insisted I not give out his name, he called around one o'clock yesterday to say he wanted it—and then he asked me to sit on his offer for a while."

"Ah." She cleared her throat. "Another secret. Been

a lot of those this summer. But at one o'clock, only three of us knew the place was for sale, ain't so?"

Derek's grin twitched. "That's correct. His offer was, shall I say . . . *less* than what we're asking."

"We Amish are a thrifty lot."

The banker's laugh rang out in the dining room. "Miriam, you're a gem! And after I saw these impressive figures," he added, tapping her ledger, "I didn't feel right about calling it a done deal, anyway. And lo and behold, around four o'clock I got another offer!"

"Jah?" She leaned forward, holding his gaze. "But you're not namin' any names."

Derek adjusted his glasses, still chuckling. "Please—I don't want to undermine your bishop's leadership or seem to make light of your beliefs, because I greatly respect the Amish. I documented both offers, however. And I liked it that this second person didn't ask how much the previous offer was. He went twenty thousand higher because he believes you belong here, serving God by serving such good food."

Tom Hostetler, maybe? He stood by me that day Hiram looked at the ledger . . . looked in on me after Jesse passed. How much milk would he have to sell—how many cows could he buy for his dairy—with that much money?

Miriam's hand fluttered to her racing heart. "Thanks ever so much for tellin' me this, Derek," she murmured. "I believed God would bring me a *gut* answer to this predicament, and—"

From out of nowhere, a perky trumpet tune began to play. "Excuse me, I forgot to turn this off," the loan officer said as he glanced at the screen of his cell phone. "Then again, I'd better take this call. Back in a few."

Miriam sat absolutely still in her chair, leaning on

the table as this new information sank in: Hiram had made a low offer and intended to make her *wait*, not knowing if she was in or out of business. It would do no good to feel insulted . . . and there was no need, since someone else had offered more. Who'd've thought this would turn into an auction rather than a cut-and-dried sale?

And while the bishop would not like it that one of the other brethren had stepped forward to keep the Sweet Seasons up and running, her heart fluttered at this unexpected development. The grapevine proclaimed that she and Hiram would be getting hitched soon, so . . . was this Tom's way of sidetracking that? Showing his support the only way he could?

As Derek came inside again, she looked up from her musings. The banker seemed as pleased as when he'd gone outside—maybe a little more. "Would you believe someone else has just called the bank, wanting to buy your building?"

Who else would it be? Zeb Schrock, keeping the peace with Mary, Eva, and Priscilla by—

"This one's from out in left field, though, because this buyer's not Amish. He asked the price and then said he'd pay it, *boom*, without missing a beat!" Derek sat across from her again, focused intently on her. "You must have some awesome connections, Miriam, because if this isn't God answering your prayers, I don't know what else to call it!"

Not Amish? Hiram wouldn't like that one little bit . . . and what if this buyer wanted to use the building for something other than her bakery café? The People hated to see parts and parcels of their property getting into the hands of Englishers. Miriam reminded herself to have some faith . . . to trust in that happiness she still saw on Derek Shotwell's face.

"Again, my intention is not to undercut your bishop's wisdom, but *now* we're doing business," he insisted. He leaned his elbows on the table and placed his chin in his hands, watching her as he considered what he'd say next. "I didn't feel right about not advertising such prime property, nor did I like the . . . interaction I saw in my office, while Hiram did all the talking about *your* livelihood. But I understood your silence, Miriam. No mistaking it for ignorance, either, after looking at your ledger."

He slipped the black book across the table to her. "As a loan officer, I consider it only right to go along with an offer that fulfills a seller's demands. And as a guy who gets a little cagey sometimes, I see this as a way to prevent those two Amish bidders from falling into the same worldly trap they were saving *you* from, Miriam."

A smile tickled her lips.

"Just maybe," Derek went on, teasing a little, "this will serve as that lesson in humility Hiram was aiming for, except it's pointed at him this time. And I will take sole responsibility for handling this highly unusual sale, Miriam. Again, I mean absolutely no disrespect here."

Miriam chuckled softly. "I like the way you think, Derek! So . . . are ya tellin' me this person's name, since he's not Plain?"

"Nope. We'll let Hiram have that point for a bargaining chip." He rose from the table and extended his hand. "Trust me a little longer. It'll all work out just like we've talked about."

As she shook his hand, she nodded. Just knowing she wouldn't be beholden to Hiram was reason to celebrate.

"Derek?" she called after him.

He turned, holding his pie in both hands, his secretive grin still in place. "Yes, Miriam? How may I help you further?"

"In a couple weeks—August fifteenth—we're celebratin' the girls' birthdays. Cake, homemade ice cream, and we'd like ya to join us!" Miriam hugged her ledger to her chest, feeling that impish impulse that often urged her to overstep or speak out of turn. "Micah's gonna show off the apartment in the smithy then, as part of the occasion, and well—if we could find out by then who's buyin' the buildin'—?"

Bless him, Derek's smile warmed her. "Absolutely. Perfect day for such an announcement, and it gives me time to see that all's in order and arrange for the closing."

The little bell jangled as he left. Miriam stood for a moment in the stillness of the dining room, surrounded by the Brenneman boys' sturdy tables and chairs . . . the Schrocks' quilted hangings on the walls . . . the peaceful sense of well-being she always felt in this room where she fed her friends. Who could've imagined this sequence of events, the way Derek's visit had ended? She didn't know who would own the building, yet her spirits soared.

She felt their gazes from the kitchen: Naomi, Rhoda, and Rachel had cleaned up and were waiting in a tight row behind the center island. Their expectant faces were the sweetest things she'd ever seen.

"Let's go home, girls," Miriam suggested. "It's been a *gut* day! I'll be along after I talk to Mary a bit. She's been hoverin' in the hall, ya know—and she'll want to know about our news."

Miriam waved them on, a bright idea shining in her mind. Their party would be a perfect day for an announcement! When the kitchen door had closed behind her girls and her cook, she quickly passed through the sunlit hall to the other side of the building. Mary Schrock and Zeb's aunts, Eva and Priscilla, were redding up the shop as though they'd been waiting for her—even if they would deny eavesdropping while Derek was here.

"Well, just that quick," Miriam said with an emphatic *clap!* of her hands, "somebody snapped up the buildin'! Haven't heard it from the horse's mouth, but I'm for sure and for certain we'll be stayin' put, here in our shops!"

Eva brightened immediately. "I was so afraid somebody'd be turnin' us out—"

"Zeb tried *so* hard to talk Hiram out of this," Mary chimed in. "But the bishop said this was for the sake of your very soul, Miriam. We couldn't afford to buy the place ourselves, so—"

"My soul's costin' him more than he bargained for." Miriam felt bubblier by the moment as she considered the outcome of her talk with Derek.

"I'll believe it when I see it." Priscilla, always as starchy as the doilies she crocheted, straightened a stack of quilted place mats with stiff, precise movements. "The way I hear it, Hiram intends to teach us *all* a lesson—especially those of us without husbands," she added with a pointed look at Eva and Miriam. "It's no secret he's been huntin' up a new mother for his children. Which explains why he eats so many meals in the Sweet Seasons."

Refusing to have her bubble burst, Miriam blew a new one. "Hiram's been outbid. But if any of ya breathes a *word* of that and it gets back to him, I'll know exactly who blabbed."

The three quilters exchanged exclamations, their thin eyebrows raised. Miriam wondered what it must be like for these women to spend every waking—and sleeping—moment together, because Zeb's two aunts lived with him and Mary. Eva, a *maidel* who'd long ago given up finding a man—if she'd ever looked very hard—glanced over the top of her rimless glasses. "Don't suppose you'll tell us who our new landlord's to be, then?"

"Can't tell ya what I don't know." Miriam headed toward the racks of fabric in the back of the shop. "But with the girls turnin' twenty-one in a couple weeks, I'm thinkin' new dresses would be a nice touch for the party we're throwin'. Hope ya can come."

"Twenty-one? How on earth did that happen?" Mary mused aloud. Her gaze followed Miriam's progress past bolt after bolt of calico, gingham, and other specialty prints for quilts. "On beyond that rack you'll see the new shipment of twill and chambray that's right nice for dresses. Don't s'pose you'll be sewin' *three* alike?"

Again Miriam's lips twitched. How was it these Schrocks never ran out of gossip and speculation? "Invited our Rebecca to the party already, *jah*. And I'm thinkin' she'll come, too! Don't even care if she's

wearin' those black jeans with her tattoos showin'."
She grinned at the three quilters watching her. "Her
last visit was a real joy, on account of how she's tryin'
to know us and our ways without any finger-pointin'
or makin' fun of us."

Miriam ran a hand over the twill, glanced at the
price, and then ignored her usual impulse to go for
something cheaper. She skipped over the black and
the navy, too, grasping a bolt of deep orchid and one
of dusty blue that would complement the girls' eyes.
"Twelve yards of each," she said when she'd carried
them to the counter. "Gonna have my own little
sewin' frolic—but not a word about this to the girls!
It's a surprise for their big day."

Chapter 26

The days flew by, filled with tour buses at lunchtime and extra orders for pies, rolls, and cakes for family reunions and weddings. Miriam found herself humming most of the time, just knowing the little secret about the building's new owner and her own fate, which looked bright indeed.

Lord, help me learn that lesson in humility—Hiram was right to point out that I can be outspoken and mighty proud of the work I love to do, she prayed. When the bishop came into the Sweet Seasons most mornings for his breakfast, she added: *And Lord, I thank You for Derek and his forthright way of doin' business, and for givin' me the what-all to keep my life runnin' along. Keep me on the path You'd have me follow.*

"You're lookin' mighty perky this mornin', Mrs. Lantz," Naomi remarked as they added raisins and dried apricots to day-old bread cubes for bread pudding. "Hiram's out there smilin' like the cat that got the canary, too. Any connections there I ought to know about?"

Miriam chuckled. "Not connections like *you're*

thinkin'," she said in a low voice. "Two sides to a secret, ya know—them that knows, and them that don't—and I can't tell ya how *gut* it feels to be on the knowin' side of this one. Can't promise a hundred percent that we'll be here come fall, but we'll be all right, Naomi. You and me'll still be cookin' and bakin'."

"Des gut, jah," her cook murmured gratefully. Then her brown eyes sparkled. "About time to be bakin' the birthday cakes for your girls? If they want the strawberry cream cake—"

"Jah, that's still their favorite."

"—it's even better comin' from the freezer. And we can stick them away, outta sight."

"Gut idea! Rachel and Rhoda're goin' to a birthday party for two of Leah's girls tomorrow night, so I've already told them I'm gonna stay late to bake pies."

Naomi thought about this as they poured scalded milk over the bread cubes and raisins. "Need to be home for dinner tonight, but I'll put the cakes in the oven for ya before I leave. How many ya think we'll need?"

"It's a big birthday and we've got lots to celebrate. And there's no such thing as too much strawberry cream cake, come the next day's lunch menu." Miriam calculated quickly and then felt a surge of happy gratitude. "I'm thinkin' we oughtta invite *everybody!* And have it here! Folks'll want to see the apartment Micah's designed—"

"And it saves ya all that reddin' up at home."

"—and we've got tables and lots of chairs here," Miriam finished. "And ya know what? I feel like life's ready to jump forward like a big ole frog! And that's somethin' to be thankful for no matter what we hear about the café sellin', ain't so?"

Naomi set down her mixing spoon to wrap her arms around Miriam. "Ya look happier than I've ever seen ya, dearie. And for that, I'm mighty thankful, too!"

"Now promise us ya won't be on your feet bakin' all evenin'," Rhoda insisted as they hung the damp towels from the morning's dishes. "Hate thinkin' Rachel and I'll be eatin' a *gut* dinner and then enjoyin' our friends while you're here workin', Mamma."

Miriam smiled over the piecrust she was rolling out. "Won't be bakin' all that long, really, on account of how you girls kept the food movin' today so's I could fill all the special orders. *Denki* for that! Go have a *gut* time with your cousins and friends!"

A few minutes later the two girls were out the back door, striding down the lane to the house. "*Gut* to see those two chatterboxes so happy," Naomi remarked as she entered the pantry. "Thought they'd never leave, though!"

"*Jah*, they have a way of frettin' over how I'll spend my time without them!" Miriam fetched eggs from the refrigerator along with the defrosting strawberries she'd hidden. She set out the canola oil and then took three big sheet-cake pans from the shelf. "*Denki* for startin' these birthday cakes, Naomi. Meanwhile, I'm gonna cut out their new dresses so's I can sneak the pieces home to sew while I'm by myself."

The longer tables in the dining room were perfect for laying out the fabric, which she'd hidden away in the pantry. Miriam grinned as she slipped her sewing scissors and pins from a package she'd tucked behind big bags of flour. By the time Naomi put the cakes in, she'd nearly finished cutting cape dresses and aprons from the blue twill.

"I'll be headin' home to Ezra now," her cook called out. "I set the timer so's ya won't forget the cakes. Say—that color's right perty! Rachel and Rhoda'll like it—but they don't dress the same, ain't so?"

"Got this orchid, too," Miriam said as she nodded toward the other fabric. "A nice color for near summer's end, I thought."

"*Jah*, I like that one even better! See ya tomorrow mornin'."

"Same time, same place," Miriam quipped. Then she grinned, listening for the closing of the back door. It was rare to keep a secret from her best friend, but Naomi didn't realize she was cutting *three* new dresses from each color! As she smoothed the deep orchid twill along the length of a table, her pulse thrummed . . . she recalled kettle cloth in a pretty shade of clay on Mary's shelves, as well as a dark fawn that had caught her eye. Could be, if all went well at the party, she'd be sewing up a few more dresses . . .

When the timer buzzed, Miriam took the four big sheet cakes from the ovens. She inhaled their heavenly strawberry fragrance. The edges were just pulling away from the pans and the tops were a rich, golden overlay on the pink cakes. By the time she finished pinning the pattern pieces, the cakes would be cooled enough to hide away—

"Say, gal, smells a lot better in here than where I've been workin'!"

Miriam glanced up to see a male form highlighted in the back door. "Tom, I believe you're right!" she teased the dairy farmer. "These're for the girls' party next week. I sure hope you'll come!"

"Why would I miss a party?" His smile looked downright shy as he held up two gallon-size ice-cream pails. "Was thinkin' ya might want some fresh cream to make your ice cream, so I brought it on over. And if you'd like a hand at crankin' that freezer—"

"And why would I turn down help like that?" she teased. "Told Naomi we'll be invitin' anybody who wants to come, so we'll be makin' up several batches. *Denki* for thinkin' of us, Tom."

Why was he here, really? Miriam took the cream to the refrigerator, sensing this man had more than homemade ice cream on his mind . . . and that he hadn't come here in his role as a preacher, either. "Your boys doin' all right these days? Don't see much of Pete nor Rudy now that they're makin' carriages— and I'm thinkin' Lavinia and Sarah must be doin' well with their families, too?"

"*Jah*, my girls're puttin' up the corn and green beans—got big gardens, ya know—and helpin' their men with the hayin' and chorin'," he replied quietly. "Sundays they bring over dinner and enough for me to eat on awhile, and they change out the clothes they've washed for what I've dirtied. Perty quick to notice I'm not one for keepin' a real tidy house, but, well—" He shrugged ruefully. "Never figured on havin' to do that. Got a letter from Lettie's lawyer this mornin' . . . tellin' me about divorce proceedin's."

The poor man looked like he'd lost his last friend along with his wife. His shoulders sagged and his sigh stumbled over a lump in his throat. Divorce was unheard-of among the Amish: she didn't know of a single couple who'd cut their ties. It meant, for sure and for certain, that Lettie would be excommunicated, while Tom would be unable to remarry until she passed on. And who knew when that might be?

Miriam put her hands on his shoulders, keeping a proper distance between them. "That's gotta be awful hard, Tom, and I'm sorry this has gone so wrong for ya," she murmured. "If there's somethin' I can do—or if the girls can come by and redd up for ya, or—"

"Nah, didn't come to cry on your shoulder, Miriam, but *denki* for the kind thoughts." He stepped away self-consciously. "Just saw you were workin' a little longer today, and . . . well, I wanted ya to know I put in an offer on your buildin'. No sense in a *gut* cook and shopkeeper like yourself worryin' about who's gonna keep ya—I mean—"

What *did* he mean? Miriam's pulse skittered while the man before her composed himself. Bless him, Tom looked a little the worse for wear in trousers and a blue shirt that could use a pressing, but his pink cheeks told her he'd gone beyond what he'd intended to say.

"Probably best if ya don't mention it to the bishop," he continued in a low voice, "and I don't want ya thinkin' I've got ideas about takin' care of your business or—I mean, what man in his right mind *wouldn't* want to look after *you*, Miriam? But I—" He stopped to shake his head in exasperation. "Mostly I'm makin' a mess of this. But if I have anythin' to say about it, ya won't be tossed outta your café. With all due respect to Hiram and the will of the Lord, I just didn't like it when he told me he was buyin' the buildin', sayin' it was for your own *gut!*"

Closing her eyes, Miriam thought fast. Tom was baring his soul—his intentions, perhaps, for the day when he was free to look for another wife—even though Lettie was a healthy sort who'd live a long while yet. The fact that Tom was an elder among them made this situation sting even more. But knowing what she knew . . .

"Can't thank ya enough for doin' that, Tom," she murmured. "And in the same spirit of respectin' the bishop's intentions, I'm gonna tell ya a third fella's made an offer, too. So now you and I have our own secret, on account of how Hiram's amount has been topped twice."

Tom's eyes widened. "Who else would—?"

"Don't know the particulars, except he's not Amish. And the banker seems mighty happy about the whole thing—which tells me the mystery man intends to keep my bakin' business here, too."

"Ah. Well, then . . ."

Miriam smiled. The relief around his eyes and forehead was a sign she'd done the right thing, telling him. "That was a fine favor ya did for me, Tom. Just didn't want ya left hangin' when so much money's involved, and you've got your herd to manage and barns to maintain and whatnot." She squeezed the sturdy hand that still held hers. "I feel real *gut* havin' ya for a friend, Tom. And I'll say it again: if there's anythin' I can do for ya, you let me know."

"I'll do that, Miriam. Appreciate ya tellin' me straight-out about this. You're a *gut* woman and a fine friend." With a grin, he bussed her cheek. "Better be gettin' on home before I stumble over my tongue any more today."

"Appreciate that cream, and"—she snatched a carry-out box from the stack on the counter and then cut a big square of bread pudding to go in it—"I'll be here Saturday evenin' while the girls are at a quiltin' frolic, so if you'd like to crank the ice-cream freezer—"

"Count on it! Bless ya, Miriam, this bread puddin'll be a real treat." He smiled as he pushed on the door. "Ya turned around a day that's laid me mighty low. It's another of your gifts, doin' that for everybody."

And wasn't that a fine compliment? As Miriam covered the cake pans with foil to freeze them and then carefully folded the dress pieces she'd pinned, her heart sighed with contentment. As she was leaving, Micah pulled up with several cans of paint and a roll of vinyl flooring in the back of his wagon.

"Thinkin' I'll be finished upstairs in a couple more evenin's," he remarked with a sly smile. "Appreciate your havin' that banker fella take a look, too. He's hired us to refurbish some apartments usin' my new wall systems, so we'll be gettin' right on that project. *Gut* money—and more jobs to come, I'm guessin'."

"Can't wait to see it, Micah." Miriam grinned and glanced at the materials in his wagon . . . soothing natural shades of blue and green and pale yellow. "Sounds like we're all gonna be busy and happy. I'm likin' that!"

"*Jah.* Gonna be real *gut* for all of us. You have a fine evenin' now, Miriam."

She knew a dismissal when she heard one. It was a fine thing to know this young man was as eager and enthusiastic about his work—and his shop's future—as she was.

As Miriam started up the lane, sewing supplies tucked into her large canvas tote, she beamed back at the sun, just now setting behind the rows of sweet corn at the back of her garden. She spotted three fat striped watermelons and several acorn squash among the fan-shaped leaves near the smithy where her Jesse used to work at his forge. Maybe . . . just maybe another farrier would want to ply his trade there someday . . .

Thank ya, Lord, for more blessin's than I can count—more than my heart can hold. It's gonna be a wonderful-gut birthday for my girls . . . and I thank ya for that, too.

Chapter 27

Saturday the fifteenth of August dawned bright and breezy, with a brisk breakfast business at the Sweet Seasons. Rachel smiled at the familiar scene: while Mamma decorated two sheet cakes for a wedding in Morning Star, Naomi turned bacon on the griddle and Rhoda plated orders for the day's breakfast casserole special. Big signs on the outside of the café announced that they'd be closed, come ten o'clock, and that the birthday party began at two.

"Guess we'll be seein' ya later for cake," Nate Kanagy remarked as Rachel set his plate of pancakes in front of him.

"*Jah*, and ice cream, too! Four flavors!"

"And you've gotta go next door to see what Micah's been doin' in his *spare* time," her sister remarked as she placed heaping plates of smothered hash browns in front of Bram and the three Brenneman boys. Rhoda tweaked Micah's nose and then giggled when he blushed. "Not like any other place you've ever seen. Or so they tell me."

"Gonna make everybody ooh and aah," Rachel confirmed. She couldn't wait to see Mamma's and Rhoda's faces when they viewed their new rooms in a couple of hours. Yesterday she'd made up the Murphy beds with new sheets and quilts from her own cedar chest so the apartment would look homey and complete—ready for whenever the two of them wanted to stay there. Again she grinned, because this event marked one more milestone on the way to her own days as Micah's bride, starting out in the home they would soon repaint and freshen for their new life together.

The bell above the door jangled, and she went to the front counter to welcome a young woman alone. Rachel paused and then grinned. "Tiffany? I—well, I hardly knew ya! Happy birthday, Sister!"

Tiffany grinned shyly. Her blue eyes sparkled in a face that looked sweet and natural, like the one Rachel saw in her own little mirror each morning. "Happy birthday back atcha!" she replied. "Felt a little funny, leaving the house this way—"

"But don't ya look perty!" Rhoda crowed as she rushed over. "Come to the kitchen! Mamma'll be real glad to see ya! So how's it feelin' to be twenty-one?"

The young woman between them chuckled. "Perty *gut*," she replied with an exaggerated accent. "I—I won't look and sound like you, but it's awesome to be celebrating my real birthday for the first time, with sisters I didn't know I had until now."

"Well, now, would ya looky here, Miriam!" Naomi called out. She set her pan of hash browns on the granite countertop. "Ya just gave your mamma the best present of all, I'm thinkin'. *Gut* to have ya here for the big day, Tiffany."

"*Jah*, I should say so!" Mamma laid down her pastry

tube to wipe her sugary hands on her apron. "And would ya look at this girl, so fresh and perty today! Happy birthday, honey-bug. It's so *gut* to have ya home with us!"

Rachel swallowed hard. Except for the low purr of the exhaust fan, the kitchen went quiet. Their mother had wrapped her arms around Tiffany and then her shining brown eyes beckoned for her and Rhoda to join in . . . an expanded version of the hug the three of them had shared ever since Dat had passed. Mamma looked so happy, why—the strings of her kapp quivered with her excitement as she gazed at Tiffany's pale blue top and white jeans . . . at the short brown hair now combed back from her face in soft, feathery layers.

"Um, Dad'll be along later for the party," she said in a hesitant voice. "He—he's really excited about coming—to meet Rachel and Rhoda, and to . . ."

What wasn't she saying? Rachel joined in the final squeeze they all shared before they separated, curious yet excited as she hadn't been for a long time. "Gonna be a real special day, Tiffany, with the both of ya here—"

"Can I—can I dress like you? Just for the day, I mean?" she blurted. "I don't think I could ever live Plain, but—if you won't take it the wrong way—I thought it might be fun for us all to look like sisters."

"Oh, that's the best idea!" Mamma replied with a clap of her hands. "So I'll tell ya your surprise now! For your birthday, girls, I sewed up new dresses, and it just so happens there's three alike! And nice new kapps to go with them. What do ya think of that?"

"Won't that be a sight!" Naomi hurried over to

sling an arm around Mamma's shoulders. "The Lantz triplets, all together again. Can't wait to see it myself."

The rest of the morning flew by: Naomi fixed a plate so Tiffany could eat in the kitchen, watching while Mamma finished decorating her cakes. Rachel bused tables and invited all the locals to come back later, while Rhoda ran the check-out and welcomed incoming customers. Even when Hiram sat down with Tom Hostetler, Gabe Glick, and Reuben Reihl, Rachel felt bubbly with energy. What a party it would be, with she and her two sisters dressed alike for the first time since—well, since that day they'd worn those little pink dresses Mamma had tucked away in the trunk. And wouldn't *that* give folks something to talk about?

"*Gut* mornin', Bishop. And what'll ya have today?" she asked cheerily.

Not even Hiram's speculative gaze dampened her mood. He stroked his beard, long and dark with spangles of gray like tinsel. "Bring me the special with a side of ham. My friends here'll have the same—and bring me the check. With a pot of fresh coffee."

"*Jah*, I can do that. Back in a few." As Rachel strode toward the coffeemaker she noted the surprised looks on the other three men's faces, as though they, too, wondered what the occasion was. Two or three of them ate with Hiram probably four mornings each week, but the bishop usually nodded cordially when one of the other elders offered to buy his meal.

"Ready for the big party?" Tom asked as she poured their first cups of coffee. "Nearly wore out my crankin' arm the past few afternoons, makin' all four kinds of ice cream your mamma wanted."

"*Jah*, and we hope you fellas'll join us for some, too.

We're mighty pleased that Tiffany, our sister, has come early," she replied. "Gonna be a big day."

"No doubt," Hiram replied with a nod.

"Wouldn't miss it," Tom agreed. He looked perkier than he had for days, smiling quietly over his first sip of coffee.

And what was all this mysterious talk? As though each man had his own . . . secret. Rachel smiled to herself. No matter what happened today, she sensed it would mark a point in time they'd not soon forget. She glanced at the clock, eager for the hands to circle it: nearly nine. Almost time for the breakfast shift to end so the celebration could begin!

"Tiffany, look at ya! Why, except for the shorter hair in front, ya could pass for one of us!" Rhoda offered her the hand mirror as they finished dressing in her room. What a treat, to giggle like schoolgirls and outfit their sister in a crisp new cape dress and apron exactly like their own: its V-shaped cape of matching blue fit at her shoulders and tucked down into the belt of her white apron, front and back, to display a figure that was identical to theirs, as well.

"She *is* one of us," Rachel chirped. "And this shade of dusty blue's the pertiest I've ever seen—and it'll dry on a hanger without needin' ironin'! Quite a nice surprise Mamma's pulled on us. What I can't figure is when she had the time to sew them!"

Rhoda's heart swelled. The way their newfound sister held the mirror this way and that, to see how her kapp looked . . . how her dress and matching apron draped around her body, well—it was a treat to watch Tiffany seeming so pleased about it all. She was going to college, specializing in computers and other newfangled technology Plain folk knew little about, yet her eyes had a real shine to them.

"Ya look like a whole new you," Rhoda murmured. "And don't be takin' that all wrong—"

"I know I was a huge shock to you when I showed up in my Goth makeup and clothes," she replied. "I— I didn't come that first day to insult you or make fun of you, but I was pretty, um . . . what's that word that means confused, like your world's gone wonky?"

"Ferhoodled?"

"Ferhoodled! Jah!" Tiffany grinned. They turned when the bedroom door creaked open and Mamma poked her head in. "And—just for today—would you call me Rebecca? To my friends I'll always be Tiffany or Tiff, but—well, Rebecca goes with Rachel and Rhoda, and here in Willow Ridge . . . it's a different world."

"It's family," Mamma answered with a happy nod. "And I just wish your *dat* could be here to see the three of ya all together again. You girls're a sight for sore eyes."

A fiercely sweet sadness hovered in the room, but then Mamma brightened again. "Shall we get on back to the café? Gotta clear the tables where the cakes and goodies go, on account of it's almost one fifteen. Micah promised Rhoda and me a private tour of the upstairs before everybody else gets here."

As their mother turned toward the door, Rhoda's jaw dropped. "Mamma! You're wearin' a new dress, too!"

"And if that's not the pertiest shade of purple!" Rachel planted her hands on her hips, raising an eyebrow. "And just when did ya whip up all these new

aprons and dresses, Mamma? And ya coulda told us
you were comin' out in color again!"

"And spoil my surprise? Why would I do that?"
Mamma looked downright shy, watching their reactions. Then a smile stole over her radiant face. "Figured it was time, after two years and a couple months
now. But whatever happens today, don't ya worry
about how it's all gonna turn out with Hiram and the
bakery and what-all. Your mamma's not nearly out of
surprises."

Rhoda considered this as they all walked downstairs and along the lane toward the café. Hiram had
looked mighty smug about something when he'd paid
for breakfast today—but who could guess what the
bishop might have in mind, given the way he'd lec-
tured them about becoming worldly and prideful a
few weeks ago?

Mamma and Rachel were pointing out the various
vegetables growing in the huge garden as they walked,
telling Tiffany—Rebecca for today—about how they
grew most of their own food and put it up for winter,
and how their aunt Leah provided the honey and a
lot of the produce they used in the café this time of
year. In her new dress, their mother looked as fresh as
the clematis blooms climbing the trellis alongside the
porch: yet another sign that things were moving along
for the good in all of their lives.

As they entered through the Sweet Seasons
kitchen, Naomi and the three Schrocks shouted, "Surprise! Happy birthday, girls!"

The tables were covered with fresh white table-
cloths. Pink roses and hydrangea blooms from Mary's
flower garden were arranged in vases. Up near the

pass-through window, a big sheet cake that said HAPPY BIRTHDAY, GIRLS! was displayed on the center table while nuts, mints, and fresh lemonade stood ready beside it.

"Oh, you ladies're too sly!" Mamma exclaimed. "And what a kindness, too, knowin' how busy we were this mornin' durin' the breakfast shift."

Eva, Priscilla, and Mary stood in a row, gawking at them. "Well, would ya look at this," Eva said in an approving voice. "Got three sisters in blue—and a mother like a fresh bouquet of lilacs. *Gut* to see ya lookin' so pert and perky again, Miriam."

"*Jah*, I was hopin' ya had somethin' like this in mind when ya wanted so much of that twill, couple weeks ago," Mary remarked with a smug nod. At the sound of footsteps behind them, she turned. "Hope ya don't mind that Micah gave the three of us and Naomi a sneak peek at the smithy loft. He wanted us to make sure everythin' was just right, like a woman would have it."

And didn't Micah look fine today in his freshly pressed black trousers and a shirt so white it nearly gave off light on its own? His dark blond hair shone and his cheeks were flushed with anticipation. "You two ready for your tour now? Almost time for folks to be gettin' here, and—"

"Mamma, come on!" Rhoda grabbed her mother's hand, giggling, and hurried over to the smithy and up the sturdy new stairs. For weeks now, she'd heard the pounding and sawing over here, and it was time to see what Micah and Rachel had been working on.

And when Rhoda topped the stairs, she just gawked—and Mamma stood alongside her doing the same. Instead of lumber studs, Dat's scrap metal, and a bare-boards floor, they saw one long wall of pale blue and the other painted celery green, with built-in bookcases the color of sunshine. Bright white kitchen cabinets and a sink filled the corner to their left, and a sitting area with cozy chairs and a small sofa sat off to the right.

"I . . . I'd forgotten what clean, new walls looked like," Mamma murmured. She looked ready to cry. "I can't believe ya did all this for Rhoda and me."

"Oh, just wait till ya see *this!*" Rachel grabbed a peg on the end of one bookcase, and as she rolled an entire section of wall toward the center of the large room, Rhoda stepped closer to observe the tracks in the ceiling . . . the way the camouflaged bookcase divider locked into place with a snap. "And looky how your beds work! Ya pull them down, come bedtime, and when ya redd up the room, they fold right back into the walls!"

"The only thing you've gotta decide," Micah added, "is who gets the green bedroom, and who wants the blue one. Got the same sort of setup for the bathroom when ya want to fix yourselves up."

Mamma walked around that section of wall, studying the sleek yellow bathroom and its new fixtures before she walked through the blue half of the loft. Cautiously she lowered the bed on that side, grinning like a little girl with a new toy. "Rhoda, I hope ya like the green room, on account of how I'm the mother, so I'm sayin' this side's mine!"

"*Gut!*" Rhoda replied, "because ya know how I've always thought green was pertier anyway!"

"And Micah!" Mamma rushed over to throw her arms around his waist. "It's even more wonderful-*gut* than I could imagine. And where'd ya come up with such a way to move these walls? No wonder Derek hired ya straightaway to rework those senior apartments!"

Micah returned her hug, grinning across the room at their visiting sister . . . Rebecca for today. "It's like I told ya when I got back from seein' Tiffany, after I'd watched the likes of this on her little bitty computer. Took a couple-three times of seein' it, but I figured out how that guy from China set up his place, and then I made it work here, too. Ran the ductwork and the pipes from downstairs, had my Mennonite friend install your plumbin', and we were all set."

"For sure and for certain, we are." Rhoda slowly strolled the length of the apartment. "Can't wait to move in, Mamma! Say the word, and we'll shift our clothes and whatnot over here. It'll be like livin' in a playhouse, ain't so?"

"Won't take but two shakes of a tail to redd up," Mamma agreed. With a blissful sigh, she beamed at them all. "Well, now! I hear folks comin' into the parkin' lot. Better fetch the ice cream from the freezer and start the party!"

Chapter 28

By three o'clock the Sweet Seasons rang with happy chatter: friends filled the tables, exclaiming over the moist strawberry cream cake and coming back for seconds—or a different flavor—of the rich home-made ice cream. Naomi dished up dessert and Mary poured drinks while Eva and Priscilla picked up dirty plates and replenished the serving tables. Micah was conducting tours of the smithy loft, beaming at the awed remarks of all who saw his handiwork. And meanwhile, Mamma collected compliments on her new dress—and smiled profusely at the three of them, her girls all together again, at last.

With their friends doing the serving, Rachel and Rhoda stood near the cake table to accept birthday wishes—and introduce their sister Rebecca to friends and neighbors who'd heard only about the girl in black. It was wonderful to turn the gossip in a different direction, to prove that good could come of even the most unsettling situations.

Rachel sighed happily. It was a fine birthday, and her spirits bubbled. Each time Micah brought visitors back to the café, he flashed her the sweetest smile . . . the one that said she was the only girl in the crowded room, as though he could gaze at her forever. Twice today he'd mentioned folks who wanted him to install a track wall system for them, to make a pantry more efficient and to build storage space in a shed for gardening tools. What girl wouldn't love a confident, hardworking man like Micah Brenneman?

Once the line of greeters had all been seated, Naomi waved the three sisters over. "Cake for you birthday girls now! Two sheet cakes're gone, but I baked ya two more, so eat up!"

"I'll have the blueberry ice cream with mine!" Rhoda insisted. "But *you*, Rebecca, have to try them all and tell us which is your favorite! There's so much we've still gotta know about ya, Sister!"

Rachel laughed. Alongside her big square of pink cake, topped with Mamma's sweet, creamy strawberry icing, she had a scoop of chocolate ice cream and a scoop of vanilla. Rebecca had just decided upon the strawberry, protesting at the size of the serving Naomi heaped on her plate, when the bell above the door jingled again.

Hiram Knepp entered. He was dressed in *fer-gut* black trousers and a freshly pressed blue shirt, and as he scanned the familiar faces in the crowd, his gaze lingered on Mamma.

Rachel held her breath, her fork still in her mouth. It was no secret the bishop had ideas—intentions—now that Mamma had made her confession and put the building up for sale. His expression confirmed that: he took in her new dress and the way she laughed at something Lydia Zook said, back at the table nearest the whiteboard. He passed up the dessert tables—

nodded at the three of them without seeming to notice that they were triplets rather than twins—and made his way through the crowd.

A couple tables over, Tom Hostetler watched the bishop as well. He sat beside Ezra Brenneman's wheelchair, nodding at the story Seth and Aaron were telling.

Rachel elbowed her sister. "Looky there, Sis. The bishop's like a bee headin' for a flower."

Rhoda grunted. "Or a stallion seekin' out a mare. This might bear watchin'."

"Oh, for sure and for certain it does."

Again the bell jingled, this time to admit Derek Shotwell and an older fellow Rachel had never seen before. The way the two of them stood together gave her pause, until Rebecca hopped up from her chair. "Come meet my dad," she urged them. "And if he says anything about my dress, well—"

"You're our sister," Rachel assured her. "Nothin' he can change about that."

"I'm not thinkin' he wants to," Rhoda replied as they went toward the door. "He looks very nice. Happy to be here, even if he and the banker are the only fellas without suspenders and straw hats!"

The loan officer smiled broadly as he took in the three of them. "Happy birthday, girls. And isn't this quite a party! Must be a hundred people here."

"Glad ya could come!" Rhoda replied. "Hope you're hungry!"

"And, Daddy, this is . . . this is Rachel Lantz, and Rhoda. My sisters." Rebecca clasped her hands tightly in front of her, looking not at all like the brazen girl in black they'd met weeks ago. "This is Robert Oliveri. He—he goes by Bob, though."

The man appeared somewhat older than Mamma, with thinning hair and paler skin than Amish men, who worked in the fields all day. As he extended a hand to Rachel and then to Rhoda, his eyes remained on Rebecca: a touching tug-of-war of emotions crossed his face, from surprise to sadness . . . and then to satisfaction.

"It's such a pleasure to meet you girls, after the way your mother came over with food that day," he said beneath the noisy voices around them.

"And quite a story he's told me, about how his toddler daughter came to him on a tree that was racing down the flooded river, all those years ago," Derek added. "Incredible, the way it's all come together."

"*Jah*, it's one mighty big miracle," Rachel replied. She gripped Mr. Oliveri's hand and then gestured toward the cake table. "Been a while since ya had the likes of Mamma's strawberry cream cake and homemade ice cream, so don't be shy! Mamma loves to feed people."

"It was the first thing I learned about her. The kind of generosity that brought me out of my deepest grief," Bob said with a nod. He smiled across the crowded café when he spotted Mamma. "Good to see her smiling again, too. And if you don't mind, I'd like to see that upstairs apartment Derek's been raving about."

"Oh, *jah*! Micah's becomin' quite the tour guide today." Rhoda pointed toward the kitchen doorway, where the blond carpenter stood with a huge helping of cake and ice cream. "Tell him to tuck his plate in the freezer so nobody'll polish it off while he's gone!"

Rachel watched the two men and Rebecca follow Micah through the café's kitchen before she leaned in closer to speak to her sister. "Have ya noticed it? When our sister has that kitty-cat grin on her face, she looks a whole lot like Mamma . . . like she knows things she's not tellin' us, ain't so?"

"*Jah*, I saw that. Ya think it means somethin'?"

"Guess we'll find out soon enough." She glanced back at Mamma, who now stood with the bishop on one side of her and Tom Hostetler on the other . . . not an unusual sight, but somehow mighty important right now. "How's that blueberry, Sis?"

"Wonderful-*gut*. Better have ya some before everybody else figures that out."

As Miriam watched Derek Shotwell and Bob Oliveri come from the kitchen, passing up the cake table, her insides tightened. Neither man's clothing proclaimed they were here on business, but, of course, they stood out because their short haircuts, open-collared knit shirts, and belted slacks proclaimed they weren't Amish. She'd expected to see them both today . . . but together?

Lord, I'm hopin' You'll stand by me, whatever happens next, she prayed quickly. *Tom'll be just fine. It's Hiram I'm not any too sure about.*

She put on a smile and stepped toward the two Englishmen. "*Gut* to see you fellas, here to celebrate our girls' twenty-first birthday. And I thank ya, Bob, for bein' so gracious as to understand how your girl's dressed today."

His grin unsettled her, yet he looked contented. More at peace than when she'd first met him. "Tiffany's had some adjusting to do. We both have." He looked around the dining room, at three thirty still full of

friends who chattered like magpies. "I can understand why she wants to come here—wants to be a part
of your family even though she was raised in a different culture altogether. But, in the ways that matter,
we're not so different at all."

"*Jah*, I believe that's the way of it." Miriam made herself breathe. Why were these men standing shoulder-to-
shoulder, looking at her so intently? Good manners
stood by her as she gestured toward the bearded man
on her other side. "Bob Oliveri, this is Hiram Knepp,
my—my *gut* friend and the bishop of our church district here in Willow Ridge."

"Honored, sir," Bob replied as they shook hands.
Hiram nodded, reverting to his reticent manner of
dealing with any Englishman: polite, but offering up
nothing he wasn't asked about.

"Shall we step outside for a moment?" Derek's gaze
encompassed both her and Hiram as he gestured
toward the door. "Got some paperwork in the car.
Might as well make this official, like we agreed a few
weeks ago."

"Yes, it's the perfect time for that," the bishop
replied with a decisive nod. "Any day that Miriam
foregoes her black clothing for such a lovely color
marks a major transformation, indeed."

They walked out into the bright sunlight, Miriam
surrounded by three men she sensed held her future
in their hands . . . but how would it play out? Although she was accustomed to Amish men making
the decisions while their women went along, she already knew how part of this story would go.

But what of the other parts? Why was Bob biting
back a grin?

"Mr. Knepp, as a successful businessman, you appreciate the importance of giving full value—and receiving it—when goods and properties are for sale," the banker began. He opened the door of a boxy gray vehicle that sat higher than the red convertible parked beside it. "So I hope you'll understand that when not one but *two* better offers came along for Mrs. Lantz's building, I did what any responsible bank officer would do."

Hiram's face clouded over. "What are you saying? We had an agreement, when I brought Miriam to your office to sign the sale papers—"

"We had a listing for a hundred and thirty thousand dollars, sir, based upon the appraised value," Derek continued as he unfolded a sheaf of papers. "That appraisal didn't include the fine handmade furnishings in the dining room or the commercial kitchen appliances."

"Which we agreed could be sold afterwards, to—"

"Mr. Knepp," the loan officer interrupted calmly, "if you had one of your prize stallions for sale and one breeder offered you less than the horse was worth, and another man was willing to pay extra because he fully appreciated the fine foals such a stallion would sire, which offer would you take?"

Hiram grunted, glaring from the banker to Miriam—and then at Bob Oliveri, whom he fully acknowledged for the first time. "We're not talking about livestock here, Mr. Shotwell!" he said sternly. "When I took you into my confidence, I explained that Miriam was selling her building to prevent her success from standing in the way of her salvation! A matter much more important than horseflesh!"

Derek's confident smile did nothing to reassure her, even though Miriam now sensed the way this discussion would end. Her pulse pounded toward a headache while her stomach twisted like a pretzel. She clasped her hands, keeping her silence. If ever there was a time to know her place and accept the decisions these men would reach, it was now.

Yet something about the soft glimmer in Bob Oliveri's eyes made her heart dare to hope . . .

"With my respect for the way you Amish separate your church affairs from the ways of the world, I won't refute your religious convictions, sir," Derek continued. "But as an officer of the bank, who holds the note on this building, and who has been entrusted to carry out this transaction, I took the better offer. It had nothing to do with personalities, or faith, or anything except buying and selling a building for far more than its appraised value. And that's what Mr. Oliveri has paid me. In full. In cash."

Miriam's heart leaped and she grinned before she could stop herself. Silently she thanked Bob with a gaze that felt prickly with tears.

"That's an outrage!" Hiram protested. "You should have called me, or—"

"You should have instructed me to do that if other offers came in," Derek countered quietly. "Just a couple hours after you made your offer, one of your neighbors offered me twenty thousand more, sir. Had you wanted to conduct an auction, we would've opened the bidding in a public—"

"That was not my intent, and you know it!"

This time it was Derek Shotwell who went silent, standing with his hands clasped around the papers . . . a stance that reminded Miriam of Bishop Knepp on a Sunday morning.

"Please understand that it was not my intent to interfere with religion or the dealings of the Amish, either," Bob Oliveri offered. "But when Tiffany came home a few weeks ago, afraid Miriam—her mother—was about to lose a business she'd invested her heart and soul in—"

"That's the problem!" the bishop interjected.

"—I suddenly knew the perfect use for my deceased wife's retirement funds." Bob sounded every bit as convinced as Derek that he'd made the right decision: he'd followed his business sense as well as his heart. "Jan's money had rolled over into accounts and CD's that weren't earning a pittance of the interest she'd originally received, and I have my own pension income. Seems more worthwhile to invest that money with a wonderful, loving woman like Miriam—the mother of the daughter I raised quite by accident. And when I saw how excited Tiffany was about the idea, that cinched it."

Miriam's pulse thrummed, yet she kept her eyes lowered: Hiram Knepp was more peeved than she'd ever seen him. It had never been her intent to prevail over the bishop quite so triumphantly . . . but hadn't the Lord just answered her prayers? Was it prideful—presumptuous—to assume her pleas to the Almighty had been heard?

"And all things considered," Bob went on in that low, steady voice, "we've accomplished your original mission, Bishop Knepp. As I understand it, *ownership* of this building was the stumbling block for Miriam, and now? She and the quilting ladies will be paying me a monthly rent while their businesses thrive, and I'll earn a better income than I would have from Jan's investments. So all things have worked out to the good, for all of us here who love the Lord."

Hiram shoved his hands into his pockets. "That's open to interpretation. And this situation is by no means settled, Miriam." Two bright pink spots in the bishop's cheeks announced his effort to restrain his temper, which didn't fit the behavior expected of their spiritual leader. He nodded curtly and stalked off to where his buggy was parked.

For a moment Miriam could only gaze at Derek and Bob, speechless. Then a laugh bubbled up from deep inside her and she extended her hands to them. "Now *this* takes the cake, ain't so? Can't tell ya how mighty *gut* I feel now, after these weeks of wonderin' about—"

"Oh, nobody was happier than I when Mr. Hostetler called," the banker said with a chuckle. "And then when Bob offered a more perfect solution than any of us could've devised—that day I returned your ledger— well, I can't think of a transaction that's ever satisfied me more. Congratulations to both of you! Just a few things to sign and our business is complete."

Chapter 29

Rachel *felt* Mamma's return to the crowd without seeing her face: a hush hovered over everyone as conversations got suspended midsentence. But then, when had they ever seen Miriam Lantz grinning like a schoolgirl—looking all the prettier because her new orchid dress and fresh kapp brought out the glow of her complexion?

Rhoda, too, turned to see what was happening, and immediately set aside her lemonade. "Well, it's for sure and for certain we're gonna hear *gut* news now. Somethin' way more excitin' than the three of us turnin' twenty-one, ain't so?"

"*Jah*! It's so!" Rebecca answered happily. "I thought Daddy and Mr. Shotwell were *never* going to get this show on the road."

The three of them stepped aside as Mamma came to the cake table, but before she said a word she just grabbed them. Squeezed them, laughing and then crying until she had to wipe her face on her sleeve. "Ya won't believe it, girls!" She blew her nose loudly into the napkin Naomi handed her. "Rebecca's *dat* bought the Sweet Seasons buildin', so now the bakery and the quilt shop can go right on doin' what we do best!"

"Oh, Mamma! That's so wonderful-*gut!*"

"Best possible news, that!" Naomi slung her arm around Mamma's shoulders for a sideways hug. She grabbed a napkin, too, to blot her huge brown eyes.

"And we've got our Rebecca to thank for it!" Mamma continued in her excited whisper. Then she picked up a spoon and loudly tapped the tea pitcher to get everyone's attention. The expectant gazes from all around the dining room had her laughing and crying all over again.

"Can't tell ya how happy I am that all of ya came to share this special birthday, now that my three girls are together again," she began in a voice choked with emotion. Then she inhaled loudly, to settle herself. "But I *can* tell ya, for sure and for certain, that I'm mighty happy about Rebecca's *dat*, Bob Oliveri, buyin' the buildin' and keepin' us here, along with the Schrocks' quiltin' shop!"

The applause and whistles were deafening. Mary Schrock clapped her hands while Eva and Priss reached for each other. Bob Oliveri looked ready to pass through a crack between the floorboards, but it was a happy sort of embarrassment—and it earned him an immediate place as a good friend among these Plain folk, who had long supported the two local shops.

From across the room, Rachel found Micah's easy grin . . . as though he'd guessed this might happen and had never believed Mamma would be out of business. The way his gaze lingered on Rachel . . . the smile that eased over his handsome face . . . foretold at least one more secret to be revealed before this

eventful summer passed into fall. Every time she'd
seen him today he was escorting someone to the loft,
and she'd overheard several folks saying they had
places in their homes or shops where a sliding wall
system would be just the thing.

Never had she felt so proud of him! Even in this
uncertain economy where large construction projects
were harder to come by, Micah Brenneman had
found a way to turn his smarts and his building skills
into a fine, steady income for him and his brothers.
All because he'd gone out on a limb to find out more
about Tiffany Oliveri, the girl in black and tattoos.
And then he'd faced the consequences, made his confession before God and all of them, and set himself
right with the world again. No complaints. No finger-
pointing or accusations.

Something about his expression made Rachel's
heart thump in her chest. She held his gaze for another teasing moment and then she cut a large square
of the strawberry cream cake, surrounding it with
scoops of all four ice creams. Micah's eyes followed
her every movement—he met her gaze then—and as
she headed for the kitchen's back door, she'd never
felt more triumphant. She hadn't conquered Micah's
wandering thoughts so much as she'd taken control
of her own. It was a wonder the handsome blond had
tolerated her pity-fits and tantrums. She could see
now that Tiffany—their Rebecca, returned—had no
romantic interest in her man. And she never had.

Rachel set the loaded plate on the kitchen counter
and returned to the cake table. She hesitated, but
when Rebecca turned, Rachel wrapped her sister in
her arms and just held her . . . felt the heart that had
beat time with hers since before they were born.

"*Denki*, Rebecca," she whispered. "Thank you so much for—for all you've done for us."

"*Jah, denki!*" Rhoda whispered as she, too, joined the embrace. "We wouldn't be celebratin' this way if ya hadn't persuaded your *dat*—"

"You wanna hear the real story?" Rebecca's blue eyes sparkled. She glanced over to be sure Mamma and the others were chattering. "Not my business, telling our mamma who to love or what to do—not my place to butt into your religion, either. But I could *not* let that bishop take over her life, ya know?"

Rhoda giggled first, and Rachel couldn't help joining in. "*Jah*, we know—"

"Ya did real *gut*, Rebecca!"

"—but can't none of us ever let on about that! Gotta be our sister secret, ain't so?"

Delight sparkled in a gaze that met theirs straight on, filled with a love light Rachel would never have believed had she not seen it herself. "Ya didn't hear about it from *me!*" Rebecca teased. "All for one and one for all?"

"*Fer gut* and forever!"

"*Jah*, sisters! *Fer gut* and forever!" Rachel squeezed their shoulders, not surprised that all of them heaved a satisfied sigh at the same time. "And now I'm gonna snatch myself a minute with Micah, before his ice cream melts. He's been givin' me a look all day and it's time I heard what's on his mind."

Rachel met Micah's gaze again. He'd stopped to talk with Tom Hostetler, but he was waiting her out . . . observing her as she embraced Rebecca. She took his plate out the back door of the kitchen, listening for his familiar tread behind her. Good thing no one was fetching their buggies, because she wasn't in the mood to be interrupted. She leaned against the sweet-gum tree that shaded the parking lot, extending the plate as bait.

Micah stopped a few feet away, his blond hair like corn tassles riffled by the summer breeze. As he stood with his feet spread the width of his broad shoulders, he looked as strong and sturdy as the oaks he fashioned furniture from; not a man to be moved by the winds of conflict or change or gossiping tongues. Micah looked ready to say something profound, but all that came out was, "Happy birthday, Rache."

She spooned up some of the melting ice cream and smiled around the creamy sweetness of it. "*Jah*, it is. Mostly Rebecca's doin', that her *dat* bought the buildin'. And mostly *your* doin' that she came around again, to really know us," Rachel murmured. "Means a lot to us, Micah. I thank ya for doin' what ya felt was right . . . and for puttin' up with me when I thought all the wrong things about your seein' her."

He shrugged, stretching his suspenders. "I was gawkin' like a clueless schoolkid. Just real glad it all turned out so *gut* for all of us. Who knew?"

"*Jah*, who knew?" Rachel cut a bite of the pink cake and held it out to him. "Seems I scooped up more than I could handle—and you're the man to help me with it."

Micah stepped toward her then, his smile still speaking of secrets. "You're tryin' to coax me into givin' out your present, ain't so? I know your kitty-cat ways, Rache." He closed his eyes over the bite of cake, taking her hand to steady the spoon. "Sweet as this is, you're even better, ya know. I love ya, honey."

Her pulse pounded. "Sometimes I wonder why—"

"Oh, never doubt it, Rache. From the time I sat

gawkin' at ya in the schoolroom, you were the only girl I could see. Hope ya won't be disappointed at what I got for your present."

Micah guided the spoon into the soft ball of chocolate ice cream and then to her mouth before taking a big bite of the strawberry for himself. He grinned. "Now, see, when I kiss ya we'll taste like both our favorites, all mixed together till ya can't tell one from the other . . . because it's a new flavor entirely," he murmured. "And that's how it'll be when we're married, ain't so? Blended. So there's no separatin' us."

Rachel closed her eyes and reveled in his kiss, cool and sweet and, yes, a perfect blending of flavors. "*Jah*," she whispered. "I'm likin' the sound of this, Micah. And the taste, too!"

"Come here. Looky what I got for ya." He led her over to where Rosie stood amongst the other horses, hitched to his wagon rather than to the buggy he was so proud of. He lifted off the blue tarp.

Rachel set the cake plate on the wagon's seat and then placed a foot on the metal step. She clasped the strong, broad hands that lifted her from the waist. "Lumber," she murmured, inhaling the fresh-cut tang of it. "And long sections of metal, and bags from the hardware store."

"Not the most romantic whatnot," Micah agreed, "but now that I've used the upstairs of the smithy as a trial run, I can whip together the same sorts of rollin' walls at the house—for *you*, Rache. So be thinkin' about how you'd wanna convert the attic into livin' space, or expand your pantry—"

"The bathroom, for sure and for certain!" she added. Her heart pounded faster as she considered all the possibilities. With a load of materials like this, why, Micah could redesign their whole house . . . create a whole new world for the two of them.

"And seein's how ya mentioned maybe openin' a B and B—"

Had this man recalled every one of her dreams? Listened to her plans and taken them seriously enough to invest in them himself? While Dat had dearly loved Mamma, he'd never been one for fixing up the house. Like most men, he'd invested money in his business—having the best farrier equipment and materials to work with—but he'd never provided conveniences for his woman. Yet here was Micah Brenneman, already indulging her whims without questioning their practicality or imposing judgment on their worth.

"Micah, I'm thinkin' now that I just wanna share that house with *you*," she insisted softly. Her heart quivered at the thought of it . . . having this man all to herself because he'd already made a cozy nest for her mother and sister. "And hopefully, now that the Sweet Seasons is still Mamma's, and you've got so many new projects . . . we won't need the income from a B and B. So we can figure out other ways to use those bedrooms. Ain't so?"

"I like the way you're thinkin', Rachel." He nuzzled her neck. "And come fall, I'm gonna make *gut* on all your ideas. And mine!"

When she turned in his sturdy arms, her heart soared. "It's been quite a summer," she whispered against his soft hair, "but there's a lot to be said for snuggle-up weather, too. Ain't so?"

WHAT'S COOKIN' AT THE
SWEET SEASONS CAFÉ?

Because I love to cook as much as Miriam and Naomi do, here are recipes for some of the dishes they've served up in *Summer of Secrets*! Some are my own favorite concoctions, while others come from Plain cookbooks and newspaper columns—where I discovered that Amish cooks do indeed use convenience foods like cake mixes, frozen hash browns, canned pie filling, Cheez Whiz, and Cool Whip. Amish cooks usually "doctor" these mixes, but they like to save time in the kitchen, same as anybody else!

I'll also post these on my Web site, www.Charlotte HubbardAuthor.com, and if you don't see the recipe you want, please e-mail me via my Web site to request it, plus bookmarks, etc. You can also learn more about me and follow my blog on this site. Hope you enjoy these dishes as much as I do! Yum!

~Charlotte

Stuffed Peppers

Feeds a hungry bunch and looks especially festive in red pepper shells—or alternate red and green peppers in the pan.

6–8 large bell peppers
2 lbs. lean ground beef
Salt, pepper, and garlic powder
1 small onion, diced
1 14.5-oz. can diced tomatoes
1 10-oz. can Rotel tomatoes with green chiles
1 pouch precooked, seasoned rice; or 2 C. cooked rice
1 can or jar spaghetti sauce, any variety
About 4 C. shredded Cheddar cheese

Cut the peppers in half lengthwise; seed and set aside. Meanwhile, cook the beef and onions, seasoned to taste, and drain. Return beef mixture to the skillet and add the tomatoes; simmer 5 minutes. Mix in the rice. Stir in about half the spaghetti sauce.

Preheat oven to 350°. Fill the pepper halves with the meat mixture, spoon some spaghetti sauce over each, and bake in a foil-covered pan about 45 minutes. Remove the foil, top each portion with cheese, and return to the oven until cheese is melted.

Kitchen Hint: 6 peppers/12 halves fit nicely into a 9x13-inch pan, but I usually have meat mixture left, so I fill another pepper or two and bake these separately to freeze for later. You can fill the peppers a day ahead and keep them covered in the fridge, too.

Cucumber-Onion Salad

Tangy-sweet, crunchy-fresh—and it keeps for several days in the fridge!

2–3 firm cucumbers, peeled
1 or 2 medium onions, peeled
1 C. white vinegar
½ C. vegetable or canola oil
½ C. water
½ C. sugar*
1 tsp. each: salt, pepper, Italian seasoning, dill

Slice the cukes and onions into a large bowl, alternating layers (a half-gallon plastic ice cream container works well, too). In a large jar with a lid, pour the vinegar, oil, water, sugar, and the seasonings and shake vigorously. Pour over the veggies, stir a bit to distribute the liquid, and cover. Chill thoroughly.

*Kitchen Hint: You can use Splenda or ¼ C. Splenda Baking Mix instead of sugar.

You can also use this dressing (even what's left over from the cukes/onions) to make **Marinated Veggie Salad:** slice carrots, celery, radishes, onions, peppers, broccoli, cauliflower—whatever you love!—into a bowl, pour in the liquid, and chill for several hours. Looks pretty layered in a glass bowl.

Frog-Eye Fruit Salad

Acini de pepe pasta gives this sweet, creamy salad its unusual "frog eye" texture. It's so yummy you can serve it as a salad, or spoon it into dessert cups!

1¼ C. *acini de pepe* pasta
1-20 oz. can crushed pineapple
1-20 oz. can pineapple tidbits
1 T. flour
2 beaten eggs
1 C. sugar
1 large or 2 small cans mandarin oranges
1 large jar maraschino cherries
2 C. whipped topping

Boil the *acini de pepe* in water according to package directions; drain and rinse with cold water. Set aside.

Meanwhile, make the sauce: drain the pineapple tidbits and *squeeze* the juice from the crushed pineapple; put fruit aside. Pour 1¾ C. of the pineapple juice into a medium pan, whisk in the flour, eggs, and sugar and then simmer over medium heat, stirring constantly, until thick. Set aside to cool.

Drain the oranges and cherries; halve the cherries. Put these with the pineapple and chill. Mix the sauce into the pasta in a large bowl and chill several hours/overnight. A few hours before serving, stir the fruit into the pasta mixture and fold in the whipped topping. Serves 15–20. (Try not to eat half of it before you share it with anyone else!)

Cherry-Pie Salad

Make this in your prettiest glass bowl!

1 can cherry pie filling
1 20-oz. can crushed pineapple
2 3-oz. boxes cherry gelatin
1 C. boiling water
1 6-oz. container cherry vanilla yogurt
1 C. whipped topping

Pour pie filling and undrained pineapple into serving bowl and stir. Mix the gelatin into the water until dissolved, then stir into the fruit. Chill until firm. Mix the yogurt and whipped topping and spread on the salad. Cover and chill.

<u>Kitchen Hint:</u> Yep, light pie filling and sugar-free gelatin are just as good in this recipe. Substitute other flavors of pie filling, gelatin, and yogurt, too.

Smothered Hash Browns

A meal in a pan! Add other fresh veggies like zucchini, broccoli, or chopped carrots for variety.

1 pkg. frozen hash browns, thawed; or Simply
	Potatoes
Dill weed, garlic powder, salt, and pepper
1 onion, sliced
1 red or green bell pepper (or combo of both), in
	bite-sized chunks
4–5 large fresh mushrooms (or 1 can of mushrooms)

2 C. diced ham; or 1 lb. bulk sausage, cooked and
   drained
1 small jar Cheez Whiz

Preheat the oven to 350°. Brown the potatoes in
about 1 T. oil in a nonstick skillet, seasoning to taste.
Spread in a sprayed 9x13-inch pan and set aside.
Simmer the veggies in ¼ C. water until nearly cooked,
season to taste, and stir in the meat. Spoon this mixture over the potatoes and then spoon the cheese
over all, spreading it as it melts. Cover and bake about
20 minutes or until heated through. Serves 3–5.

Mamma's Sky-High Biscuits

A little whole grain makes these more healthful and
very satisfying! Makes about 15, depending on the
size of your cutter.

2 C. white flour
1 C. whole wheat flour
4½ tsp. baking powder
2 T. sugar
½ tsp. salt
¾ tsp. cream of tartar
¾ C. butter or margarine
1 egg
1 C. milk

Preheat oven to 425°. Combine the dry ingredients in
a bowl and cut in the butter or margarine until mixture
resembles coarse crumbs. Add egg and milk, stirring
quickly to blend, then knead dough on a lightly floured

surface. Roll to a 1-inch thickness and cut with a 1- or 2-inch biscuit cutter (or use an overturned drinking glass dipped in flour). Place on a parchment-papered cookie sheet. Bake 12–14 minutes or until lightly browned.

<u>Kitchen Hint</u>: You can do all the mixing in a food processor! Faster and easier! You can freeze them, too.

Lemon Icebox Pie

Sweet yet tart, this easy pie makes a refreshing summer dessert.

1 10-inch graham cracker crust
1 egg white, slightly beaten
2 cans sweetened condensed milk
5 egg yolks
½ C. sugar
½ tsp. vanilla extract
⅔ C. bottled lemon juice

Preheat oven to 325°. Brush the crust with egg white and bake 5 minutes.

Meanwhile, make the filling: With a whisk or fork, blend the condensed milk and egg yolks until smooth. Stir in sugar, vanilla, and lemon juice until well blended. Pour into crust and bake at 300° for 20 minutes or until center is set. Cool to room temperature and then refrigerate several hours or overnight. Garnish with whipped cream or whipped topping.

For key lime pie: Substitute bottled key lime juice for the lemon juice.

<u>Kitchen Hint</u>: Use those extra egg whites in a healthy veggie omelet to serve with Sweet Zucchini Corn Muffins.

Sweet Zucchini Corn Muffins

Sweet and dense, these muffins accompany any meal—and they're a great way to use up zucchini when your garden explodes with it.

2½ C. white flour
1½ C. yellow cornmeal
1 C. sugar*
1 T. cinnamon
2 tsp. baking powder
1 tsp. each baking soda and salt
3 C. shredded/finely chopped zucchini
⅓ C. honey
1 C. oil
1 6-oz. carton lemon yogurt*
4 eggs

Preheat the oven to 350°. In a large bowl, stir the dry ingredients together and then stir in the zucchini. In a small bowl, blend the honey, oil, yogurt, and eggs, and then stir them into the flour mixture until well moistened. Spoon into muffin tins and bake 12–15 minutes, or just until tops are set. Leave in pans about 10 minutes and then cool muffins on a rack. Makes 2 dozen.

*<u>Kitchen Hint</u>: You can substitute ½ C. Splenda Baking Mix for the sugar and use nonfat yogurt.

Chocolate Zucchini Cake

So moist you won't miss the frosting. Try it as a coffee cake, too!

½ C. margarine
½ C. oil
1¾ C. sugar
2 eggs
1 tsp. vanilla
½ C. buttermilk, sour cream, or plain yogurt
2½ C. flour
¼ C. cocoa
1 tsp. each salt and soda
1 T. cinnamon
2 C. grated unpeeled zucchini
½ C. chopped nuts
1 C. chocolate chips
2 T. sugar

Preheat the oven to 325°. Cream the margarine, oil, and sugar. Add eggs and then vanilla. Sift the dry ingredients together and add alternately with the buttermilk/sour cream/yogurt. Stir in the zucchini and spread in a sprayed 9x13-inch pan. Sprinkle with the sugar, nuts, and chips. Bake for 45–50 minutes. Freezes well.

Mamma's Best Cinnamon Rolls

Who knew great bakery cinnamon rolls could start with a cake mix?

2 T. or 2 pkgs. yeast
2½ C. warm water
1 box yellow cake mix
4 C. flour
3 eggs
⅓ C. oil
1 tsp. salt
Melted margarine, brown sugar, and cinnamon

Dissolve yeast in the water for about 3 minutes. In a large mixing bowl, add yeast mixture to the cake mix, 1 C. of the flour, the oil, and the salt. Mix until bubbles appear, then slowly add the remaining flour to make a soft dough. Knead on a floured surface until smooth and elastic, then place in a greased bowl, turning the dough in the bowl to grease the top. Cover the bowl and let dough rise until double (about an hour with regular yeast; 30 minutes with quick-rise).

Punch down the dough, divide in two, then roll into 12x9-inch rectangles. Spread with melted margarine, then sprinkle all over with sugar and cinnamon. Roll the short sides like a jelly roll, pinch edges to seal, and cut each roll into 12 rounds. Place rounds in two sprayed 9x13-inch pans and let rise until double. Bake at 350° for 20–25 minutes.

Frosting: 2 C. powdered sugar, 1 tsp. vanilla, 3 T. melted margarine, 3 T. milk or orange juice—enough to make it drizzly. Spread on the rolls while they're hot.

Secret Ingredient Chocolate Pie

Cinnamon adds subtle richness to an everyday dessert!

2 pkgs. cook-and-serve chocolate pudding mix
1½ C. cold milk
2 tsp. cinnamon
1 9-inch graham cracker crust

Follow package directions for stovetop or microwave pudding, using only 1½ C. of milk. Cool pudding in the pan, with wax paper or plastic pressed on the surface. Spoon into a 9-inch graham cracker crust and garnish with whipped topping and a shake of cinnamon.

<u>Kitchen Hint:</u> Sugar-free pudding mix and skim milk work just fine in this recipe.

Orange Knots

Fragrant, light, and sweet . . . is it time for breakfast yet?

1 T. or pkg. yeast
¼ C. warm water
1 C. warm milk
⅓ C. butter or margarine, softened
2 eggs
¼ C. orange juice
2 T. grated fresh orange peel
5¼–5¾ C. flour

In a mixing bowl, dissolve the yeast in the water. Add milk, sugar, butter or margarine, eggs, juice, and orange peel along with 3 cups of the flour. Beat until smooth, then add enough remaining flour to form a soft dough. Knead on a floured surface until smooth and elastic, then place in a greased bowl (turn the dough to grease the top). Cover and let rise in a warm place until doubled (about 2 hours, using regular yeast).

Punch down dough; roll into a 16x10-inch rectangle and cut 10 strips on the 10-inch side. Roll and tie each in a knot. Place on a sprayed baking sheet and tuck the ends under. Cover with a towel and let rise about 30 minutes. Bake at 400° for 10 minutes or until golden. Cool and drizzle with frosting.

<u>Frosting</u>: 1 C. powdered sugar, 2 T. orange juice, and 1 tsp. grated fresh orange peel.

Italian Zucchini Stew

A great way to use up zucchini when your garden explodes with it!

2 medium zucchini, sliced
1 small onion, sliced
1 large can diced tomatoes with juice; or 3–4 large
    fresh tomatoes, peeled and chunked
1 green or red bell pepper, seeded and diced
Italian seasoning, dill weed, salt, pepper, garlic
    powder, 2 bay leaves.
Parmesan cheese

Place the veggies in a large skillet coated with nonstick spray; season to taste with the spices. Simmer over medium heat, covered, until veggies are soft. (You might need to add a little water or tomato juice if you use fresh tomatoes.) Remove bay leaves. Spoon into serving bowl and sprinkle generously with grated Parmesan cheese. Serves 4.

<u>Kitchen Hint:</u> For a meal in a skillet, add a pound of browned, seasoned ground beef; or Italian bulk sausage; or cooked chicken.

Whole Wheat Zucchini Bread

Dense and sweet, these loaves freeze well. Try a slice toasted!

2 C. sugar
3 eggs
1 C. oil
2 tsp. vanilla
2 C. grated zucchini
2 C. whole wheat flour
1 C. white flour
1 T. cinnamon
¼ tsp. baking powder
1 tsp. baking soda
1 C. raisins or dried cranberries
1 C. chopped nuts, optional

Preheat the oven to 350°. In a mixing bowl, blend the sugar, eggs, oil, and vanilla. Add zucchini and dry ingredients, mixing until just blended. Add fruit and nuts. Divide among three 8x4-inch sprayed bread pans and bake about an hour, or until a toothpick comes out clean from the split in the top. Cool in the pans for 10 minutes, and then cool completely on a rack.

Rhubarb Cream Pie

Tart and creamy-sweet. If you don't have fresh rhubarb, frozen works well. This recipe makes enough crust for 2 double-crust 10-inch pies and enough filling for one pie.

Crust
3 C. flour
1½ C. Crisco
2 T. sugar
½ tsp. each baking powder and salt
½ C. cold water

Filling
3 T. flour
2 eggs
½ tsp. each nutmeg and cinnamon
1½ C. sugar
1 T. butter or margarine
3½ C. cut-up rhubarb

Preheat oven to 400°.

Crust: Cut Crisco into dry ingredients with a pastry cutter or food processor until well mixed. Add water and mix well. Roll out and cut to fit a 10-inch pie pan.

<u>Filling</u>: Blend flour, eggs, sugar, spices, and butter or margarine. Add rhubarb.

Fit bottom crust into a 10-inch pie plate and pour in the filling. Criss-cross or weave strips of dough over the top. Sprinkle lightly with sugar, if desired. Bake 10 minutes, then reduce heat to 350° and bake 25 more minutes.

<u>Kitchen Hints</u>: Placing strips of foil around the edge of the crust keeps it from getting too brown. Put the pie on a baking sheet to keep any filling that boils over from burning on the bottom of your oven.

Oatmeal Flax Bread

Dense and chewy with whole grains, this makes awesome toast for breakfast, or a great go-along for soups and salads. Flaxseed replaces the oil and eggs used in other quick breads.

1½ C. whole wheat flour
1 C. all-purpose flour
⅔ C. packed brown sugar
½ C. old-fashioned oats
⅓ C. ground flaxseed or flaxseed meal
1 tsp. salt
1⅔ C. buttermilk

Preheat oven to 350°. Coat an 8x4-inch bread pan with nonstick spray.

In a large bowl, combine the flours, sugar, oats, flaxseed, and salt. Stir in the buttermilk just until mixed. Pour batter into the pan and sprinkle with 1 T. oats. Bake about 45 minutes or until a toothpick inserted in the center comes out clean. Cool 5 minutes before removing from pan to cool on a rack. Cool completely—at least 2 hours—before slicing.

Kitchen Hint: No buttermilk? Stir 2 T. white vinegar or lemon juice into milk and let stand 5 minutes. This bread freezes well, so I always double the recipe.

Lemon Pound Cake

An old favorite! Bake it in a 9x13-inch pan for squares or in a Bundt pan for slices.

1 box lemon cake mix
1 box instant lemon pudding mix
¾ C. oil
4 eggs

Preheat oven to 350°. Mix all ingredients and pour into a sprayed pan. Bake about 20–25 minutes (toothpick comes out clean) for the 9x13-inch version and 50–60 minutes for the Bundt version.

Meanwhile, mix glaze: 2 C. powdered sugar, ½ C. lemon juice. While cake is still warm, in the pan, gently poke holes all over it with a meat fork and pour the glaze over it to soak in. If using a Bundt pan, invert after 25 minutes to cool completely and drizzle additional, thicker frosting on the top.

Dark-On-Dark Cookies

A soft, chewy chocolate cookie that's sinfully delicious!

1¼ C. butter or margarine, softened
2 C. sugar
2 eggs
2 tsp. vanilla
2 C. flour
¾ C. Hershey's Special Dark cocoa
1 tsp. baking soda
1 bag Hershey's Special Dark chocolate chips

Preheat the oven to 350°. Cream the butter or margarine and sugar, then blend in the eggs and vanilla. Combine the dry ingredients and mix into the dough, adding the chocolate chips last. Drop by spoonfuls onto greased or parchment paper–covered baking sheets and bake 8–9 minutes. Cookies will be soft and puffy. Allow to cool on the sheets about a minute, until they settle around the chips, and then cool on a rack. Makes about 5 dozen.

No-Bake Peanut Butter Cookies

These cookies set up like fudge and they won't heat your kitchen on a summer day!

1⅓ C. sugar
½ C. butter or margarine
½ C. milk
¼ tsp. vanilla
1 C. peanut butter
3 C. quick oats

Mix sugar, butter or margarine, milk, and vanilla in a pan and bring to a boil; cook 1 minute. Remove from heat and stir in peanut butter and oatmeal. Cool and drop by spoonfuls onto wax paper. If they stay too gooey, store them in the fridge.

Butterscotch Brownies

A great fix for a sweet/salty/chewy craving!

½ C. butter or margarine, melted
1½ C. brown sugar, packed
2 eggs
1 tsp. vanilla
1½ C. flour
2 tsp. baking powder
1 C. chopped pecans
1 bag butterscotch chips

Preheat oven to 350°. Mix melted butter or margarine, brown sugar, eggs, and vanilla; add flour and baking powder and mix well. Add pecans and ½ the bag of chips. Spread in a sprayed 9x13-inch pan and sprinkle remaining chips on top. Bake about 30 minutes, just until toothpick comes out clean—don't over-bake!

Sausage Breakfast Pie

Practically makes itself, and the varieties are endless. Good for any meal of the day.

1 lb. bulk sausage, cooked and drained
1 C. shredded cheese (Colby, Cojack, or mozzarella are good)
¼ C. chopped onion
¼ C. each red and green bell pepper
½ C. Bisquick or "JIFFY" Baking Mix
1 C. milk
Salt and pepper to taste
Dill, garlic powder, parsley to taste
2 eggs

Preheat oven to 400°. Spray a 10-inch pie pan with nonstick spray. Sprinkle the sausage, cheese, and veggies in the pan. Stir remaining ingredients until blended and pour over the meat layer. Bake 35–40 minutes or until a knife inserted in the center comes out clean. Let stand 5 minutes before cutting and serving.

<u>Infinite varieties</u>: Try including ham, shredded pork, or cooked chicken and using mushrooms, black olives, diced fresh tomatoes, peas, or whatever you've got left over. Works for any meal of the day.

Italian Green Beans

Nice switch from plain green beans. If you don't can your own fresh beans and tomatoes, use equal-size cans from the store.

1 qt. green beans
1 qt. tomatoes
Italian seasoning and dried onion to taste
¼ C. real bacon bits
1 C. shredded mozzarella cheese
¼ C. grated Parmesan cheese

Preheat oven to 350°. Spray a 1-quart ovenproof bowl or casserole and pour in drained green beans. Add drained tomatoes, seasonings, and bacon bits; stir. Top with cheeses, cover, and bake about 30–40 minutes, until bubbly.

Kitchen Hint: You can also add a can of sliced mushrooms, or use fresh sliced onion rather than dried.

Cherry-Pie Bars

You can use any flavor of canned pie filling, but cherry is the prettiest!

1 C. butter or margarine
1¾ C. sugar
4 eggs
3 C. flour
1½ tsp. baking powder
2 cans cherry pie filling

Preheat oven to 350°. Cream the butter or margarine and sugar, then add eggs and mix well. Mix in dry ingredients, and save out 1 C. of the dough. Spread the rest in a sprayed 11x17-inch pan (or two 9x13-inch pans), then top with pie filling. Drop remaining dough by teaspoonfuls over the top. Bake about 30 minutes, until cookie seems firm (don't overbake!). Cool and drizzle with frosting. Cut into bars.

<u>Frosting</u>: 1⅓ C. powdered sugar, ½ tsp. lemon flavoring, ½ tsp. almond flavoring, 2 or 3 T. milk.

<u>Kitchen Hint</u>: No-sugar pie filling works just fine here!

Strawberry Cream Cake

Moist and delicious. Pretty enough for a party!

1 strawberry cake mix with pudding in it
1 3-oz. box strawberry gelatin
1 10-oz. pkg. frozen strawberries, thawed but not
   drained
1 3-oz. box of white chocolate instant pudding
1 8-oz. tub of whipped topping

Make cake in a 9x13-inch pan according to directions; cool. Use a meat fork to poke holes all over it. Dissolve the gelatin in 1 C. boiling water, cool slightly, and pour this liquid evenly over the cake.

For the topping, stir the pudding mix into the thawed berries until blended, then add the whipped topping. Spread over the cake. Store, covered, in the fridge. Freezes well, too.

<u>Kitchen Hint</u>: Sugar-free gelatin, pudding, and light whipped topping work fine.

Skillet Baked Beans

Faster than the oven variety, and keeps your kitchen cooler, too! Same great taste.

4–5 strips bacon
1 medium onion, diced
2 20-oz. cans pork and beans
¼ C. each mustard, ketchup, brown sugar
Salt and pepper

In a large skillet, cook the bacon; remove, drain, and crumble. Cook the onion in the bacon grease (then drain the remaining grease if you wish) and pour the beans into the skillet. Stir in the condiments and bacon, season to taste, and cook over medium heat, stirring occasionally, until beans are thick and most of the liquid is absorbed. Serves 10–12.

Rhubarb Crumb Cake

Moist and sweet-tart, this breakfast treat could double as dessert!

1½ C. brown sugar
½ C. margarine, softened
1 egg
1 C. buttermilk
2 C. flour
1 tsp. baking soda
1 tsp. vanilla
2¼ C. diced fresh rhubarb
½ C. sugar
2 T. cinnamon

Preheat the oven to 350°. Cream the sugar and margarine, add the egg. Dissolve the baking soda in the buttermilk and add to the creamed mixture, then add the dry ingredients and rhubarb. Spread the batter in a greased 9x13-inch pan. Sprinkle the remaining sugar and the cinnamon over the top of the cake and bake for 40 minutes or just until a toothpick inserted in the center comes out dry. Do not over-bake!

Please read on for a taste of the next
Sweet Seasons novel,
Autumn Winds.

Lord, if this rain's gonna cause another flood like ya sent Noah, I'm hopin' you'll give me a sign to get to higher ground. Can't have my bakery blowin' off the face of the earth in this wind, either, as we're countin' on these pies and cakes for the big party tomorrow!

Miriam Lantz slammed the whistling window shut. When was the last time they'd seen such a fierce wind? Rain pelted the roof of the Sweet Seasons Bakery Café, not quite drowning out the troubling thoughts that had wakened her in the wee hours. Too often these past weeks she'd dwelled upon Bishop Knepp's vow to somehow get her out of this business and into his home. Ordinarily it wasn't her way to fret so, but Hiram Knepp could stir up more trouble than a nest of ornery hornets, if he had a mind to. It hadn't made him one bit happy, when an English fellow had outbid him to buy the café building last month.

Miriam sighed. It wasn't her way to start the day's baking at one in the morning, either, but lately she'd felt so restless . . . as unsettled as the weather they'd had this fall. Now that she and her partner Naomi Brenneman wouldn't lose their building—or their booming business—she could focus on her daughter Rachel's wedding plans. Such a happy time, because Naomi's son Micah was the perfect match for her daughter! But even kneading the fragrant, warm dough for the cornmeal rolls on today's lunch menu didn't settle her.

Miriam pushed the grainy dough with the heels of her hands, then folded it over itself and repeated the process time had so deeply ingrained in her . . . sprinkled more cornmeal and flour on the countertop, and then rolled the sleeves of her dress another fold higher. "Awful warm in here," she murmured.

The oven alarm buzzed, and she pulled out six thick pumpkin pies. As she replaced them with the large pans of apple crisp on today's menu, Miriam paused. Was that a horse's whinny she'd heard outside?

Not at this hour, in this storm. Who'd be fool enough to risk life and limb—not to mention his horse—travelin' the dark county blacktop that runs through Willow Ridge?

She inhaled the spicy aromas of cinnamon and cloves, imagining the smiles on folks' faces after tomorrow's preaching service at Henry and Lydia Zook's, when they surprised the bishop by celebrating his fifty-fifth birthday. These pies, made from her sister Leah's fresh pumpkins, would be the first to go—but their hostess, Lydia, had also ordered a layer cake and sheet cakes from the Sweet Seasons for the occasion.

And if Hiram gets the notion I baked all these things especially to impress HIM, he'd better just find somebody else to court. And to raise his kids, too!

Miriam chuckled in spite of her misgivings. If anyone could think of a way to dodge the bishop's romantic intentions, it would be she and her girls. It was no secret around Willow Ridge that Hiram's young wife, who'd died of birthing complications, had borne more than just the burden of being married to their moral and community leader. While Miriam believed she could live the upright life required of a bishop's wife, serving as an example to their Old Order Amish community, she had no illusions about sharing the same house with Hiram and his rambunctious kids—not to mention his daughter, Annie Mae, who was in the throes of a *rumspringa* no stepmother would want to deal with!

A loud *crash* out in the dining room made Miriam jump. Glass tinkled over the tables and a sudden gust of wind howled through a jagged hole in the window before the power went out.

The bakery grew eerily quiet, what with the freezers and the dishwasher shutting off. This storm was a reminder of how her gas appliances at home had an advantage over the electric ones required by the health department and installed by the Mennonite quilters next door. Miriam was no stranger to the darkness, as she started her baking at three every morning, but this storm had set her on edge. And when had she ever seen a huge tree limb on one of her café tables?

"Lord a-mercy, what's next?" she murmured as she warily made her way through the darkness, between the café's tables. "Better have Naomi's boys clean this up before folks come in for the breakfast—"

Again a horse neighed, right outside the window this time.

"Whoa, fella! Easy now!" a male voice soothed.

A bolt of lightning shot across the sky to backlight the frightening silhouette of a huge percheron rearing up, frantically pawing the air. The horse's handler stood near the damaged tree, struggling with the reins, still talking as calmly as he could while dodging those deadly hooves. "Pharaoh, take it easy, fella! We'll wait out the storm right here, so—"

But another ominous flash filled the sky and in his frenzy, the horse tipped forward to buck with his powerful back legs.

Miriam heard a sickening *thud* as those hooves connected with human flesh, and then a cry of pain and another *thud* when the fellow struck the café's outside wall. The percheron galloped off, whinnying in terror, its reins flapping behind it.

Things got very quiet. Only the patter of the rain and some rapidly retreating hoof beats punctuated the darkness. Miriam rushed to unlock the café's main door, afraid of what she might find when she stepped outside. A man was sprawled against the foundation of her building. She considered herself a fairly stalwart woman, able to heft fifty-pound bags of flour and such, but for sure and for certain she wouldn't be moving this stranger—

Best not to shift him around anyway, she reasoned, noting that his head was up out of the puddles. Should she find something to cover him, and then call for help? Or hurry straight to the phone shanty in the back? *Best to call 911 and then . . . but what if he was kicked in the head? What if he's not gonna come around?*

Miriam hesitated but a moment. If the poor fellow was unconscious, at least he wasn't in pain, and if he was already gone, well, the paramedics had better come to make sure of that. She started back inside but before she reached the door, the man groaned loudly.

"Don't be tryin' to stand up! Ya got kicked mighty hard, by the sound of it." Miriam sensed that he, like most injured men, would ignore a woman's instructions, so she hunkered down beside him. The cold rain soaked through her kapp and the back of her dress, but that was a minor discomfort compared to what her visitor must be feeling. "Where'd he kick ya? A horse that big—and that scared—could've killed ya, easy."

The man winced, shifting. "I should've known better than . . . just wanted to get one town farther along, ya know?" he rasped. "Should've just stayed with my wagon instead of thinkin' Pharaoh would get over bein' spooked by this lightnin'. Smarter than I am, that horse is."

Miriam looked all around. She moved closer, under the eaves, where she wouldn't get quite so wet. "What kind of wagon are we talkin' about?" she asked. Could be this man was half out of his head after being kicked so hard. He had the nicest voice, though. And even if he was in horrible-bad pain, he was thinking of his horse's welfare.

"Smithy wagon. I'm a travelin' farrier." He looked at her then, gingerly rubbing his chest. "Lookin' to find some reasonable land for a mill, so I can settle down. I came to these parts on account of the rapids I heard about on the river."

Miriam's heart played hopscotch in her chest. "A travelin' blacksmith?" she asked in a thin voice. "We've got an empty smithy right behind the café buildin' here. Belonged to my Jesse, but he's passed now, and . . ."

Had she said too much? It wasn't her way to speak of her widowed state to strangers, yet this fellow seemed willing to reveal his own hopes and dreams to her. So what could it hurt?

"I'm sorry to hear that, ma'am." He inhaled, testing

the pain in his chest. "Ya know, I think I if I could sit up against the buildin'—"

"Here, let me help ya!"

"—and draw a few *gut*, deep breaths to clear my head—"

"Don't try to stand up just yet!" Miriam knew she sounded like a mother hen clucking instructions, but she didn't want him falling over. "If ya can wait here, I'll call the ambulance and—"

"You'll do no such thing!" He grabbed her arm, then managed a tentative smile despite the rain that soaked him. His other hand remained on his chest, massaging where the horse must've kicked him. "A fella in my line of work gets some sense knocked into him every now and again. Probably a *gut* thing."

Oh, but that smile and his touch set the butterflies to fluttering inside her! Miriam drew back, and he released her arm. She chuckled nervously and he joined her, a happy sound, even if the thunder still rumbled around them. "All right then, since you're a man and you'll do as ya please anyway, can I at least bring ya out a chair to pull yourself up with?" she asked. "Better than sittin' in this puddle, ain't so?"

"Right nice of ya to look after me this way."

Miriam scurried inside and grabbed a sturdy chair from the nearest table. Part of her wanted to call the Brenneman boys—her Rachel's fiancé Micah would be here in two shakes of a tail—yet she craved some time with this stranger. She told herself she was giving him a chance to recover before anyone else saw him in this sorry state—

"If ya don't mind my drippin' on your floor, I'll just rest here for a few."

Miriam jumped. Why wasn't she surprised that the

man had already stood himself up and come in without her help? He eased into the chair she'd pulled out.

"I'd ask what ya were doin' here at this crazy hour, in the pitch dark," he murmured as he looked around, "but I guess that's none of my business. I've got to tell ya, though, it smells so *gut* I must've passed through the pearly gates and into heaven."

Miriam laughed again in spite of her agitated state. "I'm bakin' pies and decoratin' cakes for the bishop's surprise party tomorrow. Gettin' the day's breakfast and lunch started, too," she replied. "Welcome to the Sweet Seasons Bakery Café. Can I get ya some coffee, or—"

"Seems Pharaoh knew more about where to drop me off than I gave him credit for." Her visitor leaned toward her, smoothing the wet hair back from his face. "I'm Ben Hooley, by the way, originally from out around Lancaster County. I appreciate your takin' a chance on a wayfarin' stranger."

"And I'm Miriam Lantz. So I guess we're not strangers now, ain't so?"

And where had such boldness come from? Here they were in the dark without another soul around, chatting like longtime friends. At three in the morning, no less!

Oh, the bishop's not gonna like this! Not one little bit!

The fellow extended his hand, and as Miriam shook it the kitchen lights flashed on. The refrigerators hummed, and for a moment she could believe it was the little spark of electricity passing from his hand to hers that had restored the building's power.

Ben's laugh filled the empty dining room. "Well, now. What do ya think about that?" He looked around, smiling. "The Lord's watchin' over me for sure and for certain, bringin' me here to your place on such a nasty night. A port in a storm. Just what I've been needin' for a while."

Miriam smiled at that . . . at the sound of his mellow male voice and the way it seemed to make itself at home in her little café. Then she blinked, remembering the reality of this situation: she knew nothing of this Hooley fellow, except that his clothes and speech announced he was Plain and that he'd been kicked by his horse. But now that he was recovering, and the power was back on in her kitchen, she had no excuse not to get back to work . . . and back to proper behavior.

"If you'll point me toward a broom, I'll clean up this mess and get that branch back outside where it belongs," he offered. "It's the least I can do, seein's how ya got me in out of the rain."

She'd been so busy following the lines of his smooth-shaven face when he talked, she'd made a fool of herself: there *was* a huge section of maple tree covering two of her tables and she'd all but forgotten it. "Oh, but ya surely must be too sore to heft—I can get a couple of our fellas—"

"Comes a time when I can't move that tree limb or push a broom, ya better just bury me." Ben scooted to the edge of his chair and slowly stood up, testing his balance. "See there? I'm *gut* as new. A little soggy—but movin' around's the cure for that, and a way to keep from gettin' stiff, too."

Miriam didn't know what to say . . . didn't think it proper to examine his chest, even if he probably had a huge, hoof-shaped bruise and some broken skin where his horse had kicked him. It was the first time she'd been alone with a man since Jesse had passed—

except for Hiram Knepp, and she'd ducked out of his embrace—so she felt acutely aware of Ben's broad shoulders and how his wet shirt clung to them. He was a lean fellow yet muscular—

And what business do ya have gawkin' at him? He can't be thirty yet. More Rhoda's age than yours!

Thoughts of her grown daughters—how they'd be here with Naomi in a couple of hours to prepare for the breakfast shift—steadied her resolve. She smiled at Ben but she stepped back, too. It wasn't proper for an Amish woman to behave this way even when no one was watching—except God, of course. "If you're up to that sort of work, I'd be grateful, as I've got my bakin' to get back to," she replied. "But if ya feel woozy or short of breath, like ya need a doctor—"

"Your kindness has already worked a miracle cure, Miriam. Right nice of ya to set aside a few of the rules to help me out."

Had he read her mind? Or did he just know the right things to say? A traveling blacksmith surely had all sorts of experience making deals for what he needed . . .

And what sort of fellow, in a trade every Old Order Amish family relied upon, didn't settle in one community? If Ben knew about the rapids in the river, what else had he checked up on? What if he was making up this story as he went along, to gain some advantage over her—or whomever he met up with—in Willow Ridge?

And what if you're spinnin' all this stuff out like a spider, about to catch yourself in a web of assumptions? Just because he's got a nice smile—

Miriam quickly fetched a broom and dustpan from the closet, relieved that Ben had already stepped outside to see about pulling the big tree branch from her window. She set the tools where he'd find them and then returned to her kitchen, where the lights were brighter and the serving window could be a barrier between this good-looking stranger and her work space.

Jah, he is gut-lookin'. But that's not his fault, is it?

Miriam laughed at herself. No, Ben Hooley's looks and manner were gifts from God, same as the way Rachel, Rhoda, and Rebecca favored their handsome *dat*.

"And what do ya think of all this, Jesse?" she whispered. Every now and again she asked her late husband's opinion, or thought about how he would've handled situations she found herself in, even though her own confidence had increased a lot during these past months of successfully running her business.

Miriam stood quietly at her flour-dusted work table . . . just the hum of the appliances and the aroma of spicy pumpkin pies kept her company.

Wait for the promise of the Father.

She blinked. Was that still, small voice she relied upon for guidance—be it Jesse's or God's—implying the heavenly Father might have made a promise to her? And that He was about to keep it? As glass tinkled onto the café floor and that tree branch disappeared out the gaping hole in the window, she wondered if this had been a providential morning. Meant to be, for both her and Ben.

For sure and for certain, this stranger was giving her a lot to think about.

Connect with U s

Visit us online at
KensingtonBooks.com
to read more from your favorite authors, see books
by series, view reading group guides, and more.

Join us on social media

for sneak peeks, chances to win books and prize packs,
and to share your thoughts with other readers.

facebook.com/kensingtonpublishing
twitter.com/kensingtonbooks

Tell us what you think!

To share your thoughts, submit a review,
or sign up for our eNewsletters, please visit:
KensingtonBooks.com/TellUs.

Books by Bestselling Author
Fern Michaels

___**The Jury**	0-8217-7878-1	$6.99US/$9.99CAN
___**Sweet Revenge**	0-8217-7879-X	$6.99US/$9.99CAN
___**Lethal Justice**	0-8217-7880-3	$6.99US/$9.99CAN
___**Free Fall**	0-8217-7881-1	$6.99US/$9.99CAN
___**Fool Me Once**	0-8217-8071-9	$7.99US/$10.99CAN
___**Vegas Rich**	0-8217-8112-X	$7.99US/$10.99CAN
___**Hide and Seek**	1-4201-0184-6	$6.99US/$9.99CAN
___**Hokus Pokus**	1-4201-0185-4	$6.99US/$9.99CAN
___**Fast Track**	1-4201-0186-2	$6.99US/$9.99CAN
___**Collateral Damage**	1-4201-0187-0	$6.99US/$9.99CAN
___**Final Justice**	1-4201-0188-9	$6.99US/$9.99CAN
___**Up Close and Personal**	0-8217-7956-7	$7.99US/$9.99CAN
___**Under the Radar**	1-4201-0683-X	$6.99US/$9.99CAN
___**Razor Sharp**	1-4201-0684-8	$7.99US/$10.99CAN
___**Yesterday**	1-4201-1494-8	$5.99US/$6.99CAN
___**Vanishing Act**	1-4201-0685-6	$7.99US/$10.99CAN
___**Sara's Song**	1-4201-1493-X	$5.99US/$6.99CAN
___**Deadly Deals**	1-4201-0686-4	$7.99US/$10.99CAN
___**Game Over**	1-4201-0687-2	$7.99US/$10.99CAN
___**Sins of Omission**	1-4201-1153-1	$7.99US/$10.99CAN
___**Sins of the Flesh**	1-4201-1154-X	$7.99US/$10.99CAN
___**Cross Roads**	1-4201-1192-2	$7.99US/$10.99CAN

Available Wherever Books Are Sold!
Check out our website at **www.kensingtonbooks.com**

More by Bestselling Author
Hannah Howell

More from Bestselling Author
JANET DAILEY

Calder Storm	0-8217-7543-X	$7.99US/$10.99CAN
Close to You	1-4201-1714-9	$5.99US/$6.99CAN
Crazy in Love	1-4201-0303-2	$4.99US/$5.99CAN
Dance With Me	1-4201-2213-4	$5.99US/$6.99CAN
Everything	1-4201-2214-2	$5.99US/$6.99CAN
Forever	1-4201-2215-0	$5.99US/$6.99CAN
Green Calder Grass	0-8217-7222-8	$7.99US/$10.99CAN
Heiress	1-4201-0002-5	$6.99US/$7.99CAN
Lone Calder Star	0-8217-7542-1	$7.99US/$10.99CAN
Lover Man	1-4201-0666-X	$4.99US/$5.99CAN
Masquerade	1-4201-0005-X	$6.99US/$8.99CAN
Mistletoe and Molly	1-4201-0041-6	$6.99US/$9.99CAN
Rivals	1-4201-0003-3	$6.99US/$7.99CAN
Santa in a Stetson	1-4201-0664-3	$6.99US/$9.99CAN
Santa in Montana	1-4201-1474-3	$7.99US/$9.99CAN
Searching for Santa	1-4201-0306-7	$6.99US/$9.99CAN
Something More	0-8217-7544-8	$7.99US/$9.99CAN
Stealing Kisses	1-4201-0304-0	$4.99US/$5.99CAN
Tangled Vines	1-4201-0004-1	$6.99US/$8.99CAN
Texas Kiss	1-4201-0665-1	$4.99US/$5.99CAN
That Loving Feeling	1-4201-1713-0	$5.99US/$6.99CAN
To Santa With Love	1-4201-2073-5	$6.99US/$7.99CAN
When You Kiss Me	1-4201-0667-8	$4.99US/$5.99CAN
Yes, I Do	1-4201-0305-9	$4.99US/$5.99CAN

Available Wherever Books Are Sold!

Check out our website at www.kensingtonbooks.com.